## PRAISE FOR *LOKA*

"*Loka*'s fascinating speculations about the future of technology, the evolution of consciousness, and the ethics of coexistence blend perfectly with its smart and empathetic coming-of-age *Around the World in Eighty Days* journey of a young woman seeking to forge her own path in a world that may not accept her for who she is."

—Kate Elliott, author of *Unconquerable Sun*

## PRAISE FOR *MERU*

"The world presented here is rich and complicated, [and] the love story, plus plenty of jaw-dropping space scenes, will reward readers."

—*Kirkus Reviews*

"Empathy convincingly overcomes anxiety in this thoughtful, inventive, and impressively understated space opera from Divya, [who] filters the immensity of outer space through the lens of close personal relationships, crafting compassionate and responsible characters (whatever their physical forms may be) that will surely win over readers."

—*Publishers Weekly* (starred review)

"This is a thrilling combination of traditional SF space travel and forward-thinking examinations of what 'humanity' will mean in the future."

—*Library Journal*

"Divya's latest (after *Machinehood*, 2021) is full of twists and turns to keep readers glued to the pages, with rich world-building that will truly invest them in the characters' fates. *Meru* transcends genres and will appeal to fans of science fiction, philosophy, and fantasy."

—*Booklist*

"*Meru* proves a worthy addition to the canon of posthuman space epics."

—*The Washington Post*

"*Meru* is a thought-provoking and imaginative future. With an intrigue spanning across interstellar distances, it still manages to be an intimate portrait of love."

—Mary Robinette Kowal, Hugo Award–winning author

"A breathtaking epic tale that challenges our views of humanity and how two individuals can bond. Again, S.B. Divya forges a new trail into what science fiction can be. Follow her and be amazed."

—Mur Lafferty, Hugo and Nebula Award finalist

# LOKA

# ALSO BY S.B. DIVYA

## The Alloy Era series

*Meru*

## Other Books

*Machinehood*

*Runtime*

*Contingency Plans for the Apocalypse and Other Possible Situations*

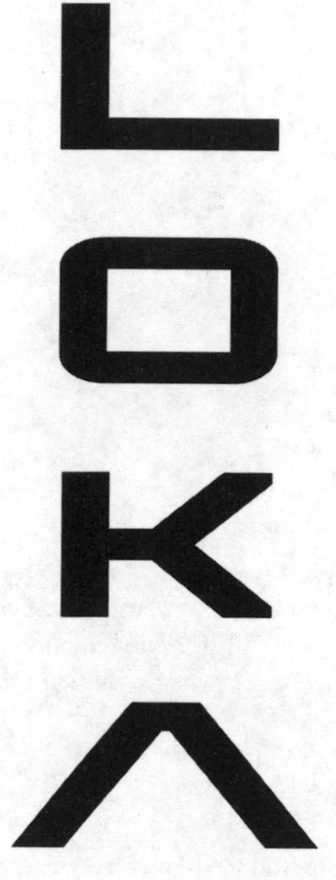


S.B. DIVYA

47NORTH

This is a work of fiction. Names, characters, organizations, places, events, and incidents are either products of the author's imagination or are used fictitiously. Otherwise, any resemblance to actual persons, living or dead, is purely coincidental.



Published by 47North, Seattle

www.apub.com



ISBN-13: 9781662505065 (paperback)
ISBN-13: 9781662505072 (digital)

Cover design by Mike Heath
Cover image: © orxy, © Gestur Gislason, © kavram / Shutterstock

Printed in the United States of America

*To Maya and to children everywhere, for what they teach us*

## The Axioms of Life

1. A life-form has a boundary, perceptible using its own sensory capabilities, that separates it from the environment.
2. A life-form has a built-in drive to live and reproduce, which implies that it must have a nonliving state.
3. A life-form is capable of accruing information about its environment and storing this information within its own structure.
4. A life-form can communicate information to other life-forms that share some or all of its sensory modalities.
5. A life-form can adapt to its environment and/or alter its environment over time and/or successive generations of itself.

## The Principles of Conscious Beings

1. All matter possesses some level of consciousness.
2. All forms of consciousness have equal value in the universe.
3. Possession of conscious4ness is necessary but not sufficient for life-forms.
4. A Being is a structure with sufficient consciousness that it has the ability to reshape matter.
5. An Evolved Being is a Being that is also a life-form.
6. All Beings should minimize harm to other forms of consciousness, with priority given to other Beings.

# DAY -46

In the old epics, heroes are born to a great destiny. They're supposed to feel grateful for that, proud that fate has chosen them over all others. I'd spent my entire life living under the weight of such expectations, except that my future wasn't foretold by the gods or some kind of magic. It was a result of my carefully crafted DNA and the choices my parents had made sixteen and a half years earlier.

A more immediate destiny lay a few hundred meters ahead, and all I had to do to reach it was keep pedaling. Behind me, my three friends—the only ones close to my age on this world—rode their own bikes. For once, I was in the lead. I suspected that Somya, my heartsib, had told the others to let me reach our destination first, since I would never make the journey again.

The path beneath our tires meandered through a grove of fruit trees. Glittering insectoid microconstructs buzzed between the blossoms while larger metal constructs tended to the care and feeding of the plants, their appendages working as both arms and legs. All of them were extensions of Chedi, a conscious megaconstruct whose vast cylindrical body formed the only home I'd ever known. She carried several hundred humans through space, traveling from one star system to another, including visits to the Solar System every couple of years. Unlike my friends, though, I had never set foot on Earth.

My parents had been exiled shortly before my birth, and they chose to serve their time inside Chedi. Because my mother was pregnant with me, the law technically included both of us for the duration of her exile, but that period was about to end. In a few days, Chedi would transit to the Solar System, and my mother, my maker, and I would leave for Earth. For the first time in my life, I would learn what human existence really meant.

I brought my bike to a halt in front of a boxlike structure that stood a bit taller than me. A doorway led into a shaft that rose along one of Chedi's flat ends, all the way to her central axis. We didn't have time to go that far up, but there were plenty of stops along the way. Somya, Huy, and Cariana arrived shortly after me. The three of them formed a spectrum—Som with their long black hair in a braid, Huy with a messy mop of loose red curls, and Cari with her blonde hair cropped short. With my black hair short and curly, I had aspects of all three.

"You came in first!" Somya said, miming applause.

I rolled my eyes. "I know you let me win."

My statement was met with three overly innocent expressions and a volley of protestations. I couldn't help laughing at my friends. It felt good to beat them, even if they had allowed it. Huy usually won our races, being both the tallest and the oldest of our small group. At eighteen, he was a year older than Somya, who led me by about four months. Cariana, fourteen, was our most junior member. She was also our newest, having come into Chedi only two years earlier, during our last visit to the Solar System.

"First to arrive means first up," Somya said.

They waved me through the doorway. Inside the housing, a squat maintenance construct slept in its power cradle. I walked past it and through another doorway into a narrow shaft that housed a ladder. With a deep breath, I began to climb. The rungs trembled as the others stepped on. The biosynthetic material felt warm under my grip. The ladder and the shaft walls glowed with pale lime-green luminescence.

The color reminded me of sunlight on the floor of a rainforest, which I'd only seen in immersives.

"Ouch! You just kicked my head," Huy protested.

I paused my climb for a second to make sure his words weren't directed at me. A downward glance revealed Somya's dark head immediately below my feet. I kept climbing.

"Sorry," Somya said, their tone cheerful. "My foot slipped."

I looked up the utility shaft and saw our destination bordered by a ring of green light. It outshone the gentler glow of bioluminescence that traced the carbon-composite walls around us, and it marked the entrance to the first hull access point.

"Almost there," I called down.

Less than a minute later, I stepped off the rungs and clambered into a tunnel. I walked forward until I found the pile of coats that we'd left on our last visit. I shrugged mine on and passed the others to my friends.

"I guess you won't need these much longer," Huy said.

"I will once we get to Meru," I said. I couldn't keep the bitterness from my tone.

After a brief stay on Earth, my parents and I would move two hundred light-years away to a different planet, one where they intended for me to fulfill my birthright.

"Come on, Aks," Somya said. They slung an arm around my shoulder and dragged me deeper into the access tunnel. "You only have to put up with Meru for five years."

"That's nearly a third of my age," I pointed out.

The air grew colder as we walked. Chedi kept her interior climate pleasant for her human residents—warm during the day, a little cooler at night to help us sleep, never too humid or too dry. From what I had heard of Loka—the latitudes of Earth managed by the alloys—it was much the same way. The weather didn't get uncomfortable until you passed into the Out of Bounds. Meru's atmosphere, on the other hand, was left to do whatever it pleased. The humans on its surface—the few that alloys allowed to live there—had to wear coats, shoes, and even hats to maintain a comfortable body temperature outside.

"What's happening in five years?" Cariana asked.

"I'll explain on the other side," Somya said.

We arrived at the hatch. Somya touched their hand to its sensor, and Chedi swung it open. The thin, cold air stung my face and lungs. We let the door shut behind us. We would have fifteen minutes to return. If we didn't, Chedi would send one of her ambulatory constructs to check on us. She understood human development enough to know that adolescents needed to exercise our independence and have a place we could talk without oversight. That was what she'd told us when we asked to go into the space between her inner and outer hulls.

A walkway about two meters wide hugged the inner wall, its surface stippled to provide grip for the feet of a construct. It worked well for our shoes, too, a good thing considering the vertigo-inducing wall of ice ahead of us. The solid mass provided radiation shielding for all life inside Chedi. Most of it loomed in darkness, but ambient light from the walkway lit the nearest surface and revealed shades ranging from pale blue to white.

I reached out and touched the ice to complete our ritual visit. The others did the same before sitting down on the walkway.

"In five years," Somya explained, "Aks will turn twenty-one." Their breath formed wispy clouds as they spoke. "At that point, she'll be a legal human adult, and she can go wherever she wants."

Cariana craned her head past Huy's bulk and asked me, "I thought your parents let you be an adult at fifteen because of your maker?"

My mother was human, but my other parent—my maker—was an alloy, a genetically engineered descendent of humankind and the current dominant species in the Constructed Democracy of Sol. Since birth, my parents had access to my bodym, a system that integrated with all my bodily functions and allowed me to access any public network. After age fifteen, my maker convinced my mother to give me full privacy, a choice that humans didn't have to make since their children didn't get bodyms. Usually only alloys had the internal networks, but I'd received one at my parents' request. It wasn't my only unique feature, but the other one was a carefully kept secret, and I hadn't yet revealed it to Cariana.

"My adult status only applies in Chedi," I explained, "because she can set her own laws within herself. On Earth and everywhere else in the CDS, I'm still considered a minor. That changes when I turn twenty-one, and when that happens, I'm going back to Earth so Somya and I can do the Anthro Challenge."

As part of Cariana's induction into our group, we had insisted that she read *A Journey of Human Power* by Rune Edersan, the only human being alive who had circumnavigated the Earth using human-era technology. He was the first to call it the Anthro Challenge, back in 691 Alloy Era, thirty years before I was born. I was determined that one day, I would replicate his accomplishment.

"After we finish the challenge," Somya said, "we're going to live in the Out of Bounds and form a society more like the one here, where people can more freely express their ambitions."

Huy snorted.

Somya leaned conspiratorially toward Cariana. "Huy thinks that's a big mistake."

"Why go to all that effort when paradise is right here?" Huy spread his arms wide. "Chedi allows as much ambition as you want, and you don't have to worry about alloys hassling you for it."

"You've never lived on Earth," Somya countered. "How would you know?"

"Neither has Akshaya," Huy said. "And you've been on Chedi since you were ten years old. It's not as if you understand what life is like there, especially in the Out of Bounds."

Huy made a fair point. All of our families lived in Loka, in the managed latitudes, so even during planet-side visits, Somya, Huy, and

Cariana had no experience with the OOB, where humans went if they didn't want to conform to Loka's behavioral requirements.

"We've read a lot about it," I said. "And we've done a lot of immersives." I couldn't help coming to Somya's defense.

Huy radiated skepticism.

"Plus," Somya said, "we'll have to pass through the OOB when we do the Anthro Challenge, so we'll get a better idea of what it's like."

The equatorial latitudes were outside of Loka, and circumnavigation meant crossing the equator. Rune had done it via sailboat, so he hadn't spent a lot of time with the people in those regions, but Somya and I could take a different approach. The challenge had no time limit. We could spend months traveling and exploring the Out of Bounds, if we wanted to.

"So what will you do on Meru in the meantime?" Cariana asked me.

"Suffer," I said.

"But you're so perfectly suited for the planet," Somya said with a grin.

I rolled my eyes at them. My mother had said those words for my entire life. How she'd crafted some of my genes for living on Meru. How our shared sickle-cell traits, combined with some choice mutations, would allow my body to thrive on the planet's highly oxygenated air. How my existence had changed the course of human history and would do so again after I proved my fitness on Meru's surface.

I was so sick of it. "I've spent my whole life here on Chedi," I said. "I want to experience being *human* on Earth. Why would I be excited about an empty planet that's barely hospitable to life?"

"Sorry to bring up a sore subject," Cariana said.

I waved off her apology. "It's not your fault. I'm not angry at you, only at my life."

Before I could wallow deeper, an alert blinked in my visual field that our time was up. I stood up, and the others followed me out without a word. I regretted that I'd brought the mood of the group down, but I didn't know how to relieve the awkward silence.

Inside the access tunnel, the others left their coats behind. I removed mine and tied it around my waist. My mother had asked me to bring it back so she could pack it with our other items. I'd begged her to bring my bike, though I wasn't sure where I'd be able to ride it, and she had allowed that, too. Unlike on Earth, where alloys would make items upon request, the resources on Meru were limited. I doubted the alloys in charge would fabricate a solar bike for me.

"First up, last out," I said as we neared the top of the ladder.

"You know," Somya said, "if you're the one making the rules, you can also change them."

"It's not much of a rule if you change it when it gets inconvenient," I retorted.

The others laughed, and I felt the knot in my chest loosen.

Cariana obligingly went first. I lingered for an extra few seconds on the top rungs, taking it all in. I would probably never see this utility tunnel again. Even if I returned to live on the megaconstruct one day, I'd probably be too old to care about clambering around in awkward places.

At the bottom, Huy pushed open the door that let us out into bright late-afternoon light. We all squinted and blinked as our eyes adjusted. Blossoming plum trees surrounded us with their honey-sweet fragrance. Several of Chedi's ambulatory constructs moved through the plants, delicately collecting and distributing pollen, but one of them sat unmoving. It listed to one side, and I could see that one leg was shorter than the others.

"I'm going to see if I can help that construct," I told the others. I grabbed my tool kit from the storage pouch on my bike's frame. "Go ahead without me."

A chorus of groans rose from my friends. I flashed a grin at them and jogged away.

"You don't have time!" Huy called after me.

I waved away his comment and headed forward. The soil warmed my knees as I knelt in front of the injured construct. The metal exterior reflected the light from Chedi's central axis, the only "sunlight" I had ever known.

"Let me look at you," I murmured.

Chedi's ambulatory constructs didn't have minds of their own, but they had basic machine intelligence, including the ability to understand human speech. I examined the malfunctioning leg. The piston mechanism had jammed, probably from all the dust and pollen in the air. I extracted a bottle of lubricant from my kit and squirted some into the joint.

"Try it again," I said to the construct.

The construct had no way to reply to me except via Chedi, but I didn't need words to understand what it was doing. After a brief whirring noise, the leg extended to its full height. The construct walked a couple of meters to the nearest tree and reached up its arms to gather pollen from the blossoms. My emchannel alerted me to an incoming message. Chedi had noticed and sent a note of thanks.

I dusted off my leggings with a smile and trotted back to my friends. They had waited for me and were laughing about something when I reached them.

"Satisfied?" Somya asked.

"Yes," I said blandly. I stowed my kit and straddled my bike.

As soon as we started to pedal, Somya—who was in the lead—called out, "Race you back," and took off. The rest of us followed, cursing in Somya's dusty wake. I was tempted to use the electric motor to boost my speed. All four of our bikes had gold photovoltaic paint over their frames and absorbed Chedi's light to charge their batteries. On our longer excursions, we would alternate between pedaling and motoring to save our strength.

Cariana had been shocked the first time Somya had called a race. That kind of competition belonged to alloy society, not humans, and she had never experienced such transgressive behavior on Earth. We didn't take the results seriously, though, and after the initial reservations wore off, she had learned to enjoy herself with us. Most of the humans who visited Chedi—including the children—did so while Chedi was passing through the Solar System, and they often chose not to stay for a longer journey. Cariana's family was one of the exceptions, which probably explained why she was able to tolerate our group's overt ambition.

I rode in last place, as usual, but I didn't fall too far behind, which was an improvement over the first few years of biking. Part of the motivation for doing all the riding and ladder climbing was so that I'd keep up my conditioning. The first year I'd tried our so-called Utility Circuit, I could only get halfway up a shaft before exhausting myself. Like my mother, I had genes for sickle-cell disease, but mine had manifested less severely than hers. After three and a half years of exercise, I could ride to and scale all ten of Chedi's access shafts in one day. My mother approved of my push to get stronger. She told me about the cliffs near Homesite, the tiny human settlement on Meru, and how she had climbed those before I was born. She wanted me strong enough to be able to do the same when we arrived there.

Huy ended up winning our impromptu bike race in spite of Somya's initial lead. By the time I caught up to the others, small knots of adults had already started to gather in the grahin. The two-story pavilion formed the social center of our village, and that's where most people preferred to rest during Chedi's reality transits.

My maker walked up to me and quirked an eyebrow. "Cutting it a bit close." Curly black hair formed a cloud around zir head, and chromatophores dotted zir bare arms, which glowed green with concern.

Technically, the body that stood before me was my maker's incarn, a mostly human offshoot of zir true body, which was a massive thing that lived and traveled in space. I'd seen my maker's true body at least once a year since I was old enough to wear a spacesuit and exit Chedi. When I was small, I accepted my maker's way of life as a matter of fact. As I got older, I struggled to understand it. Zir true body and zir incarn shared a consciousness. At night, while the rest of us slept, my maker would wake in zir true body and give it nourishment and exercise.

"Your mother is waiting in our room," my maker said. "She sent me to find you."

The atmosphere in Chedi matched that of Earth, and my mother had to monitor her activity levels to avoid complications from sickle-cell disease, like pain crises. The first time I was old enough to witness her going through a crisis, I was terrified that she would die. In later years, I feared that it would happen to me, but my genes expressed themselves differently, and I had yet to experience anything besides getting tired faster than my friends. Chedi had built my family an enclosed bedroom with an atmosphere more like Meru's, with twice the oxygen content of Earth's atmosphere—much healthier for me and my mother. We'd spend nights in there as needed, usually when my mother was sick or I'd had a strenuous day.

"Wait," I said, grabbing my maker's arm. "I was going to make this transit in the rose garden with my friends, remember?"

My sleeve fell back, and apricot light leaked from the chromatophores on my skin. My maker's eyes narrowed. I hastily covered up and forced my skin back to neutral. Somya was the only person near enough to have seen it, but they already knew my secret.

"I forgot about that," my maker said. "Do you feel okay? What does your bodym say about your vitals?"

I checked and sent zir the results via emchannel. "All good, see?"

Zie nodded. "Then we'll see you tomorrow. Rest well." Then zie flashed in phoric, <And don't get careless with yourself.>

I resisted the urge to retort with my own chromatophores. My maker wouldn't find it amusing, and my sarcasm would unfairly hurt zir. My phores were my mother's doing. She had promised me since I could remember that she would tell the world about my unusual genes after we were settled on Meru. She had been exiled in part for making me in a womb without proper assistance from a type of alloy known as a tarawan. At the time, only they had license to design and make babies—whether alloy or human—and the judiciary of the Constructed Democracy of Sol hadn't taken kindly to my mother's excess ambition. She had confidence that she could safely make me, and she was right, but if people knew that she had given me DNA outside of the *Homo sapiens* gene pool, she could get into more trouble. Or I could.

In Chedi, I had no one other than my maker to communicate with in phoric. No other alloys lived in the megaconstruct, so my maker had spent many hours in our high-oxygen room teaching me how to communicate with flashes of light, how to interpret colored moods as easily as I did facial expressions. I, in turn, had practiced phoric during my sleepovers with Somya. Their vocabulary was more limited than mine, and they could only reply with speech, but it was enough to feel like a secret language between us.

With another *be-careful* look, my maker patted my shoulder and walked away. Somya quirked a brow at me. I shrugged. My mother would probably hassle me about the slipup, but I'd deal with that when it happened. She was always lecturing me about something.

# DAY -45

When I awoke from the reality-transit sedative, my body felt like it had been rolled between two sheets of rock. While all the humans inside her were unconscious, Chedi had shifted her body to the Solar System. Somya lay on a cushioned mat between me and Huy, both of them still asleep. I sat up, stretched, and slightly regretted my decision to eschew the high-oxygen bedroom with my parents. Remarkably, my mother hadn't objected to my choice to spend the night outside with my friends. She would probably make an *I-told-you-so* face if I mentioned my aching muscles, so I resolved to keep them to myself.

The trees around us rustled in a gentle breeze, oblivious to my discomfort. Artificial morning light filtered through their leaves and painted the rosebushes with their shadows. What would sunrise be like on Earth? I'd seen it in immersives and pictures, but those couldn't substitute for the real thing. Birdsong, golden clouds, the deep blue of sky—I couldn't wait to experience them for myself.

Somya rolled and mumbled in their sleep. I reached out a hand and rubbed their back gently. They'd always been a restless sleeper. It was why we put them in the middle—so they wouldn't thrash themself out of the cot. I figured their nighttime personality gave their negative emotions an outlet. They rarely took anything seriously in their waking hours, so the bad stuff had to express itself somehow.

I fought back the sting of tears as I thought about never seeing my heartsib again. Our families lived on different parts of Earth. After our stay there, we'd reunite for a couple of months on Chedi, and then I'd end up on Meru, while Somya, Huy, and their families would travel to wherever Chedi's residents decided to go next. With interstellar distances between us, we could only exchange messages by courier. Reality transits enabled instantaneous travel between stars, but in-system travel was limited by the speed of classical physics. A transit couldn't occur until a pilot or megaconstruct had passed the edge of the local heliosphere. That meant weeks or months of delay between courier drops. In the seven years since Somya had come to Chedi, we'd only been apart when they'd gone to Earth with their parents to visit other family. How would I face the challenges of Meru without them?

Somya mumbled something again and flung an arm over my legs. I placed my hand over theirs. My parents and I would leave for Earth on the first shuttle from Chedi. She usually selected passengers by lottery, but everyone had agreed to give my family priority because we'd lived in exile for so long. I wondered if I could talk my parents into letting Somya come with us until Somya's parents arrived. It would take Chedi two hundred and forty days to travel from heliopause—the outer limit of the Solar System—to a point close to Earth and then back out again. Letting Somya join us would mean we'd get to spend two extra months together.

*If only we could spend my entire stay together, we'd have a full eight months. That's more time than it takes to complete the Anthro Challenge.*

The thought jolted me out of the drowsy slump I'd fallen into. I slow-blinked and thought-retrieved *A Journey of Human Power*, the book by Rune Edersan. It had detailed information about his route, equipment, and everything else someone would need to know in order to replicate his success. The rules of the Anthro Challenge stated that a human had to circumnavigate the Earth, defined as journeying around the entire planet and crossing its equator at least twice. The start and end points had to be the same, and most importantly, the challenger could only use human-era technology along the way. That meant no assistance from alloys, constructs, or devices that relied on infrastructure maintained by either. That's what made it so appealing to me.

When Rune had tried it the first time, in 683 AE, he'd spent a lot of days scouting for ways to avoid roads, bridges, and such. He'd also had to find community farms and gardens that only humans tended to—not an easy thing to do in Loka because the alloys had filled ecological gaps with constructs. He had run into unexpected weather delays in the Out of Bounds, where alloys often redirected atmospheric energy in order to keep Loka more livable. After eight months, he'd exhausted himself to the point that he had to quit. On his second attempt, Rune used everything he'd learned the first time and completed the journey in 155 days with less overall effort.

If Somya could come with me to Earth and take the last shuttle back to Chedi, we'd have six months together on the planet. As long as we followed Rune's successful path, we could finish with almost a month to spare. The odds of convincing our parents to let us attempt it were the longest of long shots, but I had to try.

---

"Absolutely not." My mother wore the frown that she always displayed when she had made up her mind about something.

"Jayanthi," my maker said, placing zir hand on my mother's arm. "Maybe we should take a minute to consider it?"

She turned her glare upon my maker. "There is no way Akshaya can do something that physically demanding while on Earth."

The three of us sat in the high-oxygen bedroom where my mother and I often slept, one of the few enclosed buildings in Chedi. After seeing my morning bodym numbers, she'd insisted that I spend a couple of hours in the room's special atmosphere. I had asked my maker to join us so I could tell them both about the plan I'd come up with. My parents sat on their bed while I sat on mine. Our feet rested on a hempen rug dyed with colorful geometric patterns. Artwork from my childhood hung on the painted wooden walls, a luxury available only in Chedi, according to my mother. The early scrawls contrasted with the less embarrassing pieces of recent years, but all of them featured the flora and fauna of Earth.

My mother swiveled back to me. "This Rune person, he was young and fit and healthy when he did the challenge, right? And even with all that in his favor, he faced so many difficulties that he had to quit the first time."

I'd given her ammunition by telling them about Rune's disastrous initial attempt. He did well the second time, and the route I'd created was based on what he'd written in his book. She knew that, too.

My mother took a deep breath, closed her eyes, and let it out. When she opened her eyes, she wore the expression that I called *forced-reasonable* face. She leaned across the small gap that separated us and took my hands in hers. "You don't know what it's like on Earth."

"That's exactly why I want to do the AC."

"People there aren't as open-minded as the ones here. In Loka, they won't like your ambitious nature, and the OOBers—well, who knows how they'll react."

It took my brain a second to translate *OOBers* into "people who live Out of Bounds." *Only one way to find out what they'd make of me.*

"Besides, you don't have as much time as you think. We're going to visit the Primary Nivid as well, remember? Guhaka is there. That'll take up another month."

As if I cared more about the alloys' pride and joy than the Anthro Challenge. The Nivid stored all the knowledge and data gathered by the Constructed Democracy of Sol, but the human contributions were tiny compared to the alloys', who made up the majority of citizens in the CDS. I *did* care about seeing Guhaka, who was like a grandparent to me. He had left Chedi on our previous trip to the Solar System to spend his final years at the Primary Nivid, and visiting him there would make the trip more worthwhile, but it wasn't enough incentive for me to back away from the Anthro Challenge.

My mother sighed and sat back. "I understand that you really want to do this, so how about a compromise? After we've spent a year on Meru and you've cleared all your health tests, we can do an Anthro Challenge there. We can request and build whatever equipment we need—the solar bikes, the boat, anything."

Her suggestion made no sense. Rune had relied on human-tended community gardens for food. He'd used hand-built cabins for shelter. He'd taken advice from locals on which trails to use so that he could avoid interference from alloys. Meru would have none of those resources. On top of all that, I highly doubted that the alloys approved requests for travel items like bikes and boats.

My maker kept turning zir head back and forth between us. Zie raised zir eyebrows at me in a silent question.

"It'll be so much better for your health to take on that kind of activity on Meru," my mother continued, ignoring my building irritation. "You'll understand after we've spent some time there. This feeling you have in here?" She waved her hand at the room. "You'll have it every day, all the time."

I wanted to say that life was about more than the air I breathed, more than our sickle-cell disorders, more than spending our lives in service of others. Nobody had given me a choice regarding the circumstances of my birth, and now that I could finally go to Earth, my mother insisted that I couldn't do *one thing* before banishing me to a barren planet.

"What do you think?" my mother pressed.

As if she really cared. "All right. Let's do the challenge on Meru." I lay back on my cot and closed my eyes.

Her lips pressed against my head. "It'll all work out. You'll see."

My maker kissed me as well and whispered, "I'll talk to her."

When the door shut behind them, I rolled over and stared at the wall beyond their bed. The screen where Chedi's face would appear stared blankly back at me. She could watch and listen to everything that happened inside her, but she chose to give her residents privacy because it was better for our health. Her policy didn't extend to her access corridors, and she'd known about my escapades with Somya long before my parents heard about them. My mother had gotten angry with Chedi—the first time I'd seen that happen—for not telling her. The ship had reassured my mother that she would've handled any emergency needs, and then she'd talked my mother into giving me more independence. Maybe Chedi could work the same miracle a second time.

I requested a meeting with her.

Five minutes later, the humanlike face that Chedi assumed popped up on the screen.

"Akshaya, what's going on? Are you feeling okay?"

I waved off her concern. "I'm fine. I was hoping that you could help me with my mother again."

"Again?"

"She's not being reasonable! I showed her a plan for Somya and me to complete the Anthro Challenge, a circumnavigation of Earth. It would let me see what life is like on the planet and spend more time with my heartsib. We could complete the challenge and get back here before you leave the Solar System."

"And your mother said no?"

"She thinks it's too dangerous. All she cares about now is getting me to Meru. But Earth is my heritage! I want to spend my life *there*, not on some remote planet that's going to feel like another kind of exile."

"I see. So the root of the problem lies in your desire to live on Earth."

"Yes, but I know she would never agree to that. She designed my biochemistry for Meru, and she wants to prove her work—me. I thought the Anthro Challenge was a reasonable alternative."

"She doesn't need to fuel her ego. Others have used her genetic designs on Meru already. She has waited patiently all these years so that the three of you can live together on a planet as a family. That is her dream, something she can't have anywhere else. Your maker's incarn isn't allowed on Earth's surface."

"What about *my* dreams? *My* feelings? Somya and I will have to wait until we're adults before we can be together on Earth."

"Those are valid questions."

"At least my mother could let me try the Anthro Challenge before we go to Meru. If I can complete the utility circuit here, I should have no problems on Earth. The atmosphere is the same. Please, Chedi, can you talk to her?"

"Perhaps there's a solution that would get you what you really want. You are confident of your fitness for Earth, and you would prefer to stay there from now on, but you think your mother won't agree to that. Do I have it right?"

I nodded.

"Would you be willing to enter into an agreement with your mother? If you can complete the Anthro Challenge in six months, you'll get to remain on Earth in the custody of your grandparents. If for any reason you cannot complete it, you will go to Meru as planned, no further complaints. We'll have to get permission from Somya's parents, too. I assume that you've already talked over this plan of yours with them?"

"Not yet, but I'm sure Somya will say yes. Do you think my parents would agree to a deal like that?"

"I can't say for certain, but it would give them some time to get used to the idea of going to Meru without you, and neither you nor your mother would be capitulating to the other."

Chedi's proposal went beyond what I could have hoped for. I could have kissed one of her ambulatory constructs if one had stood nearby.

"Thank you, Chedi, from the bottom of my heart."

If she could get my mother to accept the deal, I knew I could fulfill my end of it.

# JAYANTHI (DAY -44)

Jayanthi tried not to get angry at Chedi, but it was hard when it seemed like Chedi was advocating harder for her child than for herself. Raising Akshaya had never been easy. Jayanthi wasn't a natural mother. She'd spent a lot of time reading about parenting and asking for advice from the handful of other parents on Chedi. As an infant, Akshaya had been colicky and slept poorly. As a child, she'd been stubborn and sensitive and prone to tantrums, and as a teenager, she insisted that she knew best for herself. Jayanthi had kept her safe from any major health problems—not even a pain crisis—thanks to some innovative living arrangements. Did she get any gratitude for it? No. Instead, her child attempted to run off on some ridiculous and risky "adventure," and now Chedi wanted to find a way to allow it.

"Jayanthi, kindly stop pacing around the room," Chedi said.

Jayanthi stopped abruptly in the middle of the sleeping room. She forced herself to take a deep breath, then sat on the edge of the bed facing the wall screen.

"Akshaya is willing to make a deal," Chedi said. "And most likely, it will go in your favor. What are the chances that she and Somya will succeed in finishing the Anthro Challenge, especially with the time limit they've given themselves? If they fail, she'll accompany you to Meru without further complaint. That's what you want, right?"

"Yes, but not for some arbitrary and cruel reason! I want her to thrive, and she can't do that on Earth."

"In theory, she could manage there the same way you do here. Build her a special house with a high-oxygen room. You know it works, so you should have no trouble getting it approved. I can send the specifications to the alloys at Earth. The truth is that you want her to go to Meru so that you, Vaha, and Akshaya can live together, am I correct?"

Jayanthi nodded as her throat closed. She'd held to that dream since before Akshaya's birth—seventeen years of patience and penitence, and now that very child wanted to ruin it.

"Akshaya is meeting you halfway with this bargain. Why not let her try the challenge?"

"Because she has *never* really been sick. She's only experienced mild pain and discomfort. She doesn't understand what a real sickle-cell crisis is like. What happens if she gets that bad midway through this challenge? Who's going to treat her? What if she tries to ignore it? She's so stubborn."

"If that happens, then she fails, and you get what you want."

"Except that I also don't want to risk my child's health for some ridiculous challenge."

"And how often did you risk your life without a second thought when you were younger? You can't protect her forever."

Jayanthi fought with herself to deny the truth of Chedi's words. She had once hiked alone across Meru's barren surface. She had nearly died in space, abandoned there by another megaconstruct until Chedi had come to her rescue.

"That's exactly why I don't want Akshaya doing this."

"Meru is your dream," Chedi said gently. "The Anthro Challenge is Akshaya's. She wants to linger on Earth, to experience human life there. Can you blame her? She'll have no peers on Meru, hardly any human beings at all. You speak of her bodily health, but what about her spirit?"

"We've waited so long for this," Jayanthi said, unable to keep the pleading tone from her voice. "The whole world has."

"I know." Chedi's expression was all sympathy, but she didn't relent.

"And if Akshaya succeeds? Then what, she lives on Earth by herself? What about us, her parents? Are we supposed to split up? Vaha can't live on Earth, not with zir incarn. Has she given any thought to that?"

"How much does any young adult consider their parents' lives? Akshaya is looking at her own future, and who knows, maybe after a few years there, she'll get the itch to experience Earth out of her system. She might mature and go to Meru on her own. For now, she is willing to stay with your parents. I think she expects you and Vaha to move to Meru as you have planned. You can still fulfill that part of your dream."

Jayanthi growled. "Or I could insist that my child—the one who's perfectly designed for Meru—go there with us."

"You could, but she might never forgive you for it."

"So she'll hate me. She's halfway there already. Maybe I should have designed her to have less ambition."

Chedi's expression didn't change. Jayanthi had seen it several times over the years, whenever she'd grown frustrated with parenting her equally stubborn child. It meant *you're being overprotective and you know it.*

"All right, I'll spend some time thinking about it while I pack, and I'll talk to Vaha. Zie has to be part of this decision, as do Somya's parents."

# VAHA (DAY -44)

Vaha sat in a corner of the grahin and faced Jayanthi and Somya's parents, Gamo and Zohel. The remains of their dinner sat on the table between them.

"They're not children anymore," Gamo said. "I'm in favor of them doing the Anthro Challenge. What better time than when they're young and healthy?"

"Akshaya might not have good health on Earth," Jayanthi replied.

Gamo made a placating gesture. "Yes, yes, of course, she needs to take care not to overexert herself. If she gets sick, or if they run out of time, we send someone to pick them up, but if they manage to complete the challenge successfully, they'll have something to be proud of for the rest of their lives."

"It will be difficult to get to them quickly in the Out of Bounds," Vaha said, "and they don't have much time, not if you want Somya back here before Chedi leaves the Solar System. The first shuttle departs in three days for Earth. Allowing for a week or so of adjustment and the travel time in space, that leaves them roughly one hundred and seventy days to work with."

"They're planning to use the solar bikes on land," Gamo pointed out. "And the rest by boat. Based on Akshaya's estimates, they'll complete their journey in a hundred and fifty days, which means they'll have some margin for unexpected delays."

Vaha envied Gamo's ability to accept the idea with such ease. The thought of Akshaya roaming the Earth by herself didn't sit so well in zir mind, especially not after what Jayanthi had gone through in her younger days. Then again, Akshaya was a year into adulthood by alloy standards, and she was an intelligent, thoughtful, and adventurous person. Zie could believe that she and Somya would finish the challenge. Doing so in time for them to get back to Chedi before her scheduled departure from the Solar System—that would be the hard part. Leaving Akshaya behind on Earth—if she succeeded—that would be even harder.

The hope of a life together on Meru had sustained Vaha and Jayanthi throughout their exile. It was the only planet in the universe where such an existence would be allowed. The alternatives were to leave Akshaya behind or for Vaha to live in stasis around Earth while Jayanthi stayed with their child on its surface. Vaha's heart broke at the thought of either one. To zir surprise, Jayanthi had wavered in her commitment to Meru. *I promised Chedi I would consider it with an open mind,* she had said.

Zohel sighed. "I'm also worried about Akshaya. Unlike Somya, she has no experience with life on Earth, and as Jayanthi said, neither of them understands how Akshaya's disorder might progress. If we could monitor her bodym along the way and know their location at all times, we could intervene when necessary, but their insistence on shutting off all alloy-supported technology will make that impossible."

When Vaha had first held Akshaya in zir incarn's hands, she had seemed so tiny and fragile, just as Jayanthi had when she had floated into zir true body. All of Vaha's protective instincts as a pilot had kicked in over their infant child. It was Jayanthi who had encouraged Akshaya to take her first steps, to climb up to Chedi's central axis, to ride a bike and swim and do all the things that Vaha had never learned because zie had grown up as an alloy, without the constraints of gravity. The vast emptiness of space was so much safer. Yes, the occasional micrometeor or solar storm could cause injury—as zie knew all too well—but they had safeguards for those, and worst case, an alloy could be remade or reborn. Humans didn't have those options.

Years spent in the company of the people on Chedi had taught Vaha that humankind had more resilience than zie had first thought. Zie had discovered that about Jayanthi before Akshaya was born, but zie hadn't known at the time if she was unique among her kind. In many ways, it turned out that she was, but so were the residents of Chedi. The humans who eschewed risk stayed on Earth, and the majority of them lived in Loka, where alloys could shape the land and climate. If only Akshaya and Somya didn't have to go to the Out of Bounds—but they had to cross the equator. Loka encompassed the area between the fifteenth and forty-fifth parallels on both hemispheres of the planet. The equator fell squarely within an OOB zone.

"That's exactly my concern, too," Jayanthi said. "This challenge needs to accommodate certain kinds of emergencies. At the very least, they should allow us to monitor Akshaya's bodym."

The terms of the challenge meant that Akshaya couldn't use her body's internal network to communicate with anyone. With the right permissions, Vaha could observe them visually from orbit, but those would take too long to procure, assuming that Earth management would grant them at all.

"What if we had a way to track them passively?" Vaha said. "Someone who can observe from orbit and has clearance for atmospheric flight. It wouldn't give us as direct a window into Akshaya's physical health, but I'm sure we could infer a need for help from her behavior."

"That's a good idea," Zohel said. "Do you know someone who would do that?"

"No," Vaha admitted. Another thought came to mind. Zie turned to Jayanthi. "What about Nara?"

"He lives in stasis," Jayanthi said. "How could he help?"

The documentarian had once approached Vaha and Jayanthi during their visit to the Solar System. Like many alloys, he spent the majority of his time in mindspace. Stasis allowed alloys to use minimal resources to maintain their bodies while pursuing academic or creative interests—anything that didn't require interaction with the physical world. Nara had wanted to make an immersive about their lives, something accurate and nonfictional, unlike the many others that had been produced. Jayanthi hadn't wanted to expose Akshaya to the public gaze, so they had refused.

"If we agree to his project," Vaha said, "and permit him to document Akshaya and Somya's journey, he'll have to find crew on Earth to record them."

"You mean from orbit, like they did when we were on Meru?" Jayanthi said. "Yes, I suppose that could work. There are plenty of atmospheric pilots who could get closer, too." She turned back to Gamo and Zohel. "What do you think? Would you consent to having Somya participate in a documentary?"

"They're still a minor," Zohel said. "I would want contractual oversight and approval before anything gets released to the public."

"I'm okay with that," Gamo said.

"Then I'll send Nara a message," Vaha said. "Communications take roughly thirty-two hours, round trip, from here to his stasis location. We can inform the children after we receive his reply."

# DAY -42

"Oh no," I groaned. "Why him?"

My mother, Somya, and I sat under the shade of the rose-garden pavilion. Our parents had made us wait nearly two days as they considered the offer from Chedi. In the end, they had agreed, with one major condition.

"Because Nara will find the right people who can watch you along the way," my mother said. She frowned. "At least that's what he said to your maker. He'll contract with them to record your journey and use that as the focus of his documentary. He's pitching it as a semi-live show, with new episodes released to the public close to real time for more excitement."

My mother's voice held a whiff of derision, like the scent of an overripe melon from across the room. I couldn't help but smile in response, though it quickly turned into a grimace. Nara had left an impression four years earlier, during one of our Solar System visits, when he first approached us about the project. He spent the majority of his time with his body in stasis and his mind in an immersive virtual world. In spite of seeing him only as an image, he'd exuded an undeniable charisma—fashionably dark green skin, silver wings, and light-brown eyes full of excitement. <We'll show everyone in the CDS what your lives truly mean, who you are, and why they don't need to fear you,> he had flashed in phoric. The more he had enthused, the greater my skepticism had grown. I had zero desire to have my life scrutinized by the citizens of the CDS, especially the alloys. Most of them would watch because of my parents' past, and the few who took an interest in me would see me as a curiosity at best or an example of human excess at worst.

Somya, on the other hand, lit up at the idea like they'd seen fireworks. "We'd get to star in our own show," they said. "Come on, Aks, it'll be great! And just imagine—we can show everyone that humans don't need alloys as much as people think we do."

They had a point. If we succeeded in the challenge in real time, no one could dispute it.

"What about the Out of Bounds?" I said. "Will Nara's people follow us there, too?"

My mother nodded. "The alloys don't manage the land and weather there like they do in Loka, but they can make aerial observations all over Earth."

"We'll have even less privacy than we do here in Chedi," I said to Somya.

"So?" They grinned. "We'll be famous!"

"Will Nara's people promise not to interfere with us unless we want them to?" I asked my mother. "We can bring some pencils and paper so we can write *SOS* if we need help."

"Very funny," my mother said. "They won't get involved unless you're both obviously injured and need help. You don't know—"

"What it's like on Earth," I interrupted. "Yes, I understand. You've said that about a hundred times already."

"But you don't understand," she said. "That's exactly my point, and you clearly aren't going to unless you take on this ridiculous dare. We'll do our best not to violate the terms of the Anthro Challenge, but if we think you're in danger—"

"No," I said. "If we're unconscious and about to die, then you get to make the call. I'm sure it'll seem like we're in danger a lot of times.

You can't jump in because you're scared for us. If that happens, the deal is off, and I get to stay on Earth."

"You two really do resemble each other," Somya said. They laughed as my mother and I turned our glares their way. "Okay, I'm going to step out of this. Aks, you know how I feel. Whatever it takes to get us going, let's do it, please!"

They sauntered away, lines of their body showing absolutely no tension. Of course not. Their fate didn't hang in the balance, not like mine did.

My mother shifted to sit next to me and put her arm around my shoulder. "I just want you to come back safe and sound."

"And to come live with you and Maker on Meru."

"I would like that very much, yes, but safe and sound is more important. Promise me that you'll ask for help from Nara's people if you need it, please."

"If I get sick enough, then yes, I promise, but you have to agree not to send any alloys to interfere with us until I make that call."

"Okay," my mother said. "I'll trust you to take care of yourself."

---

We ate dinner that night with Huy and Cariana as usual. The meal doubled as something of a farewell party, since some people wouldn't return from their journey to Earth. I hoped I would be one of them. People kept crowding the buffet tables to enjoy the abundance of dairy-based foods. Chedi didn't carry animals other than humans, so our dairy supplies were limited to what we picked up when she visited the Solar System. Personally, I'd never been a big fan of the taste, except for ice cream, and that day we had three different flavors to choose from.

"I'm going to eat this every night while I'm on Earth," I said, spooning more delicious frozen chocolate creaminess into my mouth.

"You should," Huy said.

Like me, Huy had been born on Chedi, but his parents had taken him to Earth during every Solar System visit, and they'd skipped one tour on Chedi to stay on the planet.

"I still can't believe that you two talked your parents into letting you do the Anthro Challenge." Huy gave me a *that's-impressive* nod. "And that you might actually get to stay permanently on Earth."

"I'm done," Somya announced. They pushed their chair back and turned to me. "You ready, or are you going for a third helping?"

The meal had lasted ten times as long as usual, thanks to the people who kept interrupting us to say goodbye and wish me luck. I felt a little guilty that so many of them expressed sadness when my own thoughts were dominated by excitement. I loved many of the adults in Chedi, especially those like Huy's parents who had known me my whole life, but as long as we finished the Anthro Challenge, I would get to see them every two years.

I lifted my bowl and licked it clean. "Now I'm done."

Our friends laughed. Huy gave me an extra-long hug before we walked away. The shuttle would leave early the next morning, long before they would all wake up. Somya and I had to finalize the items we wanted to carry to Earth. The list had changed after we decided to do the challenge. Much of the gear that we brought on our multiday excursions around Chedi would serve us equally well for the AC.

One of Chedi's ambulatory constructs met us in a clearing. Next to it lay an assortment of items. I slow-blinked and called up the checklist that Somya and I had made earlier in the day. I called out each item as Somya confirmed that it was included in the pile before us.

"Solar bikes—two. Spare tires—four. Spare parts: derailleurs, brake pads, battery packs, photovoltaic paint. My tool kit. Our bike helmets and gloves. A two-person tent. Two bedrolls and pillows. Two backpacks and four water sacks."

"That's everything," Somya confirmed.

We'd get the rest, like raincoats, food, cooking gear, and printed maps, after we arrived on Earth. Chedi would have had to learn to make those since no one in her body used them, and we didn't want to waste her energy or resources.

Somya grinned at me. "I can't believe we're really doing this."

"Me neither."

I looked around at the only home I'd known. On Earth, the ground would look flat rather than curving upward. I'd have an open sky above me. Real sunlight. Wind. My stomach fluttered at the thought, mostly excitement, but partly an undeniable nervousness. I had always known that my life would change after my parents' exile ended, but I hadn't expected my dreams to come true so quickly.

Somya slung an arm around my shoulders. "Don't worry, it's going to be great."

"How do you know?"

"Because I'm always right."

I had to laugh. No matter what happened along the way, at least I'd get an extra six months with Somya, and if we succeeded, I'd see them every two years thereafter.

We strolled back toward the grahin, where our parents waited. Microconstruct insects worked at the night-blooming bushes along the way, their backsides pulsing with a gentle glow. My brain tried to interpret their signals as words, but they were nonsense, like the coos and gurgles of a human baby. I inhaled deeply and tried to memorize the scents and sights around me. *Farewell, home,* I thought. *See you in two and a half years, I hope.*

# DAY -14

The Earth holds an iconic place in history: the birthplace of life, home of humanity, a sanctuary for plants and animals of all kinds. Its blue-green-white form is as well known as the golden hemisphere of the Primary Nivid, and I saw it for myself twenty-eight days later. Chedi's disc-shaped shuttle took us as far as an orbital station. Through the craft's viewing bubbles, I watched the planet transform from a bright point of light to a colorful orb, a contrast to the monochrome palette of the Moon.

We waited at the station for a day so that an alloy pilot could carry us down to the surface. I spent my time at any window with a good view of the Earth. As I gazed upon the broad stretches of blue, I imagined myself standing upon the shore at Banbhore, the first coastal town on our route. To see an *ocean* in real life, to have water that stretched to a convex horizon—I could taste the salt spray from the immersives that I'd replayed. We were going to sail across that vastness. We'd practiced with a small craft on Chedi's largest lake. I knew how to work a sail and a rudder. Chedi had even built some turbines to generate variable breezes. The open ocean would have real wind, though, and swells and currents and marine life.

My mother floated down the corridor toward me. She grabbed a nearby handhold, steadied herself beside me, and gave me a sealed packet of bhojya. The majority of the station's residents were alloys.

They didn't eat food the way humans did. Alloys had specialized digestive systems and subsisted on drinks full of nutrients and microbes. I took the packet and sipped at the warm, broth-like liquid. It was salty with flavors of cinnamon, fennel, and oregano. Not terrible, but a far cry from the meals that we ate in Chedi.

"It's beautiful, isn't it?" my mother asked. "I've missed it."

I could only nod.

"You should look out the other side, too, at the berths. You've only seen your maker's true body. This is your chance to see others."

I shrugged. Most alloys in orbit were in stasis while their incarn bodies lived on Earth. A few, like my maker, were pilots who transported cargo from Earth to other parts of the Solar System and beyond. They held little interest for me compared to the destination that floated outside the window.

"They're part of your heritage, too," she said.

"Don't remind me."

"Akshaya—"

"Okay." I cut her off before she could lecture me again on how she'd made me a *hybrid*—someone not entirely human, someone with DNA from my maker, someone who might be the future of life on Meru—all while insisting that I hide that part of myself from the world.

I pushed off and drifted to the other side of the corridor, grateful for the time I had spent in Chedi's zero-gravity viewing bubble since an early age. The station was technically in microgravity, held in Earth's orbit, but it made no appreciable difference to how I moved. Outside, I could see rows of berths—ovoid structures that held individual alloys. I'd seen my maker's true body many times after I was old enough to spacewalk. While zir humanlike incarn lived inside Chedi with us, zir true body—large enough to hold several passengers and designed to live in a vacuum—rested on a sheltered portion of Chedi's exterior, a kind of makeshift berth. Most of the alloys orbiting Earth were much smaller, two to three times the length of a human. I spotted only a few massive pilots.

"I wish Maker could've flown us here," I remarked.

"So do I," my mother said, her tone wistful.

I tried to imagine her coming to Earth orbit and meeting my maker for the first time. "Is it strange for you? Coming back after so long?"

"Very much, though I'm looking forward to it. I'm definitely not the same person I was when I left. I wasn't a mother then. I was only a few years older than you."

And yet she'd not only left Earth, she'd crossed two hundred light-years to go to Meru, a planet that had no other humans at the time. My maker had carried her there. They'd fallen in love. She'd gotten pregnant with me. It was a whole big saga, and people had written books and made immersives about their story. Somya had watched some of them. I found it too unsettling to see fictionalized versions of my parents, but I knew that my mother had taken incredible risks with her life.

"Can we look at Earth again?" I asked.

We drifted back to the other side. The orbital station was passing over Asia, and my mother pointed out roughly where my grandparents lived, the home where she'd grown up. The great curve of the snow-capped Himalayas was unmistakable. I'd studied Earth's geography, but seeing it in person made me giddy. In another two hours, an alloy would carry us to the surface, and I'd finally set foot on my home planet.

---

"Come in, come in!" My grandmother, Kundhina, ushered us into the family home, a squat building whose exterior walls were made with soil and covered in plants. Most of the dwellings we'd seen between the landing point and my grandparents' house were built in the same style. I'd never seen anything like it on Chedi, whose structures were made of biosynthetics. Also strange: The houses on Earth didn't have doors.

They had synthetic privacy curtains, which blocked the view from the outside but allowed small animals and some air to pass through.

My grandfather, Vidhar, pulled me and my mother into an embrace. His hairless incarn's face expressed a feeling of glad-sad-fond while his chromatophores glowed with the same emotions in purple, yellow, and pink. He and my grandmother had visited Chedi during our passes through the Solar System, often staying for several months. I had memories of playing and swimming and exploring Chedi with them when I was small. I gloried in being able to speak phoric with them in out-of-the-way places where no humans could observe us.

Like my maker, my grandparents were alloys whose true bodies lived in space and shared a consciousness with their incarns. The law didn't allow alloys on Earth to take forms that resembled human beings, but my grandparents had received an exception in order to raise my mother, who was entirely human. Other than their lack of hair, they had bodies similar to my maker's—dark skinned with chromatophores swirling across their arms, cheeks, and neck.

"Welcome home," my grandfather said, his gaze fixed upon my mother.

To my surprise, she blinked, and a couple of tears fell down her cheeks. I'd never seen my mother act sentimental. She brushed them away and regained her composure. My grandmother and Somya stood by the entrance and beamed at us.

"Let me show you to your room," my grandmother said to me and Somya.

As we walked down a hallway, she pointed out various pieces of art—paintings, ceramics, small sculptures—all made by human hands, some dating back to the Human Era. My grandparents were anthropologists, and they'd spent years collecting works from across the continent.

Our room was just big enough to fit two beds, a couple of sling chairs, and a chest of drawers. A door in the back led to an open-air tub made of stone and set into the ground next to a vine-covered wall.

“There’s a shower around the other side,” Kundhina said, “but the tub is really nice at night.”

I looked up and saw the vast black sky sprinkled with dancing points of light. For a moment, the beauty took me away. Then the world swayed under my feet, and I had to close my eyes. I felt my grandmother’s hand steadying me.

“Don’t worry, you’ll get used to it.” She guided me back inside.

I had experienced immersives of Earth, but standing under an actual sky affected me in an entirely different way—something to do with inner-ear mechanics. I lay back on my bed and anchored myself by staring at the ceiling. Inside, everything felt the same as it had while in Chedi. My grandmother left the room.

Somya started to put their clothes away. “I wonder how long it’ll take you to adjust. Can’t get very far until you can handle being outdoors.”

I slow-blinked and activated my emchannel. Earth’s public network interface worked much the same as Chedi’s had. I connected and did some research on vertigo after space travel. Most of it had to do with time spent in microgravity and the effects on fluids in the human body. Few people like me had spent their entire lives in an enclosed space.

“According to the experts, it’ll take one to two weeks for my body to adapt,” I said aloud. “I hope I don’t have to spend most of it indoors.”

“Enjoy it while you can. We’ll be outside for the next six months. I’ve gone trekking with my family before, and I can tell you that after a few days, you’ll be wishing for a roof and a soft bed.”

---

That evening before dinner, we received a custom-printed atlas. The book held the latest data on the terrain and trails along our planned route. We would have to rely on it for the entire challenge since the rules prevented us from accessing updates.

We sat down to review our itinerary with my mother, my grandparents, and my mother's childhood friend, Mina. We would start by heading west to the coastal city of Banbhore, then continue past Ormara along the Gulf of Oman until we reached Hormirzad. From there, we would turn inland, heading north and west through the Fertile Crescent. We would then hug the northern coastline of Africa until we reached the bridge to Nuberia. There, we would have to find someone with a sailboat large enough to cross the Atlantic Ocean.

While at sea, we would follow Rune's original path to Cueva, through the strait into the Pacific Ocean, then head south and west across the equator. We'd have to sail all the way to Australia, stopping at Out of Bounds islands along the way. According to Rune's book, the people in Ganjdija would welcome ocean travelers and help us with supplies. Then we would head back north, threading through Nusantara, crossing the equator again, and leave the boat behind in Mawlamyine. Somya's family lived a bit east of there, along the borderlands, and we wanted to see them. We would make the rest of the journey over land through Loka, back to our starting point.

"With the slight detour to visit Somya's family," I said to the group, "we expect that the whole trip will take a hundred and fifty days. We have a hundred and eighty days before Chedi's final shuttle run from here, but we're going to lose a week or two to my vestibular system. The biggest unknown is the ocean, especially the winds in the Out of Bounds."

The alloys who managed Loka redirected a certain amount of Earth's energy to push extreme weather into the OOB, where it would harm fewer humans. Rune had described only two trips in his book, and he'd encountered calm seas as well as boat-damaging storms in different places and at different times. We had to prepare for both.

"You'll be spending a lot of time on the water," my grandmother said, sounding a little stunned.

The others murmured in agreement.

"According to Rune," Somya said, "it's safer than traveling overland through the Out of Bounds, especially if we stick to established sailing routes. Plus, it allows us to bypass getting approval from the Committee for Intercontinental Travel."

"Who's going to take you on their boat?" my grandfather asked.

"We should be able to find someone at Nuberia," Somya said, their voice confident as usual. "We have to arrive there before the end of November, which is when the regatta starts, and we think we'll get there a week before."

"The regatta?" Mina asked.

"A group of boats that sails together," I explained. "They attempt to cross the Atlantic Ocean around the same time every year."

"What happens if you don't reach Nuberia in time?" Mina asked.

I exchanged a glance with Somya. We didn't have a good answer.

"Hope that someone is still there?" I shrugged.

My mother, who had been unusually quiet, finally spoke up. "Maybe we should reach out to this Rune person. He seems to have a lot of knowledge, and he might be able to introduce you to someone in the regatta."

I had to admit that her idea was a good one. Somya raised their brows and nodded at me.

"I'll send him a message," I said.

I slow-blinked and thought-retrieved his full name, Rune Edersan, then looked up his contact information. I sent a brief message introducing myself. I explained that Somya and I planned to attempt the Anthro Challenge in the near future and asked for advice about finding a boat and crew who could help us, as well as any other information he'd be willing to share.

By the time I'd sent it—after reading it over five times—the conversation had moved on to our supply needs. We decided to add a trailer to Somya's bike for camping equipment, food, water, and, in an emergency, me. Our list of items to obtain on Earth included a print copy of Rune's book and outerwear to protect us from rain and snow. We had to traverse a couple of higher-altitude locations across eastern Asia, and despite the alloys' efforts, the weather there could turn cold and wet. I secretly hoped that we would get to see snow, something I'd experienced only in immersives.

"What about medical supplies?" my mother asked.

"According to Rune," I said, "the purpose of the original challenge was to prove that humans don't need alloys to live harmoniously with the Earth. We can get medical help as long as it's entirely provided by human beings using only human-era technology."

"It's ridiculous that you can't make an exception for illness." My mother shook her head. "Who invented the rules of this challenge?"

"People like you and me," Mina said with a wicked grin.

While growing up, my mother had discovered that only a few other humans cared about accomplishing big, demanding goals. She'd found a few of her age, including Mina, and they had formed the Society of Humans with Ambitions. The name was ridiculous, but they were part of the reason that she'd gone to Meru the first time. Since then, especially after people voted to allow humans to travel in space, many of those with similar inclinations had moved to Chedi or the Primary Nivid. To me, they didn't seem strange, but according to my mother, the majority of people on Earth were very different. Somya agreed. They had told me that their relatives had no interest in travel or studies or accomplishments of any kind. I found it hard to comprehend.

Alloys had kept humans constrained to the same way of life for hundreds of years. They held all the power in the Constructed Democracy of Sol by virtue of outnumbering humans by five orders of magnitude. Alloys used exile as a consequence for their own kind's worst transgressions, which ruined people's lives, including my maker's and one of zir good friends. They applied a similar principle to the humans in Loka, sending anyone who refused treatment for behavioral excess, including Aspiration and Avarice Disorder, to the Out of Bounds. If Somya and

I succeeded in our ultimate goal, to create a new kind of society there, like the one we had in Chedi, we would give those people a better life. I had tried and failed to get my mother to see why our idea was important. She had lost interest in political action during our time in exile, preferring to start over on a new planet rather than agitate for better laws for humankind.

<I think the Anthro Challenge sounds like fun,> my grandmother flashed in rapid phoric. <I wish I could come, but I suppose that would be breaking the rules.>

I smiled, grateful that she pulled me away from my thoughts, and pulled up my sleeves. <I wish you could, too,> I flashed. <Sorry.>

"I put in the fabrication order," Somya said. "Everything should be ready in five days."

So unless Rune said something extraordinary to dissuade us—assuming he replied at all—that meant that we could leave as soon as I felt fit. I almost couldn't believe it. After dreaming about the Anthro Challenge for so long, I would actually get to try it. *No, trying isn't good enough. I have to complete it. I have to succeed so that I can stay on this amazing, beautiful, powerful planet for the rest of my life.*

---

Halfway through dinner, Rune's reply arrived: "Delighted to make your acquaintance and to discover a new generation of enthusiasm for the AC, especially from someone in such a well-known family. I'm free in a couple of hours to converse, if it isn't too late in the day for you?"

I wouldn't have refused, regardless of the time. I tried to be patient through the rest of the meal and for the hour that followed. When the call request came, I thought-shared my visual and audio with the others. Everyone in the house wanted to be involved, even Mina, who delayed their return home so they could listen in.

Rune's camera showed him from the waist up, perched on a chair with a dark wooden wall behind him. Bright blue-gray eyes stood out in his brown-skinned face. Teal-colored hair fell to his shoulders in gentle waves, and a bushy gray beard hid his neck. His waistline was paunchy and saggy, but his shoulders and arms had well-defined muscles. He wore a sleeveless tunic patterned with a geometric design, its colors faded by sun or time or both.

*It's really him!* All other words fled from my head.

"Hello, I'm Somya," my friend said, coming to my rescue.

They introduced me and the others in the room and enthused about meeting Rune with the perfect amount of admiration and respect.

"I'm flattered," Rune said with a smile. "I know it's getting late for you there, so let's get right to it. I'd like to offer myself and my boat for the sailing portions of your journey."

I held myself back from saying, *Aren't you too old?* But perhaps my expression betrayed me.

"I promise you that I'm fit enough for it, and so is the *Svapna*," he said. A grin gleamed through his shaggy mustache. "In fact, I'm on my boat right now. It's been my home for the past fifteen years—no, almost twenty years. Time gets away from you when you're my age. Anyway, I have a young assistant by the name of Halli Kangas on board as well. Between the two of us, we've sailed around the entire world twice, and it would be my great honor to help you cross both the Atlantic and Pacific Oceans. You mentioned trying to find someone at the regatta, but the attendance for that is quite poor—fewer than ten boats lately—and they like to race. They won't want to wait around for you if you miss the start date."

He offered to pick us up at Alanya, on the eastern edge of the Mediterranean Sea. From there, we would sail west, through the Strait of Gibraltar, and then follow his previous Anthro Challenge route. Somya and I nodded along as he outlined the stops. We recognized the names from our plan.

"The harder part," Rune added, "will be the land crossings. I looked over your route, and it seems good—in theory. What you'll come to realize is that the weather won't be your only challenge. You'll also have to deal with unexpected terrain, the people you encounter, and yourselves."

"We've trained a lot," Somya said. "We can handle it."

"Perhaps your bodies can, but your minds will betray you. It gets tedious, crossing those kilometers day after day. No entertainment, no rest, no diversions. At least you'll have each other for company, but I've heard from other adventurers that a group isn't always a benefit. The stress of the journey can test even the best of relationships. I'm not saying this to dissuade you but to make sure you're as prepared as you can be."

"And what about people being a problem?" I asked, finding my tongue at last. "Should we bring something to defend ourselves?"

"What?" Rune looked almost comically startled. "No, nothing like that. The danger isn't one of violence but of good intentions gone wrong. Humans like to help each other, and they're so used to relying on what the alloys provide that they might cause you to violate the rules of the challenge. Stay cautious and think twice before accepting assistance from strangers. If you send me your proposed land route, I'll see if I know people along the way who you can trust, who will understand what you're trying to do. The Anthro Challenge isn't a popular undertaking. Many people have never heard of it."

That didn't surprise me, given that no one had completed it since Rune's successful attempt. With Rune picking us up at Alanya, we wouldn't have to make the trek across Northern Africa, which meant that most of our time on land would be at the start and end of our journey. I had trouble believing that those few weeks could pose any real problems, but Rune was the expert.

I half listened as the adults in the room asked him questions about food and water and potential illness. Alanya wasn't much of a detour from our original itinerary, so I modified our route and sent the details to everyone. We probably wouldn't need to find Rune's friends along the way, but it couldn't hurt to know who they were.

After an hour, the conversation began to devolve into speculation and outlandish contingencies. Somya and I exchanged a look of understanding. At the next lull, Somya pounced.

"I think we're as prepared as we're going to be," they said firmly. "Thank you for the help, Rune. We're hoping to leave in a week or so, once Akshaya has adapted to the open sky. We'll see you in Alanya three weeks after that."

With that, our meeting ended, and everyone retired to their beds. I listened to the sound of raindrops outside, the wind spattering them in bursts every few minutes. *A rainstorm!* My eyes refused to stay closed. Not only were we going to do the Anthro Challenge, we'd be sailing with Rune! It seemed almost too good to be true.

"Are you awake?" Somya's whisper carried over the noise of the rain.

"Yes."

"I can't sleep."

"Neither can I." I rolled over so that I faced their bed.

"Nervous?" they asked.

"Of course. Aren't you?"

"Nah. I'm excited."

"Rune made it sound like so many things could go wrong, and he didn't finish the first time. What if—"

"Don't go there. We'll make it, Aks. We have to. *You* have to. With Nara's documentary, everyone will know what we're doing. Your parents will have to hold up their end of the deal. Remember, the real goal isn't the Anthro Challenge, it's letting you live on Earth for the rest of your life. No more Chedi and *never* Meru."

I had almost forgotten, with all the preparations for our journey. *Never Meru.*

"Thanks, Som. You're right."

"I always am."

I reached across the gap between our beds and smacked them with a pillow.

"Hey!"

I cackled. Somya began to laugh. We fed off each other until my body shook with helpless mirth, my sides ached, and tears leaked from my eyes. After several minutes, I caught my breath.

"Good night, Som."

"Sweet dreams, Aks."

# NARA (DAY -5)

Nara needed to recruit eyes on Earth, and fast. He had narrowed the list significantly based on the need for the person to A) be a pilot, B) have atmospheric flying skills, C) have permission to fly everywhere on Earth, and D) exhibit some interest in artistic pursuits. Only one name remained: Reshyan. The pilot enjoyed making immersive art in zir spare time, and Nara had become a fan after seeing a series of pieces on the solitude of interstellar exploration, something that Reshyan had done before zie remade zirself into a weathercrafter. Really, Nara couldn't have invented a more perfect fit.

And yet, Reshyan refused the commission.

<Not interested,> the pilot flashed, zir phores glowing with aquamarine indifference.

The two of them floated in Nara's office, a custom-designed mindspace that gave the illusion of floating under a dark ceiling streaked with pale orange and above a bowl-shaped canopy of trees. White marble carved into delicate filigree ribs curled around them and formed the outlines of a sphere. Nara had chosen the design to create a sense of tasteful elegance without crossing into gaudiness. Over the years he had planned everything for this project, holding on to a sliver of hope that Jayanthi and Vaha would agree to it one day. That day had finally come. Nara was ready with interview questions and a production crew, but he had to scramble to get permits for working on Earth, an angle he hadn't anticipated. With those in hand, he had turned to recruitment. The majority of Nara's crew lived in stasis, like himself, but some tasks required an alloy who primarily existed in the physical world, in this case, a pilot who could also make competent artistic decisions in the field. Reshyan was Nara's best hope. If zie refused, Nara would have to settle for a worse fit, but he kept his anxiety from leaking into his phores.

<I care little for the matters of humankind,> Reshyan flashed. <I'm here for the research and deployment of weathercrafting. Taking time to follow a couple of people on the surface will distract me and incur an opportunity cost in terms of energy and time.>

Nara examined the other alloy's aspect. Reshyan hadn't altered zir physical appearance for mindspace—pale-green eyes, blue-black skin with simple rectangular black wings, phores dotted at random, and a single-fin tail. No clothing. No headpiece. No adornment of any kind. Nara had crafted his own appearance with far greater care, enhancing the green of his skin, setting his tail to a fashionably fluttering style, and wearing a tailored sleeveless tunic worked with silver embroidery. The effect was wasted on Reshyan. Nara should have expected that. Reshyan was the kind of person who enjoyed spending a lot of time in zir own head. Hence the voyages outside the Solar System. Zie had little interest in documentaries or entertainment in general. Nara had done his research, and Reshyan hadn't turned up in any of his fan groups. He had found the pilot's social presence across three interests: atmospheric science, immersive art, and microgravity flight. Nara hoped he could entice Reshyan through the second category.

<You'll receive full credit for the footage and camera deployment,> Nara flashed. <In addition, I'll list you as an assistant art director. If you remember three or four varshas back, the number of fictionalized shows and books about Jayanthi and Vaha were incredibly popular—many still are—but no one could produce a documentary work. They wouldn't even give interviews from Chedi! Now they've agreed to let me follow

their child—someone who's grown up on a megaconstruct, far from most of society—as she attempts to cross the Earth. It's a massive breakthrough, and I guarantee that this show is going to be huge, especially with the format that I'm planning. When that happens, your name and your art will reach a much wider audience.>

The blue-green hue persisted in Reshyan's phores. <I make immersives to relax. I'm not looking to build a reputation.>

Nara quelled his frustration before it could show. He scanned the notes from his extended memory. There had to be something he could use to persuade Reshyan . . . aha! Perhaps a personal connection would do it. He phrased his next question with care.

<Does your genetic relationship to Pushkara have something to do with your disinterest? Perhaps you'd like this documentary to cover another side of Vaha and Jayanthi's story?>

Reshyan's expression turned thoughtful. <I'm not a fan of my ancestor's political leanings, however . . .>

Nara waited. As a person who liked to think, Reshyan wouldn't appreciate being pestered with questions, and *however* implied that perhaps zie would propose something, in which case Nara could figure out how to make that happen.

At last, the pilot's phores flashed. <I take issue with the exile.>

<You think Pushkara's term is too long?>

<No. He accepted his fate. I think that the policy is fundamentally wrong and should be abolished.>

Well, that had certainly not turned up in Nara's research. Were his skills slipping? How had he missed Reshyan's views on such a significant political topic?

<Is there a referendum coming up that you'd like me to endorse?> Nara asked. He wasn't averse to trading his vote, especially on a policy to which he'd given little thought.

<Nothing yet. First we need greater awareness on why exile is punitive rather than consequential. There are many aspects of it that can go

wrong physically, and it costs all of us to remake exiles, or in the worst cases, to give them a full rebirth. On top of that, the memory degradation doesn't necessarily change the exiles' fundamental worldview, which is what the worst offenders require in order to be rehabilitated into society. It would be far more efficient to treat them the way we do humans—remake them with modified gene expression, assign them a social helper, and allow them to continue as active members of society. Alternatively, give them the choice of true exile, to live somewhere far removed from the populous areas of the CDS.>

<I see,> Nara flashed. He had never heard of a social helper, and he wasn't sure he agreed with all of Reshyan's declarations, but he could see the passion in the pilot's words. Here, at last, he had some leverage to work with. <And how can I help you to bring about this beneficial change?>

<I'll sign your contract,> Reshyan replied, <if you'll include a clause to collaborate with me on another documentary, one that shows people why exile is so terrible.>

<That's . . . a significant request.>

<You're asking a lot of me, too,> Reshyan flashed. <I'll have to fly many extra hours in order to get the recordings that you need.>

Nara had always worked on projects that inspired him, that piqued his artistic interests. Did he really want to commit to one without knowing more about it? At the very least, shouldn't he convince himself that he could produce the narrative that Reshyan demanded? Then again, what choice did he have if he wanted to make the best possible show about Jayanthi and Vaha? Other alloy pilots worked on Earth's atmosphere and climate, but only Reshyan had the eye for visuals that Nara needed. He really couldn't settle for second best.

<Very well,> Nara flashed. <I'll propose your idea as my next project, and if voters approve the necessary resources, I'll produce it. Do we have an agreement?>

Reshyan flashed in the affirmative. Nara allowed his phores to glow indigo with satisfaction. His previous documentaries had received acclaim, but they had struggled to find a wide audience. This one, he was certain, would make his name known to every living alloy.

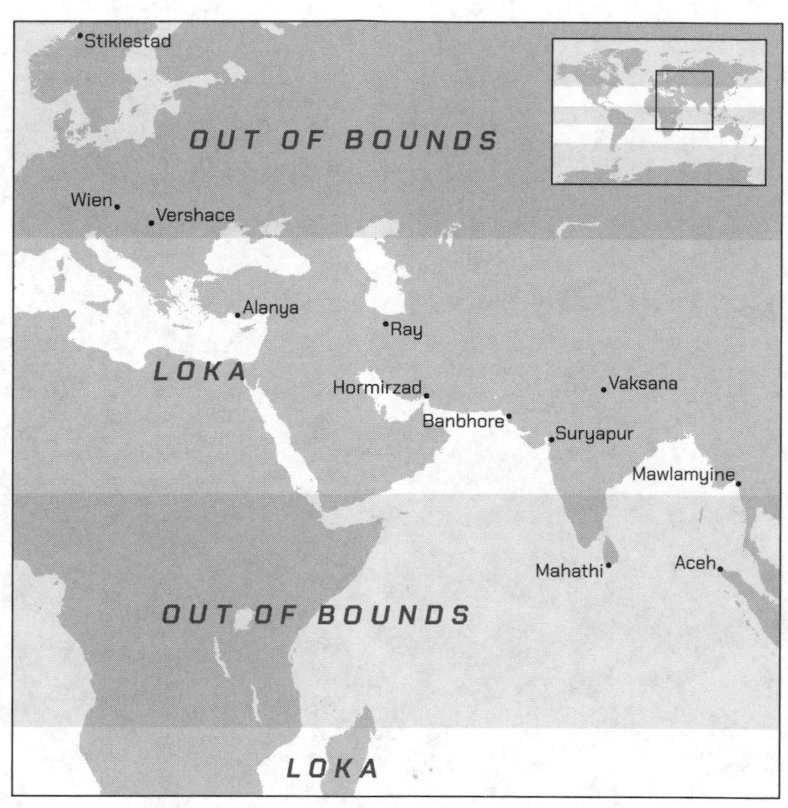

Stiklestad
OUT OF BOUNDS
Wien
Vershace
Alanya
Ray
LOKA
Hormirzad
Vaksana
Banbhore
Suryapur
Mawlamyine
Mahathi
Aceh
OUT OF BOUNDS
LOKA

# DAY 1

Somya and I left exactly fourteen days after we arrived on Earth. It annoyed me that my body took that long to adjust to the surface, but we needed the extra time anyway. Getting the rest of the camping gear had also taken longer than we'd expected. Chedi would have fabricated whatever we needed after a simple request, but on Earth, we had to take a trip to the heart of Vaksana, the town where my grandparents lived, to explain why we needed the items, and then to provide evidence that we didn't own much and didn't suffer from avarice, possessiveness, or hoarding disorders.

We'd spent the better part of a day packing and repacking our gear until everything was stacked in a stable fashion on the trailer. I'd also spent two hours talking to Nara, who wanted an interview before we began our journey.

"I love you," my mother said as we shouldered our packs.

She put on a *brave-not-worried* face and gave me a kiss. I almost felt guilty for what we were about to do, but then I remembered Somya's words: *Never Meru*. If I quit, I'd end up stuck on a planet two hundred light-years away for the next five years of my life. I embraced my mother and told her I loved her, then did the same for my grandparents. Somya and I had sent our recorded farewell messages to our parents in Chedi the night before.

Outside, the sun rose into a partly clear sky and lit the treetops. *Clouds.* Those alone would have made the journey to Earth worthwhile. I'd only observed a couple of types—thin and wispy cirrus, or puffy and scattered cumulus. Surely we'd see more during our travels. I was especially eager to witness thunderheads and coastal fog.

We stayed on the roads until we reached the forest trail that would lead to our first camping site on the outskirts of Dandur. I'd seen my first dog, cat, cow, and goat already, but when we stopped for lunch, I spotted birds in the canopy above us. I pulled out my print edition of *The Field Guide to Earth Flora and Fauna*, a gift from my parents on my fifteenth birthday, along with a small pencil. I had memorized most of the book's contents, but I wanted to mark everything I could identify.

"Look, a rose-ringed parakeet," I called out to Somya, pointing at the brilliant-green bird. "And there, a verditer flycatcher!" Its feathers had an iridescent shade of blue with a hint of green. "Aren't they amazing?"

Somya grinned and swallowed a bite of their sandwich. "Are you going to do this the entire time? Because there are a lot of trees on Earth, which means a lot of birds, too."

I playfully smacked the back of their head with the guide. "Maybe you don't appreciate how amazing the biodiversity is here, but that doesn't mean I won't."

I kept up the commentary in spite of Somya's groans. Not only did I see a variety of birds but also lizards and snakes. I spotted a lone jungle cat on one of the slower uphill sections of our ride. Microconstruct insects flitted around, glittering wherever they caught a sunbeam. Those I ignored after a couple of glances. They appeared identical to the ones on Chedi.

We also saw alloys and constructs along the way. The latter were easy to spot from a distance, their metal bodies glinting in the light. The former, however, often had skin that blended with the environment. They ranged in size from that of a deer to as large as a house, and their bodies had strong animallike characteristics—hooves, tails, feathers and wings, four-legged bodies. Sometimes the only reason I could identify them was because I knew which animals still existed on Earth. We did our best to pull onto side trails and stay out of their sight, but I couldn't help holding my breath when they spotted us. Luckily we received some *confused-but-not-enough-to-care* looks, and no one stopped to question us.

I would have preferred to stay on wilderness trails. The solar bikes could handle the terrain, but the trailer that held our gear made it awkward, and as my mother had correctly predicted, the rough surfaces took more pedaling effort than the roads. Somya towed all of the heavy items on the trailer, except for our packs, which we wore. Somya's pack held half the maps, and I kept the rest along with my field guide, a blank sketchbook, and Rune's book. We didn't bother with any recording devices because somewhere above us, an alloy named Reshyan kept watch.

The pilot flew too high for us to notice zir, and the self-guided indriya devices—about the size of an apple—stayed mostly out of sight. Since any alloy interference would invalidate the challenge, Reshyan couldn't drop down to interview us or intrude on our journey in any way. I liked that. It allowed me to pretend that we were on our own. It also provided a good disincentive if we were ever tempted to cheat.

The temperature was pleasant, well suited to the lightweight pants and long-sleeved tunics we wore. Breezes cooled our sweat. The planet had so much life to it. Not just the creatures, but also the plants. No place on Chedi grew this wild. She maintained wooded areas, but her ambulatory constructs had cultivated those carefully. In a closed environment like hers, she had to keep everything in balance, from trees to bacteria, whereas on Earth, a forest could mostly sustain itself. I'd never seen or heard or smelled anything like it. Every kilometer we traversed convinced me that I'd made the right choice. I belonged on Earth, not Meru.

---

We arrived at the outskirts of Dandur with about three hours of sunlight left. A narrow dirt path took us away from the main road and up a gentle hill. My legs begged for mercy, so I switched the bike to powered mode. Eventually, the incline eased, and we reached a flattened crest. The view brought me to a stop. The slope beside us dropped away to a lake, its far shore bounded by a crumbling wall. Above it rose the sandstone walls of a vast fortress, punctuated by rounded towers topped with domes and graceful arched windows. In the center of the lake floated a square stone platform covered in wild greenery. The blocky artificial lines of the construction screamed Human Era.

"I wonder how old that place is," Somya commented.

"Around 700 HE," I said. I'd spent hours each night looking up our waypoints and learning about them. "It's called Amber Fort, though it was also used as a palace."

"More than fourteen hundred years old," Somya exclaimed. "I'm impressed that people could build like that before we had constructs or alloys to help."

After the catastrophic years, humans had genetically engineered their behavior to have less attachment to permanent structures, like buildings and roads. They'd made concessions for sites of historical value, protecting them from the degradations of nature and time, and the alloys had continued the work. A couple of ruminant alloys cropped at the plants growing along the base of the fort. I turned away and looked for a place we could set up our tent. I found a reasonably clear spot near a small grove of trees and called out to Somya to join me.

"I'm glad that humans invented solar bikes before the Alloy Era," I said as I dismounted. I stretched and bent from side to side to loosen my stiff back. We'd ridden for nearly seven hours with only a short break for lunch. The bikes' solar paint could draw a good amount of energy from the sun, which I needed, because there was no way I could have pedaled the entire day.

"Tent or food?" Somya asked.

"Definitely food. I'll give you a hand with the tent if you need it."

"How do you feel?"

I began to set up the cooking gear. "My neck and shoulders are bit stiff, and my butt is sore, but otherwise I'm doing okay. I pedaled for a quarter or maybe a third of the day. No worse than some of the rides we did around Chedi."

"Remember that time when we were halfway around and my gearbox broke?"

I groaned. "Yes, that was the worst. I felt like my legs were going to fall off by the time we got to Orange village."

We'd gotten stranded in an undeveloped part of Chedi. With no constructs around and no easy way to get the ship's attention, we had abandoned our bikes and walked for two hours. Afterward, I had to spend almost a week in my high-oxygen room getting infusions to help my body deal with the stress. My parents had not been happy about it.

Somya had apologized to them profusely—though the malfunction was in no way their fault—and came to visit me every day. I'd never seen them so worried. The incident happened less than a year after they arrived on Chedi, and it was the first time they'd seen me get sick. I had laughed it off at the time, but looking back on it, I realized how scared they must have felt. We were still kids at the time.

"Don't worry," I said. I placed a pot of dried chickpeas and water on the stove. "I'm not feeling nearly that bad."

"Good." The tent sprang to life. "So what's for dinner?"

"Couscous with onions, peppers, and beans." As I spoke, I chopped the vegetables. "Since I'm making dinner, you get cleanup duty. How about riding down to the lake and getting us more water?"

"We could trade?"

"No way." I laughed. "I've tried your cooking."

"Point taken." Somya stood beside their bike and gave it a baleful stare. "Actually, I think I'll walk."

I dropped the onions in a pan of hot oil. The aroma made my stomach gurgle. I kept one eye on the food and the other on Somya's shrinking form. I wished we had enough time to visit the fort, but that would've required us to apply for permission in advance. *It doesn't matter,* I told myself. As long as we finished the challenge, I'd have the rest of my life to explore Earth. Our first day had gone well. I took it as an omen. If the rest of our days went like this one, we'd have no trouble completing our journey.

# DAY 4

Over the next three days, we averaged about 350 kilometers per day. The terrain gradually shifted from dry and hilly to flat and wet. We found more out-of-the-way paths to avoid alloy traffic, but our gear got splashed as we rode through one stream after another. Our timing was fortuitous—this was supposedly the start of the dry season. I couldn't imagine taking these routes while the water levels were high. Alloys running on four legs wouldn't mind the wet roads, but the bikes were a different story.

We approached Banbhore toward the end of the fourth day. Before we reached the city, we arrived at the coast. My first glimpse of the Indian Ocean was simply a deeper blue line along the horizon. As we rode west, that line grew in thickness and transformed into a dazzling array of hues, many of which I had no words for. Sapphire, silver, lapis—jewel tones could hint at the beauty of the sea, but they failed to capture its living, breathing nature.

When the ground turned sandy, we abandoned our bikes in favor of our feet. The unceasing rush of waves had a musicality that I'd never noticed before, and I stood for many minutes just listening to it. Meanwhile, Somya took off their shoes, pulled their leggings above their knees, and waded in. The vastness of the water awed me. I'd seen immersives of the ocean, but nothing could compare to the reality of its mass. So much water! I tasted the saltiness in the spray, felt the sting of sand on my shins, watched the sun's light shimmer on its surface.

I sloshed past Somya into deeper water. Each wave tried to carry me back to shore, and I watched as my friend demonstrated how to swim between the crests. The water was cooler than lakes in Chedi, but my body adapted. We made our way to a more sheltered spot and dove under. The sight of striped damselfish and angelfish greeted me. Parrotfish nibbled at coral, and a turtle larger than either of us clamped a bit of seagrass in its jaws.

I popped up to get some air and yelled to Somya, "Did you see the turtle?"

"Yes," they said.

We grinned and dove down for another look, then another, and another. Eventually, and with reluctance, I pointed out the setting sun, and we swam back to the beach where we'd entered. My limbs ached with the exertion of the swim, and my skin prickled with salt as it dried, but I didn't care.

"Let's go again in the morning," I said.

Somya nodded and handed me a towel. We changed into dry clothes and headed onward to Banbhore. The city occupied a section of coastal plain about fifty kilometers long. We rode around the outskirts until we spotted a community garden, one tended by humans for pleasure. We needed to restock our fresh produce, so we parked the bikes outside the garden's edge and grabbed a couple of sacks and shears. The sun had set, and we hadn't seen anyone at the beach or along our ride, but a couple of people attended the plots of vegetables and fruits. We gave them a wide berth.

"I'll get fruits and nuts," Somya offered, pointing to a small grove on the northern side.

I nodded and walked past the grain storage to the vegetables. At this time of year, beans hung from vines, and early season roots and greens were nice and tender. I finished collecting what we'd need for the next several days and returned to our trailer. As I secured the bag, I saw motion in my periphery. I turned and saw someone beside me, close enough that their identifiers popped up in my visual via near-field access. Her name was Ebra, and she had light-brown skin with wide, dark eyes perched over her thin nose and lips. A braid of blue hair draped over one shoulder and fell to a decorative belt around her waist. A beautiful gown of indigo with turquoise leaf embroidery draped over a slender, adolescent body similar to mine. I felt comparatively unkempt in my mud-splattered tan leggings, matching tunic, and windblown hair.

"I've never seen devices like these," she said. "What are they, and how do you use them?"

"My friend and I are traveling across Asia," I said, a little taken aback at Ebra's directness. "They're called solar bikes. They're powered by sunlight and also our legs."

"It looks like you're camping." She waved at our other gear. "You're welcome to stay overnight with me and my family, if you'd like. We can offer you a kitchen and a hot bath." Her smile was open and offered no insult.

I noticed Somya walking toward us. "Let me check with my friend," I said. I strode toward Somya before Ebra could object. I wanted to talk in private.

"What's going on?" they asked.

"This person named Ebra has invited us to stay in her house tonight."

"Great! Let's go!"

"Just like that? We have no idea who she is."

On Chedi, I could identify every resident, and I knew that Chedi herself could always be alerted in case of trouble or bad behavior. But Earth had millions of people, nearly a billion if you counted the alloys and constructs. Human nature had changed a lot in recent centuries, and violence had been greatly reduced, but it wasn't gone.

My thoughts must have shown on my face, because Somya said, "It's not that scary here, I promise, and if you start to feel uncomfortable, we can always leave. Let's at least meet the family. We have nothing to lose."

But we did. "What if they do something that counts as alloy interference?"

Somya shrugged. "Let's tell them what we're about so they don't accidentally make us violate the challenge." They smiled and put a hand on my shoulder. "Aks, ease up. Humans here aren't dependent on alloys for everything. It'll be fine."

With reluctance, I agreed. Somya could befriend people easily, and things usually went right for them. My instincts, especially as a newcomer on the planet, would probably steer me wrong. Better to trust in my friend's experience and take their lead on unfamiliar matters.

We walked back to Ebra, who was crouching to examine our bikes. I made introductions, and Somya offered Ebra a ride on the trailer, which she happily accepted. She directed us to her family's home, and we arrived in less than five minutes. From the outside, the house resembled those I'd seen in Vaksana and others along our journey. It rose from the ground in a low rounded rectangle, its walls and roof covered by plants. Two windows faced the street, and a colorful privacy curtain hung across the doorway.

We parked the bikes and trailer to one side of the house and left our shoes on a covered shelf beside the entrance. Inside, the stone floor cooled my bare feet. The furniture was different than that of my grandparents' house. In place of low-slung chairs and a regen-redwood table, they had rattan sofas with small side tables made of matching wickerwork.

"Ammi, Dadi," Ebra called out.

Then she said something in a language I didn't understand. She had spoken fluent Terran to us before—the same language that everyone on Chedi used—but I'd learned that many human beings on Earth were bilingual. Regional languages persisted from centuries past, as did their cultural associations. If I'd had an active network connection, I could've heard a translation of Ebra's words, but I guessed their meaning as an older person emerged from a dim hallway.

"This is my grandmother," Ebra explained, switching back to Terran. "Please, sit down. I'll get everyone something to drink."

A two-legged construct with the name Yan carried Lilis, the grandmother, into the room and stopped near one of the sofas. The artificial being lowered into a squat and extended an arm to help Lilis move to a sofa. I wondered how Yan compared to someone like Chedi, given the difference in size and function.

"Thank you, Yan," Ebra's grandmother said. She patted the construct's side. "He's been with me for nearly three decades now, well past the expiration of his original contract."

I smiled politely.

"So what brings you to Banbhore?" Lilis asked us.

"We're on an adventure." Somya flashed her a grin that always won them new friends. "Our hope is to bike and sail all around the world, entirely on our own, with no help from alloys or constructs."

Ebra emerged with a middle-aged person whom she introduced as her mother. She set down a tray of tumblers made from coconut shells and handed us one each.

I took a sip of the mostly clear liquid. It was cool and slightly sweet, with an earthy undertone.

"Coconut water," Somya identified with delight. "I haven't had this in a while."

"It's delicious," I added, though I found the flavor strange. "Thank you."

"What an interesting journey you're on," Ebra's mother said. "Is there a reason you're doing it?"

"Just to prove that we can," I said quickly. I didn't feel like advertising that I was the child of Jayanthi and Vaha. Too many people had heard of my parents, and I wanted no special treatment, positive or otherwise. "We're doing something called the Anthro Challenge, an attempt to go around the Earth using transportation from the Human Era."

"Sounds difficult," Ebra's mother said. "And quite ambitious."

"It's also a lot of fun," Somya said.

They shot me a reassuring glance, then continued on, telling the others about the animals we'd seen along the way and explaining our mud-splattered clothing. After a few minutes, Somya had Ebra's family laughing so hard that tears streamed from their eyes. I grinned and allowed myself to relax, glad that my friend was happy to do the talking. When Ebra stood to cook dinner, I offered to help.

"I can chop whatever you need," I said.

Ebra put me to work, and I lost myself in the repetitive motions. Neither of us spoke much, other than to direct or be directed, and I found the silence as companionable as the conversation that continued in the front room.

Our meal consisted of flatbread spiced with garlic and chilis, a stew of vegetables with chunks of pea protein, and fried red legumes sprinkled with coconut and cumin seeds.

"It's delicious," I said around a mouthful. "Definitely better than what I could've made on the camp stove."

"You were an excellent assistant," Ebra said.

After dinner, Somya and Ebra's mother cleaned up while I took a hot bath. The water felt divine as I soaked my sore, aching body. After I got out, I gave my dirty clothes a quick rinse in the tub and hung them to dry.

We were sharing a bedroom with Ebra. I found her sitting on her bed, her gaze fixed on a viewing wall. I guessed that she was reading or in an immersive. Somya lounged on the other bed.

"You should sleep on this," they said in a low voice. "I'll set up my bedroll on the floor."

"No, let's share it," I said. "Might as well be comfortable for tonight. I re-ran the bath for you."

Somya left. I lay down and decided to close my eyes for just a minute. The next thing I knew, I awoke with a start to a dark room and Somya's sleeping form stretched out beside me. The sleeves on my nightshift had bunched around my elbow, and the phores on my arms glowed white with alarm. I took a deep, calming breath and forced them back to neutral, then lifted my head to make sure Ebra hadn't noticed.

Her bed was empty.

*Probably in the bathroom.*

I tried to fall back asleep, but my heart still thumped in my chest. Had a bad dream awakened me? If so, I couldn't recall it. I yawned and tried to let sleep take me, but part of me waited for Ebra to return. *Surely it doesn't take this long to use the bathroom at night. Is she getting a drink of water? Is something wrong?* I sat up carefully, trying not to disturb Somya. Was I ridiculous to worry? Probably. But my brain wouldn't stop churning, so I decided to investigate.

I crawled awkwardly past Somya and padded into the hallway. No light shone from the kitchen. A creaking noise sounded from somewhere, and I walked toward it. It came through an open window on the side of the house. I peered outside and saw Ebra and her mother rolling our bikes and trailer into a small shed toward the back of the house. *A storage place of some kind?* The night sky was clear and full of twinkling stars, so they didn't need to protect our gear from rain. *Why move them in the middle of the night without waking us?*

I returned to the bedroom and gently shook Somya awake.

"What?" they asked groggily.

"Sh, be quiet," I said. I relayed what I'd seen. "It's strange, right?"

"It is." After a pause, they said, "Maybe there's a good explanation for it. They're just putting our stuff somewhere sheltered. We don't have network access, so they might know something about the weather that we don't. I think we can wait until morning and ask them. It's not like we can ride off in the dark anyway."

Somya's explanation made sense. Maybe Ebra and her mother were trying to be considerate and let us get our rest. My heartsib shifted toward the wall and patted the bed. I lay down beside them and let their arm fall around me. After a few minutes, Ebra came back and got into her bed. My mind finally quieted after that. The slow rise and fall of Somya's chest against my back lulled me to sleep.

---

Dim gray light shone through the bedroom window. I felt a hand on my shoulder and turned to see Somya holding a finger against their lips. I went from half-asleep to fully awake in a second. Somya stood and beckoned me to follow them. In the other bed, Ebra slept, unmoving, her mouth hanging slightly open.

Somya led me through the hallway, out past the privacy curtain, and several meters down the street before they stopped.

"Something is definitely not right," they whispered in the predawn stillness. "I woke up a little while ago and started thinking about the conversation last night. I think I know what's going on. Ambitious."

"What?"

"Ebra's mother called the Anthro Challenge ambitious yesterday. I remember her using the word a few times."

"And?"

"That's one big difference between Chedi and here. If someone in Loka thinks you have Aspiration and Avarice Disorder, they can demand that you get evaluated."

"Som—"

"Don't say it." They held up a hand. "Yes, you were right. We shouldn't have come here."

"So what now?" I glanced at the sky. Blue washed over the eastern horizon, and only the brightest stars still showed in that part of the sky. "There's enough light to start riding. Should we get our bikes and go?"

"Yes, but quietly. If they notice us leaving, they might try to stop us. I don't think they'd get violent, but they could try to follow us. They'll probably try to figure out who our parents are so they can reach out to them and get us help, and if that doesn't work, they'll escalate to the alloys in orbit. Some of my extended family kept bothering Gamo Papa about their AAD a long time ago. That's one of the reasons they moved to Chedi."

I only knew the basics about how Aspiration and Avarice Disorder was handled on Earth. If it caused people to behave in ways that troubled the other members of their household or locality, they were given a choice: they could attempt to self-regulate their behavior, they could get treatment to reduce the effects of the disorder, or they could relocate to the Out of Bounds or somewhere away from Earth, like in Chedi.

Somya's description of what Ebra and her family might do to us didn't sound all that bad, but I trusted that they knew better than me what our course of action should be. We walked back to the house, and I led the way to the side building where I'd seen Ebra and her mother take our bikes. I held the privacy curtain aside while Somya wheeled my bike out first, then retrieved theirs. The trailer wheels squeaked, and we both froze for a heart-pounding minute. When no one emerged from the house, we continued, walking our bikes to the street and then riding away as quickly as we could. The electric motors were nearly silent. The only noise we made was the crunch of the wheels over the dirt.

We headed toward the community garden and the back road that had brought us into town. Staying off any main roads had become necessary in my mind. Not only would we have to avoid alloy interactions, but we'd also have to tread carefully around humans, keeping our identities and intentions to ourselves. It seemed like traveling in the Out of Bounds would make our journey easier. Rune had advised against it because of the harsher weather, but he hadn't said whether he dealt with obstruction from people in Loka. I wondered if human attitudes had changed in the intervening years, or if he'd gotten lucky.

Taking side and back routes meant more uncertainty in our navigation and timeline. In getting to Banbhore, we had stopped several times a day to check our maps. The roads often shifted. Main avenues ran between each of the major cities, but smaller routes drifted to accommodate natural forces. Anyone with network access could see the current conditions and find their way, and most humans traveled by alloy or construct, but Somya and I had to make our best guesses using old human tools like compasses and the maps we'd printed. Rune had tried to warn us about unexpected obstacles, but I hadn't thought that the very humans I shared the planet with would be the first.

# DAY 9

We made it all the way to Hormirzad with only one stop for food at a small town named Gwadar, and we managed to avoid seeing any other humans along the way. Alloy encounters, though, had occurred a little more frequently. Even on the wilderness routes, we spotted them, often in the distance, nibbling at ground cover or tree leaves, digging at the ground to channel waterways, running at full speed along the trails. Sometimes I had to look closely to determine if they were indeed alloys or if they were Earth animals. Most of them didn't give us a second glance. Other than rare exceptions like my grandparents, alloys didn't live on Earth willingly. Most were assigned a period of service to make amends for breaking laws. I couldn't tell by looking at the ones we passed which category they belonged to.

Back when the Constructed Democracy of Sol was formed, alloys and humans signed a compact that allowed alloys, who lived in space, to take a certain amount of Earth's natural resources. In exchange, they would assist in the management of the planet and provide technology to assist the humans living on its surface. There were strict rules about the forms that alloy incarns could take, most especially that they couldn't resemble human beings, like my maker did. I had never given it too much thought, but now that I saw so many of them, I realized how unique my childhood had been.

The first buildings marking Hormirzad appeared on the horizon around midday. It was a medium-size city where we were supposed to find Pazir, a friend of Rune's. They had offered to help us cross the mountains that stood between Hormirzad and the city of Ray, about 1,300 kilometers to the northwest. We hid our bikes outside the city limits, shouldered a few essentials in our packs, and entered the city on foot. Our encounter with Ebra and her family had made it clear that our bikes could draw unwanted attention, and we wanted no trouble this time.

We arrived at Pazir's house a little after the sun's peak. The architecture had shifted from the verdant constructions we'd seen in the first few days. The buildings in Hormirzad still blended with their surroundings, but the arid climate meant that they were built from stone the color of sand and had none of the lush green plant coverings of Vaksana. Windows were cut into the domed buildings with beautiful geometric patterns. Solar paint covered every solid surface with colorful murals or abstract designs.

Somya stepped in front of Pazir's doorway and called out a greeting.

A middle-aged person, with dark hair peppered by gray, pulled the privacy curtain aside. Her identity popped up in my visual: Shalma Abbasi, a resident of the household.

"Hello. How can I help you?"

"We're here to see Pazir," Somya explained. "We're friends of Rune."

"Ah, of course." Recognition lit Shalma's eyes. "We're expecting you. Please come in."

The cutout windows cast patterns of dappled light on the cool stone floors and walls. We passed through a shadowed hallway into an open sunlit room. A warm breeze blew in, carrying scents of the sea mixed with something that reminded me of the areas near Chedi's engines. A simple cot occupied one end of the room. Next to a window, an older person rested in a reclining sling chair, eyes closed, feet propped on a rounded cushion.

"Pazir," said our host softly, touching their shoulder. "The people Rune mentioned are here to see you."

Pazir's eyes—a washed-out blue-gray—opened. After a second, they smiled and beckoned us closer. Shalma brought over two more cushions for us to sit on.

"So you are the two doing the Anthro Challenge?" Pazir asked.

We nodded.

"And how is it going so far?"

I hesitated, wondering how much we should trust this person with the details of what happened in Banbhore.

"We're doing well," Somya said with an easy smile. "The bikes have been great, and we've had no trouble finding our way or meeting our distance goals."

"Good, good," Pazir said. "I helped Rune with this leg during both of his attempts. I'm afraid that I won't be able to take the journey with you, but my grand-nibling Freni is an experienced trekker and camper. She knows the mountains well, and she'll help you get to Ray. She's at her dance lesson right now, but she'll be back soon."

"Are you not feeling well?" I asked. Rune hadn't mentioned anyone except Pazir, and it felt rude to ask if we could trust Freni.

Pazir's gaze sharpened. "You're the one who grew up on a megaconstruct?"

I nodded.

"I have decided that the time has come for my andoly. I'm not sure if you saw much of that where you were."

I shook my head. The word sounded vaguely familiar, but I couldn't recall its meaning.

"Death comes unexpectedly, but andoly is a deliberate decision. As stated in the Axioms of Life, we must all pass into a nonliving state one day, and for me, that time has come. I've lived a long and full life, and I've chosen to make room for new people, like yourselves."

I knew about death, of course, but I'd never seen it happen to anyone on Chedi. Our oldest resident, Guhaka, had two decades over Pazir, but Guhaka had always taken treatments for illnesses, as we all had. Letting infections go uncontrolled on Chedi was dangerous to everyone who lived inside her. Guhaka had undergone additional procedures to slow his aging, as well. In my many conversations with him, he had never mentioned andoly or that he might choose to end his life. I didn't know how long humans on Earth typically lived. Alloys could go for centuries thanks to partial rebirths, and they decided when to stop. It shouldn't have surprised me that humans could also make that choice.

"You'll stay the night with us?" Pazir said. It was barely a question. "That will give Freni some time to get ready. It's a long journey on foot, but I imagine that the bikes will cover much more ground. How fast have you been going?"

"About three hundred and fifty kilometers per day," I said.

Pazir made a thoughtful noise. "You should expect slower going for the next part of your journey. The mountain passes are narrow and rocky. You won't have as smooth a ride as you've had so far. I'd say four or five days to reach Ray if the weather holds, longer if it gets stormy. According to the rules of the challenge, I can't tell you what to expect, but even if I tried, the mountains are notoriously fickle. The weathercrafters in orbit have a hard time predicting what will happen at the higher elevations."

A tinkle of bells drew our attention, and our heads turned in unison.

"Ah, Freni, you're back," Pazir said. "Meet Akshaya and Somya, your travel companions."

Freni wore a lightweight sky-blue skirt that fell to her ankles. Tiny golden bells bordered its hem, and another set hung from a short blouse. Her dark hair was pinned back, and her equally dark eyes lit upon hearing our names. She had deep-brown skin like mine, a long nose, and a generous smile. At nineteen years old, she had two years on Somya.

"A pleasure to meet you," she said. "If you don't mind, I'll go freshen up and change out of my dance clothes."

"Of course, my dear," Pazir said.

The chiming of bells chased her departure.

"Freni is Shalma's child," Pazir explained, "and Shalma is my nibling."

Just then, Shalma brought us a tray with cups of steaming tea and a bowl full of some brown oblong things. Pazir popped one into their mouth and passed the bowl to Somya.

"What are these?" Somya asked, bravely eating one. "Other than tasty?"

"A type of fruit called dates," Pazir explained.

I took a nibble and was pleasantly surprised to find it sweet and soft, almost like a paste. The tea was also slightly sweet, but its astringency complemented the fruit nicely.

"Thank you," I said and placed the bowl back on the tray. I turned to Somya and said, "Do you think we should bring our bikes here?"

"Are they not in the house?" Pazir interjected, brows raised.

Somya explained what had happened in Banbhore with greater diplomacy than I would have. As they talked, I ate through a few more dates. Perhaps they were a local delicacy, in which case I wouldn't get a chance to eat them again anytime soon.

"Your things should be safe where you left them," Pazir said. "I doubt any animals would care, nor any alloys who pass by. You're probably right that the humans here would get curious and possibly concerned. Nobody tried to stop Rune, but neither did he get a lot of support for his endeavors along the way." Pazir shrugged. "Conservatives turn to alloy therapeutics at the slightest whiff of an illness, and they're extra sensitive to Aspiration and Avarice Disorder. Their attitude leaves little room for those with globe-spanning visions."

Alloys weren't much better, I thought to myself.

Freni returned just then, wearing brown leggings and a layered tunic made of the same gauzy fabric as her dance skirt. She held a roll of paper in her arms, knelt on the floor, and spread it as flat as it would go. The topmost page was covered with squiggly markings crisscrossed by dashed lines.

"These are topographic maps," Freni explained. "Each of these contours marks a particular elevation above sea level, and these lines are the last known positions of wilderness trails. The blue is for water, and the pink-shaded areas are protected from all human, alloy, and construct traffic." She patted the floor beside her and looked at Somya. "Have a seat. I'll show you the route I'm thinking of."

Somya joined her, and I scooted my cushion closer to get a better view. Freni began to mark up the papers with a pencil. Pazir sat up so they could see what she wrote. Somya and I mostly watched and listened as the two of them argued about the best route for our bikes and trailer. The maps we'd brought didn't show elevation markings and lacked enough detail to plan our route so carefully. We were fortunate that Rune had connected us with these two. On our own, who knew how much longer it would've taken us to make the crossing? I realized how little we knew about what we faced.

Nine days into a five-month journey, and I'd already faced two rude awakenings, first Ebra and her family's obstruction, and now the complexity of mountain traverses. What more lay in wait for us? Rune had told us to focus on the end goal and daily activities. *The medium-range worries will destroy your willpower,* he'd said. *Tackle each challenge as it comes. Don't waste your energy solving problems you might never face.* I tried to follow his advice, but in the back of my mind, doubts gnawed at me. Would the bikes hold during our crossing? Would the weather cooperate? And most of all, could someone barely older than Somya and me successfully guide us across a treacherous mountain range?

---

Because we'd arrived in Hormirzad so early, we had some time to relax that evening. Pazir's house was not far from the beach, and my dip in the ocean at Banbhore had left me eager to take another swim. Freni led Somya and me to her favorite spot, a stretch of soft sand with views of two islands, one small and the other quite large. A number of white-and-gray seagulls pecked at the sand along with light-brown plovers, adorably plump sanderlings, and speckled curlews with long, narrow beaks. I regretted leaving my guide and sketchbook with our gear. Small swarms of microconstructs flew around the birds, most likely as replacements for long-extinct insect species. The sun hung low in the sky, scattering its pale-orange light across the waves.

Once again, I was overcome by the power of the sea, the rushing arrival of each wave followed by the gentle retreat in its wake. The sheer quantity of water overwhelmed me. We were going to sail on a living, breathing ocean!

"I wish I could take you over to Qeshm, that big island," Freni said. "There are some amazing rock formations, and you can look out across the strait. The ocean is more active there."

"But here, it's good for swimming," Somya said. They grinned and stripped down to their underwear. With a whoop, they ran into the waves, arms outstretched, and dove in.

Freni followed more slowly, fully clothed, and walked into the water until it lapped at her knees. I followed her example, leaving my outerwear on to keep my chromatophores covered, and plunged in. The sea had a pleasant temperature that balanced the heat of the afternoon sun as I bobbed on the surface. My body floated easily. *The salinity makes us more buoyant,* I recalled from an old science lesson. I looked around until I spotted Somya's head and waved at them.

"Isn't this great?" Somya called out.

"I love it!" I lifted my face to the deep-blue sky and shouted, "I love the ocean, and I love Earth!"

We swam closer to the shore and Freni.

"Join us!" Somya beckoned with one arm.

Freni shook her head and called out, "I don't know how to swim."

How could someone live this close to the sea and not swim in it every single day? Was this another facet of humans who lacked ambition?

"I'll teach you," Somya offered.

They splashed out of the water and went to Freni's side. She shrieked playfully as Somya caught her by the hand and led her deeper. Eventually, Somya convinced Freni to let them hold her by the waist and support her atop the gentle waves.

I floated on my back, listening to their shouts and laughter, until the sun fell behind Qeshm. We returned to the beach and lay on a blanket while the sea breeze dried us off. My skin itched with salt. Freni showed us how to scrub the worst of it off with sand. I took care to keep my phores neutral as I followed her instructions.

"Feel how soft my skin is," she said, but she held out her arm to Somya.

My friend stroked Freni's arm with the back of their hand. Their gazes locked on each other, and I suddenly felt like an intruder. I couldn't help a stab of irritation. I had no romantic feelings toward Somya—we were too close for me to see them as anything but my heartsib, and I'd never felt that kind of attraction toward anyone—but Freni didn't know that. She'd made her interest in Somya known from the start, and her presumption annoyed me.

Somya had always made friends easily. I'd only seen them romantically involved once before, two years earlier. None of us took it too seriously because the other kid—Earth born and raised—came to Chedi for a transient visit. I told myself not to take Freni too seriously, either. She'd only be with us for a few days.

I stood and brushed the sand off my legs. Somya could have their fun, but I didn't have to stay and witness it. I made my retreat quietly and walked farther down the beach. They'd let me know when they were ready to return to the house.

The sand turned to pebbles and then large, water-rounded stones. I found a small boulder to perch myself on. Not far away, a couple of hippo-like alloys sat in a pool of water fed by a culvert. Freni had mentioned earlier that we could ignore them. The alloys' skin fostered various bacteria that broke down human effluvia in the water. Once the pool was fully purified, it would drain into the ocean. The plumbing system's location was centuries old, from a time when polluted water went straight into the sea. Like all cities in Loka, Hormirzad had gone through a rebirth in the Alloy Era, taking on a new name and mostly new construction. In the biggest cities, like Vaksana, they still hadn't finished breaking down the old materials. As much as I despised the alloys for exiling my parents, I couldn't help but appreciate the work that the ones on Earth did.

Clouds massed on the horizon in shades of pink and gold. I still found it hard to believe that they were made of little more than vapor. On Chedi, rain fell at scheduled times from her central axis. Somya said that they usually had advance warning on Earth, too, at least within Loka. Alloy pilots could herd clouds in ways that avoided major droughts or floods in the managed regions. We'd had no rain so far along our journey. I couldn't tell if the clouds on the horizon would precipitate, but I hoped so. In spite of Pazir's warning about the mountain trails, I wanted to see another storm, like the one at my grandparents' house. Rain meant wind and gloom and a fresh smell that I'd never experienced growing up. Everything on Earth was so *alive*, even the very air!

I glanced back at Somya and Freni. The pair had merged into a complex silhouette against the fading western light. *Still not ready to leave, then.* The sun had set, and while the twilight had its own beauty, it had lost its charm. I walked back to Pazir's house alone, the stone pathways still warm under my feet.

# DAY 11

The storm found us on our second day in the mountains. We woke to a dark, chill morning with heavy drops falling intermittently on the ground beyond our shelter. Freni had brought us there the day before, calling it "not enough of a cave to attract wildlife, but protected enough for human needs." Rock the color of sand surrounded us in a rough hemisphere. Toward the back, a barely noticeable shift in the texture marked a sealed mining hole from the previous century. Alloys would dig with their bodies, like giant moles, and then fill the tunnels up to restore the land as best as they could after they extracted whatever they needed. The fruits of their labor included the ultralight thermal fabric that kept us warm, though the design for our underclothes predated the Alloy Era. Humans had managed to be clever for a long time on their own. They'd only stopped when their descendants had taken up the mantle and moved most forms of manufacturing to hard vacuum, away from the delicate ecosphere of Earth.

The previous day, we had ridden through a rocky, severe landscape that reminded me of the recordings from Meru that my mother forced me to watch. The hills rose from the ground in great banded pleats, topped by almost vertical thrusts of stone. Freni had taken us on a slight detour to see a salt glacier. Knife-edged waves of smooth white, pink, and orange stood apart from the surrounding sandstone. I'd made a rough sketch of it in my notebook even though it didn't count as flora or fauna. From that point, the scenery shifted to more green plants, though they were still low and shrublike. Barren gray mountains loomed ahead. As we gained altitude, I increasingly relied on the bike's power, and by the time we arrived at the cave, every part of me ached. I slept poorly that night and awoke with a throbbing head, grateful for the lack of sun.

I leaned out from under our rocky overhang and peered up. Dark clouds blanketed the sky, their bottoms wispy and moving fast. A gust of cold wind stung my exposed face, and something hard pelted my forehead. I pulled back. A tiny whitish ball skittered against the ground. A few more followed, falling from the sky.

"Are these . . . hailstones?" I asked.

Freni stopped combing her hair and looked past me. "Yes." She put down the comb and pulled a hooded jacket and a pair of gloves from her backpack. "That's not a good sign. I'll find a high point and check the forecast in case there's an ice storm coming."

"Wait, no," I sputtered. "You can't!"

"Don't worry, I'll be all right."

I gaped at her. Had she already forgotten the rules of the Anthro Challenge?

"Freni," Somya said gently, "we're not allowed to use anything built by alloys as part of the AC, remember?"

She gestured at the bikes. "Everything you own is made by alloys."

"All of the items we use existed in the Human Era," I said.

"So did weather forecasts."

"Not with the resolution or the control that alloys have, especially over Loka." My annoyance wasn't helping my headache.

"Look, this is a matter of safety," she said, as if she were the arbiter of our journey. "Going out in this storm could risk our health and possibly our lives. Besides, no one will know if I access the network for a minute, not even the alloy who's shadowing you."

"*We* would know," I snapped. "And we'd have to lie to the world about it. We're not making any exceptions, and we're not cheating."

Freni crossed her arms. "I no longer consent to your methods."

"Fine. Then you can stay here and wait out the storm," I said. "Som and I will find our own way."

"Good luck with that."

"All right, both of you please take some deep breaths," Somya said. They put an arm around Freni's shoulders and kissed her on the cheek. "I understand your concern, but Aks is right. Using the public networks is a violation of the challenge rules, and it's traceable if someone bothers to check. Let's put our heads together and figure out a safe way through this." Somya shot me a classic *help-me-keep-the-peace* look over Freni's head.

I took a long drink of water and tried to find a kernel of charity, for my friend's sake. "Sorry for my tone," I said at last. "I woke up with a headache, and it's making me touchy."

Freni nodded. Her tight expression relaxed a bit.

"Rune once got surprised by a snowstorm," I continued. "He walked his bike through it, so that's a less risky option than riding. Another would be to reroute to a lower elevation and hope that it's warm enough to rain instead of hail."

"Let's take a look at the contour maps," Somya said.

We spread them out on the cave floor.

"The only way down is to backtrack," Freni said. She pointed to a trail that branched off from the way we'd come the day before. "This will take us along the bottom of a canyon, but we risk getting caught in a flash flood if the rain gets heavy. Alloys usually redirect storm energy away from the coast and into these mountains, where there aren't any cities or villages. They wouldn't expect anyone here to get taken by surprise. In your case, though, they're following you and know your situation, right? That you won't check the forecast?"

Somya nodded.

"So perhaps they'll weaken the storm's energy to keep you safe."

"That would count as interference," I pointed out, my newfound patience wearing thin. "They won't do that. It sounds like it might be less dangerous to stick to the ridges and continue on foot if necessary. It'll be slow going, but some progress is better than none. Are there other places along the way where we can take shelter if the storm gets worse?"

"Only a few," Freni said. "The next one is eleven kilometers away, at the high point of this trail. Not far by bike, but not exactly close on foot."

"What do you think?" I asked Somya.

"It's not coming down too hard out there, so I think we should try it. Better to stay ahead of the storm while we can and take advantage of what riding time we get. If the conditions aren't too bad, we'll make eleven kilometers quickly. Are you okay with that, Freni?"

She bit her lip and then nodded.

With that settled, I rummaged through my pack and found one of my headbands. The stretchy cloth fit snugly around my forehead and eased some of the pain. Since Freni didn't know how to ride a bike, I couldn't sit on the trailer and rest, so I had to nurse my headache while pushing on. Somya and I slipped into thermal hoods and waterproof jackets. Freni zipped up her coat and donned her gloves.

"I'll take the lead," I offered. "That way I can warn you if the ground gets slippery."

Concern shadowed Somya's eyes. "Are you sure? If one of us has to slip and fall, I'd rather it be me."

"I can do it," I said, with more confidence than I felt. I recalled Rune writing that doubt was often his worst enemy. I couldn't allow it to be mine.

---

As we rode, the pain spread from my forehead, behind my eyes, and down to the base of my skull. I pulled up to the summit shelter—another hollowed-out not-a-cave in the mountainside. My gut tensed and heaved. I flung myself off the bike and got to the side of the trail. Vomit wrenched out of my body, once, twice, and a final time. I barely registered the sound of Somya's bike arriving as I knelt, trembling and breathing hard, my eyes focused on a small lizard half-hidden under a rock. It had a pale-green head and yellow-brown body with a long, tapered tail like that of many alloys in space. I couldn't recall its name through the static in my head.

"Here," Somya said from behind me. "Your water bottle."

I rinsed and spat the lingering taste of bile from my mouth. When I turned, I saw two concerned faces watching me. I wanted to say, "I'm fine," but I wasn't sure of that myself. I'd seen my mother throw up during some of her pain crises.

"It might be the altitude," Freni said in a soft voice. "We should let her lie down in the shelter for a bit. I'll set up her bedroll."

I nodded in gratitude.

"Come on, young one," Somya said. They reached out a hand.

"You're barely older than me," I whispered. The effort of talking made my stomach churn.

"That still makes me the elder, doesn't it?" They grinned and pulled me up gently. "Don't worry. I'll use my wisdom to take good care of you."

I laughed and instantly regretted it.

With one arm around my waist, Somya helped me walk slowly inside. As I leaned back against the rock wall, they said, "I'll mix some salt into your water. It might help."

The early morning squall of rain and hail had passed quickly, but the dark clouds and wind remained. I didn't want to hold us up in case the storm worsened, but at that moment, I had no choice. Riding my bike was an impossibility. I sipped at the salty water that Somya brought me. They left my side and stood in the open near Freni and the bikes. I could see them speaking, but I couldn't make out the words.

After ten or fifteen minutes, my stomach started to unknot itself, but my head still felt like it wanted to split open. I'd never felt such pain before. Was this a sickle-cell-induced crisis? My mother had always described it as a fire that spread throughout her body, but did it work the same for everyone? I could hear her voice in my head: *You don't know what it's like.* Or maybe this was an effect of altitude, like Freni suggested. We were barely twenty-four hundred meters up. I checked my bodym. It showed a higher-than-average heart rate, widespread neurological activity, and a slight decrease in my blood oxygen levels. The sensors for my lungs and blood circulation looked fine. The altitude seemed the likely culprit.

Somya came over and knelt by my side. "It's mostly downhill from here. Freni thinks you might feel better if we can get you lower."

"I agree," I whispered. "But I can't ride like this. Sorry."

"It's okay. Not your fault. We're thinking you can sit on the trailer, and we'll walk the bikes. I'll put mine in power-assist mode so I won't have to work too hard to pull you."

The wreckage in my head didn't allow me to think beyond a basic understanding of Somya's words. I would have to trust that they and Freni were making good decisions. I nodded at Somya and let them help me up and over to the trailer. Freni tucked the bedroll behind me, and I curled up in a fetal position on my side, head resting on the soft bundle. After a minute, the trailer began to move.

At first, Somya and Freni kept a moderate speed, slowing when the trail became particularly rocky or steep. Every bump and bounce sent a stab into my skull. I tried to breathe through the misery, but I had to throw up two more times.

Then it began to rain. They both picked up the pace. I pulled my hood over my face as much as I could. *Be careful what you wish for. It might come true.* Why had I ever thought that seeing a storm in these mountains would be fun and exciting?

At some point along the way—my time sense was off, and accessing my bodym had become too painful—Freni asked if we could stop. I assumed she needed a break or had to relieve herself. I didn't bother to move or open my eyes to check.

"Akshaya?" Freni's voice was soft and nearby.

"Hmm?"

"I've brought you an herb that usually helps with altitude sickness."

I cracked my lids just enough to see a few greenish-brown leaves in her hand. What I really needed was an analgesic, but I didn't have the energy to argue with Freni again, and I didn't know if any natural pain reducers grew in the area. I took the herbs from her with a heavy hand and placed them in my mouth.

"Let them soften a bit," Freni instructed, "and then chew on them slowly for as long as you can. You can swallow or spit after a while."

The leaves had a slight astringency mixed with a sharp sweetness like mint. I left the pulp tucked between my teeth and my inner cheek until it became a tasteless mass.

After some more time, we reached the next shelter. My internal clock informed me that it was early afternoon. I couldn't tell if it was the lower altitude or if Freni's herbs had helped, but my headache had abated. I thanked Freni just in case.

The rain thinned while we ate lunch. Freni's mother had packed a generous container of soup, and the warm liquid eased my sore throat.

"You're looking a little better," Somya said. "How do you feel?"

"Not as bad. I think I can try riding for a while."

Freni took my place upon the wet trailer, and I hopped on my bike. I let Somya take the lead in case I needed to ride more slowly. Another hour went by. Water pooled in some spots, but most of the trail was just wet rock, which wasn't too slippery. The rain pelted my face, and the wind tugged at my clothes, but overall, the ride wasn't too difficult. The lower we got, the better I felt. We had one more mountain range to cross before we reached Alanya, and we'd have to go even higher for that one. I wondered if anything in our stores would help with altitude sickness.

I recalled stories of mountain climbers carrying their own oxygen, but that was something we would need specially made. Stopping and asking for help like that didn't seem like a wise idea after our encounter with Ebra. The only other relevant thing I recalled from my reading was that humans eventually adapted to living at high elevation. Entire civilizations had existed on mountaintops. How long that would take, I had no idea, but perhaps going uphill a little more slowly would help. That meant more delay, though, and we'd already lost half a day with the stretch of walking. Why couldn't my body act like Somya's and Freni's? They'd had no trouble. I wanted to blame my mother. She had designed my DNA. I knew why she'd given me sickle-cell disorder, but couldn't she have saved me from altitude sickness? I had to hope that she hadn't burdened me with seasickness, too.

I swallowed my wounded pride at our next stop and asked Freni to gather some more of the herb for me if she spotted it. No one could argue that a wild plant violated the Anthro Challenge, and it had worked well enough once.

—

We made better time for the rest of the day. The farther we went from the mountain peaks, the less rain fell upon us. Behind us, dark clouds swam through the sky like an inverted ocean. Sometimes they lit up from within, a magical sight. The brunt of the storm raged above and beyond our path. I wondered if it had started to snow up at the pass where we'd sheltered overnight. Part of me regretted not witnessing the phenomenon, but another part was relieved to be away from the danger and discomfort. The hail had caused enough concern.

I needed more time—to linger at high altitudes until my body adapted; to take in all the different types of weather, the play of light and shadow and color. We were less than two weeks into our first Anthro Challenge, and I couldn't help but dream of the day I could do it again. Unlike Rune, who wanted to make a faster time on his second attempt, I would aim to slow down.

The few humans I'd seen on the road didn't seem to be traveling for pleasure. In the old days, tourism had grown to the point that it endangered the natural phenomena that people wanted to appreciate in person. Humans had used machines that polluted the planet or ridden less intelligent animals who couldn't consent to the labor. After the Directed Mutation Catastrophe and the ruination of Mars, humans started to engineer themselves to do less and want less. They only rode alloys or constructs who had the ability to accede. The desire to stay home dominated.

People like Ebra now disapproved of unnecessary journeys. The Committee for Intercontinental Travel set limits and gave approvals for projects that required frequent or long transits. On one hand, I wanted to be a good person, to respect the Earth and all the living and nonliving beings it harbored. On the other, I had always loved to explore. The bike tires we rode upon would accelerate erosion, and if enough people used them, they would create more work for the alloys who managed Loka. It was to our advantage that others didn't travel on wheels, but I did feel a little guilty about it. One Anthro Challenge was a privilege.

Two would be a luxury. More would be excessive enough to warrant a diagnosis of Aspiration and Avarice Disorder followed by treatment or a life in the Out of Bounds. I had no desire to push my luck.

At least we could keep our journey mostly private. Nara's documentary would end that, but by then, we'd be done with our circumnavigation, so it wouldn't matter. Had Reshyan captured our adventures in the mountains? Could zie peer through the clouds, or had the storm blocked zir access? I hoped for the latter. I didn't relish the thought of the world seeing me getting sick and sitting atop the trailer.

We reached the foothills before dark, but we stopped almost a hundred kilometers short of our goal. My headache had returned, low and dull. Somya insisted that I rest while they and Freni set up camp and made dinner. It turned out that Freni was a much better cook than Somya, for which I was very grateful. She had foraged for fresh greens to add to our grain-and-legume stews, and she used local spices that combined sweet and savory in ways I hadn't tasted before. We finished the meal with a few dates. We didn't have many left, but Freni assured us that we could pick up more in the days to come.

A light rain pattered against the waterproof cover over our tent. I tried to place my bedroll a little apart from theirs, but I couldn't get any real distance in a two-person tent. If only we'd had a second shelter, I would've gladly given Somya and Freni some privacy. As it was, I kept my back to them and tried to ignore the whispers and rustles behind me.

"Aks," Somya said softly. "Are you still awake?"

"Yes," I said. I rolled over to face Somya.

"I'm a little worried about tomorrow. Back home, you'd probably sleep in your high-oxygen room tonight. Out here, we don't know how your body will respond, right?"

I didn't want to admit that Somya was right. I had been so relieved to feel better and ride my bike again that I hadn't thought ahead to further consequences. Would I wake up feeling okay? Or would my body decide not to cooperate again?

"So I was thinking," Somya said, filling my silence, "that it might be good if Freni stayed with us a little longer to help out—if you don't mind—especially to cross the Alburz Mountains between Ray and Alanya."

My instinctive reaction was a resounding no. The only way Freni could really help was to learn to ride. Otherwise, we'd be restricted to a walking pace and fall further behind. I didn't relish the idea of teaching her—another time cost—nor of sitting on the trailer while Freni rode my bike. I was also irritated that Somya had put me on the spot. It would seem rude to say no with Freni listening in.

The more reasonable part of my brain pointed out that if I continued to push my body past some tipping point, I'd get so sick that my parents and our alloy minder would swoop in and end the challenge anyway. Somya's suggestion made sense. Freni could cook. She knew her way around mountainous terrain. Even if she'd almost broken the AC rules, she'd been more help than hindrance. I suspected that Somya's romantic interest biased them toward having her company longer, and as much as I felt like a spare part at times, I couldn't begrudge my heartsib their happiness.

"It's a good idea," I said finally. "She'll have to learn how to ride. You're okay with that, Freni?"

"Yes," she replied immediately. "I've never had the chance to explore so far beyond Hormirzad, and I'm sure no one else would offer to teach me how to use a solar bike."

"Then let's spend a little time tomorrow morning doing that."

"Thanks, Aks," Somya said.

Somya reached out and squeezed my hand. I gave one back. They pulled away and rolled back toward Freni. The warmth of their palm faded, and I curled up inside my bedroll. The chill of the night air seeped through the tent wall. I turned over our conversation in my mind, already regretting how quickly I had agreed to Freni's company. What if she turned into a real love interest for Somya? Would they abandon the challenge? Would they abandon me? The chatter of raindrops gave me no answer.

# DAY 12

Daylight brought a steady cold breeze and clearing skies. My body ached all over, but still no fire in my veins, not the way my mother would describe it. We packed up as efficiently as we could while the wind attempted to defeat us. I welcomed the ride. It warmed me up and eased some of the soreness in my muscles. The way forward took us through rolling foothills covered in scrubby green bushes and sprawling oaks. Here and there, I spotted clusters of pistachio trees, something that I'd only seen in tidy orchards in Chedi. We hadn't seen any signs of civilization since we'd left Hormirzad. Even the animal life seemed reclusive in these parts, with only some cattle or a lone hawk in sight.

Our map put us on a trail that barely supported the designation. Other than a little less greenery on the ground, nothing marked the way. Freni thought it was created by migratory animals. I could believe her. Not one part of the track went in a straight line, and the constant twisting slowed our progress.

I'd never felt so connected to my surroundings. Chedi had many areas without humans, but she had sensors nearly everywhere in the form of her ambulatory constructs. I'd spent my whole life knowing that help was never far away. Earth's wilderness felt different, more open and barren. *But we aren't truly isolated,* I reminded myself. Somewhere above the circling birds flew our alloy watcher. Try as I might, I couldn't make out anything reflective in the sky. *What would it feel like to be out here and all alone?* Humans had gone off on solo treks in the distant past. Could I ever dare to attempt something like that? My mother had done so on Meru, a planet with no other life at the time, no trails or plants or animals. I granted her a lot of respect for that.

We stopped for lunch on a grassy plain. With a closer view of the ground, I noticed small burrowing constructs, their metallic bodies proclaiming their nonliving nature, their size about the length of my finger joint. What extinct creature's function did they fill?

Freni offered me a date. "Last one."

"Thank you."

Somya stood and wandered off to answer the call of nature. Given the terrain, they had to walk pretty far to find privacy.

"So why are you doing this, anyway?" Freni asked. "The Anthro Challenge, I mean."

Nara had asked me the same question during our predeparture interview.

"To prove that humans don't need alloy help to get around," I said, giving Freni the simplest answer.

"Do you have something against alloys?"

I hesitated. "Do you know about my parents?"

"No. Amoo Pazir asked if I would help you cross the Zagros, and I said yes. Beyond that, I only know what you've both told me."

"I'm Jayanthi and Vaha's child," I said.

She gave me a *that-means-nothing* face. I explained the basics, and Freni's expression grew increasingly astonished as I spoke. "So you're half-alloy?"

"No," I said. "I'm human. My mother didn't use any of my maker's Z chromosome."

Mostly true. Technically, the chromatophores made me a hybrid—altered enough not to be entirely human, but not so different as to count as an alloy. I was something the world hadn't seen since the Human Era. My mother had made me learn about the ugly history, when people had the technology to tinker with chromosomes but before they had the skills to do it well. Diseases and disorders were eliminated, including the sickle-cell genes that I carried. Human beings had optimized for what they considered wellness and left no room for chance mutations, not only in their own DNA but in all life on Earth. After a couple of centuries, the lack of genetic diversity in the ecosphere led to a collapse, and many species went extinct. People sickened and died young. Human- and hybrid-kind tried to save themselves by doubling down and modifying their children even more, like tying layers of cloth around a leaky pipe. Alloy historians called it the Directed Mutation Catastrophe.

After that, people made rules about genetic engineering to include chance mutations. They learned to accommodate for the difficulties that resulted. Eventually, they discovered how to add instructions, including a new chromosome that allowed a body to tolerate more metals. That was the birth of alloys, who eventually moved off the planet, became humanity's caretakers, and did their best to restore biodiversity to Earth. The alloys maintained *Homo sapiens* as a separate species, not allowing hybrids.

My mother had broken that rule, along with several others, when she made me. My maker said I got my ambition and my stubbornness from her, though I felt like hers were a lot louder than mine. She promised me that one day, after we settled down on Meru, the world would know what I truly was. A handful of people on Chedi, including Somya, shared my secret, but I would never reveal my hybrid nature to anyone I didn't trust completely. Freni seemed like a decent person, but she was far too recent an acquaintance to tell her the truth, never mind showing her what I could do with my phores. I hadn't forgotten about Nara's watchful pilot and the indriyas recording us, either.

"You haven't answered my original question," Freni said. "Or maybe I missed something. Do you hate your maker? Is that why you're doing the challenge?"

"No, my maker is great. It's what the alloys did to zir that I hate. They exiled my maker for one small act of violence. Alloys are supposed to be able to regulate their behavior better than us, but when they fail, they don't get a chance to undergo treatment like we do. They get forced out of their lives." I paused. That still didn't answer her question. "I'm not doing the challenge because of the alloys, though. I'm doing it for myself, to prove that I can thrive on Earth in spite of being designed for Meru, and to see this amazing planet that should've been my home."

I told her about the deal I'd made with my parents and why I had to succeed in completing the challenge.

"Aren't there some humans on Meru already?" Freni asked.

I nodded. "Twenty-five of them, including five made children. Two of them have genomes based on mine. But I think the real reason my mother wants to go back to Meru is so she can live there with my maker's incarn. I don't blame either of them for that, but I'm almost a full adult. I don't need to go with them. If I can finish the AC, then I'll prove that to them."

Somya sauntered up to us. "I found a good spot nearby for Freni to try riding. What do you say?"

They looked at me for confirmation, and I nodded. I stretched my limbs and lay back as the two of them wheeled a bike a little ways off the trail. There was much laughing and kissing and toppling over at first. I fought the urge to dislike Freni—Somya was *my* friend—and I had to credit her good attitude. She picked herself up with a smile after every fall. I hadn't been nearly as easygoing when I first learned. Somya couldn't take their eyes—or their hands—off Freni. Would they be able to leave her behind when we reached Alanya?

I made myself comfortable on the trailer and closed my eyes. The sun glowed orange through my lids. The wind had slowed since the morning, and the air around me was warm and heavy with the scent of drying soil.

I dozed for a while. By the time I got up, Freni had figured out the basics of balance and pedaling. We resumed our journey, and she rode for an hour, wobbling frequently and forcing Somya to slow their pace. After that, I took over. Freni would need to build up muscles for long rides as well as a tolerance for the bike seat, and I could ride faster. We had already lost time to the storm and my illness. We would have to push hard over the next two days if we wanted to reach Ray on schedule.

# DAY 19

As the days passed, I started to understand some of Rune's warnings better. The initial excitement of getting underway faded, and starting out each morning got harder. Inertia applies to human behavior as much as it does to inanimate objects. It's compounded by our inherent laziness, especially those of us who hate doing the same thing over and over again. Wake up. Make breakfast. Pack up the gear. Pedal until the sun charges up the motors. Ride. Ride. Ride. The landscape was scenic, and I loved the clouds and wind and mountains, but they didn't have the same thrill as when I first experienced them.

Freni added an hour to her riding time each day, which helped ease the tedium. All three of us took turns resting on the trailer. With those breaks, we were able to go faster and farther, and we made up for lost time. We arrived at Ray on Day 13. The city sat at the foot of a broad, flattened mountain range. White glaciers nestled in the uppermost peaks. Somya and Freni went to an isolated community garden while I stayed outside the city limits with our things and got some rest.

In the city, Freni connected to the network briefly to send a message home, telling her family that she was safe and planned to travel farther with us. We figured that didn't invalidate the Anthro Challenge rules since Freni didn't check weather or land conditions, so it had no impact on our travel plans.

From Ray, we turned westward and traversed the northern section of the Zagros Mountains. That part of the range was a lot greener and more wooded than the southern portion that we'd crossed from Hormirzad. Freni proved to be an excellent resource for foraging delicious things to eat, and we harvested pistachios, almonds, and pomegranates along the way. The sun shone upon us and made the crossing easier.

The rain started as we entered the plains, and it didn't stop. Everything got wet. The bike motors had very little power. Our easy cruising turned into mud-caked slogs. The only saving grace was that the terrain had been landcrafted to handle the runoff. We resorted to the main roadways, which followed contours that didn't collect water. Wooden bridges helped with the numerous stream crossings. Other than the occasional alloy running by, we didn't see anyone along the way, not until our approach to the Euphrates River. A few kilometers before the river bridge, our road fed into a larger one. We stopped at the intersection for a short break. A cluster of trees with branches espaliered into a dense weave formed a protective shelter. As we rested and snacked, we saw a small group of alloys pass by with passengers on their backs.

"I thought this was supposed to be the dry season," Somya grumbled. "If people need to be out in this weather, why don't the cloudcrafters give us a break and take the rain elsewhere?"

I assumed it was a rhetorical question, and I understood Somya's irritation. Chedi would never have allowed her showers to go on for days. I had expected life in Loka to have a similar level of comfort, but managed weather meant something very different on Earth. If it could get this bad in these parts, how much worse would it be in the Out of Bounds?

"The weathercrafters can only do so much," Freni said. "The planet has needs, too."

"I know that," Somya snapped.

There was a moment of silence.

"Sorry for being irritable," Somya said. "I just wish we could have a chance to get truly dry."

"Me too," Freni said.

"The day after tomorrow, we'll reach Alanya," I said, surprising myself. I hadn't often found myself in the position of soothing Somya's temper. "I'm sure Rune's boat will have a nice, dry cabin, and once Freni leaves us, she can stay somewhere comfortable in town."

Somya and Freni exchanged a glance. Her hand crept into theirs.

"Could I perhaps," Freni said tentatively, "continue on with you?"

I should've seen the request coming. Once we embarked on the boat, we'd be sailing for the bulk of the journey until we reached Asia again—more than a hundred days.

"It's okay if you don't want me to," she added.

But the expression on Somya's face said otherwise. How could I call myself their heartsib if I broke their heart? I'd been the odd person out since Hormirzad, but once we met up with Rune, I would have others to talk to. I wouldn't need Somya's companionship.

"You're welcome to come," I said before my silence could turn awkward. "As long as there's enough room on the boat, of course. Your family won't mind? You'll be gone for months."

"When I talked to them at Ray, they said I could go as far as I want with you. Amoo Pazir still regrets not spending more time with Rune, and they told me this is a once-in-a-lifetime opportunity. They convinced my mother to give me permission." She paused and gave Somya a light kiss on the cheek. "If Rune can't take me on the boat, then I'll turn back. Even two more days with you both will be a blessing."

With that settled, we got back on the bikes and headed out on the main road. We didn't get far before we reached a small crowd of people. A cluster of identification tags popped up in my visual. Beyond them, I could see a brown, turbulent course of water: the famed Euphrates, one of the cradles of human civilization. We stood upon a raised bank with the others. A wooden bridge extended from our side to the other, twisting and bouncing on barrel-shaped floats. Two alloys stood in front of it. The first one appeared somewhat human, though twice as tall as an average person and with dark-orange down covering their skin. The other resembled a cross between a bat and a pterosaur, standing about three meters high with a brown, furred body, a humanlike mouth, and vast leathery wings. The first alloy directed two humans to climb on the back of the second, who then took flight and carried the passengers across the river.

I turned to Somya and Freni. "Looks like they're not allowing people to cross the bridge."

"It must not be safe," Freni said. She shrugged. "We'll have to ride the alloy across. I'm sure they'll bring over the gear, too."

I pointed out the obvious. "That would violate the challenge rules."

"We literally don't have any other choice," Freni said. She turned to Somya for support. "The rules must allow some kind of exception for situations like this, right?"

Somya hesitated, then said, "No exceptions. We have to find somewhere else to cross by ourselves."

"It's days to the next bridge, north or south," Freni exclaimed.

She was right. We had all seen the maps. The road to Zantep was one of the few that crossed the river, and that was why we'd chosen the route.

The giant humanoid alloy was looking at us with an expression of concern. "The other nearby bridges were also damaged by high winds yesterday," they called out toward us. "We'll carry you across after these others."

That was the last thing I wanted.

"Let's go back to the shelter and discuss this," I murmured.

I turned my bike around and started to ride away before Somya or Freni could argue. Better that they get annoyed with me than for that alloy to insist on helping us. Within minutes, we had parked ourselves under the protection of the trees.

I turned to Freni. "The whole point of the challenge is to complete a circumnavigation without assistance from the alloys, as humans used to do."

"Then we should ask how far it is to a working bridge," Freni said.

"That's still alloy help!" I said.

"What do you suggest, that we walk along the river until we find a safe place to cross? With no idea how far out of the way that will take us?"

Somya pulled out the map book. "This should give us an idea if there's an alternative route."

"Are you both mindless?" Freni threw her hands out. "The Euphrates is the longest river in this part of the world. The mountains to the north drain into it, and to the south, it goes on for more than a thousand kilometers."

After a minute of studying the map, Somya admitted that she was right. "Maybe we can find a bridge that isn't monitored," they said without much conviction. "Then we could take our chances and cross anyway."

"I don't think that's wise," I said. "If the bridge breaks while we're on it, we'll lose our gear."

"I agree with Akshaya," Freni said. "The alloys wouldn't close multiple bridges without good reason."

"I said it would be risky." Somya shrugged. "I know, that's a bad word around these parts."

"For good reason," Freni retorted. "What use is ambition if it leads you to harm?"

"Yes, yes, Ratnam's famous quote." Somya raised their hands in surrender.

"What quote?" I asked.

Freni turned her glare toward me. "You don't know who Ratnam is?"

"Of course I do," I said. "Ratnam published a treatise that helped shape the compact." That much I recalled from basic history. Perhaps students on Earth went deeper. "Do you have to memorize all of the compact?"

*"Ambition and materialism lead to greed and exploitation,"* Freni recited. "It's inscribed on the archway into Hormirzad. Didn't you see it when you entered?"

I shrugged. "I noticed it, but I didn't know that's what you were referring to."

"People on Chedi don't hold so closely to Ratnam's philosophy," Somya explained to Freni. "Aks's parents even less than others."

"What about the axioms and principles? Did they at least teach you those?"

"Yes," I said, annoyed. I assumed she meant the Axioms of Life and the Principles of Conscious Beings, part of every CDL citizen's basic education. "Now can we please get back to the more imminent problem of how we're going to cross the river? Because I have an idea. Som, remember that time when Huy tried to ride his bike off the minicliff and fell in the lake?"

Somya nodded.

"The bike sank, so Chedi remade them all to float," I said.

"So?"

"Maybe the trailer floats, too. If it does, we can swim across and tow our gear with us. If not, we can abandon it and carry our gear until we can build a new one. We might drift downriver a ways, but that'll be less of a detour than biking for days until we find a good bridge."

"It could work," Somya said, looking thoughtful. "We'll have to find somewhere to test the trailer, like that lake we passed an hour ago."

Freni looked back and forth between us. "Are you serious?"

"Yes," Somya and I said together.

"I can't swim, remember?"

"You can ride on my back," Somya said, putting their arm around her waist. "I promise I won't lose you."

She pulled away. "No. This is as terrible an idea as risking the bridge. Maybe worse. It's too dangerous. We could drown."

"Sailing over the ocean," I pointed out, "is also potentially deadly, and you're willing to do that. Why is this different?"

Freni shook her head. "Swimming across a river isn't the same as sailing on a boat."

"In ancient times," I said, "plenty of people died at sea."

"Aks, you're not helping," Somya said with a wry smile. They stared at our gear for a moment, then sighed. "Freni, I won't ask you to put yourself in danger, but I will ask that you don't try to stop me and Aks from doing so. Swimming across is our best option." They took Freni's hands in theirs. "I would really like for you to come with us, but . . . if you don't want to, I understand."

I resisted flinging my arms around Somya in gratitude. They had left Freni with a hard choice, but they had drawn a line at abandoning the challenge.

Freni snatched her hands back. "In that case, I choose to stay here. I won't watch you do this. If something happens and you need help, I hope your alloy in the sky can see you through all this rain." She turned to me. "This is *exactly* why Ratnam wrote those words, because the old way of being human was flawed. It led people to do selfish things like this, risking their own safety as well as the health and happiness of the people who love them."

Her words stung. I knew they held a kernel of truth, but I wouldn't apologize. "Thank you for sharing your feelings," I said, "and for helping us get this far."

Freni started to cry. Somya tried to put their arms around her, but she pushed them away. She turned her back to us, and we wordlessly separated her things from ours. She would have to walk to the bridge, but it wasn't far. The alloys could help her get home.

"Freni?" Somya said to her back. "I'm sorry. I hope you'll watch the show and see that we get through this. Thank you for taking us this far."

Freni shrugged and crossed her arms, still refusing to look at us.

I touched Somya gently and inclined my head. The pain on their face made my heart ache, but I suspected that anything I said would only make the situation worse.

—

I didn't think we could get any wetter, but a dip in the lake to test the trailer's buoyancy proved me wrong. We tried it without any items on it, and it floated. It couldn't take the full load of our gear, though, so we figured out a way to tie some of the items to our bikes. With that done, we put everything back on the trailer and rode south, past the turnoff to the bridge, until we had put a few kilometers between us and the intersection. The shelter had been empty when we passed it. I hoped that Freni was somewhere dry.

The rain continued in a steady state. We had to walk our bikes off the road, slipping and sliding through the grass and mud until we reached the banks of the river. The Euphrates ran swift and brown. Water pooled in every shallow depression along its edge. Somya and I worked in silence to rearrange the gear in the way that had worked at the lake. Unlike the dramatic storms from our first week on Earth, this dull gray soaking had worn out its welcome. When we reached Zantep, it would be difficult not to seek out some real shelter and a set of dry clothes.

But I was getting ahead of myself. First we had to cross the river.

"Swim diagonally to the opposite shore," Somya said. "The river is moving fast, so we'll probably end up in different places. I'll try to see where you land before I go in. Either way, I'll come find you, okay? If we both go looking, we might miss each other."

I nodded.

On Chedi, I'd considered myself a strong swimmer, but I'd never gone in water like this, churning and flowing like a living being. No wonder ancient humans had embodied rivers with divine spirits. I sent the Euphrates a silent prayer for our success, just in case its consciousness could sense mine. I glanced upward. Was Reshyan actively watching us, or had zie left the indriyas to track us? In the former case, the alloy pilot could send help if we needed it, but in the latter, we'd be on our own until someone reviewed the footage. I closed my eyes and pretended that we had traveled through time to the Human Era. That no one knew our whereabouts or activities. That if we got hurt, or died, we would return to the Earth, and that was that. *But I would much rather we both get across,* I told the river.

I turned to Somya. "If I don't make it, go back to the bridge and get help."

They threw their arms around me and squeezed. "You can do it," they said, pulling back. "My cousins and I used to catch driftwood and cruise down rapids much worse than this. Don't try to fight the current. Just keep your eyes on the far shore."

"Self-doubt is your worst enemy," I said, quoting Rune.

"Exactly."

We had fashioned makeshift harnesses with our tent cords. I stuffed my outer clothing into my sack, pulled the straps over my torso, and waded in. The river was only a little cooler than the air, which had been warm since we entered the valley. The current urged me forward, tugging insistently at my legs. At first I towed the bike, but as I got deeper, it floated on its own and took the lead. I held on to the frame, using its buoyancy to help keep my head above water. I kicked as best as I could at a shallow angle to the current, as Somya had instructed. The Euphrates tasted nothing like the sea, its grit metallic with only a hint of salt.

I had no sense of time as I swam, only that for a long while, the opposite shore seemed no closer. With the speed of the river, I lost sight of Somya after the first minute. The water seemed to flow faster than it had appeared from the shore. As the seconds ticked by, my existence shrank to my grip on the bike and my legs working like scissor blades. *Breathe. Kick. Look.* And repeat.

On and on I went as the rain-driven river carried me. My shoulders ached. My thighs and calves burned. I merged with the Euphrates and wondered if I would ever be Akshaya again. But no, there was a rock, thrusting itself into my view, attached to land. The bike sped by it, but I had to be close to the far shore. I pumped my legs harder. *There!* A stretch of open land, green with welcome. Using a burst of desperate energy, I thrust the bike ahead of me and pushed my body harder than I had ever done. Wet branches grasped at the frame, clung to it, and held fast. With a gasp of air, I heaved myself onto solid ground. I yanked the bike out, dragged it up the embankment, and collapsed at the top, my chest rising and falling like the surges of the river.

After I caught my breath, I stood and looked northward. Somya was nowhere in sight.

*I'll come find you,* they'd said, so I lay on the soggy ground in my underwear, exhausted and glad that I didn't have to move. The ancient books on wilderness survival said to stay in one place if you knew someone would come looking for you. The old ways didn't have a lot of practical advice for modern times. Back then, they advocated the killing and eating of animals, chopping down tree limbs, lighting fires, and other illegal activities, but I enjoyed learning about how humans had managed, and sometimes I found information I could use.

After I'd caught my breath and my muscles stopped acting like jelly, I checked the time. The clouds hid the sun, but my bodym told me that it would set in two hours. It also informed me that my vital numbers were less than optimal. I needed water, food, and someplace warm and dry to rest. Of the items we had tied to my bike, I still had my pouch of fresh water, its integrated filter, and a dry sack with my clothes—damp but not soaked—a bruised pomegranate, and some shelled walnuts.

My bedroll had slipped its noose, as had my pack with the rest of my clothing and toiletries. The self-heating blanket had disappeared, too. I felt a stab of guilt knowing that I had polluted the river with my lost items. *I hope no animal gets harmed because of them.*

I pulled on the somewhat-dry clothes, but they did little more than stick to my muddy, wet skin. Hunger gnawed at my stomach. I ate the nuts first, then shelled the fruit and chewed on the rosy pods, the juice sharp and sweet in contrast to the pithy seeds. I buried the remnants and washed my hands in a puddle of river water. I refilled my drinking pouch, then I had nothing to do but sit on the riverbank and wait.

Minutes passed into hours. What little light had shone through the clouds faded, with no sign of Somya. Even if they were nearby, they would struggle to see me. Would we end up spending the night apart? Had they passed me in the water when I hadn't noticed? The thought of spending the night alone sent a shiver down my spine. *Rune spent plenty of time alone in the wilderness. It's not dangerous. The wolves that live around here don't like the smell of humans.* As part of restoring the Earth, the alloys had tinkered not only with human behavior but that of animals and plants. I had nothing to fear, so I kept telling myself, but I started to worry.

What if something bad had happened to Somya? I had told them to seek help at the bridge if the river took me, but they hadn't said anything back. *Careless.* We should have planned better for worst-case scenarios. At what point should I give up and signal for assistance? If I waited until daylight, it could be too late to save them. *It might already be too late,* whispered a vicious part of my brain. On Chedi, no one could get lost or die by accident, but Earth was a planet, wide open, uncontrolled, unpredictable. The enormity of the situation squeezed at my heart. Maybe Freni had been right all along. Maybe we'd taken too big a risk.

I could picture waking up in the morning alone. I could imagine the devastation of learning that the Euphrates had taken Somya forever.

Then what? I could hear my heartsib's voice in my head: *You can't quit the Anthro Challenge, Aks. You have to keep going by yourself. Never Meru, remember?* I shuddered. Would I have the strength—the courage—to journey alone like Rune did? My thoughts bounced off the idea. It seemed impossible. Better to break the rules of the AC and call for help.

I tried to shield my eyes from the rain and peered up into the gloom, hoping for a glimpse of the indriyas. They hadn't followed us at all times, and I'd found their occasional absence a relief, but at that moment, they would have given me a sense of security. I could see nothing above me. *It's too soon to give up. Imagine how angry Somya would be if you panicked and ruined the challenge, and it turned out they were almost here.* I took some deep breaths. Patience. Courage. Calm. The words were part of Rune's litany in his worst moments. I wouldn't allow fear to rule me, not yet.

Night fell, and the world around me slipped into darkness. Somya could have passed a few meters from me, and I wouldn't have known it. I didn't have any of our bioluminescent lights with me—we hadn't expected to be separated so late in the day—but I had my body. I had waited long enough. I had to risk exposing my secret if there was any chance of Somya finding me. I flashed *hello* as brightly as I could with every phore I had. After a few minutes, I repeated the word. I lit my phores again and again, desperate for any kind of response.

"Aks, is that you?"

Somya's voice sounded like sunshine.

"Yes," I called back. I stood and waved my arms like a child. I flashed, <Over here!>

After a minute, I spotted their figure moving like a hole through the night. I stumbled forward to meet them, sloshing through the puddles along the way. We flung our arms about each other and held tight for a few breaths.

"Sorry I took so long," Somya said, pulling back. "I had to find high ground for the bike and trailer, and then I wasn't sure how far you'd gone, so I packed for the night. Are you okay?"

"I am now. How about you?"

"I'm all right, though I lost some things from the bike."

"Me too," I admitted. "What about the trailer?"

"It's fine, but it's a long way back, and it's too dark to find our way."

If we'd had clear skies, the starlight would have been enough for us to see, but the murk of a rainy night was absolute. We would have to wait until morning.

"My bedroll is gone," I groaned.

"You can share mine."

Then I noticed the bulk of the pack that Somya carried. They had brought our tent, their bedding, and more food. No wonder the walk had taken them a long time. I helped Somya set up our shelter. Despite the damp interior, it was absolute bliss to have the rain off my face. Somya rummaged through their pack and handed me an apple, a hard yellow cheese, and some more walnuts. We ate and drank by the glow from my phores.

"I didn't bring any clothes," Somya said. "Everything got wet in the river. I guess a dry-sack only works so well. Let's huddle up for warmth."

Wet clothes cooled the body, according to survival basics. Better to strip down and get close to share heat—the more people, the better.

"I'm sorry about Freni," I said softly. "I wish we didn't have to leave her behind."

Somya's shoulders brushed mine as they shrugged. "Would've happened eventually. I think she liked the idea of adventure more than the reality. It's better that she figured it out now rather than somewhere in the middle of the Atlantic."

Their light tone relieved my guilt. Perhaps ten days wasn't enough to make their attachment serious.

"She's probably begging the alloys to treat her for AAD," I said.

Somya snorted. Then laughed. They laughed so hard, they leaned into me. I couldn't help but join in. The day's tensions melted away until I lay there, breathing deep, my friend's warm body at my side. Their lanky arm curled around mine, and my phores glowed pale violet in response. I ached in a hundred places, but I was too exhausted to care. We had crossed the Euphrates, I had survived hours of being alone, and we were together again. In that moment, nothing else mattered.

# RESHYAN (DAY 20)

The storm front was dropping too much rain over the plains to the east. It had stalled over inhabited areas, and Reshyan needed to redirect the energy to the Eastern Alps. The mountains lay mostly outside of Loka and could absorb the excess heat and moisture produced by the Mediterranean, which had grown overly warm. Others would do the hard work of crafting the elements. Reshyan had a more cerebral task: to observe, analyze, and instruct. Zie could have asked someone else to collect the data for zir, as Olanma did underwater, but firsthand experience gave zir an intuitive sense for what needed to happen, which allowed zir to be more efficient and responsive.

Reshyan folded zir wings up and back. Zie plummeted a hundred meters as the air pressure dropped. Raindrops pelted zir face shield and cleared almost immediately, pushed away by the wind and the hydrophobic material. Far below, in the warm waters of the Mediterranean Sea, zir research partner, Olanma, swam in the depths and sent sensor readings via emchannel. Reshyan squeezed air through zir pectoral funnels and unfolded zir wings, stabilizing zirself in the clouds before examining the data.

"Looks like we'll need to pull more warm water to the surface," Olanma sent via emtalk.

"Agreed," Reshyan replied. "We also need to speed up this front and give it a westward heading, then reduce some of the energy from

North Africa to slow the front over the sea. Looking at the data from the Atlantic side, that shouldn't be a problem. It's pretty mild over there."

Weather and cloudcrafting were as much art as science. Simulations could cover a lot of variables, but chaotic systems like Earth's would rapidly hit asymptotic complexity, the point where the computational load would include every molecule and become infeasible. Crafters needed a certain amount of intuition and a tolerance for uncertainty. Reshyan had an excellent track record, but zie never took success for granted. People had learned to make accurate predictions about the weather many centuries earlier, but trying to control it, as they had on Mars, turned out to be another matter entirely. It required a delicate touch, patience, and a nimble attitude.

"I'm going to take some more wind-speed readings," Reshyan sent. "Can you repeat your measurements one more time? We're not within error margins yet."

"Close enough, don't you think?" Olanma sent. "I'm hungry."

"So grab a mouthful of plankton and keep going."

"I can't. At this time of day, all the zooplankton stay in the depths. I could dive down and take some readings there?" Zir words were olive and pansy colored with wry hope.

Reshyan didn't take the request seriously. Olanma knew as well as zie did that data integrity superseded a trivial issue like hunger.

"Such a workaholic," Olanma sent, teasing. "I know the real reason—you love to fly."

Olanma was right, but Reshyan would sooner admit to sensor tampering than tell zir so. Flying through Earth's atmosphere, especially the storm clouds, posed unique challenges. Zie hadn't expected to enjoy it when zie had arrived at Earth. Zie had to maintain a serious demeanor, though, especially after zie became a senior-level researcher. Still, Reshyan couldn't help but enjoy the air buffeting zir body as zie flew through the nascent heaps of precipitation. Updrafts, drops, wind shear forces—they allowed Reshyan to use zir body in ways that zie never could while growing up. Hard vacuum didn't support atmospheric maneuvers.

After half an hour, Reshyan had taken enough samples for zir satisfaction. For fun, zie folded zir wings back and dove down, below the cloud deck, until zie could see ripples on the gray sea below. Rain hadn't precipitated this low, and as zie leveled off, zie caught a glimpse of Olanma's sleek, aquatic form breaching the surface. The only water Reshyan had felt were the droplets in the atmosphere. Zie had often wondered what swimming was like. Not good for zir true body, that much zie knew. Perhaps when zie got bored of atmospheric work, as zie had eventually done with interstellar travel, zie would apply for an aquatic incarn and spend some time in Earth's oceans.

"I'm all done for today," Reshyan sent to Olanma. Zie waved at zir colleague, who raised a fin in acknowledgment before submerging again.

Reshyan called the weather sensors back to zir body and stowed them in zir hip pouch. Zie slow-blinked and thought-retrieved a map of the land below. The two humans who Nara wanted zir to follow, Akshaya and Somya, ought to have reached Zantep. They had lost half a day to their river crossing because they'd backtracked to retrieve their gear. That much Reshyan had observed via the orbital cameras the day before. Zie wasn't sure if they would stay the night in the city, which would put them two days behind schedule, or if they'd taken a break and then pushed on.

Akshaya's maker, Jayanthi, had taken note of the extended rain in the area and contacted Reshyan the day before.

"The river they need to cross is flowing at unusually high levels," she'd sent in a message. "Do you know if the weather will clear soon? Will they have safe passage?"

Reshyan hadn't told her about the straight-line winds that had blown out multiple bridges. Zie had a moment of pity for the two little humans and their ignorance, but zie had a job to do, and that had meant letting those winds blow. They hadn't harmed any populated areas or wildlife. Avoiding that was the primary mandate for weather-crafters. Reshyan couldn't protect a couple of children who refused to access information from the public networks. Instead, Reshyan kept their danger to zirself. There was no sense in telling Jayanthi. She would probably find out eventually, as part of Nara's documentary. The director was too competent to ignore the high drama of the river swim.

As part of the contract with Nara, Reshyan had agreed to take immersive recordings from zir perspective at the end of zir workdays. For the remaining daylight hours, zie deployed indriyas to auto-follow the humans from an unobtrusive distance. Reshyan could guide the devices individually, and Nara had given zir the artistic license to do so, but the children's activities grew dull and repetitive after the first two days. Instead, Reshyan kept in mind the promise of Nara's next documentary—the piece on exile reform—and used that as motivation.

Reshyan's interstellar journey had left zir with an acute sense of isolation. Zie imagined that alloys in long periods of exile—like zir ancestor, Pushkara—would experience something similar. The practice was intended to be less cruel than imprisonment or other such punitive actions that people had used in the past, but this was a lie that the CDS told itself. Reshyan wanted to see it abolished in zir lifetime.

It had taken Reshyan many varshas after returning to the Solar System to rebuild zir psyche. Zir ability to tolerate interactions with other people still hadn't returned in full, but at the same time, zie couldn't stand being alone. Earth orbit had provided a good balance. The space around the planet teemed with people and goods traveling to other parts of the Solar System. Someone was always in sight. Zir primarily worked alone, though, so zie could enjoy the presence of others without socializing.

Nara's contract brought Reshyan closer to the surface and within range of human sight than Reshyan had previously experienced. Zie had yet to communicate in real time with any of them. Jayanthi was the first human zie had ever messaged. Her words and tenor resembled those of an alloy, and Reshyan wondered if the children spoke differently.

Zie flew in a zigzag pattern along the pair's anticipated route, moving from west to east and searching the ground for the characteristic infrared shape of a warm-blooded biped. How humans had accomplished so much with their limited visual spectrum, zie would never understand. About seventy-five kilometers west of Zantep's outer limits, Reshyan spotted them. They had stopped to set up camp near an offshoot of the Taurus Mountains. Not a very productive day for them in terms of distance, but perhaps they were still worn out and saving energy for the mountains they would have to cross.

Reshyan deployed a fresh set of indriyas, gathered the spent ones into zir pouch, and slow-blinked to start an immersive recording. Zie sharpened zir gaze and flew in wide circles above the campsite. Both subjects appeared to move in a healthy fashion. They had their bikes, the trailer, and the tent—all of the essentials. With that established, Reshyan flexed zir tired tail muscles, squeezed zir oblique funnels, and rose upward.

Zie threaded between lingering cumulus clouds, relaxing as the pressures of atmosphere and gravity eased. The platform where zie berthed orbited about eighty kilometers above sea level, higher than most clouds but below the Kármán line, where atmospheric flight became impossible. Reshyan had vents all over zir body, like a typical alloy, so zie could fly in vacuum, but zie had no reason to waste water and energy on that.

Home was a simple but comfortable sheltered berth. Several others attached to the orbital platform's center like eggs arranged around a plate. The units were more plush than those found in the padhrans of outer space, with the exception of the ones at the Primary Nivid. Reshyan slipped into zirs and relaxed into its cushioned hold. Luxuries like these sweetened the work zie did on Earth.

Reshyan first transferred the day's weather data and analysis to the local Nivid repository, then moved the immersive recordings to a private location where Nara could retrieve them. With that done, zie perused the daily menu of bhojya flavors. Zie settled on one spiced with za'atar and cinnamon. It seemed appropriate given the region zie had worked on that day. As zie sipped on the flavorful liquid, zie thought-retrieved the painting of the Alps that zie had started a few days earlier. To keep the mind sharp, one had to give it other tasks, much like cross-training the muscles of the body. Reshyan chose a virtual brush, then put it aside. Zie had forgotten to send a message back to Jayanthi, which zie had promised to do, and zie always kept zir word.

"All well," zie sent. "The children are seventy-five kilometers west of Zantep."

With that done, zie settled in and began to paint.

# DAY 22

The village of Alanya hugged a small, jewel-toned bay that reflected turquoise skies and sparkled in the sunlight. Somya and I stood astride our bikes and admired the view from atop a bluff. We'd lost a day after the river crossing at Zantep, but we'd made it through the mountains and along the rugged coastline without any further delays. It helped that the weather had cleared up—at last—and that our route never took us above a thousand meters in altitude.

As had become our habit, we stashed our bikes and gear a little ways out of town and made our way down to the beach.

"Let's take a quick dip before we meet Rune," I said. "We look a mess."

We hadn't found a clean body of water to camp by, so our skin and hair still held traces of mud. As eager as I was to meet Rune, I wanted to make the best first impression that I could. We plunged into the crystalline waters of the Mediterranean Sea, admiring the brightly colored fish, and then scrubbed the dirt off using beach sand. The grains were finer and softer than at Hormirzad, and I could almost imagine that I rubbed myself with a towel.

We had nothing clean to wear, so we rinsed our travel-weary clothes, pulled them on, and walked along the coast. We headed west toward the setting sun. Rune had told us to look for the *Svapna* at the second pier we encountered from that direction. A few people glanced curiously at us as we passed the first pier, a floating construction made of braided wood about as wide as an average human's arm span. They asked no questions. The second pier was four times broader and extended farther into the sea. Two sailboats were tied to it, one about halfway and the other at the very end.

"This is it," Somya said.

I answered their grin with my own.

We ignored the first boat, which clearly didn't belong to Rune. At five meters long, it was too small for an ocean crossing. A middle-aged person with a round belly and curly black hair sat in the open cockpit. Identification stated her name as Isin Erdemir. She waved as we walked by and called out, "Hey, are you Rune's friends?"

I stopped and reflexively nodded. Isin stood and stepped nimbly onto the dock. The floating surface rose and sank gently under my feet.

"I'm captain of the *Zephyros*," she said. "Also a friend of Rune's."

"Nice to meet you," Somya said. They glanced toward the end of the pier. "We're headed for the *Svapna*."

"That's not Rune's boat," Isin informed us. "It's about to go into dry dock for repairs, and I'm afraid Rune's is in a similar situation. The *Svapna* took some damage during a recent storm, and it's stuck in Nuberia for the time being. Rune said he needs to get the work done before you all can cross the Atlantic." She shrugged apologetically.

I exchanged a look with Somya. *What should we do now?* We didn't need to ask the question aloud.

After a moment, Isin said, "I've got a small house in town. You two look like you could use a warm bath and a hot meal, maybe a bed for the night. Why don't you stay with me, and I'll help you figure out what to do next?"

As she spoke the words, a bone-deep heaviness settled into my body. The thought of Alanya and Rune had kept me going since the Euphrates. My bodym had raised multiple alarms about my need to stay off the bike and get some rest. To have the boat ride taken away was too much to handle. I felt Somya's arm settle lightly around my shoulders.

"That would be wonderful, thank you," they said.

Isin led us away from the beach. Alanya had architecture more like Vaksana's, rectangular and made of dirt and growing plants. Isin's home nestled in a hillside beside a grove of pine trees. She had us sit in her front room and went to get us some food and drink.

I turned to Somya and spoke in a low tone so that Isin wouldn't overhear. "So what do we do now? We budgeted a week to get from here to Nuberia. Do you think Isin could take us? She hasn't offered us a ride. Would it be rude to ask?"

Somya held up a hand. "Take a breath, Aks. I think she wants us to get some rest first, and she's probably right. I'm exhausted, which means you must be ready to fall over."

"I'm . . . not as bad as I thought I might be."

Somya made an *I-don't-believe-you* face.

"Some of my numbers aren't great, but I don't feel awful, not the way my mother does when she has a crisis." I shrugged. "She changed my gene expression in ways that go beyond the sickle-cell effects. On Chedi, she always made me sleep in the high-oxygen room after an active day, but what if I didn't need it? My body has held up really well so far. Think of everything I've put it through." I smiled through my weariness. "Maybe I'm as well suited for Earth as I am for Meru."

Somya chuckled. "Wouldn't that be ironic?"

Isin entered the room. "I'm glad to see you both smiling."

She handed us cups of cool water and set a plate of some kind of baked biscuits on a low table made of wood and stone. I took one bite and fell in love with the buttery, crumbly deliciousness.

"Thank you," I mumbled around a mouthful.

"I'm sure you're both worried about the next part of your journey," Isin said. "Rune and I discussed some ideas, but I want to fix you a hot meal before we get into it. I've put out some towels and robes by the bath, and there's a basin where you can wash your clothes. I'd offer you the microcleaner, but Rune told me that's not allowed. Get cleaned up, and after your bellies are full, we'll talk."

With that, she showed us to the bathroom. I let Somya wash up first while I kept eating. When they finished, I took my turn. The stone-tiled room was already warm and steamy, and the clean, hot water felt divine. I closed my eyes and submerged my entire body in the tub for as long as I could hold my breath. After I dried off, I pulled on the simple robe and knelt by the small washbasin. I didn't have much skill at laundering, but after the previous week's adventures, a little bit of soap and a lot of water worked a miraculous transformation. I hung my dripping clothes next to Somya's and stepped into the hallway.

"In here," Somya called.

They beckoned me into the kitchen. A small round table with four chairs sat in one corner. Somya patted the seat next to theirs. The aromas that filled the room made my head spin. I had to clench my hands against my thighs as Isin placed several steaming dishes in front of us, otherwise I would've started eating before she joined us. I had no name for what she dished onto my plate, but it was hot, heavily spiced, and it tasted like the best meal of my life.

---

We sat under the pine trees after dinner to watch the sunset. Sol painted the clouds with unreal colors ranging from coral pink to gold. The waves of the Mediterranean complemented the sky with sapphire tones and white froth. Every minute, the view changed in some way, and I couldn't take my eyes off it. When a day ended in Chedi, there was never the kind of drama that happened on Earth on a regular basis. As the sky darkened, a cool breeze blew in from the north. I wrapped my arms around myself and tilted my face up. The first stars glimmered in the gaps between the clouds.

Isin handed each of us a mug of hot tea. "As you could probably tell, my boat's a bit small for the journey you're taking. I use it to hop between the islands of the Aegean Sea. It can sleep three people, but it's cramped, and once we get your gear on board, we really won't have much space."

I nodded along and blew on my tea. It surprised me that our bikes and the trailer would fit on the *Zephyros*. We planned to bring them to the house under the cover of night. Alanya would shut off its light three hours after sunset—as most cities in Loka did—and its streets would lie quiet after that.

"Rune and I think your best course of action is to sail to Thessali with me. From there, you can head north through the Balkan Mountains. I could take you up the Adriatic, but then you'd either have to backtrack east or cross the Alps. November is early in the season but not too early for snowstorms. The Balkans will make for an easier passage, and from there, you can head northwest above the Alps before heading west and south to Nuberia."

"We would like to avoid high altitudes," Somya said, diplomatically omitting that I was the reason.

I thought back to the maps I'd studied. "If we have to skirt the Alps to the north, that will put us into the Out of Bounds."

Isin nodded as if I'd said the most ordinary thing in the world.

"Rune said we should avoid traveling over land in the OOB," I said.

Isin pursed her lips. "It's not ideal, but without a boat, you can't avoid it. The alternative is to go along northern Africa, but that would require crossing the Mediterranean—which I can't do in the *Zephyros*—or backtracking east and taking a land route. Rune estimated that it would cost you two extra weeks to do that. You would only lose a week by going north."

I groaned and looked at Somya. I didn't like any of the options. "What do you think?"

Somya shrugged. "Rune's the only experienced one among us. If he thinks it's okay for us to go through the European OOB zone, then let's do it."

"It might be safer to take the extra week and head south and east," I said. "That keeps us in Loka and on land. We'd make good time along the north African coast. No mountains to deal with. Warmer weather, too."

"Perhaps you should take tonight to think it over," Isin said. "You have maps?"

We nodded.

"Good. They won't be as accurate for the Out of Bounds as for Loka, but they should show you enough to plan ahead. People in the OOB have settled in and around the major cities of old. You'll find resources, though you might have to trade for them. You can stock up in the borderlands."

We finished our tea and headed inside. The night had grown chilly enough that it reminded me of the stormy pass we'd crossed with Freni.

"If we're going to Europe," I said to Somya as we settled on the sofas in the front room, "we're going to need warmer clothes."

They agreed. "We can probably pick some up in Thessali, closer to the borderlands." Somya grinned at me. "You do realize what this means?" They continued before I could answer. "We'll get to spend some time living in the Out of Bounds, after all! Maybe we'll find a good site to go back to and establish our new society."

If my friend had phores, they would have glowed with excitement. I tried to share their eagerness, but after our misadventure crossing the Euphrates, I couldn't help worrying about what complications we might encounter in the OOB. I nodded with as much enthusiasm as I could muster.

"Come on, Aks, aren't you curious about what life is like over there?"

"I am," I said, "but I'm also nervous about timing." I opened our map book and placed it on the low center table. A bioluminescent tube hanging from the ceiling filled the room with a gentle pink glow. I turned to the page that showed where we'd be crossing the border and frowned. "We're already going to lose an entire week because of this, and we don't know what we'll run into in Europe."

"Doesn't your grandmother go there for research?"

"She does, but she's an alloy. She flies in and out, and she's got her bodym tied to the network at all times. Nobody's going to bother her."

"Bother?" Somya propped themself on their elbows. "Do you really think the people there will try to stop us?"

I lifted my gaze from the book. "They might. Or maybe they'll get violent or steal things. People who won't take treatment are the ones who get sent out of Loka, right?"

"That's not exactly how it works—at least, that's not what I heard while I was on Earth. The tarawans and alloys have engineered violent behavior away in humans. It's only things like Aspiration and Avarice Disorder or Empathy Deficiency where we have a choice about taking treatment."

"And for end of life," I said, remembering Pazir.

"Yes, for andoly, as well. Anyway, I don't think you need to worry so much about the OOB. Rune said that conditions there would be unpredictable, not that it would put us in danger from humans." They laughed lightly. "It's not like we got a warm welcome from everyone in Loka, either. At least the OOBers won't hassle us for having excessive aspirations."

"That's a good point," I admitted. "It sounds like you really want to take the northern route."

"Don't you? I'll be an adult on Earth one day, and I can go where I want and see what I want then. You might not have that option."

"Thanks for the vote of confidence."

Somya's teeth flashed in a grin. "Take nothing for granted."

"And cherish every day," I finished.

On Chedi, I never knew when a family might decide to return to Earth. Friendships sometimes lasted only a year or two, and after a few rounds of getting my heart broken, I had invested less of myself in them—until I met Somya. They had taught me to open up, to allow myself to fully enjoy what I could in the moment rather than holding back in case of loss.

"Okay, but this challenge isn't all about me," I said, "and our motto applies as much to your situation as to mine."

"So we're going to the Out of Bounds?"

I closed the map book. "Let's do it."

# DAY 23

We loaded up the *Zephyros* before sunrise. The eastern horizon glowed with the promise of day, but above us, the stars held on to the darkness of space. Somya, Isin, and I spoke in hushed tones as we took apart the bikes and trailer and stowed them in the small cabin. The boat had a V-shaped berth at the bow, a small stove and sink for cooking, and an even smaller closet with a toilet and hose for washing. We worked as efficiently as we could, but Somya and I had yet to get our "sea legs," so we spent a lot of effort trying not to fall over on the bobbing vessel. Once we had everything secured, we sat on deck and had our breakfast. Dark-gray-and-black cormorants floated beside us, fishing for their own meals.

"Let me give you an overview of sailing," Isin said as we ate. She sat by the steering wheel, and Somya and I settled on a bench along the stern.

"We have some experience," I said, unable to keep the note of pride from my voice. "Chedi has a lake big enough for a two-meter skiff, and she has constructs that can generate wind. The *Zephyros* is bigger, of course, and has a jib, but I'm sure we can learn quickly. We've looked at everything that seemed relevant in our local copy of the Nivid."

Isin smiled. "I'm glad to hear that, but it's one thing to read or watch immersives and another to be out on the sea. I'm used to sailing alone, though, so it's no trouble. Once we're underway, I'll let you practice. Until then, let's go over some safety basics." She gave us each a self-inflating life vest and a pair of gloves, the latter to avoid rope burn in case we had to hoist or lower the sails. "If I'm going to tack or jibe, that means this big, beautiful beam's going to swing across the deck. I'll give you a warning first. You know why they call it a boom, right? Because that's what it sounds like when it hits your head." She kept a solemn expression as Somya and I exchanged an *is-she-serious* look, then she burst out laughing. "Had you there, didn't I?"

After breakfast, she showed us the basics of the kitchen and taught us how to wash the dishes efficiently. The boat had a desalination pump that would provide fresh water, but it filled the tank slowly, so we had to be mindful of our usage. Solar paint covered the mast and deck and would provide a limited amount of electric power. We went above deck as the first rays of sunlight washed the landscape in pale yellow.

"We'll motor out for the first bit," Isin said. "Who wants to take the wheel?"

Somya waved in my direction. "Let Aks do it. She's been waiting for this day her whole life."

I threw my arms around them in a thank-you hug, then swapped places with Isin. She threw off the deck lines, started the motor, and said, "Let's go."

We headed south for a short while, getting clear of the bay, and then turned west. Seagulls circled and cried out above us. A pretty black-headed gull alit on top of the mast and stared at me with its dark, round eyes, so much like an alloy's. I held the steering wheel steady and matched its gaze until it took wing.

Isin showed Somya how to raise the sails. The little skiff we'd used in Chedi had a much simpler rigging system and only one sail, but from my observation, the same basic principles applied: head into the wind, get the main sail up, fall off until it catches, then tighten the sheet. Repeat the same process with the head sail, except with a winch to help get it tight. After that, it was a matter of fine adjustments in bearing and tension until the telltale ribbons flew straight back.

With the motor off and the wind from the port side, we headed northwest, following the coastline. The sails snapped and sighed. The rigging clanked. Waves slapped against the hull. Salt spray coated every exposed surface on my body. The *Zephyros* gave us a comfortable ride at a moderate speed, not heeling the way I'd seen racing boats do. Somya sat at the bow, leaning over the rail on the leeward side from time to time to vent the contents of their stomach. I felt bad for them and simultaneously relieved that I hadn't drawn the short straw for seasickness. Isin promised that Somya would get used to the motion in a day or two.

In between Somya's bouts of nausea, Isin taught us some basic maneuvers—how to tack, zigzagging across the direction of the wind; how to bear away from the wind and jibe if we need to turn the boat around; how to quickly take the sails down in case of inclement weather. We each took a turn with the three primary tasks—steering, adjusting the mainsail, and adjusting the jib. Our actions lacked coordination, but I could see a future where Somya and I worked in perfect synchronicity. This was exactly what I'd dreamed of when I had first read Rune's book: to journey on the open ocean like humans had for thousands of years, harnessing the power of the Earth and coaxing it to our aid, the sea below and the sky above.

I couldn't stop grinning.

How had humanity lost its connection to such activities? Even my mother and her friends, the so-called Society of Humans with Ambitions, had never gone on this type of adventure. Freni, similarly, failed to tolerate this kind of danger. Was that the cost of protecting the Earth from the rapacious nature of our past? Humans had chosen to engineer their behavior after the catastrophic years, to reduce violence and greed, to change their biochemistry so that we could live in balance with other forms of consciousness, whether living or not, but in the process we had lost our thirst for exploration as well as our tolerance for risk.

As the boat rose and fell with the rhythm of the waves, the wind whipped at my clothes and hair. We had a steady heading, and Isin had left me and Somya to keep watch while she prepared our lunches, though I didn't expect Somya to eat much. They stood at the wheel, their gaze distant.

"How are you feeling, Som?" I asked.

They took a deep breath and nodded slowly. "Not terrible, but it's better if I don't think about my stomach."

"Right, sorry. It's beautiful here, isn't it?"

A couple of islands rose from the sea in weathered geometric shapes. Isin told us that once upon a time, many of them were inhabited, but alloys had rewilded them. They had saved a few structures of historical interest, as in other parts of Loka, but they had digested most of humanity's artificial structures back into soil and rock. When we passed close to land, crowds of monk seals raised their round gray-brown heads and barked at us. At one point, a small pod of striped dolphins swam alongside our boat, pacing us and playfully leaping out of the water. I wished we could take the time to explore all of it.

"I've never seen anything like this," Somya said. "My family lives too far inland to explore beyond the beach." They flashed me a smile. "Maybe instead of doing the Anthro Challenge again, we should sail around the world."

"It's a deal."

*But first we have to finish this journey,* I thought to myself. I didn't raise my concerns about the Out of Bounds again. We had to get through it, one way or another, and our travels had already proved unpredictable. A hundred more things could go wrong as we crossed Europe, but at that moment, I put them out of my mind and let the sea carry us forward.

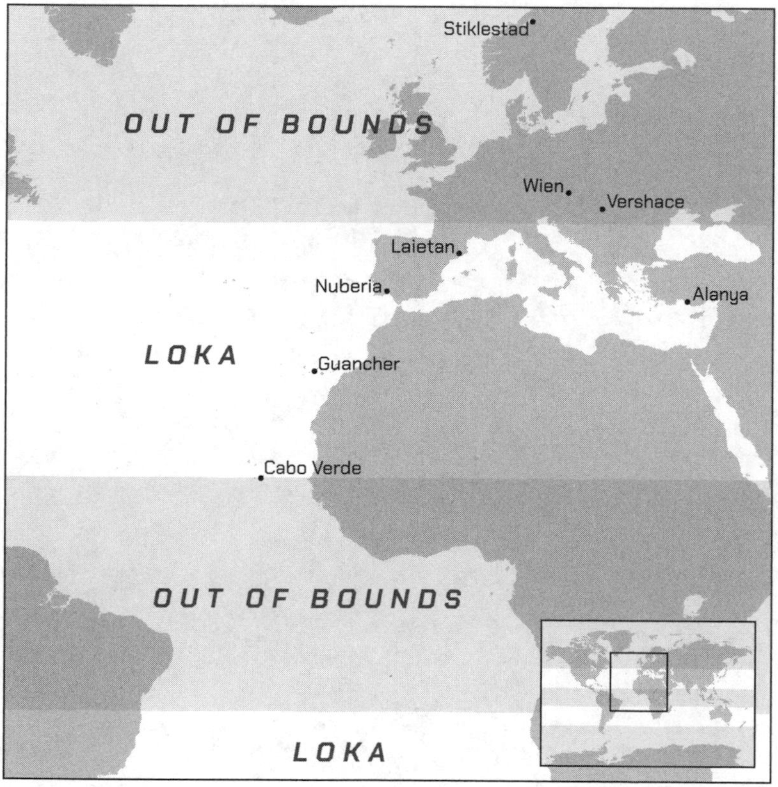

Stiklestad

OUT OF BOUNDS

Wien

Vershace

Laietan

Nuberia

Alanya

LOKA

Guancher

Cabo Verde

OUT OF BOUNDS

LOKA

# DAY 26

On our fourth day aboard the *Zephyros*, as the sun sank into the western horizon, we arrived in port at Thessali. Along the way, we'd seen countless wonders of Earth life—basking sharks, sea turtles, a multitude of fish, a megapod of dolphins that numbered in the thousands, and more birds than one guidebook could possibly hold. I had made only the roughest of sketches in my notebook. The constant motion of the boat made detailed drawings tricky. I promised myself that I'd fill them in on land while the memories remained fresh.

We'd also come across some alloys that I'd first thought were whales. They traveled solo or in pairs, sometimes paralleling our boat for a while before disappearing into the depths. Isin didn't seem bothered by their presence, but I couldn't help feeling nervous for the same reasons I didn't like to see them on land. I expected that we'd encounter more alloys in Thessali, close as it was to the border between Loka and the Out of Bounds.

The city's famous White Tower reflected the orange light of sunset, standing like a proud guardian along the coastline. Much like in Alanya, the harbor was more of a sheltered bay with a couple of floating piers than the massive structures of old, but Thessali itself had more people and buildings than Isin's hometown. Still, we saw no other boats as we tied the *Zephyros* to the empty posts.

"I usually sleep here," Isin said, "but you're welcome to find more comfortable lodging if you wish. I assume you'll want to set off in the morning?"

I exchanged a *where-do-you-want-to-stay* look with Somya and confirmed that they also preferred the *Zephyros* to a stranger's home. "We'll spend the night with you," I said, "though we might want to scout a place for our gear and get everything stored there tonight."

"To avoid unwelcome attention in the morning," Somya added.

Isin nodded. "Could you two head into town and pick up some fresh food first? It'll be an hour or so until full dark."

Somya and I agreed. I swayed as I walked along the dock and grabbed on to Somya's arm. They fared no better.

"Is this pier really bouncy?" they murmured.

We set foot on the beach. The horizon insisted on moving up and down.

"Not the pier," I said with a laugh. "Just our brains, I guess."

I'd heard of people getting their sea legs, but I hadn't realized that we would have to find our *land* legs once back on shore.

We staggered into Thessali, leaning on each other like a couple of drunks. Our giggles didn't help. People smiled at us, though. They sat on verandas supported by carved columns or waved at us from wickerwork balconies. For the first time since arriving on Earth, I saw two-story houses. The structures were made of pale stone. Vines hung from flat rooftop terraces, which also harbored compact olive trees.

The first community garden we found was set in an open area near the center of town. In addition to fresh fruit and vegetables, the storehouse had sacks of millet and jars with olives, honey, or cheese. We took some of everything. We even found a small jug of wine for Isin. Whatever we didn't consume that night, we would pack for the next few days. Remembering the advice to find items to trade in the OOB, we also found artwork and clothing in a different area. We didn't take too much—only what we could comfortably carry.

Isin laughed at our laden arms on our return. Night had fallen by then, but we waited until after our meal, when darkness blanketed the city, to extract our bikes and the trailer from the boat's cabin. The motors had no charge, so we pedaled our way through quiet, empty streets. We stayed on the outskirts, avoiding the routes that we'd taken earlier, and found our way past the last buildings. A few kilometers to the north, the land rose in gentle hills dotted with laurel, oak, and poplar trees. We left our gear behind some bushes and walked back to the *Zephyros*.

Isin handed us hot mugs of watered-down wine sweetened with honey and fruits. The warm drink coated my throat and settled like a blanket in my belly. Above us, the sky was dark with clouds. We'd met with one storm on our way to Thessali and had taken shelter by one of the larger islands until it passed. I'd already gotten used to the luxury of having a roof over our heads.

"Thank you for all your help," I said softly.

"And to you both for yours," Isin said. "It's not often I get other hands to sail with."

"Will you head back home tomorrow?" Somya asked.

Isin shrugged and smiled. "Depends which way the wind blows."

"We'll miss you," Somya said. They patted the bench. "And the *Zephyros*, too."

"You can miss it more tomorrow," Isin said. She stood and gathered our mugs. "You want the inside bunks? One last night of comfort?"

We nodded gratefully. I crawled into the narrow space first. Somya followed, and Isin rinsed the mugs and then climbed the ladder. The waves lapped against the hull, their gentle slap-slap a nice counterpoint to the swaying of the boat.

"We did it, Som," I said. I yawned. "We sailed."

"I can't wait to do it again. I wonder how different Rune's boat will be."

I groaned. "We have to get to Nuberia first."

They reached out a hand and squeezed mine. "Try not to worry, Aks. I know that's like asking you not to breathe sometimes, but look, we've already come this far. We swam across the Euphrates. We survived hail and floods and high mountains. There's nothing the Out of Bounds can throw at us that we can't handle."

"I hope you're right."

"I'm always right."

I smacked them lightly on the shoulder. Somya's back warmed mine as I settled in. I hoped their words came true.

# DAY 29

By our third day out from Thessali, our time on the *Zephyros* with Isin seemed like a dream. The first day wasn't too bad, but as we rode north through the mountains on the following day, the weather turned against us. Not only did it rain, but being mid-November in the Out of Bounds, it got cold. I had never experienced temperatures so low, and neither had Somya. The so-called warm clothes we'd packed kept our bodies dry, but our hands and faces grew damp and numb. As we neared Vershace, I developed a sore throat. I did my best to hide my misery. My body ached like it had been run over by a boulder, my eyes burned, and no amount of tea eased the pain of swallowing. I ignored the various reports of elevated this and depressed that from my bodym. None of the numbers related to my blood oxygen or hemoglobin, so I assumed I had some normal Earth-based illness and did my best to ignore it.

That night, Somya went into Vershace while I rested in our tent. The city sat at the edge of the Out of Bounds. No sign or fence marked the border. It looked like many other places in Loka, with earthen buildings covered in plants. After Somya returned, they reported that the people seemed used to strangers, a departure from our other stops. I wished I could have experienced it for myself, but my body demanded rest. We were only two days into a two-week journey, and we couldn't afford more delays.

My attempts to push through my misery fell apart the next day at Donji Miholjac, a small town on the bank of the Drava River. As we approached the crossing, my legs gave out. My body began to tremble uncontrollably, and when Somya put their hand against my cheek, it felt icy cold. A blocky, medieval-style manor house was the only structure visible on our side of the river. Its empty gables and turrets looked over a stone bridge that crossed the water into the main part of the village, similar in size to the ones we had in Chedi.

I lay in a miserable heap on the muddy ground while Somya worked with quiet, fierce efficiency to pitch our tent. We'd picked up replacements for the gear lost to the Euphrates while at Thessali, including a portable electric heater. With the incessant rain, we didn't have much power in the solar batteries, and I welcomed every bit of warmth and dryness. Somya helped me change into dry clothes and wrapped me in my bedroll. At least the rain hadn't soaked those.

I grabbed Somya's arm. "Wait! We're camped in sight of the town. We can't—"

"We're in the Out of Bounds now," they said, gently removing my hand. "It doesn't matter if people see us."

I lay down then and closed my eyes, the tension cut from my body like a puppet string. Shivers racked me until my teeth chattered. Somya held me up and gave me hot soup to drink. I sipped at it with no enthusiasm. After some coaxing, they gave up and let me sleep.

According to Somya, I moaned and tossed relentlessly. They became worried and went into town seeking help. I'm not sure what exactly transpired, but that's when they met Lumo and his traveling companions. Lumo came to our tent and, after seeing my condition, pronounced me as having a fever, an illness that neither Somya nor I had knowledge of. Lumo provided some edible medicine—entirely developed in the Out of Bounds by humans—to help reduce my temperature. I had only the vaguest sense of swallowing something that left a bitter aftertaste.

Fever is a strange thing. Chedi took care of herself such that no harmful pathogens multiplied in her. I understood sickle-cell disease and its effects, but I'd never experienced an infection of such severity. Somya probably had when they were younger and still on Earth, but they had no memory of it and no idea what to do for me. In Loka, the alloys would have treated such conditions easily. In the Out of Bounds, humanity largely fended for itself. People could return to Loka and receive help, but they had to accept the conditions of life imposed there by law, which meant treatment for harmful behavioral disorders. If they wanted to avoid that, they had to rely on leftover materials from the Human Era or whatever bits of alloy technology and resources made it across the border.

Lumo wasn't a doctor, but he'd lived and traveled on his own long enough to know the basics of care. At one point, after the medicine and a nap, I woke and heard him say, "I've done all I can. If she needs further care, we aren't too far from Loka, and I have a walker-wagon. I can give you a ride there."

"No!" I sat up, panicked. "Som, don't let him take us back!" I stood, my bedroll tangled around me, and I stumbled into Somya's arms.

"Hush, Aks." Somya's grip tightened around me. "You need to rest. Lie down!"

"We have to keep going," I cried. "We've come too far. I can ride. I can—"

"No, you can't," Somya said. "Not if you want to get better."

"Don't call my parents," I begged. "Or . . . or Reshyan, or Nara. Please!"

"I won't. I promise." They pulled me down to the tent floor and kept me tight in their embrace.

"She's delirious," Lumo said. "We need to get her cooled off."

"No," I groaned. I clutched at the bedding, but they pried it from my hands.

"You're going to be okay, Aks," Somya said. "You'll be okay."

I struggled a little more, but I had already spent my strength on the day's ride. Eventually, I allowed Somya to place me atop the bedroll, which Lumo had spread on the ground. My heartsib sat beside me, stroking my hair and exchanging words with Lumo that I could no longer process. My body turned to lead, and my eyes burned under heavy lids.

*We can't stop here. We'll fall behind. Don't let the alloys near us.* I wasn't sure if I spoke the words aloud or only in my head, but it didn't matter. We weren't going any farther that day.

# DAY 30

They called themselves "bounders." Besides Lumo, there was Mezei and Brana. All were young adults in their twenties, with Lumo acting as the parent and driving the walker-wagon. They had no fixed place of residence other than the family homes where they'd grown up, and they chose to live as itinerants who crossed between Loka and the OOB at will.

Lumo had purple hair that fell to his shoulders in loose waves. Brana had hair the color of fire, and almost-white skin—lighter than anyone's on Chedi. Freckles dotted her nose and cheeks. My feverish mind transformed her and Lumo into magical creatures, like those from old fairy tales. Mezei's appearance was the only one that grounded me. They had medium-brown skin and green eyes with ordinary dark-brown hair cropped close to their head. Mezei looked like family.

The morning after Somya met Lumo, the three bounders came to our campsite. Brana and Mezei helped me walk to their wagon while Lumo and Somya packed up. The rain had eased overnight, and the clouds had broken apart, leaving a bitter cold in their wake. I was lucid enough to see my breath fog in front of my face. The bounders' mobile home had a rounded rectangular shape, kind of like my maker's womb but much smaller. It rested on six struts that resembled short legs. It also had four wheels that were raised above the ground and windows on the front, back, and right.

Inside, there were two bench-style beds. Brana got me settled into one of them and tucked my shivering form under a soft, fluffy blanket. When I looked up, I could see blue sky through a clear pane in the roof.

"Don't worry, darling," Brana said cheerfully. "We'll have you all better in no time. Your friend said that it's okay for you to ride with us since our vehicle is based on an old human invention, like your bikes, so you just rest easy, okay?"

"Thank you," I whispered.

Brana's words put my biggest worry to rest. If we could keep moving forward while I was sick, we wouldn't fall further behind schedule.

I lay in the bunk with my eyes closed, my fever-heightened hearing picking up every little noise. Soft murmurs of conversation preceded thumps and thuds from overhead. Inside, clinking sounds punctuated by the gurgle of running water indicated the presence of some kind of kitchen. Something clanked near my head, and I cracked open my eyelids.

Brana had set a plate with toast and a mug of steaming liquid on a small table next to me. "Try to eat. I made you a special tea, as well, that should help with your fever and taste better than the straight medicine."

She helped prop me semi-upright against some pillows. The toast had a generous spread of butter on it, and it tasted like heaven. The tea had a bitter undertone mellowed by honey and lemon. I sipped at it slowly and looked around. We were in the rear segment of the wagon. The second bunk was folded against the wall above me. On the other side was a miniature kitchen, complete with sink, stove, and chiller. A small window above the sink shone with sunlight. To my right, against the back, was a bench seat behind a long table, and to my left were two tall closets forming a short passageway that ended in a door. I could hear voices on the other side, including Somya's.

Brana glanced that way and said, "I think we'll be underway soon."

"I've never ridden in a vehicle like this before," I said, "but I've read about them. Did you build it?"

She grinned. "Not me. I haven't a mechanically inclined bone in my body. Lumo found it somewhere and got it fixed up. He picked me up a few years ago in Paris, and we added Mezei in Wien. In fact, that's where we're headed next."

The city names conjured up memories from my history lessons. The major cities on Earth had broken down with the exodus of alloys into space. Eventually, the alloys returned to rehabilitate and rewild those places, starting with the ones at temperate latitudes. Humankind had settled into a new way of life in the wake of this work, which marked the borders of Loka. Residents often paid tribute to ancient civilizations when choosing names for the new cities. In the Out of Bounds, though, in places like Northern Europe, the original locations and labels still held. I hoped I would be well enough to appreciate whatever I could see of Wien the next day.

The door between the cabins opened. Lumo's purple-topped head poked through it. He gave me a surprised smile, then turned to Brana. "Time to lock down, Bee."

"Aye, aye," she said.

Lumo disappeared. Brana busied herself in the kitchen, pressing against every cabinet door, then putting a cover over the sink and stove. She flipped the table in the back against the wall and latched it. My small table had an arm that attached below my bunk, and she left it in place. After a quick knock-knock against the door, she sat on the rear bench and picked up a book from a small shelf above it.

A whirring noise preceded the motion of the vehicle. I held on to my mug, and we began to move. The walking sensation wasn't like riding on the bike trailer, but more like being carried by a construct. The legs absorbed most of the bumps that the ground offered up. My tea lapped gently against the walls of the mug. I nibbled at the toast, trying to make it last as long as I could, and watched the cold, wet world through the window.

---

The wagon didn't go much faster than our average biking speed. Many of the roads in the Out of Bounds were not well maintained, if at all, and the vehicle, which ran on a combination of solar and plant fuel, didn't have a lot of power.

By the time we arrived in Wien, nearly nine hours had passed, and the sun had set. I missed the incoming views of the city because my fever had come roaring back. Somya had taken a turn riding with me. They helped me to the small toilet, which turned out to be inside the right-hand closet, and then nursed some more soup into me. After that, I fell asleep and didn't wake until the wagon stopped moving. My body felt bruised. Every motion sent a lightning bolt of pain through my head. Lumo laid a hand on my forehead and pronounced me in need of medical help.

"There is a hospital here," he said to Somya in a low voice. I was lucid enough to parse his words, though I didn't open my eyes. "It's run by humans. I'm not sure what working technology they have—it's unpredictable in the OOB—but they can do more for her than we can."

"Let's go," I said, the words like fire in my throat.

I could imagine my mother's mounting concern, first at seeing people helping me into a strange vehicle, and then not seeing me at all. She would know that something wasn't right. I decided to risk the hospital over having Reshyan or some other alloy swoop in and fly me back to her.

We rode a little farther in the wagon. When I emerged, darkness had descended on the sky, but lights—bright and harsh—shone from the windows of the building in front of us. Its tall, blocky shape betrayed its age. I leaned on Somya as Lumo led us through a solid double-door entryway and into a large room dotted with armchairs, some framed in regen-based wickerwork, but others built out of solid wood. People—all human—filled about half the seats.

Lumo told Somya to sit with me and went to a person behind a counter. They spoke for a few minutes. He returned holding a soft, sleevelike device, which he told me to place around my upper arm. It tightened itself to a snug fit. The outer surface lit up with various numbers.

Lumo took the chair beside me. "Now we wait until they call you back to a treatment room. Don't worry about payment. The desk nurse said that care here is no cost, though they will accept donations of any goods you can spare."

His words didn't entirely make sense to me. Everything had a cost. A place like this clearly expended energy, labor, and other resources to keep itself going, and it would generate waste products that would incur additional costs to process.

"What is payment?" Somya asked.

"Do you know what money is?" Lumo asked.

The answer came to me through the fog of illness: a social convention that represented resource allocation and individual property. People in the Human Era used it as a means of trading and accumulating wealth. Based on Lumo's question, I guessed that *payment* and *money* indicated some kind of transactional relationship in the Out of Bounds.

"They still do that kind of thing here?" Somya asked.

"Yes," Lumo said, his tone wry. "Property ownership exists in most parts of the OOB. It serves the people who come here with avarice and possessiveness."

I leaned my head on Somya's shoulder and half listened to their conversation. Alloys would give humans what they needed in any part of Earth, but those in the Out of Bounds might not be content with the same kinds of things that satisfied the majority of those in Loka.

"Couldn't the OOBers rebuild human-era technology using materials from Loka?" Somya asked.

"Sure, but they are still subject to the laws of the CDS. That means no extraction of natural resources by humans, limits on environmental waste, rules about construction and agriculture and infrastructure. OOBers can own items without limits on hoarding. They can trade. They can live in isolation or get in fights. They can even hunt some animals, but they can't live like humans did before the Alloy Era."

So the alloys had oversight in the Out of Bounds. That meant that we couldn't exactly replicate society in Chedi, who could set her own laws within her body. I wondered how many CDS laws she chose to violate. Based on what I'd seen during my six weeks on Earth, the rules weren't all that different, so perhaps we could establish the free society we hoped for in the OOB.

After an eternity, the device on my arm beeped.

"That's your summons," Lumo said.

He started to help me up. I turned and grabbed Somya's arm.

"Som, I want you in there with me," I said. I knew it made me sound like a child, but I couldn't face the unknown by myself.

My heartsib stood and took me by the hand. A nurse named Devika held open another solid door and smiled kindly at us. She made no comment as she led Somya and me to a small room with a comfortable bed, and she indicated that I should lie down on it.

"Based on your diagnostics," Devika said, "you have a bacterial infection, likely from exposure to dirty water. We have microconstructs that can easily take care of it."

"Do you have an alternative treatment?" Somya interjected. "Something that doesn't involve alloy technology?"

She paused. "Why would that matter?"

Somya explained it to her, and to my surprise, she made a *thinking-about-it* face and didn't raise any objections.

"We do have some synthetic antibodies available," she said after half a minute. "We usually give them to people who are headed to remote areas. They should help with this kind of infection. I'll need a few minutes to figure out which ones to use. You can wait in here."

“Thank you,” I said. “Would it be possible to get an infusion for hydration as well? I have sickle-cell disease, and an infusion will help my recovery.”

This time, her expression indicated *never-heard-of-it* and *is-the-feverish-person-delusional.* Luckily Somya recognized it and backed me up. Devika shrugged, nodded, and left the room.

I smiled weakly at Somya. “Thanks.”

“Bet you caught the infection from the Euphrates swim,” they said. “I must have had immunity. Benefits of being born here, I guess.”

“Lucky you,” I murmured.

After another small eternity, the nurse returned. She placed a small round device against the back of my hand. I felt a brief tingle there and a pinch on the other arm as Devika activated a hydration sleeve.

“I’ll be back in an hour,” she said.

“Do you mind if I leave and get something to eat?” Somya asked me.

I shook my head. The minimal exertions of the waiting room and conversing with the nurse had worn me out. Somya closed the door behind them, and I dozed until I heard it open again. Devika entered first, followed by Somya.

“All done,” the nurse said as she detached the sleeve. “I included some fever reducer and immune enhancements with the hydration solution. Your temperature should improve by morning. If it doesn’t, come back here, and we’ll take another look. The antibody treatment can take a week to resolve the infection fully, so don’t strain yourself even if you start to feel better.”

I sat up and waited for the dizziness to pass. Somya put their arm around me as we walked out to the waiting area.

“Good thing we met up with the bounders,” I said. “I won’t be fit to bike for a while. Sorry.”

Somya gently poked my side. “It’s not your fault, and yes, I’m glad we have a ride. They’re an interesting bunch. I’ve been talking to Lumo about our idea to establish a self-sustaining society within the Out of

Bounds, and he says that not only does he think it's doable, but there are already places where humans have lived independently since before the Alloy Era. Lumo thinks they might have a way of life that we'd enjoy, so maybe after we finish the Anthro Challenge, we can find ourselves a wagon and visit them."

I pictured the two of us roaming the Out of Bounds together and instantly fell in love with the idea. "You're the best, Som."

"I know."

# DAY 31

Sometime in the predawn hours, I woke with sweat dampening my clothes. My mind felt more lucid than it had for the previous two days. Somya was in the bunk above me, and Brana lay on the bench along the back of the wagon, both so deeply asleep that I couldn't hear a sound. A half-moon shone through the small kitchen window. I propped myself up on an elbow and took a drink of water. It eased the tight, dry sensation in my throat. My stomach gurgled. I hadn't felt hungry while I'd been feverish, but my appetite had returned at the least convenient time. I filled my belly with more water and lay back. My heart raced from that small exertion.

Whatever fate had brought Lumo and his bounders into our lives had also brought luck. I wouldn't have made it much farther on the bike, and neither Somya nor I would have known about the hospital. I hoped that the antibodies the nurse had given me wouldn't cause other problems. With what I understood of biochemistry, they shouldn't, but bodies were chaotic systems and not perfectly predictable. I took my improved mental state as a good sign.

My eyelids grew heavy. I closed them for a moment, or so I thought. When I opened them again, the sky outside had grown light, and Brana was busy at the stove. She turned when she saw me stir.

"Good morning. How are you feeling?"

I sat up slowly. "Exhausted, but better than yesterday. Also, ravenously hungry."

Her brown eyes crinkled as she smiled. "Great! Lumo says we'll get underway as soon as the sun's up. I'm making a porridge for breakfast."

"It smells great."

My stomach reminded me again how desperate it was for food. It growled audibly when Brana handed me a steaming bowl. She laughed. Somya stepped out of the bathing closet just then, a towel wrapped around their long hair.

"Welcome back to the land of the living, Aks," they said. They sat beside me and blew at the hot cereal in their own bowl. "If you're feeling up to it, I recommend riding up front next to Lumo. You'll get the best view up there."

"Maybe for a little while," I said. "Did you get to see Wien yesterday?"

"The parts we drove through, yes. Most of it was in ruins. Lumo said that alloys come through once a year and do maintenance on the important landmarks, but they let the rest decay. The actively inhabited part is pretty small. I'd guess maybe a little bigger than Hormirzad."

I recalled Wien featuring prominently during certain parts of European history, but it hadn't played much of a role in the later centuries of the Human Era or during the Alloy Era. As we ate, Mezei entered from the front, nodded at us, and stepped into the wash closet. Brana's porridge settled in my stomach like a warm hug. I got up to rinse my bowl, but Somya pulled me back down.

"Remember what the nurse said? You're to rest for several more days, even if you start to feel better." Somya cleaned both of our dishes and stowed them. Somehow they had already memorized exactly which cabinets the bowls and spoons belonged to.

After that, they helped me through the door into the front part of the wagon, which had taken on an almost mythical function in my imagination. There I found a small cabin with four C-shaped chairs, two facing a large front window and the other two against two side windows. Lumo sat in the forward chair on the right, a steering wheel in front of him. His face lit upon seeing me.

"How are you feeling?" he asked.

"Better, thanks," I said. I padded forward. "Can I sit here?"

"Of course."

I took the copilot's seat. The wagon stood on an ancient slab of concrete. Cracks ran through the surface like a river delta seen from orbit. Plants had sprouted in them. Nature would reclaim it eventually, if the alloys didn't intervene first to speed up the process. One day, Loka and the Out of Bounds would merge into the same entity, but that could take centuries—more than enough time for me and Somya to accomplish what we wanted in the OOB. Crumbling buildings surrounded the wagon, only a few with their walls and orange roof tiles still intact. The architecture had that classically human style—blocky and rectangular—so distinct from the living structures I saw everywhere in Loka, but similar to what I was used to from my childhood in Chedi.

Somya took the chair behind me, and Mezei sat in the one behind Lumo. Brana said she preferred the back. Once she gave the ready knocks, Lumo began to drive. It didn't look much harder than steering Isin's boat, but then I realized he was doing something with his feet—not quite pedaling like we did on the bikes. When I asked, he explained that the foot levers controlled the speed of the wagon.

"Since it's your first time here," he said, "I'll take you by the famous sights."

He turned onto a broad avenue paved with stones. It looked well kept and modern. He flipped a switch, and the wagon lowered and started to roll forward.

"Do the alloys maintain the roads here?" Somya asked.

"No, that's all done by the locals. The alloys only look after historical buildings. They let the OOBers take care of themselves for the most part, but they'll intervene if someone acts destructive or too aggressive."

He frowned and glanced back at Somya. "Even though they don't manage the OOB, they never stop watching, not even in the most remote parts of the Earth. That will make it challenging for you to establish a truly free society. One of the reasons I love this wagon is that it makes me harder to observe from orbit. The alloys would have to dedicate resources to tracking me. As long as I don't give them a reason to do so, I can take a lot of liberties. As with your Anthro Challenge, I prefer to keep myself independent of alloy interference."

A manicured garden appeared on our right. It surrounded a large pond full of all kinds of ducks—I spotted eiders, ring necks, teals, and mallards—and terminated at a multistory building made of whitish stone and topped with a green roof.

"That's Belvedere Palace," Lumo explained. "It houses some famous works of European art, or so I've heard. You have to apply to go inside."

As we continued, I saw a few people walking beside the road. Others sat on balconies, soaking in the autumn sun. The OOBers didn't look any different from other humans I'd seen. I don't know why I expected them to, but even their clothing—tunics of various lengths worn over pants—looked standard. What would it take to live in this part of Earth? It certainly didn't resemble life in Chedi. For one, everyone had to take care of themselves. I hadn't seen any community gardens or farms, but surely they grew food somewhere.

We drove past another palace and a crumbling circular structure with a vertical column in the middle.

"What is that?" Somya asked.

"Used to be a fountain," Lumo said. "A device that circulates water in an artistic way."

He turned left. Many of the buildings had fallen into rubble, but the street terminated at one that stood intact, with arched doorways and windows.

"That's the opera house," Lumo announced, as if we should have heard of it. I only knew about the one in Australia. "The alloys open it up for concerts on the first day of each month."

I had started to get used to the blocky architecture, and while I didn't find it very attractive, I could admire the craft and detail that humans of that era had put into it. From there, we drove past a couple more palaces and planned gardens, their forms as rigid as the rest. Lumo took us down a few other streets, and the number of pedestrians increased. Many headed in the same direction.

"The market," Lumo explained. "In fact, I need to make a quick stop there. I'm always looking for replacement parts for the wagon, and Wien is large enough that I might have some luck."

"It's a great place for antiques, too," Mezei said.

It was the first time I'd heard them speak. They had a low, musical voice. I turned back, gave them a smile, and received a nod in return. Somya insisted that I rest in the wagon while they and the others left to explore. My heartsib took some of the items we'd brought over from Loka, including artwork. I could see the periphery of the market from the wagon—a sprawling array of people and wares that matched the historical images I'd seen. Walking through it would have exhausted me.

Wien was a place outside of time. Unlike some of the other cities we'd seen, I wasn't sure I liked it enough to come back, but I could see why anthropologists like my grandmother would find it interesting. Did she study the OOBers themselves or just the history of the place? Perhaps one day I'd ask her to take me along on one of her research trips.

The bounder crew came back with smiles. Lumo had found something to patch the wagon's solar skin. Brana carried a stack of books. Mezei held a small, exquisitely detailed bird made of painted metal, which I identified as an alpine swift—the white throat and belly gave it away. Somya carried one of our sacks. From inside, they pulled out a small book covered in dark-green fabric that fit in the palm of their hand.

"A gift for you," they said. "I traded some clothing for it!" Their voice held a note of pride.

Inside, I found a series of sketches of insects—beetles, centipedes, butterflies—all drawn in colored pencil. Small, fine handwriting named each one and described where the artist had found it. The pages were yellow and brittle with age, but the images and text were clear. I stood and gave Somya an unsteady hug.

"Most of these are extinct," I said. "It's wonderful!"

Somya grinned. "I figured you'd like it."

"I love it!"

Halfway through the notebook, the drawings stopped. The book had no name, no indication of whether the artist had been a scientist or simply an enthusiast like me.

"What about you?" I asked Somya. "Did you find anything for yourself?"

They shrugged and shook their head. "You know me. I prefer to travel light."

People might call Somya ambitious, but they could never accuse my heartsib of avarice. Somya had arrived on Chedi with almost nothing, and they hadn't accrued much beyond personal necessities since. The solar bike was the one exception, though technically it was part of Chedi and would return to her someday.

After the trading excursion, we left the city. The well-paved cobblestone streets gave way to ribbons of synthetic pavement, warped and cracked over time. Lumo shifted the wagon into walk mode.

"The wheel was once considered the greatest invention of humankind," Lumo said. We rose higher above the ground, and our motion changed to the familiar gait of a hexapod construct. "Turns out that it's only good if you're willing to trample the Earth with roads. Nature had evolved a better solution all along. It just took us a while to figure out how to replicate it."

The buildings grew progressively more weathered until they stood open to sky and wind. Trees grew through the gaps, their branches reaching up and out as if to claim the homes as their own, and the leafy canopies formed a pleasing roofline.

Just past the last of the city structures, I saw a series of square vats. Each must have been five or six meters to a side. Some kind of dark liquid filled them, its surface covered in bubbles. A terrible stench entered the wagon.

"What is that?" Somya said, making a *trying-not-to-vomit* face.

"Slurries," Mezei said.

"A place where waste gets broken down," Lumo added.

"Isn't that called sewage?" I asked.

"Not that kind of waste," Lumo said. "Garbage. Inorganic items that people can no longer use."

"You mean castoffs?" Somya asked. "That's what my family calls them—things that people used and then abandoned because they didn't know how to remake them."

"Exactly," Lumo said. "The slurries were developed around the time of the Directed Mutation Catastrophe to deal with the heaps of human waste. They decompose things in a similar way to alloy digestion. It's a slower, less efficient process, but we can maintain the slurries without alloy assistance, and they're an improvement over burying the items in the ground. They feed into farmland that you'll see farther on."

The DMC had precipitated a lot of changes in how people behaved, including humans' willingness to modify themselves so that they could coexist in equilibrium with their surroundings. The slurries smelled awful, but once upon a time, they had been an innovation to help realize a better world. I could appreciate that. Nevertheless, I was glad when we left them behind and the odor cleared from the wagon.

Around that time, my head began to feel heavy, and my joints started to ache. “I think I need to lie down,” I said.

Lumo glanced at me. “Good idea. You’ve seen all the exciting stuff. Go get some rest.”

I moved to the back of the wagon and stretched out in my bunk. Brana was lost in a book, so I stayed quiet and closed my eyes. Sitting up had used more energy than I would have expected. I fell into a deep sleep as the wagon stepped and swayed its way toward our destination for the night: Munich.

# DAY 32

On the way from Munich to Zurich, the first snowflakes fell. The bounders didn't think it was wise for me to stay out in the cold, and after catching a few of the icy crystals on my tongue, I agreed with them and admired the view through the window. We stopped for the night a little east of Zurich, in the foothills of the Alps. The peaks were shrouded in gray clouds, so I never got a good look at them.

A few hours after we fell asleep, the moan of the wind and the shuddering of the wagon woke us all up. The darkness outside was absolute, but I could see snow and ice crusted around the window from the gentle interior lights. Lumo and Mezei, who slept in the front cabin, came into the back with *this-is-serious* expressions.

"It's coming down fast out there," Lumo said. "If we stay here, we might get snowed in."

"Meaning what?" Somya asked.

"We could get stuck here for days. If we're lucky, the storm will end quickly, and we can walk the wagon out. If it continues long enough, we'll be buried too deep to move, and we'll have to call for help. Depending on how bad the conditions are, it could take a rescue team weeks to dig their way here from Zurich."

Somya and I exchanged a worried glance. Not only would that set us back on our schedule, but I doubted that we had enough food and water in the wagon to last five of us that long.

"If it turns into a life-threatening emergency," Brana said as if reading my mind, "we can call to orbit to send assistance."

"No," Lumo said with a hard edge to his voice. "We will not bring alloy attention to this wagon. I don't want them anywhere near me."

I could empathize with his sentiments.

"I can walk us out," Mezei said in their quiet voice. "I've navigated conditions like this when I was at home."

Lumo shook his head. "This is my wagon, and no one drives it but me."

The declaration of ownership startled me. Did Lumo have Possessiveness Disorder? Had that led to his expulsion from Loka?

"You won't know what you're doing," Mezei said. "If you don't control the speed of the legs on an icy surface, they'll slip and break."

"Then you can sit beside me and guide me," Lumo said.

"I need to go by feel." Mezei's tone rose. "I can't do that just by watching you drive. You're being unreasonable, and your PD is going to get us in trouble."

Mezei's words confirmed my suspicions.

"And your Empathy Deficiency is making you act like an ass," Lumo shot back.

I found myself inching closer to Somya as the two argued. Something in Lumo and Mezei's body language made me afraid—of what, I wasn't exactly sure, but my instincts told me to escape from it.

Brana stood up and placed herself between the other two bounders. She held out a hand to each of them, palms outward. "Stop this! Insulting each other isn't going to help our situation. You both need to calm down and think about what's best for all of us." Her tone was firm but not harsh. "If we end up stuck here for weeks, Akshaya and Somya will fail their Anthro Challenge. You both need to recognize that and rise above your problems."

After a few seconds of silence, Lumo let out an audible exhale. He held up his hands in a placating gesture. "Okay, I'm sorry. The wagon *is* mine, but I will allow Mezei to drive it because of the unusual circumstances."

Brana turned and gave Mezei an *it's-your-turn-to-make-peace* look.

"I apologize for raising my voice," Mezei said, back to their usual placid self. "Thank you, Lumo, for allowing me to guide your wagon out of this storm."

I relaxed as the tension in the room dissipated. Brana smiled and offered to make some hot tea, which we gratefully accepted. Lumo and Mezei moved to the front cabin.

"Let's watch," Somya said to me, their eyes alight with excitement.

The prospect of navigating through a dark, snowy wilderness filled me with trepidation, but I followed my friend through the doorway and took the second passenger seat beside them.

Mezei placed a couple of drops in each eye, sprayed their hands, and slow-blinked. They glanced back at me and Somya. "Don't worry. I'm only using the interface to control the wagon. I won't connect to the public network." They made a gesture that lowered a lighting boom in front of the vehicle, illuminating the snow with a lime-green glow.

The freshly fallen crystals sparkled as powdery flakes swirled in the air. How could something so beautiful be so treacherous? The wagon shuddered in a gust of wind. Mezei raised it up on its legs and worked the pedals and steering wheel. I wanted to ask how they'd learned to operate a wagon, but I didn't dare break their concentration.

Our forward progress seemed impossibly slow, especially with few landmarks visible around us. Every so often, the wagon would lurch to one side as a leg sank deeper into the snow than the others. It took me a while to realize that I had clenched my jaw and gripped the seat beneath me, and I forced myself to let go. When I looked at Somya, they grinned back at me from a relaxed sprawl. I shook my head slowly in disbelief. The arc of Lumo's spine indicated a mental state more similar to mine. Every so often, the bounder's hands would twitch as if he wanted to wrest the controls from Mezei. Brana knelt in the space between the seats, her gaze alternating between the two. I couldn't see her full expression, but I imagined she was trying to keep the peace while also maintaining her physical balance.

The snowstorm blew relentlessly for the first hour of the midnight journey. None of the others seemed the least bit sleepy, but I could sense exhaustion creeping up on my body. It mingled with heartbreak for every bush and sapling that we trampled. With the visibility so low, I couldn't fault Mezei's driving, but at the same time, I felt guilty that we were causing harm to life on Earth. Somya winced as much as I did at the damage. The bounders didn't react as strongly, and I wondered if they'd grown numb to such actions by living in the Out of Bounds.

When the density of the falling snowflakes thinned and the gusts of wind abated, I decided to lie down. I wasn't helping anyone, and I had a sense that Mezei had taken us through the worst of the danger. We could see farther ahead, and we'd picked up some speed. Lumo wanted the wagon well away from the storm, so he and Mezei were going to take shifts until we reached clear skies. Brana took my seat with a grateful smile as I exited the cabin. I had a brief pang at leaving the snow behind before I could appreciate it in daylight, but the feeling was overwhelmed by relief that we wouldn't get trapped.

# DAY 35

Over the next two days, we rode along the northern edge of the Alps. The storm front passed behind us, continuing north while we headed west. We passed through the remnants of a few more major cities—Zurich, Bern, Geneva, Lyon. After a while, I got tired of the blocky palaces and opera houses with their ornately carved facades. Geneva had a beautiful espalierum, one of the first of its kind, a multifamily dwelling built in 433 HE entirely from engineered vines and trees trained to grow into livable structures. After the environmental disasters on Earth and Mars, human ingenuity had turned toward bending nature to its will, but espalieri required too much care and had eventually fallen out of favor. A society of OOBers tended this one, though not perfectly, and its form blended naturally with the contours of the hill it grew on.

We saw three massive lakes, Constance, Vierwald, and Léman, and many rivers. A lot of the old bridges had washed out during the last warming age, but the bounders had driven through these places often and knew how to get around. They had friends in almost every town and stopped frequently to deliver goods from Loka, usually taking nothing in return other than fresh food. Most excitingly, we saw the eastern Alps, and they were covered in snow! Under clear, brilliant-blue skies, Lumo took us into the foothills of the famed mountain range. The bounders lent me and Somya their snow clothes—warm jackets, waterproof gloves and boots, knit hats. Even with all that, I started shivering after a few minutes, but I pelted Somya with a snowball and waded into a drift as deep as my waist.

My health gradually improved. I traded the fever for a cough that left my stomach aching. The irregular numbers from my bodym crept back to the ranges where they belonged. I couldn't imagine how Somya and I would have navigated the journey on our own. Even if we'd abandoned my bike and had me ride on the trailer, the cold air would have made me miserable, never mind that our maps didn't reflect the true conditions in the Out of Bounds. They had neat little lines marking the major roadways, but with the state of the surface in many places, we wouldn't have been able to ride on those routes, and unlike Loka, where animals and alloys had established trails, the Out of Bounds wilderness was largely uninhabited. Birds and small rodents had taken residence in the towns. Every other creature had either gone extinct or had yet to be repopulated by the alloys.

We crossed back into Loka on our sixth day with the bounders, at Narmont, a small town on the Mediterranean Sea. Lumo estimated that we'd reach Nuberia in another five days. With the improved road conditions, the walker-wagon kept a brisk pace, and we passed several inhabited towns. The bounders had developed travel habits similar to ours. They didn't try to hide their vehicle, but they always parked it away from buildings and approached on foot to get food or clothing. The alloys knew about and tolerated their activities as long as they didn't show too many symptoms of avarice or possessiveness, and like Rune, the bounders had discovered which locales didn't mind their unusual ways.

Late in the day, we took a detour from the main road to visit a natural hot spring a bit north of Laietan, the largest city in the region. It had some famous buildings, including a stone church built in an organic style that Lumo thought I would appreciate. We intended to spend the night there after taking a dip in the healthful mineral baths.

"The water is a little stinky," Brana warned me. "It's because of the sulfur, but that's also what makes it good for you, especially for your skin."

Lumo switched the wagon to walking mode as we climbed some low hills. He parked in the middle of an open area with low-growing shrubs and rocky soil. The sun was sinking in the west, but the day had been unseasonably warm, and we all stripped down to our underwear outside. A low wall of stacked rocks marked the boundary of a small pool. Brana's promised odor emanated from it, but it wasn't as bad as I'd imagined and was a far cry from the stench of the slurries outside Wien.

"Let me check the temperature," Mezei said. They sat on the side and swung their legs into the basin. "Could be hotter." They opened a tap, and steaming water poured from it. "Come in. It's not cold. There's a bench below the surface that you can sit on."

Mezei sank down to demonstrate, submerging up to their shoulders. Brana gave me an encouraging smile. Lumo and Somya stepped over the wall and into the pool. I followed them, but my foot slipped as it made contact with the bench. My tailbone landed on the rim, and I cried out. Lumo grabbed my elbow to steady me, and his eyes went wide. The phores on my arm glowed brilliant white, an instinctive reaction to the pain. I got them back under control, but it was too late. Four faces stared at me, three of them shocked and one worried.

Lumo dropped my elbow like it had burned him. "You have chromatophores. Who . . . *what* are you?"

Mezei inched away from me. "I thought humanlike incarns weren't legal," they said. "Have the laws changed? It's not like we pay a lot of attention to them."

"Is that what you are?" Brana said, her eyes narrowed with suspicion. "Are you some new form of alloy surveillance?"

"I'm human, I swear on the Nivid," I said. My heart pounded. "Ask Somya."

Brana grabbed Somya's wrist and pulled their arm out of the water. She examined their skin.

"I don't have phores," Somya said, their tone casual with an expression to match. "Aks is also human, but she's got some special genes."

Brana looked disgusted. "By *special*, you mean *alloy* genes. You should have told us when we picked you up."

"Why does it matter?" Somya said.

"Because," Brana said, "you pretended that you don't like alloys. You lied to us."

Lumo surged out of the pool and strode to the walker-wagon.

Why did everyone think that doing the Anthro Challenge meant that we hated the alloys? I had no love for them after what they had done to my maker, but I was too taken aback by the bounders' hostility to defend myself. On one hand, the bounders clearly had their own biases, but on the other, they shared our love of adventure and had never criticized our ambitions. To have them reject me on the basis of my phores hurt as much as my bruised spine.

"We didn't lie," Somya said. "You made an assumption."

Lumo returned and loomed at the edge of the pool. "I looked her up. She's that kid they designed to live on Meru. One of her parents is an alloy." He turned to me. "Get out, both of you. Put on your clothes and pack your things. Whatever your true purpose here is, we're not going to be part of it any longer. Mez, help me get their gear off the roof."

"She's not half-alloy," Somya insisted. "She was made by a human, and her DNA is human, too. Maybe you should look that up before you jump to conclusions."

*Mostly* human would be more accurate, but my mother had sworn me never to disclose my hybrid nature, and I wasn't about to use the word in front of people who no longer considered themselves my friends. How could I have been so mindless about my clothing? I'd grown too comfortable in the wagon, and I'd let down my guard. I wouldn't make that mistake again.

I clambered out of the hot pool. "Come on, Som. Let's go."

For a few seconds, my heartsib looked at me as if I had betrayed them, and I had to swallow hard to avoid tears. The situation was entirely my fault.

Mezei gave us a half-apologetic shrug and followed Lumo. Somya and I dried off as we trailed after them.

"Why aren't you defending yourself?" Somya demanded in a quiet voice. "We need to convince Lumo that we're friends. He's our best guide to settling somewhere in the OOB."

My mistake had not only affected our present but also our future—especially Somya's. Creating a new way of life in the OOB was their long-held dream, and I'd sabotaged their newfound hope.

"What am I supposed to say that's going to convince them?" I asked, wishing I could rewind time. "I *do* have DNA that doesn't naturally occur in humans."

"That doesn't make you part alloy. Their suspicions are totally wrong."

"I know that, but what can I do about it?"

We stared at each other in helpless frustration. Somya heaved a sigh and stepped into the wagon. I followed. We dressed and grabbed our personal items, and by the time we emerged, Lumo and Mezei had our bikes, trailer, and other gear in a heap on the ground. Brana walked past us, dripping wet, and I almost spoke up to thank her, but the sentiment stuck in my chest like a stubborn bite of food. These people had helped us—helped me—so much, to get over my illness, to drive us more than halfway to Nuberia. How could they turn their backs on us so quickly? If the bounders could reject us so thoroughly, how would the true OOBers feel if I tried to settle among them?

Somya and I stared at the receding walker-wagon. I felt a lot healthier than when the bounders picked us up, but I wasn't sure if I had regained enough strength to bike three hundred kilometers a day. It would take us almost a week at that speed to reach Nuberia. What if my illness got worse again? What if we couldn't find our way? We were back in Loka, but Lumo hadn't given us a specific indication of where we were.

Somya turned to me and said blandly, "Well, those three clearly need some empathy therapy."

The unexpected joke startled a laugh out of me. Somya shot me a mischievous grin and started assembling the bikes and trailer. I worked alongside them, our habits ingrained from weeks on the road, my thoughts temporarily distracted. I should have kept better control over my phores. I should have *remembered* to stay conscious of them, especially when we stripped off our outerwear. I'd grown complacent. Comfortable. *Trusting.* I could hear my mother's words in my head, scolding me as she'd often done when I was younger, reminding me to be careful. *People won't understand. One day, the world will know, I promise, but not until we get settled on Meru.*

The thought reminded me of Nara. *By the Nivid!* I looked upward and froze. Somya noticed and tracked my gaze. The characteristic glint of an indriya sparkled high in the sky. The warm weight of my friend's hand pressed on my shoulder.

"It's all recorded, Som." I'd ruined everything for my mother, exposed her secret—my secret—to the world.

"Don't panic," Somya said.

"Too late."

"Our parents are going to review all of it, remember? Because we're not adults. They can demand that Nara edit this part out."

"If he did that, there would be no explanation for why the bounders abandoned us like this. Besides, Nara will know. Reshyan, too." I felt like the air was being squeezed out of my lungs.

Somya cupped my face in their hands. "Hey, look at me. None of this is your fault. Let your mother handle it. Right now, we need to focus on getting to Laietan before full dark and getting some food. Okay?"

I nodded, but my thoughts still spun like air currents in a storm. My body worked on its own, loading our gear on the trailer, getting everything secure. Somya kept up a stream of chatter, narrating their actions, talking about what we might cook that night, guessing what we might find in Nuberia. I couldn't focus on the words, but the sound of their voice kept me grounded enough to keep moving.

We rode in a direction opposite to the sunset. East would get us to the coast, and whether we found Laietan or some other place, once we had a city name, we could orient ourselves with our map book.

Along the way, I worried about having given away my secret. Back at the Euphrates, I'd remembered to check for indriyas. I should have thought of it at the mineral springs, too. I should have kept my clothes on. I should never have agreed to let Nara record our journey. Somya was wrong—our situation was entirely my fault.

I had to hope that my heartsib was right that Nara would give my mother a chance to hide what she'd done to me. If not, I wasn't sure what would happen. Would the alloys let me stay on Earth? Send me back to Chedi? Forced relocation to Meru? Whatever the outcome, it would likely mean the end of the challenge. My carelessness had placed our entire journey in jeopardy. But it was also deeply unfair that I had to keep part of myself hidden. If only my mother had disclosed the truth before I was born. Why couldn't everyone accept me for who I was?

# NARA (DAY 37)

Nara blinked away the mental afterimage of space that lingered from his hour of embodied activity—all those tedious mandatory exercises while staring into the void, the sun burning one side of him, impossible cold on the other. He would never understand people who preferred physicality to life in stasis.

The details of his mindspace home gradually filled his senses. Graceful curves of glass and flowering bushes surrounded him. The blaze of sunlight in a clear blue sky scratched some deep atavistic need that vast amounts of genetic tinkering hadn't erased. Nara's custom-designed skin draped him in the palest of pinks. Intricate patterns woven in white-gold threaded their way over his sleeves and up his neck to the crown of his head, where they fell in hairlike waves. He needed one last thing: music. He scrolled through his usual favorites for creative work and landed on a recent mix from the starsong genre.

With a thought-command, he recalled the last state of Project Anthro, the working title he had chosen for his documentary. Bubbles filled the space around him, each one showing a brief loop from the recorded snippet it represented. He had reviewed the raw footage as it came in from Reshyan, throwing out all the repetitive or boring bits. The blocked bridge at thc Euphrates was the obvious ending for the first episode, but he still had to find a narrative arc and a theme that could last through the entirety of Akshaya and Somya's journey and tie back to their parents, whose story had to be told. He also needed dialogue to go with the images and provide color cues to alloy viewers who didn't—or couldn't—appreciate music.

The project's assistant director had proposed that they focus on cultural conflict, with Akshaya and her mother as examples of people who mixed alloy and human ways. Nara had considered it seriously, especially after seeing Akshaya's skin light up in a distinctly alloy-like manner at the mineral pools. It seemed that she had more of her maker in her than most people knew, a little gem to reveal, perhaps in the second episode. First, he needed to get an honest reaction from Jayanthi, who had designed Akshaya's DNA, and second, he had to consider whether the revelation might affect the way people reacted to the two subjects later in their travels. He couldn't allow the show to inadvertently violate the parameters of their challenge.

The genetics couldn't carry the whole documentary, though. The cross-cultural aspects of the story would make a good secondary theme, but they didn't fit with the Anthro Challenge. He pulled forward the bubble with Akshaya's interview. The child obviously took issue with alloy management of human life. How could he make that personal? He reviewed the snippet.

"Because of my parents' exile," she said, "I never had the chance to experience Earth. I want to see it—feel it—the way humans did long before alloys were around to help."

"Is that so you'll feel prepared to take care of yourself on Meru?" Nara had asked. "Do you see a future where humans manage that planet on their own?"

Akshaya shrugged. "I'm more interested in Earth than in Meru right now." She hesitated, clearly wanting to say something more. What had she held back?

Nara tried to put himself in her situation. Akshaya identified as human. She had primarily interacted with her maker's incarn, who took on a very humanlike form. She felt that she had grown up in exile from her true home, the only planet that humanity belonged to. She wanted to prove that she didn't need help from modern civilization—no, from *alloy* civilization—to have a fulfilling life. Like her mother, she was determined to follow her own rules, but she preferred to do so on Earth. Why the resistance to Meru?

With a satisfying pop, the answer jumped into Nara's mind: Akshaya wanted to have control over her own life. Like many adolescents, she longed to rid herself of the demands of adults, and the Constructed Democracy of Sol loomed large in her thoughts as another form of authority. Going to Meru, fulfilling the ambitions of her mother—in her mind, these would conflate with the strictures that alloys had placed not only on Earth but on her maker. The Meru Exploration Committee chair had accused Jayanthi of having excessive ambition. Clearly her child had even more, at least by human standards.

Nara began to sort the bubbles. The start of Akshaya's story was not at the moment of her birth but at the trial of her parents. Vaha's exile, Jayanthi's choice to follow and to raise her child in a spacefaring megaconstruct rather than on Earth.

He would start the episode with the archival recordings of the sentencing. Cut to an external view of Chedi flying away. Cut again to Akshaya and Somya leaving for the Anthro Challenge. Next, flash back to the moment of the infant's birth. Pull in snippets of her growing up, but intersperse them with footage of human children on Earth. He had to show the contrast, the factors that shaped Akshaya, that funneled her to the point of rejecting half of her heritage. If it weren't for the circumstances of her early life, she wouldn't have needed to do the Anthro Challenge. *Because of my parents' exile, I never had the chance to experience Earth.* He let her words form the narration for the montage. At last, he had the shape of the story. Whether Akshaya succeeded or failed at the challenge, she would fulfill her true ambition, the one created by the actions of the CDS judiciary and her parents.

A new thought formed, this one growing slowly, like a cloud in atmosphere: Reshyan had demanded that Nara's next documentary portray the negative consequences of exile. Perhaps Nara didn't need to wait that long. Perhaps he could accomplish two goals with this series. Akshaya and her family's banishment was very different from standard alloy practice, but it had accomplished the same objective: it had removed them from their society for a period of time and reshaped their thinking, and in the process, it had exacerbated Akshaya's penchant for ambition, to the point that she risked her very life. With that, Nara knew he had the perfect title for the series: *In Exile*.

# JAYANTHI (DAY 38)

Jayanthi pressed her hands against her mouth. She knew from Reshyan that Akshaya and Somya would survive the swim across the Euphrates, but watching the turbid water carry each of them away evoked a visceral fear that she couldn't repress. Nara was recording her reactions, both visually and through her bodym, so that he could have a full picture to present to his audience. She hated the exposure. Other than those brief moments at the Primary Nivid seventeen years earlier, she'd stayed clear of public attention. She didn't have enough practice at controlling her reactions. Then again, that was exactly what Nara wanted.

A new video clip appeared in Jayanthi's field of view. It showed Akshaya crawling out of the river, then Somya, much farther to the north. Somya's figure began to walk south. The ambient light dimmed and then darkened to the point that Jayanthi could see nothing but vague shadows from the elevated perspective of the indriyas. She guessed that more information was visible to alloys, who could see into infrared and ultraviolet bands of light. Dramatic music built in the background, along with an edge-glow of green and brown, the phoric hues of worry and fear. Jayanthi tensed in response to both cues. The music reached a crescendo, then faded along with the image, replaced by Nara's expectant face.

<What do you think?> he asked, his phores flashing.

Jayanthi remembered a time when she would've needed to use emtalk or a translation to understand phoric, but she had practiced diligently with Vaha and grown fluent over time. It seemed only fair, considering that her life mate had given up zir people to live with her and Akshaya.

"I'm still processing it," Jayanthi said, "but I couldn't see anything toward the end. What happened next?"

Nara's phores gleamed with mauve smugness. <That will come in Episode Two, but you already know from Reshyan that the children find each other and continue on. Unfortunately, the indriyas couldn't capture their reunion through the precipitation—too much interference.>

Jayanthi nodded. Knowing and seeing were different experiences, and she couldn't help craving the proof that Akshaya was not only alive but also well. Reshyan had told her about the detour into the Out of Bounds, the ride in some strangers' vehicle, then the kids being on their own again. She had asked after their health, and only then had zie mentioned that they had gone to some kind of hospital. After they separated from the wagon group, they had ridden off on their bikes, and Reshyan had assured her that they looked fine. Zie had no idea what had sent them to the medical facility, and neither did Nara.

<I haven't started to assemble the second episode, but in the meantime, I'd like to show you something more recent—something I found quite interesting.>

A daylight scene appeared in Jayanthi's visual: Akshaya, Somya, and three strangers stood outside in the wilderness somewhere. Behind them, a strange-looking object rested on six articulated legs. Four wheels were tucked in between the limbs. Jayanthi guessed that these were the strangers and the vehicle that Reshyan had mentioned. As the scene played out, the five humans stripped down to their underwear—including Akshaya. Jayanthi's stomach clenched. *What is she doing, baring her skin to these people?* The group stepped one at a time into a large stone pit full of water. When it was Akshaya's turn, she slipped and fell. Her chromatophores blazed with pain for a fraction of a second, but everyone noticed.

The knot in Jayanthi's belly turned to ice. "Pause playback," she snapped.

The recording froze, and Nara's face appeared in its place. Jayanthi closed her eyes and breathed. She had granted Nara permission to record her as she previewed the show. She could prevent him from making footage of Akshaya public, but he could do whatever he wanted with her reactions.

She exhaled and forced her muscles to relax. *Think of calm. Be unfazed.* She would find a way out of his trap. She had to, for her child's sake.

"You can't use those last few minutes," she said.

<Why not?> His phores flickered with the faintest hint of amusement.

*Careful.* "I think that would be obvious to any decent person."

Nara smiled, lips together in the alloy style. <Very well. That's your prerogative.> His demeanor changed. <I had a feeling that's what you'd say. Let's talk off the record. Obviously you've tinkered with more of Akshaya's genes than the ones that affect sickle-cell disease. How have you kept her ability a secret for so long? Did you plan to hide it for her entire life, because if so, what was the point?>

Jayanthi didn't have to answer any of Nara's questions. He might claim that this conversation was off the record, but he wasn't a news construct, so he had no restrictions on his behavior when it came to reporting, and being an alloy, he could save everything she said to extended memory and recall it when he needed it.

But he was right. She hadn't intended to keep Akshaya's chromatophores hidden forever. Over the sixteen years of their child's life, she and Vaha had often discussed what to do. They'd dressed Akshaya in long, opaque sleeves when she was too young to control her reactions. Their closest friends in Chedi knew—Sunanda, who'd helped with Akshaya's birth, as well as Guhaka, Huy's parents, and of course, Chedi herself. The first time that Akshaya revealed herself to Somya, she had been ten years old.

"You should know better," Jayanthi had scolded her.

Her child's scornful expression had burned itself into her memory. "I know who I can trust," she had said, and she'd proven herself right, then and on many other occasions.

Had Akshaya chosen that moment with her companions to expose her phores to the world, or had it happened by accident? *By the Nivid, I wish I could talk to her!* Humans had developed globe-spanning communications in the fourth century Human Era, but those systems had been replaced many times over, and every present-day method relied on alloy manufacturing and upkeep. Jayanthi had no way to reach Akshaya without violating the rules of the Anthro Challenge. Was this another opportunity for Jayanthi to trust her child's decisions?

Equally frustrating, she couldn't talk to Vaha. Zie was still too far away for a real-time conversation, which was why Nara didn't have Vaha participate in live reactions to the documentary. Vaha would have a chance to respond asynchronously. Had Nara sent the preview of the episode to zir as well? Should she ask him about it?

Jayanthi had long held on to a vision of revealing Akshaya's phores on Meru. She had pictured the three of them—Akshaya, Vaha, and herself—standing by the lake near their home, the amethyst sky darkening at twilight, holding hands and allowing the phores on Vaha's and Akshaya's arms to light up. She wanted the world to see it as a positive moment, a celebration of the introduction of alloy DNA into a human. Her mentor, Hamsa, had once told her to never do such a thing. The alloys had outlawed the practice after so-called hybrid humans had paved the way for genetic stagnation and the Directed Mutation Catastrophe. Jayanthi blamed the social practices of the times more than the science. Both had radically changed since then, and she was ready to defend her choice to add chromatophores to her child's genome, but if Akshaya succeeded at the Anthro Challenge, then Jayanthi's imagined moment on Meru might never happen.

Nara waited for her with studied patience. What had Jayanthi's expression given away to him while she was lost in thought? She arrived at a decision and met his gaze.

"I'm speaking on the record," Jayanthi said. "Akshaya has an inclusion of nonhuman genes in her DNA. Like a gemstone, it makes her more interesting and beautiful. I chose to give her chromatophores because I wanted her to have a biological connection to Vaha and her alloy heritage." Jayanthi took a long, shaky breath. She had rehearsed the words so many times, in so many different ways, and now they would go out into the world and take on a life of their own. "I retract my earlier statement. If Vaha has no objections, you can use the recording of Akshaya's ability."

<And you did all this seventeen years ago, when you were still on Meru and before you and Vaha had entered into a committed relationship?>

"I was already in love with zir."

<That's quite a gamble. You're lucky that the relationship worked out. You trained with Hamsa to learn tarawan skills, correct?>

"Yes."

<Several years after your exile began, the law changed to allow humans to become tarawans. There are now four humans on Earth who have earned their licenses. Will you become the fifth?>

"I—I don't expect so. I had assumed I'd be busy with other concerns on Meru, but I suppose that if Akshaya succeeds in the Anthro Challenge and we stay on Earth, then I might consider it. I'm not sure if the Tarawan Ethics and Standards Council would approve me for a license, though, given my history."

Nara's phores flickered with amusement, and Jayanthi responded with a tight smile.

<Perhaps Akshaya will sway them in your favor,> he flashed. <I'm not sure which episode will include that demonstration of Akshaya's chromatophores. Not everything will go in chronological order. I have some concerns about the reception of the news, especially if Akshaya and Somya are still traveling, so I might hold on to it for a while, until the right moment reveals itself.> Nara paused. His phores took on a hue of concern. <I have one last snippet to show you. This one is from yesterday, very raw, but I thought you might want to see it.>

The clip began. Seen from above, a dark speck moved along a grassy field, expanding until it resolved into a figure on a bike towing a trailer. Closer still, and Jayanthi could see that Somya was the rider. The second bike lay on top of the trailer, held in place partly by Akshaya's prone body. Had the equipment broken? The visual closed in more. Somya's expression held an unusual amount of tension, and Akshaya . . . Akshaya's cheeks were wet with tears, and her spine curled in a comma of unmistakable pain.

Jayanthi's stomach twisted. She knew exactly what that implied because she had experienced the same thing many times.

"How much farther to Nuberia?" she asked Nara.

<Another thousand kilometers, roughly,> he flashed. <Akshaya became ill a few days after the river crossing. She seemed improved just a couple of days ago, when they got dropped off by the walker-wagon—>

"The what?"

<The vehicle that you saw earlier. The humans who use it decided to abandon Somya and Akshaya after seeing her chromatophores.> Nara added more information about the hospital visit and explained that the OOBers had helped Akshaya get there. <They got back on their bikes after the others left,> Nara concluded. <I suspect that the exertion caused a relapse.>

"No—well, maybe, but she's clearly having a pain crisis due to her sickle-cell disorder. It was probably brought on by the illness or the ride or both. Regardless, she needs medical treatment or it will get worse."

<Do you want us to intervene?>

*Yes,* screamed every nerve in Jayanthi's body. "Not yet," she said aloud. "I'll keep a closer watch on their situation through Reshyan, if you'll allow zir to share the daily recordings with me."

Nara nodded.

"As long as Akshaya rests and stays warm and hydrated, she has a chance to recover," Jayanthi said, forcing herself to believe it. "A thousand kilometers means another three or four days, depending on the pace that Somya can maintain. Akshaya can get treatment in Nuberia, if she needs it."

<She might not take it,> Nara countered, <considering that they're in Loka and any medical care would involve alloy methods.>

He was right. Jayanthi could only hope that Akshaya's crisis would pass without further complications, both for her child's sake and so that she didn't have to crush Akshaya's dream. Jayanthi's own body responded with echoes of remembered pain. She wished she had wings so she could swoop down, take her child in her arms, and give her the palliative that would bring her relief. Instead, all she could do was watch and worry.

# DAY 41

The world blurred through tears of pain. Nearly a week had passed since the bounders left us at the hot springs. My fever had lifted, replaced by an entirely different kind of burning, one that ran through my blood with a thousand little thorns and pierced everything in its path. The sensation started subtly. For the first two days, I thought that being back on the bike had caused the throb in my muscles, but the ache grew and sharpened, transformed from a mallet to a cluster of needles, until I could no longer hide it from Somya. They insisted that I ride atop the trailer and rest my body. Luckily the weather held in our favor, with plenty of sunshine. The bike had power, and our pace didn't slow down much.

We arrived in Nuberia in the late afternoon, a little over a week behind our original schedule. Somya left me on an isolated bluff while they went to look for Rune. I briefly saw the turquoise hues of the ocean just beyond a stretch of sand, but the glare of the western sun forced me to close my eyes. By then, I knew what was happening. I had watched my mother go through it several times, first when I was five. She hadn't wanted me to see her in distress, so my maker tried to leave me with Sunanda for the night. That had scared me even more, and eventually they let me back into the high-oxygen room to sleep with my parents. I hadn't truly understood then—or later—how terrible she felt.

My bodym confirmed my suspicions, raising every alarm for a sickle-cell crisis. The pain distorted time. My entire existence narrowed to one sensation, and I desperately craved relief. I had to force myself to eat and drink, to stay alive and conscious of the world even as part of me begged to let go.

*We need to reach Nuberia. We'll find Rune. He'll know what to do.* Somya repeated those words like a vow every night. They held me, warmed me, coaxed me into accepting their care. They even tried to make me laugh. At times in our friendship, Somya's relentless positivity had annoyed me, but in the middle of my first pain crisis, I clung to it. Only when they were fast asleep did I allow myself to break down, to allow fear to wash over me—that I wouldn't finish the challenge, that I was doing irreversible damage to my body, that I had made a terrible mistake in taking on the AC. More than once, I considered activating my network connection and calling my mother. For Somya's sake more than mine, I forced myself to wait until Nuberia. I refused to consider what would happen if we had a repeat of Alanya and didn't find Rune there.

The sun's rays warmed me, and a cool breeze blew in from the water. I opened my eyes and saw a bank of clouds lining the horizon and hiding the last of the light. I still hadn't gotten used to the length of day changing. We didn't have seasons on Chedi. I extracted my bedroll and wrapped it around me, letting my eyes fall shut again.

Just as I started to wonder what had happened with Somya, I felt their hand touch my shoulder.

"Aks, you awake?" they asked softly.

I nodded and opened my eyes. Behind Somya's familiar face loomed another, creased by sun and wind and surrounded by hair the color of the sea.

"Rune!" The shock of recognition sent a jolt of adrenaline through me. I sat up. "You're here."

The old sailor nodded, his brow furrowed with concern. "Somya told me about your condition, but I have to say, you look worse in person. It's a ways up the beach to my boat. I think you're better off camping here tonight. Let's get you set up, and then we'll talk."

I tried my best not to curl back up into a ball while Somya and Rune pitched the tent and unpacked some basics. After getting the bedrolls in place, Rune had me lie down and sent Somya back to the boat to get food from his crewmate, Halli.

"I wanted to talk to you privately," Rune said. "I can guess how much the Anthro Challenge means to you, but, Akshaya, you need rest, and you need real medical attention. According to Somya, you've been feeling like this for several days already."

"I can rest on the boat."

"The open ocean is no place for someone in your condition. What if you get worse? I won't take you aboard like this."

I shook my head. "Not giving up."

"Don't think of it that way." He ran his fingers through his beard. "You're both young. You can try again in a few months, or even a year or two."

"No." I didn't have the energy to explain the deal I had made with my parents. If I didn't finish the challenge, I wouldn't be back for a long time. My life would belong to Meru. "I need oxygen. Fluids. Blood. Ask Som. Seen my mother . . . handle this."

With the right treatment, my body would heal. We needed a portable solution, one that would let me continue the therapy while we sailed.

"All right," Rune said. "I'll wait until Somya returns and ask them, but if alloy assistance is the only way to treat your condition, then that's what you have to do. The AC isn't worth ruining your life."

*It'll be ruined either way.*

By the time Somya returned, the sky had darkened enough that we needed lanterns to see our food. Dinner was a hearty stew with potatoes, onion, white beans, and various herbs. I had to force every bite, but my stomach welcomed the warmth as the food settled.

I listened as Somya explained to Rune about the room in Chedi with the high-oxygen air. They told him that my body needed extra hydration and possibly a blood exchange. The latter required a special machine and time to culture clean blood that matched mine—weeks of delay that we couldn't afford.

"I can't help with the blood exchange or the oxygen room," Rune said, "but I can provide hydration. I have a medical sleeve with a reservoir that I can fill with saline and electrolytes. It's useful when I'm ill and far from shore. Do you think that alone will be enough?"

"I don't know," Somya said. "I guess we'll have to try it and find out. I didn't pay attention when her mother went through her pain crises."

It always took my mother a few days to recover from the worst of it, and then another few weeks to feel fully herself again. I couldn't do the math through the fog of pain, but a few days of delay didn't sound too bad. My mother had access to the full spectrum of treatment, though. I didn't know any more than Somya whether an infusion alone would relieve my symptoms.

An hour later, Rune returned. He hooked up the sleeve to its reservoir and slipped it over my bare forearm. The device tightened itself around me like a firm hug. He interfaced with its screen for a minute.

"I've set it to provide hydration as well as pain relief," he said.

The sleeve had an old electronic display. It emitted a harsh, bright light that could only come from a Human Era design. As soon as Rune finished setting it up, I unclenched my hands and draped my blanket over it. The blanket didn't entirely block the glare, but it helped to dim it.

Rune's brow furrowed. "I'll come check on you in the morning, but let's not set our expectations just yet. Take heart, Akshaya. Whether this year or another, I'm sure you'll complete the Anthro Challenge."

"Thank you," I whispered.

Rune nodded, collected the dinner dishes, and left us.

"This has to work," I said, my voice cracking.

"Sh, don't talk," Somya said. "Just rest. The sooner you're well, the sooner we can leave. I can't wait for you to see Rune's boat. The *Svapna* is amazing! So much bigger than Isin's. It has two masts and three sails, and you can stand fully upright in the cabin. It has a double bed in the bow, like the *Zephyros*, plus two extra bunks that fold down from either side of the hull, kind of like the berths in the walker-wagon. I met Halli briefly. Not that they're part of the boat." Somya laughed. "Though they almost could be. Halli doesn't talk much. Oh, and I almost forgot Paasha! She's the ship's cat. Apparently she adopted the *Svapna* as her home during one of Rune's stops and hasn't left. She's very friendly."

My eyes closed, but I listened to Somya's every word and tried to picture life on the boat. *A friendly cat!* I'd seen a few around the towns we visited, but they had always kept their distance. *Please, please let the hydration help me,* I begged the universe. I couldn't think of anything else to do. It was November 29. We had managed to arrive one day before the departure of the regatta. Between the weather delays and having to go over land, we had already lost half of our two-and-a-half-week margin. I had a week to get well enough to sail or we wouldn't return in time for Chedi's last shuttle—assuming that the rest of our journey went according to plan. Given everything that had already happened, that seemed highly unlikely. I recalled Freni's comment about Ratnam and wondered if I was being selfish. But if I quit, I would let Somya down. Completing the Anthro Challenge was their dream, too, and it wouldn't be fair to ask them to go on alone. The two thoughts circled each other like binary stars, neither one the obvious right choice.

# DAY 42

The next morning, I tried reducing the pain relief dispensed by the sleeve. I had woken with a dull ache throughout my body rather than the fire of a million needles. I had a brief hope that I had improved, but a couple of hours later, the hope fled in the face of reality. The burning sensation returned with full force, and I had to adjust the sleeve back to the previous night's setting.

Somya kept themself busy, refilling the bag of water that fed the sleeve, making breakfast, and washing our clothes. They did their best to hide it, but I could sense their disappointment that we would miss sailing with the regatta. The night before, I had thought that asking them to continue the AC without me was unfair, but perhaps not giving them the choice was worse.

When my pain levels subsided again, I detached the sleeve and crawled out of the tent. Tepid sunlight warmed my skin. Seagulls circled beneath a pale-gray sky and cried out their joy. The ocean lapped at the sand below our campsite, murmuring promises of adventure. I inhaled the scent of the sea and worked up my courage.

"Som, come sit by me for a minute."

They dumped out a basin of dirty water in the nearby grass and then obliged, their shoulder touching mine. "Feeling better?"

"A little, thanks to the sleeve. I had to increase the pain treatment back to the original level, but it's helping. Som . . . I don't know if this will be enough for me to get well. My mother always had hydration, the high-oxygen room, and a blood exchange. I remember going to sleep with her and her waking up feeling a lot better, but it took her weeks to get back to full health, and I'm—"

"So you need more time. Is that so surprising if you're using a third of what she did?"

"We don't have more time. We burned through most of our buffer when we crossed Europe. Any more delays, and we'll miss the final shuttle back to Chedi. We'll fail that part of the deal with my parents."

"So what are you saying?"

I took a deep breath and met their *puzzled-and-wondering* face. "I think maybe I should quit, and you should keep going." As understanding dawned on their face and their jaw started to set, I rushed on. "The rest of the way is mostly on Rune's boat, and by the time you get to Asia, you'll be close enough to reach your family within a day or two of riding. You could finish this on your own."

"Aks, no—"

"And like everyone keeps saying, I have five more years until I'm a legal human adult. At that point, no one can make me stay on Meru. I can get the gene therapy for SCD and come back here, and we can do the Anthro Challenge together, without a time constraint."

Somya looked away, out across the sea. They said nothing for several minutes. I waited, my heart working double time, half from the sickle-cell crisis and the other half pure anxiety.

Finally, they said, "You can't put this on me. It's not fair, Aks. I get that you're feeling guilty, but we're in this together. Imagine how you'd feel if I told you to go on without me."

I thought about that and couldn't imagine it. I concluded with a heavy heart that Somya was right. By asking them to choose, I'd transferred my burden to their shoulders, and they had already carried more than their share of our load.

"Go ahead," they said, flashing a brilliant grin at me. "I can see it on your face, but I want to hear you say it out loud."

"Okay, fine, you're right."

"Ha!"

"But Som, that means we both have to quit." The last word tasted like acid.

Somya twisted and held me by the shoulders. "Together or not at all, right? If you can wait five years, so can I, but, Aks . . . are you sure?"

Every word my mother had said about sickle-cell crises replayed itself in my mind—every complication, every lost piece of medical knowledge, every reason why past humanity had eliminated people like us from the gene pool. I would rather have proved her wrong, but my shrieking flesh declared otherwise. I could barely hold a coherent thought together without pain relief. How could I continue our journey? It didn't matter what I wanted if my body wouldn't cooperate. Half the point of doing the challenge was to prove that I could thrive on Earth. *But this situation isn't my fault. We had to go to the Out of Bounds, and then the weather got bad, and I got sick, and then the bounders abandoned us before I could fully recover.* My excuses sounded whiny, even to myself. So I could survive on Earth under ideal, managed conditions. How was that any different from living in Chedi or on Meru? I had failed to prove my fitness on this planet. Like the people we'd met along the way, Earth, too, had rejected me.

"I'm sure," I said. "Let's go watch the regatta start and then call for help."

"You should probably put your sleeve back on first," Somya pointed out.

With their help and some creativity, I set up my sack to hold the bag of fluids that fed the sleeve. We secured the tubes so that I could still move my arms.

"If this is it, I might as well pack up," Somya said.

"I can take the tent down."

To demonstrate, I stood up and stepped toward it. I couldn't stop myself from wincing, but I gritted my teeth and tugged at one of the ground stakes.

"Sit down, Aks," Somya said from behind me. "I don't think you can will-power your way out of sickle-cell pain. Otherwise, your mother wouldn't have had any problems."

I hesitated, swayed, and did as Somya ordered. Not that I had much choice. My legs refused to hold me up.

"Sorry," I said. "I want to help."

"I know." They yanked the stake out with ease. "Don't worry, you can make it up to me after you're well again. Let's say . . . fifteen rounds of g-ball."

"I hate g-ball."

"Then it's lucky for me that you're in no position to negotiate."

"You're terrible."

"I love you, too."

Somya worked with brisk efficiency, packing the tent and our bedding and securing them on the trailer. I sat with my eyes closed and ran my fingers through cool grains of sand. The morning air was chill, welcoming the sun as it struggled through the hazy clouds.

We moved off the beach and up to less sandy bluffs. Somya pedaled over grassy hillocks that tugged at the wheels. Every bump sent a jolt into my bones. I tried to distract myself with the scenery. Who knew when I would see the ocean again? A lot could happen in five years. What if Somya changed their mind? What if they fell in love and committed to someone who didn't care about the Anthro Challenge? Or worse, what if that person made Somya get treated for Aspiration and Avarice Disorder?

Tension spiked at the base of my neck. *Relax, Aks! Focus on the sea! Look how it blends into the sky at the horizon! Look at the gulls! They're leaving adorable little three-toed prints everywhere in the wet sand.*

A triangle of pale green gleamed up ahead.

"Sailboat," I cried out.

"I see it," Somya called back from the bike.

"Are we too late? Did they already leave? Go faster!"

"I don't know, and I'm going as fast as I can!"

I propped myself up and shaded my eyes. The horizon showed no other boats. Was it the first or the last of the regatta? I could only wait, impatient and anxious, as the bike and trailer trundled along over the unfriendly terrain. A low hill blocked my view of the land ahead of us. Somya huffed as they pedaled up. We came over the crest and saw a wide bay full of beautiful boats, their hulls gleaming with oiled, braided wood, their masts rising straight and tall.

"We made it, Som!"

"I can . . . see that," they panted.

We left the bike at the end of the dock that led to the *Svapna*, the only boat still tied up. I half limped, half ran toward it with Somya's arm supporting my shoulders. Surprise and concern warred on Rune's face, but he helped me step off the gangway.

"Welcome aboard," Rune said. "How are you feeling, Akshaya?"

"Better thanks to the sleeve's pain relief," I confessed. "Without it, not so great, but I couldn't miss seeing the regatta."

"You have a sailor's heart already, eh?" He guided us to the port side. "You'll get a good view from here."

The *Svapna* was easily twice as large as the *Zephyros*. The main mast rose higher, and a second mast added a third sail. A steep, narrow staircase led down to the cabin. Somya pointed out places that had been repaired, where the newer wood had a lighter tone.

"It took so long to fix up," they said, "because they can only use natural wood-fall, and it takes time to soften, treat, and weave the pieces together. The bigger the boat, the longer the wait."

The other vessels in the regatta were of similar size. I'd studied enough to understand why. Too small and they couldn't safely cross the

Atlantic. Too big and they'd need machinery or additional crew, both of which were in short supply.

Someone sounded a horn, and the boats began to move, their sails still down. Rune stuck his head into the stairwell and called, "Halli, it's time!"

A tall person with a head of blond hair emerged from below deck. They looked like a ghost, or more accurately, like a historical figure with pale-blond hair and eyes the color of the sky. On Chedi, Sunanda had the lightest-colored skin of anyone I knew. Halli's was closer to Brana's but with a hint of tan. In spite of that, they wore a sleeveless tunic dyed in deep indigo over brown leggings. They appeared only slightly older than me and Somya, with a fuller figure and well-defined shoulder and arm muscles.

Halli nodded at us in greeting and stood on Rune's far side. A second horn drew our attention back to the bay. Sails went up, and the boats moved into the open ocean in a staggered formation. After a couple of minutes, some of them began to turn southward. They would follow the same route we had planned, heading southwest along the coastline to Guancher and Cabo Verde before turning west toward the Caribbean, with the winds of millennia in their sails. The course lay entirely within Loka, where the alloys managed the ocean currents as well as the winds.

My heart soared at the sight of the regatta, the brightly colored sails like seabirds taking flight. For a few minutes, I forgot about my overly viscous blood, my suffering, and my failure. I rode the waves and soared on the wind until the triangular forms dwindled to distant spots of color. An inadvertent sigh escaped my lips.

Somya put an arm around my shoulders and gave me a gentle hug. At least I had them to share my disappointment with, though the end of our journey also meant that we didn't have much time left together. The oldest child on Meru was two years younger than me. Would we have anything in common other than a few shared genes? *This is all my mother's fault—my sickness, my failure at the Anthro Challenge, my obnoxious destiny! Why couldn't she make me healthy and human, like everyone else on Earth?*

I gripped the boat until the woven strips of wood dug into my palms. *Maybe I should let myself die. Then she'd regret what she's done to me.* But as I looked out over the waves, I realized that not only had I no desire for my life to end, but hurting my mother wouldn't relieve my own disappointment.

"Here, sit down, Aks," Somya said, pulling me gently to a bench.

Every muscle shrieked as I moved, but I did as they asked. I took a deep breath. "We have to tell Rune."

"I know."

The old captain stood in front of me, blocking the sun. "Tell me what?"

I could neither meet his gaze nor force the bitter words out of my throat. Waves slapped at the boat.

"We're quitting the AC," Somya said. "Aks thinks she's going to need more treatment than the sleeve can provide, and that her recovery might take more time than we have."

"Probably a wise move," Rune said, his voice gentle. "A moment deferred is a lifetime earned, eh?" After a pause, he continued, "How about an afternoon of sailing before you call for a rescue? Are you feeling well enough to be a passenger, Akshaya?"

I would have preferred to hide in our tent, but I didn't want to deny Somya the experience, so I said yes. I increased the pain relief from the sleeve. It no longer mattered if I used it up quickly. Whatever alloy came to fetch us could deliver better therapeutics.

Rune decided that we should eat lunch before getting underway. I picked at the food to be polite, my appetite having vanished with the regatta. The sea breeze, the gulls, the turquoise waters—none of it mattered anymore.

---

After lunch, Rune invited Somya to steer the boat out of the bay. I gave them the best smile I could manage. Somya hadn't said much to me, which told me they were also struggling with disappointment. I decided not to sulk so that at least one of us could enjoy our last excursion.

Halli and Rune raised two of the sails, enough to give us a pleasant speed. As I gazed out over the water, something bumped into my calf. I looked down. A pair of wide, pale-green eyes met my gaze, and I took a sharp startled breath. The cat!

In all the pain and anguish of the day, I had completely forgotten about Paasha. She had fur as black as deep space, except for her feet, chin, and a patch on her chest, which were pure white. She nudged my leg with her head—small enough to fit in my hand—and rubbed her body against me as she walked by. Somya reached down and stroked her back. To my amazement, she stopped and allowed them to continue.

"Could I?"

"Of course," Somya said.

Her fur was much softer than I expected. She turned and sniffed at my fingers, tickling them with her pink nose.

"I see you've met the ship's cat," Rune said with a grin. "They used to be standard. Good for catching rodents and keeping them out of the food stores. That's not a problem we have these days, thank goodness, but she seems to like it out on the sea, and who am I to stand in her way?"

He scooped Paasha up and gently scratched under her chin. She started to make a faint rumbling sound, but she didn't struggle to get away. Rune set her on my lap. She pushed at my legs, made a few circles, and settled down. The rumble started again. I found the sensation soothing, especially when combined with her warm body. Paasha blinked slowly at me a couple of times, then closed her eyes. I did the same as exhaustion overcame me. A steady breeze blew as the bow rose and fell.

I must have fallen asleep, because when I opened them again, the boat had slowed down. Halli was taking down the sails, and Rune and Somya were standing beside a bin full of various things I didn't recognize. Paasha had disappeared from my lap. I sat up and looked around.

"Aks, you're awake," Somya said. They grinned. "Rune's going to take me diving!"

"That's great," I said automatically. It took a minute before I registered my own disappointment at not being invited. Of course not. My body was in no shape even for a swim.

Rune started pulling items from the bin and dumping them on the deck. He held up something that resembled a gray vest. "This should fit, I think. Hold out your arms." Rune slipped it on Somya like a jacket, then ran his hand along the seam. The vest shrank a little until it fit snugly around Somya's torso. Rune pulled on a vest of his own and extracted another device. "I'll talk you through it a little more once we're in the water, but the basic idea is that the vest will keep your buoyancy neutral so that you can easily swim up or down. We won't go too deep, just far enough for you to see the shipwreck."

*A wreck!* I was missing that? I wondered briefly if I could set the sleeve to numb my pain completely so I could dive with them, but it was a ridiculous thought. Too many of my red blood cells had deformed, and my tissues weren't getting enough oxygen. Exercise would only make the underlying sickle-cell problems worse.

"Good. Now, you also need a breather." Rune pulled out a transparent, jellylike mask shaped like a face. A hose ran from the chin part to an oblong device about half a meter long. Like the medical sleeve, the device had an old-fashioned electronic screen for its interface. "Most people who dive recreationally have help from microconstructs," Rune explained as he placed the mask over Somya's face, "and an alloy guide who can produce oxygen and nitrogen. Halli and I often dive in the Out of Bounds, so we have these old breathers. Let me set it up for standard air and run a quick systems check to make sure that everything works. The last time Halli and I used these, we were doing a deep dive with additional oxygen."

Halli lowered the anchor. I peered over the side of the boat and watched as the metal sank through clear-blue water. Rune talked Somya through some more instructions about the equipment. They attached the masks to their faces, pulled some gray fins over their hands and feet, and jumped off the back of the boat. After a reassuring wave, they disappeared beneath the surface.

A shadow fell over me.

"Some water?" Halli held out a cup. They spoke Terran with a slight accent.

I took it gratefully. The sleeve might keep my body hydrated, but my throat was parched. "What's it like under there?"

"Depends on the conditions. Sometimes clear as glass, sometimes cloudy with silt. Lots of silvery fish of various kinds. Occasionally some sharks or whales, though they prefer the waters around the strait. And some alloys, too. Usually watercrafters or researchers."

"Those breathers, do they work like gills?"

"Kind of. Gills are more like lungs. They draw oxygen from the water, but we can't breathe pure oxygen. The breather extracts a mixture of nitrogen and oxygen from the water. In an emergency, it can electrolyze to make hydrox, too."

I didn't know what that meant, but I was more interested in the first part. "Rune said something about diving with additional oxygen."

"Yes, that's useful for staying longer at depth, to avoid decompression sickness."

I didn't know what that meant, either, but it was irrelevant. "Would the breather work if you submerged it in a bucket of water?"

Halli shrugged. "Probably. Why?"

"One of the things that helps my sickle-cell disorder is to breathe air that has forty-five percent oxygen, like the atmosphere of Meru. I'm wondering if I could use a breather to do that. I don't suppose you have another one?"

Halli walked to the bin. "Rune likes to keep spares of everything. Stuff tends to break in the most remote places." They rummaged around and pulled one out. "You want to try it?"

I nodded.

Halli dumped the rest of the bin's contents on the deck, then dipped the empty container into the ocean. They placed the bin next to me and dropped the breather into it.

"Forty-five percent $O_2$, you said?"

"Yes."

While Halli set up the device, I held the clear mask to my face. It sealed itself to my contours and inflated enough so that I could move my mouth. I took a deep, slow breath. Cool, dry air entered my nose and throat. Halli submerged the breather in the bin.

"When this indicator light goes from green to yellow," Halli said, "that means it's getting low on either nitrogen or oxygen, but it should last a couple of hours."

"Thanks, Halli."

They nodded. "I hope it helps."

They left me alone and started tidying the boat. I tried to relax and keep my breathing even. A pain crisis resulted from a buildup of hemoglobin in the blood as sickled cells broke down. A blood exchange was the fastest and best way to clear it up, but my mother had tinkered with my genes to give me additional ways to deal with the problem. In Chedi, I had never needed anything except the high-oxygen room. I'd never had a true pain crisis, either, but it was possible, however small the chance, that the breather would be enough to help me through it. A tiny voice in my head whispered, *Maybe I don't have to give up on the Anthro Challenge after all.*

A giant grayish-brown pelican alit on the deck rail a couple of meters from me. It had an enormous lower beak, and it stared back at me with bright eyes. After several very long seconds, it spread its wings and flapped away. The first one I'd seen. I grabbed my sack and pulled out my sketchbook. When Halli noticed, they came over and glanced at the drawing.

"You're good," they pronounced.

I smiled and shrugged. "Not as good as this person."

I extracted the notebook that Somya had found in Wien's market and showed Halli the images in it.

"You're almost as good," they said.

I considered their tone and expression and couldn't find any sarcasm in either. I shrugged off the compliment again. Perhaps Halli was being kind to me.

Half an hour later, Rune and Somya emerged from the water. As soon as Somya removed their mask and vest, they sat down beside me and demanded to know why I was wearing a breather. It didn't take long for them—and Rune—to understand.

Somya's dark eyes lit. "Does this mean we're not calling for a rescue today?"

I nodded. "I'll check the numbers from my bodym tomorrow and try turning down the pain meds again if I can."

"With three breathers," Rune said, "we can rotate so that one is always ready go. You can have high oxygen all night, though you'll have to wake up every two hours to swap units."

"I'll help with that," Somya offered. "Aks and I can sleep up here so it's easier to refill the bin."

We sailed back to the harbor at Nuberia. I stayed awake for the return journey, trying my best not to get my hopes up. Somya allowed themself to be optimistic, of course, but I couldn't shake the memory of intense pain from earlier in the day. The sleeve had worked its magic. I didn't relish the thought of having to dial it back only to discover that I'd made no progress.

At least I'd had one more glorious day at sea. The salt breeze coated my skin and hair. Flying fish caught the sunlight and sparkled like diamonds. Even if I hadn't been able to sail or dive, I had seen the pelican and met Paasha. For the rest of the evening, I set aside thoughts of the next day and just lived on the waves, as my ancestors had done for thousands of years.

# DAY 43

I waited until after breakfast to check my bodym. My numbers had improved enough that I decided to reduce the pain meds. As we waited for the change to take effect, Somya did their best to distract me with stories about diving. Tension built between my shoulder blades. Rune and Halli went into town to pick up fresh food and other supplies. Paasha returned to the boat shortly after their departure, sauntering up the gangway and leaping gracefully onto the deck. She found her way to my lap uninvited and settled there to sleep.

The burning sensation came back gradually. It built for the first hour or so, but then, to my relief, it stabilized to a bearable level of agony. I didn't tell Somya, not until after Rune and Halli came back and we'd eaten some of the fresh chirimoya and jujubes they had found. The pain dulled my appetite, but the fruits tasted sweet enough that I could force some down.

As Rune and Halli cleaned up, Somya sat beside me and nudged me with their shoulder. "So?"

I couldn't help smiling.

"It's working?"

"The pain is less than yesterday, but"—I held up a hand—"my numbers are nowhere close to baseline. Don't get your hopes up too much."

"Too late!" they said gleefully. "We'll do this for a couple more days, and if you keep getting better, we'll continue on. You can use the breathers as often as you need to."

I nodded.

When Rune and Halli emerged from the cabin, Somya broke the news.

"That's a good sign," Rune said. "And a good plan. We need to be certain that Akshaya's health is stable before we set sail. Getting an alloy rescue in the middle of the ocean is a lot harder than it would be here. Pilots aren't like birds. They can't launch from water."

Halli said nothing, and their face didn't give away their thoughts. I wondered how they felt about all of it—having me and Somya aboard, helping us with the Anthro Challenge. The most they'd spoken to me was while setting up the breather the day before. Did they resent the intrusion? Did they wish they had more authority over the *Svapna*? Halli treated Rune like a captain, and as far as I knew, he hadn't given Halli a choice about this plan.

"Are you okay with this?" I asked Halli.

They nodded again, their expression neutral.

"That settles it," Rune said. "I'll head back into town later, in case I can resupply the medications in the sleeve. It's unlikely this far from the border, but perhaps I'll find something that we can adapt. We're low on some other emergency medical treatments, too, so I'll stock up on whatever I can."

"Thank you," I said. "Sorry I can't help."

Rune grinned. "Don't worry. There'll be plenty for you to do once we're underway and you're feeling well. Meantime, young Somya, perhaps you can give me and Halli a hand below? We came up with an arrangement that we think will be more comfortable for a four-person crew."

The three of them disappeared into the cabin. I lay back on the bench and squinted at the sky. A couple of indriyas glinted in the distance, as they usually did, but where was our watcher? Had zie figured out why we had missed our departure? Two or three more days . . . would I be able to sail by then? For the previous week and a half, I'd been carted around by others, first in the walker-wagon and then on our trailer. I wanted to participate in the Anthro Challenge. How long would I have to rest on Rune's boat like a piece of baggage?

I wished I could ask my mother if my body would heal. She would know best if the method I'd contrived would be sufficient to overcome a pain crisis. I had so many questions. Would I have to keep using the breather for the rest of our journey? Could I leave it off during the day? Would warmer weather, especially after we crossed the equator, improve the condition of my blood? If the pain went away completely, did that mean I had returned to good health, or could my body fail me again without warning?

My mother had drilled a lot of information into me on Chedi, but she liked to focus on the science. As a tarawan, she understood genetics better than physiology, and since no one on Earth had dealt with sickle-cell disease in many centuries, the only information she had about dealing with it in modern times came from her own experience and whatever we could look up in the Nivid. I doubted that she would have been able to answer all of my questions.

I had set out on the Anthro Challenge not knowing what to expect from Earth. That was part of the adventure. Strange to think of my body as a world, but if I applied the same attitude to my internal state, then my health was another journey, another opportunity to embrace surprises and setbacks along with plans and uncertainties. Every morning brought something new. The only way to find out what lay beyond the horizon was to move forward.

# DAY 50

We waited three additional days at Nuberia. Somya slept at my side the first two nights, waking every two hours to swap the breather and refill the water tank. On the third night, I was able to let them sleep through one round and do it myself. I gradually dialed back the pain relief on the sleeve as the days passed. My progress wasn't perfectly linear, but I only had plateaus, not setbacks.

On December 5, almost a week after the regatta left, we set out to cross the Atlantic Ocean. Although I didn't have the strength to hoist a sail or trim a sheet, I was able to take one watch each day because the *Svapna*, unlike the *Zephyros*, had a lot of electromechanical automation, including switches and sliders to control the sails remotely. Rune had been alone until he picked up Halli, and he couldn't have managed it with fully manual controls. I continued to use the breather overnight, letting whoever was on watch help me with the swaps. Halli had rigged a pump so that we could easily refill the bin without slowing the boat.

On December 8, we put into port at the main island of Guancher. A pod of Atlantic bottlenose dolphins accompanied us until just outside the harbor. Somya and I couldn't stop watching their graceful blue-gray forms as they leapt and dove and did backflips. We even saw a couple of calves swimming alongside their parents.

Guancher had long been famous as a stopping point for those sailing west from Europe or Africa. Clouds covered the interior skyline, hiding a massive volcanic peak. According to Rune, it had last erupted over a century earlier. I walked into town with everyone else to pick up food and other supplies. The houses on the island were built from brown-and-black volcanic rock, their exteriors rough and their silhouettes uneven. Lush green plants grew from divots in the walls and roofs. The air had the familiar thickness of the tropical zones in Chedi, but the island breeze kept it from feeling stifling. We found many fruit trees, especially bananas, mangoes, and papayas. The community gardens had sprawling patches of melons and gourds, both of which Rune favored for the crossing. We would have another stop at Cabo Verde, but no one lived there, so we would have to forage and rely on luck.

The people in Guancher seemed unfazed by our arrival. We were the only ones who had arrived by boat, but others had come via flying alloys, including a few human geologists and recreational divers. Rune had friends in town who tolerated his ways and invited us to dine at their home. Like him, they were older humans, with two adult children and several grandchildren, all of whom came to eat with us. Somya made quick friends with the little ones, including the two-year-old, who wailed in disappointment and clung to their neck when we had to leave.

That night was cool and clear, and we set sail under the light of a nearly full moon. If Somya and I hadn't been there, I suspect that Rune would've stayed longer at Guancher, but we had to make up for lost time and couldn't afford to linger. As I set up my breather mask, I heard a strange noise off the starboard side of the boat. Rune and Somya were in the cabin getting ready to sleep, and Halli sat at the steering wheel.

I glanced at them and said, "Did you hear that?"

They shot me a rare smile, let the sails slacken, and pointed out at the water. "Whale spout. There—see it?"

A glistening arc rose from the water's surface, then submerged again. It was hard to judge in the dark distance, but it looked to be half as big as my maker's true body.

"It's huge!" I said. "I wonder what kind it is."

"Need to get a better look." Halli stepped over beside me. "Now that it's up, it should hang out for five or ten minutes before diving back down."

Any thought of sleep fled. I kept my eyes trained on the same area and tried hard not to blink. Moonlight and starlight caught on the wave tops. A rounded rectangular shape rose from the surface—above the water!—and then fell back in with a loud splash.

"Breach," Halli said.

"Som," I yelled, not taking my gaze off the ocean. "There's a sperm whale! Come see it before it dives down again!"

A groan emerged from the cabin. "Too tired," Somya called back. "I'll see the next one."

Halli raised their brows at me. "You know your cetaceans. Does your field guide cover them?"

"No, only land animals." I hesitated, then volunteered, "I kind of obsessively studied Earth fauna for the last couple of years."

Halli's grin caught the light. "Same, but only the sea creatures. That's how I convinced Rune to go diving."

"When I'm well again, maybe I could join you."

"Yes."

The whale surged out of the water again. This time, only its back showed, but I heard the strange sound again and matched it to the spume from its blowhole.

"Sometimes it's hard to tell the mature whales apart from the alloy watercrafters," Halli said, "especially at night. The blowhole is the giveaway. Alloys have nostrils, so you'll see their faces surface to breathe."

I envied the alloys' ability to be part of ocean life. As a human, I couldn't have an incarn or be remade into a vastly different kind of body. Not only did alloys have a third set of chromosomes, their DNA was custom designed for specific genes and gene expression, starting in the enormous wombs that gestated them.

"What got you so interested in Earth animals?" Halli asked.

"We didn't have any in Chedi."

"None at all? Not even small domesticated ones?"

"No. It wouldn't be fair to them if something went wrong with Chedi's artificial gravity. They wouldn't understand space suits or zero-g."

"I can't imagine having no animals around," Halli said. "Where I grew up, we had dogs and cats and rabbits everywhere." They moved from the rail to the cockpit. "I don't think our whale friend is coming back."

I sat down again. "Where was your home, Halli?"

"A small village in far northern Europe called Stiklestad, in the Out of Bounds. It's part of the Principality of Norseland."

"Was it hard," I asked, "growing up in the OOB?"

Halli shrugged. "Not for me, but I didn't know any different. Still don't. We followed an old way of life. Mostly self-sustaining with fish and foraging. Alloys would drop off supplies for emergencies. We're too far for the bounders to come and trade. I met up with Rune in the borderlands. We never spend much time off the boat in Loka, so I only get small windows into life here. The weather is better."

"Is that why you left?"

"No." Halli laughed. "I liked my life in Stiklestad, but I have restless feet. That's what my parents said. Rune understood. When I stepped onto the *Svapna*, I knew I had found my second home."

"Makes sense to me. If you're descended from Vikings, then the sea is in your DNA."

Halli was only a few years older than me. I imagined their life as a child, running around an idyllic village perched on the edge of a great fjord, living independently through whatever the planet gave them and whatever the alloys herded away from Loka. Why did we need Meru when we had the OOB? Loka would one day expand to include all of Earth, but the work would take the alloys centuries more to complete. In the meantime, we could carve out more independent places to live, sanctuaries for those who didn't fit within Loka's constraints. I didn't know how closely my imagination matched the reality of Halli's home, but I added it to my mental list of places to explore in the future.

On Meru, we would live side by side with alloys in their true bodies, not the incarns who inhabited Loka. It would be a collaborative existence. That was my mother's dream. She'd chosen to go into exile with my maker so they could be together, which they weren't allowed to do on Earth, and she saw Meru as a place where all three of us could coexist as equals. I didn't see why we couldn't have that life in the Out of Bounds. The laws of the compact stood in our way, but they could change. My mother had helped make it legal for humans to travel in space. Could I do something similarly transformative for the OOB? She never talked much about what she'd done, and I knew that the Nivid had archived recordings of what happened, but I had never cared to watch. I didn't enjoy politics, much less public speaking, and I wasn't good with strangers the way Somya and my mother were. *Maybe I can recruit Som to the cause. They'd be much better at winning over the hearts of alloys and humans.*

Then I thought of the bounders' reaction to my chromatophores. Would the humans in the OOB accept alloys living among them as residents, or was there too much history? Between their behavioral engineering and the passage of time, maybe humans had lost the ability to change their attitudes. I had even less of an idea how the alloys might feel. I glanced over at Halli. I hadn't revealed my unusual ability to them or to Rune. The reactions of Lumo, Brana, and Mezei, who had all seemed so friendly and like-minded, had made me wary of putting too much trust in anyone, even those who held my life in their hands. How was I going to win the minds of voters? Never mind that I knew so little about CDS politics. The enormity of changing the compact seemed like trying to count all the stars in the sky. I didn't know where to start.

"What was life like in space?" Halli asked.

"Small." I glanced upward. The stars twinkled above me. It still took me a second to get used to their unsteady light. My instinct was to think that my eyesight had a problem, then I would blink and remember that I was on a planet with atmosphere. "You could walk around Chedi in a couple of days. We had a few small villages. About two hundred people lived in the main one, and about fifty to seventy-five in the others."

"Wow. We have over twenty thousand in my town. I've thought about applying for a spot in Chedi. I would love to see the world beyond Earth."

"Restless feet."

Halli laughed. "Exactly. Someday, I would love to visit Meru. Another world—just imagine it!"

"I won't have to, not if I fail the Anthro Challenge."

Halli turned a quizzical expression my way.

"Rune didn't tell you?"

They shook their head.

"My parents are Jayanthi and Vaha." I got a blank stare in response. So Halli didn't pay much attention to politics, either. I gave them a brief history.

"I envy you," Halli said. "You're younger than me, but you've seen so much more, and you have the ability to explore a place that few will. I really hope they open Meru up in my lifetime. I've heard if you volunteer for genetic treatment, you can apply to live there."

"Why would you do that?" I spread my arms wide. "You have all of this amazing planet. Plants, animals, history—why would you trade that for an empty, barren hellscape with a dozen humans on it?"

"You're not looking forward to it?"

"No. In fact—" I hesitated, then told them about the deal I'd made with my parents.

"But you're so adventurous. You'll sail across the ocean, but you have no curiosity about an entirely new planet? Think of all the places you could see before anyone else, human or alloy or construct."

Their *I-think-less-of-you* face was clear to me even in profile. It stung, and I tried to shrug it off. "Maybe I'm spoiled from all the years flying around our galactic neighborhood. I want *life* around me. Meru is dead except for some cyanobacteria."

Halli made a noncommittal sound and walked away to check our heading. They didn't have to express their disappointment—or perhaps disapproval—for me to feel it. We hadn't known each other for long, but Halli had helped me with the breather. They shared my love for sea creatures. I had started to believe that we were kindred spirits.

I slipped the breather mask on and lay back. The long day had worn me out, and the high-oxygen air tasted sweet. My body relaxed, though the effect was probably more psychosomatic than real. A lifetime of breathing an atmosphere like that, free to go on excursions without worrying about my health . . . was Halli right? Would that be as good a life? But there were no whales on Meru. No pelicans or cats or bushy-tailed foxes. No trees except for the few that humans cultivated. Maybe one day, I would be okay with a place like that, but there were years' worth of experiences left on Earth, and I wanted them all.

OUT OF BOUNDS
Jadnut-
Udebiga
Tongvana
Kado
Tequestan
LOKA
Nitaynoa
Oloubera
Cueva
Guayaquil
OUT OF BOUNDS
LOKA

# DAY 62

By the time we reached Cabo Verde, three days later, I felt well enough to stop using the medical sleeve all the time. We sailed west from there, expecting to take roughly ten days to arrive at Nitaynoa, depending on the winds and weather. Instead of solo shifts, Rune switched us to working in pairs on a staggered six-hour schedule so that two people were always awake. That meant we never had to stop, and we made up for a bit of lost time. The *Svapna* was built for a single sailor, but given our lack of experience, it was easier for me and Somya to have Rune or Halli as backup while on duty. My health continued to improve, and I tapered my use of the breather. We navigated by the sun and stars using a sextant, an ancient and very annoying instrument, along with some old maps from Rune's successful attempt at the Anthro Challenge. People in the Human Era had more sophisticated tools, but none of those existed anymore.

"As long as we're generally headed west," Rune told us, "don't worry too much about our course. I'll check and make adjustments when I'm awake if necessary."

Somya and I did our best to maintain the correct heading during our shifts. A week out from Cabo Verde, the barometer started to rise. Rune turned us south to avoid an area of building high pressure. The last thing we needed was to get stuck in calm seas. Two days later, we crossed the border out of Loka. My shift started a little after sunset, and I put all three sails up and picked up a good amount of speed. I couldn't stop grinning as the *Svapna* skimmed over the inky waves. I even practiced letting the boat heel under Halli's supervision, while Somya perched on the rail, feet dangling over the side. A little after midnight, Somya took over, and I descended into the cabin. Halli's praise left me glowing as I went to sleep.

I woke up a few hours later to frowning faces. By the time Rune had done the predawn reckoning, we'd gone much farther into the OOB than planned. Halli hadn't yet gone to bed. Clouds streamed across the sky to our south. The wind picked up, and our telltales flew straight back. We clearly didn't have to worry about getting stuck in a high-pressure area, but too much wind would cause a different set of problems.

"Damn this thing," Rune muttered at the sextant. "I'm out of practice with it."

I looked at Halli, who shrugged. "I grew up sailing the local fjord. We didn't need much in the way of navigation tools. Even in Norseland, we have access to the public network."

"The currents around the border are less predictable," Rune said. "We usually sail well to the north, but for some reason the alloys left that high-pressure system in place." He squinted up. "I suspect they're herding a storm. Those aren't birds up there. Halli, we need to bear away and head north as hard as we can. You take the jib. I'll handle the main and mizzen. Somya, help Akshaya make some food, please."

In the cabin, Somya chopped a melon with quick, sharp motions while I brewed tea. Their shoulders were hunched and taut.

"I'm sorry," I said.

They looked at me, eyes round and startled. "What for?"

"I got carried away last night. If I hadn't picked up so much speed—"

They put the knife down. "It's as much my fault as yours. Maybe more. I didn't even check the compass last night. After all these days at sea, I thought I knew what I was doing."

"We can share in the blame," I said. It didn't make me feel better.

We took the food and drink up to the deck, but it was clear that neither Rune nor Halli would get a chance to eat. They had decided to adjust the sails manually. Rune had told me early on that in rough or racing conditions, he preferred to feel the tension in the ropes rather than adjusting them by sight from the helm. Their shoulders and biceps bulged with the effort. Rune called out warnings as the boom swung from port to starboard, the wind at our backs. Stray hairs whipped at my face and neck, and the gusts snatched my breath away.

"Maybe you'd better sleep early," I yelled to Somya, pulling them toward the cabin. "You can swap shifts with Halli later."

Below was only a little quieter.

"I wish we could do something to help," Somya said from their bunk.

"Me too. Get some rest so you can do more during your shift."

I went back above in case Rune needed anything and tucked myself out of the way as best as I could. I slipped on a harness and clipped myself to a railing, then trained my gaze on the sky. High above us, dozens of dark spots flew in complex spiral patterns. Rune had said they weren't birds. *Weathercrafters.* Alloys working to keep atmospheric energy directed into the Out of Bounds. To our south, the clouds continued to build. I couldn't tell whether they'd come closer or my mind was playing with my fears. The farther north we could get, the less severe a storm would be.

Was our alloy watcher among the people above? Zie ought to know the position of our boat, and zie would have tracked its voyage as part of the documentary footage. If we had continued into a truly dangerous situation, would zie have contacted us somehow? Or would Nara tell zir to let us risk our lives for the sake of entertainment? He hadn't stopped us from swimming across the Euphrates, but he couldn't have anticipated that we would do something like that. Sailing into a bad storm was a different matter. I couldn't imagine they would allow it, even if it meant violating the Anthro Challenge parameters, but we hadn't discussed it when we made our plans. Perhaps they had someone following us undersea, someone who could come to our rescue in case of a shipwreck. That made more sense than an air-based rescue in bad weather, and Halli had said that alloys could provide divers with oxygen, so they could keep us safe underwater and carry us to land.

The wind built, and the waves smashed into each other, sometimes washing over the railing. The deck bucked and bounced like a trampoline. Even Rune and Halli had put on their safety harnesses. *Surely the alloys wouldn't let us die out here.* I squinted and searched for the telltale glint of an indriya, but I couldn't see one. If they couldn't stand the winds, then it was possible that we were on our own, after all. I crawled back down into the cabin. I couldn't do anything above deck except get in the way. Somya rose from their bunk as soon as they saw me and pulled me down next to them. We held each other as the world roared around us.

# RESHYAN (DAY 63)

Reshyan's muscles ached, but not in that sweet way that followed a day of hard flying. An unusually severe hurricane had required the efforts of every alloy who could herd clouds or water, including researchers like zirself. They had spent nearly thirty-six hours working, with only four hours of sleep in the middle, and they had succeeded in redirecting the worst of the storm's energy south of fifteen degrees latitude. The Caribbean Sea in Loka would still receive plenty of wind and rain, but not as much as the waters in the Out of Bounds. Zie had returned to zir berth with a level of exhaustion zie hadn't experienced since zir time as an interstellar pilot.

Nara had released the first episode of *In Exile* a few days earlier. Reshyan had been too busy to watch it right away, but now, with a full day of rest ahead of zir, zie decided to wait no longer. Zie activated full immersive mode with a thought-command. The opening sequence showed a megaconstruct flying through space with Sol in the background. It took Reshyan a few seconds to adjust to the perspective of interplanetary space. Zie hadn't left Earth's orbit in so long that zie had forgotten how it felt out there. The edges had a somber tint that overlaid dramatic colors. Human vocalizations and music accompanied it, but Reshyan had never bothered to learn either. Zie disabled the audio and focused on the phoric subtitles.

<Five varshas ago,> flashed an unseen narrator, <an unlikely couple left the Solar System to live together in a unique form of exile.>

The visual cut to an interior room with Jayanthi and then Vaha talking about their decision and motives. Their words carried over non-immersive clips of Akshaya doing human-child things inside the mega-construct Chedi. Reshyan couldn't relate to any of it. Until the contract with Nara, zie hadn't paid much attention to human lifestyles. Another interview snippet followed, this one with Akshaya, who talked about her reasons for attempting the Anthro Challenge, and then Somya, who had a less compelling motive but far more ease on camera.

After that, the episode got into the actual journey. Reshyan recognized quite a bit of the footage. Strange to see it presented in such a cohesive way with mood lighting and immersive clarity. Nara had taken hours of recordings and turned them into a dramatic series of events with none of the daily tedium. No one experiencing *In Exile* would have the least idea how much time and effort Akshaya and Somya spent each day on simple necessities like making and striking camp, cooking, and cleaning. Reshyan only knew because zie had reviewed so much of the raw footage for Jayanthi's sake. Nara had made use of nonaerial perspectives, too, and the indriyas that Reshyan had deployed had picked up audio. That modality wouldn't matter to alloys who watched the show, other than the small segment who consumed a lot of human entertainment, but nondeaf humans ought to appreciate it.

The episode concluded with a moment of high tension at the Euphrates. Reshyan knew the outcome of the river crossing, but anyone else would worry and wonder. The children's latest predicament carried an equal if not greater concern. Reshyan had caught a glimpse of their boat at the edge of the hurricane's eye before recalling the indriyas. The craft was crawling northward, the correct choice of direction, but powered as they were by the wind, Reshyan wasn't sure they could outpace the weather. Not that zie could change anything about their fate either way. The work zie and the others had done wasn't for the benefit of a few fragile humans on a bit of wood and fabric. They had managed to mitigate the speed and moisture that the storm would pick up, but it had taken a massive effort. Zie looked forward to resuming zir research work, which was far less strenuous.

Reshyan scanned the reviews of the show. It had reached many more alloys than zie had anticipated, given Nara's level of fame. About a third of the responses came from humans. Their feedback mostly expressed dismay. Quite a few of them lobbied for outlawing activities like the Anthro Challenge. Not surprising, but also less relevant to Reshyan's interests. The voting population of humans was less than a percent of the total in the Constructed Democracy of Sol. Their opinions held little sway, especially among the alloys in stasis.

The show had a more favorable reception across the rest of the populace. Quite a few alloys commented that exiling Vaha and Jayanthi might have been a mistake and that the practice in general was outdated. Much to Reshyan's pleasant surprise, someone had compiled a list of proposed policies that would modify or abolish the practice, and others had pledged their support. Reshyan added zir name to it and broadcast the pledge to zir small network of like-minded friends. Zie hoped that people continued to like the rest of *In Exile* as much as the first episode and that its audience continued to grow. The wider the reach, the more it would propel exile reform into the spotlight, and sufficient momentum would make voter approval for Nara's subsequent documentary more likely.

A call request from Olanma interrupted Reshyan. Zie hoped that didn't mean their day of rest was getting cut short. Zie opened an emchannel with the watercrafter.

<I've been immersed in this new show that everyone is talking about,> Olanma flashed. <It's called *In Exile*. Have you seen it?>

<Yes,> Reshyan replied. <I just finished watching the first episode.>

<I have to admit that it's pretty good, but, Resh, I noticed an interesting name in the credits—yours.> Zir words glowed ultraviolet with suspicion. <Are you using our assigned resources for a parallel project?>

<Of course not,> Reshyan flashed, letting zir irritation show. <Nara has provided me with all the constructs used for recording. All I've done is deploy them.>

<But you're taking extra time and energy for that,> Olanma pointed out. <Did Nara contract with your orbital station for the additional bhojya you're drinking or the extra repairs your body will need?>

Reshyan didn't know the answer. <If I'm flying along that route anyway, there's no extra expenditure.>

<Aren't you worried that you're choosing your data-collection locales based on what Nara needs rather than what's good for Loka? This extra labor seems like a conflict of interest. Our contracts specifically state that you can't take on additional work without the approval of the Earth Ground-Based Service Committee.>

<I appreciate your concern,> Reshyan flashed, keeping zir phores neutral. <The recordings I'm taking for Nara will not impact Earth or my research project.> That was true, and zie didn't think that the contract with Nara would violate the terms of zir research project, but zie hadn't thought to check.

<Why would you help Nara? Are you friends?>

Reshyan hesitated. Zie certainly wouldn't call Nara a friend. What could zie tell Olanma that would get zir to stop prying? Reshyan had no interest in telling zir colleague about zir political motives or zir distant relationship to Pushkara, but zie had to come up with some plausible rationale for taking on the collaboration. If Reshyan lost the respect of zir colleagues, they would refuse to work with zir, and zie would lose the contract for atmospheric research.

<We have some mutual interests,> Reshyan flashed, <and I'm curious about human life on the surface.> The statement came out

of nowhere, and zie hoped it would be enough to quell Olanma's suspicions.

Olanma's phores still glimmered with ultraviolet, though the intensity dimmed. <You never mentioned that before.>

<You never asked.>

<Don't expect me to go chasing after the humans for you.>

<I wouldn't dream of it. They don't want us to interfere with their journey, and if Nara needs underwater footage, he will find his own way of obtaining it.>

<All right, I'm taking you at your word. Enjoy the rest of your day off.>

Reshyan thanked Olanma. They ended the call, but zie couldn't shake a glimmer of anxiety. The excuse zie made to Olanma wasn't entirely untrue. Zie had grown curious about the fate of the two young humans, and zie took pride in having contributed to the show, especially after seeing the prospect of reform starting to coalesce around it, but zie didn't relish the thought of choosing between atmospheric research and the project for Nara. Reshyan pulled up both contracts and began to read.

# DAY 64

We motored into the bay on the northeastern side of Oloubera with our sails down. Rain and wind lashed every millimeter of exposed boat and body. Poor Paasha insisted on hiding under a blanket in the bow's berth. Rune said that we needed to find shelter in town, somewhere safer than the *Svapna*, but none of us could convince the cat to leave. In the end, Rune grabbed her, blanket and all, and carried the writhing bundle in his arms.

The floating dock twisted and pitched like a leaping dolphin under our feet. Land rose quickly beyond the beach under cover of dense foliage. A muddy lane led the way between green bushes that whipped us with their wet leaves. At the top of a hill that left my legs aching, we found a small empty village. The homes were woven into flexible trees that bent under the weight of the storm. They had neither roofs nor furniture, which struck me as odd until I noticed the squat stone structures near each building. I guessed that those provided storage for the household items. Where had everyone gone? We ran down every path we could find until Somya spotted a door-shaped hole in a large boulder. The three of us followed them over a low barrier wall and down a spiral ramp, also cut from stone, and lit by traces of pink bioluminescence in the walls. The roar of the storm faded as we descended.

After a few minutes, we arrived at a large, dimly lit space crowded with humans. The ones nearest the ramp moved away to give our dripping forms some space. A hunched figure threaded through the gaps and approached us.

"Welcome, friends." Identifying information popped up in my visual. "I'm Makuya, I'm the local greeter." He handed us each a blanket and peered at our faces in the dim light. "You look familiar. Have you been here before?"

"We just arrived by boat," Rune said. "It's been many years since I stopped here."

"Welcome back," Makuya said. He scratched at a chin stubbled with gray hair. "It's the youngsters who I've seen somewhere recently." After a pause, a broad smile spread across his face. "Yes, I remember now—you're the ones from the pledge . . . Somya and Akshaya, right? Doing that challenge to go around the planet? I watched your show last week."

"Yes," I answered automatically. "That's us. It's called the Anthro Challenge. Is that the pledge you meant?"

"No, no. I suppose you wouldn't have watched your own show, but people love it, so of course there is political controversy. An alloy started a pledge to vote in favor of exile reform if you successfully finish your journey. Quite a few people have signed it. Some humans have started a similar movement to stop sending people to the Out of Bounds. They think we should have more options for those of us who want to practice an alternative lifestyle."

I tried to absorb this information. Nara hadn't given us a date for the first episode's release, so the recognition took me by surprise.

"That's great news," Somya said. "I'm glad people are seeing our efforts as more than personal gratification."

I thought of the pledge and what it would mean for my maker. Zie had finished zir term of exile, but zir old friend Kaliyu still floated in a cold and distant orbit around the sun, along with many others. I didn't know the number, but it wasn't small. Could our trivial circumnavigation of the Earth really bring an end to the practice? It would depend on how many alloys had signed the pledge. I couldn't connect to the network to find out, nor could I ask Makuya to look it up. He had already divulged more than he probably should have, given the parameters of the Anthro Challenge. Knowing about the show's reception wouldn't affect our travel decisions, but at the same time, it was information that we shouldn't have had access to.

"We will be happy to do what we can to help you," Makuya said.

"That's very kind of you," Rune said.

"Have you brought some precious goods with you?" Makuya nodded at the bundle in Rune's arms, which had finally gone still.

We all smiled, and Rune filled Makuya in on the joke. He set the blanket on the ground and let Paasha out. She bolted up the circular ramp, disappeared for a few worrying minutes, and then returned to sit with only her twitching tail in sight.

"If you need anything during your stay, please come and find me," Makuya said. "We expect the hurricane to pass around midday tomorrow. Other than access to the public network, we don't use alloy technology here. We have extra food and water, which we'll gladly share, but I'm afraid these blankets are all we have to offer in the way of physical comforts. The washrooms are over that way, and refreshments to our right."

With that guidance, Makuya left us. After some time, people started to bed down for the night. In our rush to get away from the sea, we hadn't brought any of our things, so we sat on the stone with our blankets. Halli and Somya brought over some water and fruits. Rune left half a cup of water on the stairs for Paasha. We took turns using the three private toilets carved into the back of the shelter. As I waited, I glanced around and estimated that there were a few hundred people. I caught some of them staring at us. They smiled when I made eye contact, but they gave us space and didn't press any of us to talk. Somya, of course, had already made friends. It wouldn't have surprised me if the shelter held everyone who lived on the island. We had motored around most of it on our way to the bay, and we hadn't seen any signs of human habitation until we arrived at the dock.

Somya and I had spent most of the previous day staying out of Rune and Halli's way. They both had a lot more sailing experience than we did, and with the boat frequently turning to keep the wind at our back, we were better off in the cabin than underfoot. A few hours from Oloubera, the gusts had gotten so strong that they had to furl the sails. Motoring was slower but safer, though without any idea of the storm's speed or heading, we had no idea if we could outrun it.

Watching the clouds darken and build into a wall that chased us across the ocean was the most terrifying thing I had ever experienced. I didn't admit it—not even to Somya—but I was glad I had an excuse to hide belowdecks. I realized then how much I had yet to learn, not only about sailing but about the planet itself. People described Earth as a living, breathing sphere of nonintelligent consciousness. In those hours on the boat, at the mercy of the elements, I realized what that meant. It would take me years to understand the planet at the instinctive level of someone like Rune or Halli, especially in the Out of Bounds, where the alloys put little effort into shaping it. How naive I'd been to think that Somya and I could handle the Anthro Challenge alone.

I rolled up part of the blanket to make a rudimentary pillow and set up the breather. My pain crisis had abated, but with all of the stress from the boat, I didn't want to take any chances with my health. If the storm ended by the following day, we wouldn't lose much time. Oloubera lay south of our intended destination of Nitaynoa, but both islands were en route to Cueva, the strait that connected the Atlantic and Pacific oceans. The hurricane might give me nightmares, but I could rest knowing that it wouldn't cause us further delay.

# DAY 65

The storm raged through the morning. We waited until the locals decided that it was safe to emerge. The drip-drip of wet branches and leaves greeted us, along with a glimmer of sunlight. We followed the crowd through a muddy, slippery tangle of flattened bushes and bowed trees. After a brief sampling of the ground conditions, Paasha leapt to Halli's shoulders and settled there.

The village remained resilient in the face of the hurricane's fury, with a few of the larger structures showing minor damage. The air had cooled, but without the breeze, it thickened around me like invisible fog. At just past the winter solstice, the ambient temperature was as comfortable as a night in Chedi. I could understand why people in the equatorial OOB would live in such lightweight shelters. Homes that could withstand frequent wind and rain were more important than airtight protection.

After sharing some food and drink, Rune, Halli, Somya, and I continued toward the beach. The closer we got, the more signs of destruction that greeted us. Greenery lay shredded and scattered as if an alloy had chewed through it and spat it back out. Sand had deposited itself on patches of ground where it didn't belong. Past a point, we couldn't tell the path apart from the surroundings.

I picked my way across the damaged plants and sent silent apologies for trampling them further. When we arrived at the shore, the *Svapna* sat upon the narrow strip of beach that remained. It listed to the port side and faced backward, the bow aimed out at the water. The mizzen mast had snapped halfway up. A long gash scored the starboard side, large enough that I could see into the cabin. Detritus floated in the bay, which looked utterly serene. There was no sign of the dock. Without the presence of the boat, I wouldn't have known that we stood in the same harbor we'd put into the day before.

Rune walked up to the *Svapna*, placed the palm of one hand upon it, and touched his forehead to the hull. Halli, Somya, and I exchanged grim looks. Paasha leapt off Halli and found her way onto the deck.

Somya took a step toward Rune. "Should we—"

"Best give him a minute," Halli said softly. "Let's see what we can recover from the water." They rolled up their sleeves and splashed out into the bay.

Somya and I followed Halli's example. A ray of sunlight broke through a gap in the clouds, and a bright gleam caught my attention. I waded in its direction through the waist-high water and discovered one of our bikes. I looked around in a panic. If one of them had washed out, what about the other? And the rest of our gear? For a moment, I wanted to sink into the water. No boat. No bikes. No way to keep going. Perhaps our venture had been cursed from the start. If I hadn't gotten sick and we'd left with the regatta, we wouldn't have gone so far off course. Or if we'd had more time, if this had happened in Loka, we could have had new equipment fabricated. Self-recriminations threatened to drown me. Rune stood in the same position, and I forced back rising tears. The *Svapna* had taken a lot of damage. I was selfish to think of the Anthro Challenge when the storm had caused pain to everyone. I dragged the bike back to shore.

Somya joined me with one of our bedrolls. They put a hand on my shoulder. "Don't."

"Don't what?" I asked through clenched jaws.

"Go over the cliff. I can see you hanging from the edge. We'll find a way through this."

*"How?"* I hissed. "The *Svapna* is going to need major repairs. We might have lost half our gear. *How can we possibly find a way through this?"*

Somya recoiled, and I felt a stab of guilt for lashing out. This wasn't their fault, and I knew that, but their equanimity made them an easy target. They shook their head, brief and rapid, like Paasha when she got splashed with seawater.

"Because we have no other choice," Somya said.

After a gentle squeeze of my shoulder, they turned and waded back into the bay. Halli had accumulated a small heap of wood high up the beach, on a matted section of the greenery. I recalled something about tidal forces. I couldn't tell if we were at low or high tide, and if we guessed wrong and left our things too close to the water, they would all get washed away again. I dragged the bike farther and left it near Halli's pile.

I channeled my frustration into my motions, using it to power me through the next few hours as we removed everything useful that we could find from the ocean's grasp. At some point, I noticed that Rune had joined our efforts. It made sense. The wood he needed to repair the boat was the same wood that had washed out during the storm, including the downed trees and branches that could replace what we couldn't recover.

We worked in silence, lost in our thoughts. Somya had no jokes. I offered them a quiet apology at one point, and they graciously accepted it, but the light in their eyes had dimmed. We managed to retrieve both solar bikes and our tent. The trailer had disappeared, along with one of our bedrolls and both our daypacks, which had held our spare clothes. I avoided thinking about it. *Get back what you can from the sea today, then worry about tomorrow.*

A little before sunset, Makuya emerged from the brush holding a wooden crate with bowls of hot soup. We sat on a cluster of rocks and sipped gratefully.

"Looks like you'll be here awhile," Makuya said evenly. "We'll be sending some of our island hoppers up to Nitaynoa for supplies. It's the nearest good-size city that has a decent fabricator. Would you like us to bring anything back for you?"

"What's an island hopper?" Somya asked.

"A type of canoe. We use them for local ocean travel, and we always have several ready to go in case of emergencies like this."

Rune and Halli exchanged a glance.

"Could one of us go with you?" Rune asked. "We're going to need quite a few items to repair the boat."

"I'll let you know tomorrow after we finish taking stock of what we need," Makuya said. "The cargo hopper is pretty big, and it can easily carry an extra passenger. Takes about three days each way, plus whatever time our people have to wait around to get what we need. The bigger question is how much you'd be able to bring back for yourselves." Makuya stood and collected our empty bowls. "Come on up to the village before it gets dark. We'll get you a proper meal and a comfortable place to spend the night."

"Thank you," Rune said. He turned to us as Makuya walked away. "I think all three of you should be ready to leave tomorrow."

"Shouldn't we stay and help you with repairs?" I asked.

"No, quite the opposite. I don't know what the people of Nitaynoa have on hand, and if we have to wait for fabrications from orbit, it could be weeks or even months to get the *Svapna* seaworthy again. You can't afford that kind of delay."

"Then we're finished," I said. I failed to keep the dejection from my tone. "You want us to go with Halli so an alloy can take us home."

"That's one option," Rune said.

"What's the other?" Somya asked.

"At Nitaynoa, you find a boat to take you to Tequestan. The regatta will have moved on, but sometimes people decide to stay and enjoy the islands for a while. Tequestan is on the east coast of NorthAm. From there, you can make your way overland to Tongvana on the west coast. That's a popular departure spot for sailing across the Pacific. Another alternative would be to head west from here to SouthAm and over to Guayaquil or Cueva, though the terrain will be less hospitable. Between the jungles and the mountains, you'll have tough going on your bikes, plus the entire way lies in the OOB. The NorthAm route keeps you in Loka. A third alternative—if you get very lucky—is that you find a sailor who's willing to take you through the Cueva strait and across the Pacific."

"What happens if we get to Nitaynoa and there aren't any boats?" I asked.

"Then you make a new plan, perhaps another island hopper," Rune said. He gestured at the *Svapna*. "No journey is without setbacks and detours, not unless you take the easy way and let the alloys fly you around. You have to decide whether the Anthro Challenge is worth the effort. You have close to a hundred days left, if I estimate correctly. A lot can happen in that time. Not all of it will go according to your plans—most of it probably won't, if we're being honest—but if you give up now, you'll never know how far you could've gone."

Somya looked at me and raised their brows. I didn't know how to respond. None of Rune's options had any degree of certainty, and after our disastrous reroute through Europe, I didn't relish the idea of striking out on our own again. Those first few weeks across Asia seemed like another lifetime, simpler and more comfortable. Traversing the mountains with Freni, swimming across the Euphrates—we had done those things on our own, without Rune or Halli. Going by land within Loka would be easier than in the Out of Bounds.

Rune stood and motioned us to get up as well. "I think we've done enough work today. You can sleep on it and decide in the morning, after we know whether there's room for you in the hoppers."

We made our way up to the village and found Makuya, who placed Somya and me with a small family. They shared their meal and their home with us. The evening breeze set the woven walls swaying. A brief squall passed over us, the raindrops muted and scattered by woven mats that formed the roof. Two young children kept us entertained with their relentless questions. The adults told us they would keep watching *In Exile* and that they had signed the pledge.

"What do you want to do?" I asked Somya as we bedded down for the night.

"I think it's our sworn duty to keep going," they said, their serious tone offset by the quirk of their lips. "Why go home when we still have time? Even if we don't finish the Anthro Challenge—maybe especially if we don't—you should see as much of Earth as you can."

I wrapped an arm around them and squeezed. "Thanks, Som. I know you're right, and so is Rune, but I can't shake the depression. I feel sick thinking about the *Svapna* . . . and the bounders . . . and Freni. What if—what if we *should* give up?"

Somya pulled away gently and lay on their back. "When I was nine, we had a storm that flooded our house and many others in our town. People were upset that the alloys hadn't managed the weather better, but I remember the alloys coming a few days before it happened to help relocate all of us and our household items to a safe location. I was annoyed because we were supposed to travel to the beach and instead we had to spend those days somewhere else. The planet has needs, and sometimes they have to take priority over ours. That means we have to accept a certain amount of destruction."

"So you're saying it's fine if we leave a wake of unhappiness because the planet does it, too?"

They grinned at the ceiling. "I guess I am."

I snorted.

They rolled to face me, resting their head on their arm. "What do you want to do?"

"I want to finish the Anthro Challenge with you, and I want to live on Earth for the rest of my life. It's hard to let go of the end goal and make exploration the priority when it was supposed to be a secondary benefit. It's a different kind of giving up, I suppose."

"The paths we walk matter more than the houses we build—my grandmother used to say that. Now, she wasn't a big fan of my parents or me and thought all three of us needed treatment for Aspiration and Avarice Disorder, but I can see how the saying might apply in a different way."

"If our paths matter," I said, "then let's go north. Jungles and mountains in the Out of Bounds might be fun under the right circumstances, but we need to get to Tongvana as quickly as we can."

"You want back on a boat."

I grinned. "Is it that obvious? I know we didn't have mountains or even hills on Chedi, but the ocean—I love it so much. It has personality in a way that the land doesn't. And, you know, I never did get to dive."

"Then let's hope there's room for us on the island hoppers tomorrow." Somya yawned. "I'm dead tired. All that splashing around in the bay was exhausting."

"Good night, Som."

The gentle sound of rain filled the house. It pained me to think that we'd come halfway around the world to face yet another detour and more unknowns. I was beginning to see why so few humans attempted the Anthro Challenge. Could I put the goal aside and learn to enjoy the journey for its own sake? I wasn't sure, especially with Meru hanging over me.

Somya's breathing evened out, but I couldn't sleep. The sound of raindrops stopped. After tossing around for a while, I gave up and tiptoed outside to get some fresh air. Across the clearing, I spotted Rune sitting on a bench with a light shawl over his shoulders. I picked my way over storm-tossed twigs and leaves and sat beside him.

"Can't sleep, either?" he asked.

"No."

A steady breeze had cleared up much of the sky, and the universe dazzled me with its infinite beauty. The rich vein of the galaxy's center ran above us like a crumpled ribbon, the glow broken up by an occasional cloud. Outside of Chedi, the stars had often struck me as cold in their unwavering luminance. On Earth, the atmosphere softened and warmed them, transforming their arrangement into a work of art. The vastness impressed me more from the surface of the planet, where I already felt puny and exposed.

"Do you think we're doing too much damage because of the AC?" I asked softly.

Rune sighed. "Life encompasses creation and destruction. You eat, you make waste, you build houses and vehicles. Even the alloys living in space need to consume a certain amount of resources, though their needs are much less than ours. We can minimize our impact on our environment, but we need to balance that with the joy of living. If millions or even thousands of humans did the Anthro Challenge every year, I would argue that it causes more destruction than the Earth can handle, but the wreckage in the wake of your journey is minimal. The storm has done far worse."

"That's what Somya said."

"You grew up in Chedi, and I imagine you didn't have natural disasters there."

"No."

"It's hard to accommodate the desires of one person and the needs of a group," Rune said. "Sometimes pursuing a dream means causing some harm along the way. Only you can decide if the benefits outweigh the costs for yourself. Society will make a collective assessment, and it won't always agree with yours, but that doesn't make yours wrong." He glanced sideways at me. "How are you feeling about the show?"

"It makes it harder to give up on the Anthro Challenge," I admitted. "Not only because of the pledge—that's really important—but also because people are watching us." I lay back on the bench and stared upward. "I knew from the start that our journey would be well documented, but I didn't expect that they'd go live with the show so soon. I guess it builds more excitement this way since nobody—not even Nara—knows whether we'll succeed. I guess we have to, though. How can I quit now? I can't be forever known as the person who abandoned the AC and ruined a great chance for exile reform. People will hate me."

"Something I've learned in my seven decades of life—the public has a very short attention span. Alloys can remember a lot thanks to their extended memory, but that doesn't mean they care. If you have to postpone the challenge until later in your life, they'll pay attention to the sequel. Some will try to follow your activities in between, but most will move on to something else. Plus, your failure could generate as much discussion as your success in the near term. People have pledged to vote for exile reform if you finish the AC, but they haven't done the opposite. They can still support it."

"I figured that voting against was implied."

"You never know. If the movement takes on a life of its own, your actions here might not have such a big impact."

Rune's logic didn't make me feel better. I liked the idea of our journey having a significance beyond our own lives. The pledge allowed me to take charge of my destiny. Rather than being the child who was made for Meru, people would know me as the person who helped reform the practice of exile. Thanks to Nara's work, the Anthro Challenge meant that Somya and I could sway millions of voters—or however many had signed the pledge. If we succeeded, we could hold on to that influence, use it to make other positive changes on Earth.

Makuya had mentioned changes to the rules for the Out of Bounds, too. The OOBers also lived in a kind of exile. They weren't entirely removed from society like the alloys, and they didn't lose their memories, but many of them had left their families and way of life behind in Loka. If the law could change regarding alloys, perhaps it could also accommodate a different culture in the OOB. It could feed into Somya's dream of establishing a new kind of society there. There were so many potential benefits to finishing the Anthro Challenge.

I sighed aloud, and Rune laughed gently.

"I'm sorry. I was trying to relieve you of pressure, but I think my words had the opposite effect."

I smiled. "Not your fault." I sat up and faced him. "Thank you for helping us. We couldn't have made it this far without you."

He made a dismissive gesture. "I'm sure you would've found a way, but I appreciate the sentiment. It has truly been my honor and privilege to accompany you. I can't think of a better use of my time."

I looked upward again. Somewhere out there orbited the many exiled alloys who had broken the laws of the CDS. "I hope we make it worth your while."

"Don't think of it that way. No matter what happens, no matter where in this universe you end up, you will carry these experiences with you. Let that be its own reward."

I knew he was right, but I struggled to feel it. I could appreciate the wonders of Earth, but would that counterbalance the disappointment if I failed to complete the AC? I'd started out doing the challenge for myself and Somya, but in that moment, my original motives seemed selfish and immature. My life—whether it continued on Earth or Meru—had little importance compared to those affected by exile.

# DAY 68

The next day, we learned that the island hoppers could carry Halli, Somya, and me. They were willing to take our bikes and salvaged gear on the cargo hopper since it was a one-way voyage for me and Somya. Saying goodbye to Rune brought me to tears. I could've spent the rest of my life on the *Svapna* with him, sailing all over the Earth, but instead, I had to leave him with a broken boat. He gave me and Somya long, tight hugs and told us to keep our eyes on the horizon. At least we had Halli's company for a few extra days.

Sailing on the outrigger canoes was a different experience from our Atlantic crossing. Halli, Somya, and I rode in three different boats and learned what we could along the way. It felt disconcerting to sit so close to the water, but I got used to it after a few hours. Although they had access to the public alloy network, the locals navigated using landmarks and ocean currents. The sailing principles were the same as anywhere else, and it didn't take me too long to learn the new mechanics. At night, we'd shelter at one of the many small islands in the Caribbean.

On our third day, we reached Nitaynoa. My heart sank as our three hoppers pulled ashore. The lone dock that formed the harbor sat empty, not a single boat in sight. We should have expected it. Nitaynoa lay within the borders of Loka. Most of the humans who lived there would never leave the island, and the few who did would get carried by alloys.

"Now what?" I asked aloud as we off-loaded our things.

"Maybe I could bring back one of these hoppers after we deliver what Oloubera needs," Halli offered. "I could sail you to Tequestan, then return the craft. It'll take time for Rune to make repairs to the *Svapna*, and he can spare me for a week or two."

After some consideration, Somya and I agreed that it was a good backup plan. The Oloubera sailors said that it would pose no problems for them. I chafed at the idea of more lost time, though, and hoped in my heart that luck would bring us a boat in the meantime.

We parted ways with the Oloubera sailors and made our way into the island's main city, which bustled with morning activity. Halli led us to a marketplace, where several humans—a mix of locals and OOBers, judging by the clothing styles—stood in a line in front of a construct that took fabrication orders. Halli joined the queue while Somya and I picked through a general-goods depot. We found some items to replace what we'd lost and also to build a makeshift trailer. Nitaynoa tolerated OOBers, but we didn't want to push our luck while we waited, so we planned to spend our days in the wilderness. From there, we made our way to a community garden, where we filled our new daypacks with food.

By the time we finished that, the sun had dropped close to the horizon. The three of us walked away from the city center to find a place to camp for the night. A little to the west, we came across the start of a vast ocean-crossing aqueduct. We stopped at the base of a causeway that sloped upward about a hundred meters into the sky, where it leveled off. A plaque near the start of the ramp gave us general information about the structure.

The aqueduct system spanned much of Human Era NorthAm, especially the United States, and was built centuries earlier as part of an effort to mitigate the changing climate. The structure was considered low priority for rehabilitation due to its elevated location and organic nature. Massive plant-based pylons grew downward for support. The people back then had engineered the megastructure to repair itself, but as with anything organic, it had failure modes. No one had maintained the hydrophobic layer that had kept the water contained, and the surface had turned porous over time. Visitors were allowed to climb up and look around, but the sign cautioned that parts of the aqueduct might have gaps and to tread carefully.

I looked at Somya. "We have to go."

"Of course," they said. "If it can be climbed, we must climb it."

That had been our motto back on Chedi, and it pained me to think how many times we'd set it aside on Earth so we could push on with the AC. Since we had to wait around for a boat, we had an excuse for the diversion.

We left our things at the bottom and walked up the causeway. It was wide enough for the three of us to stroll side by side with room to spare. The higher we got, the more we could see of the rest of the island. The city of Nitaynoa nestled against the sea in the distance, the domed earth houses resembling a cluster of mushrooms in a bed of greens. Halfway up, I regretted not using the bikes, though it would've meant leaving Halli behind.

By the time we reached the top, all three of us were breathing hard and covered in sweat. The ramp had been made of plant fibers and clay, but the surface at the top was very different. It had a pale-green tinge and felt springy underfoot. Reddish-brown rootlike structures threaded through it. The same material curved upward on either side, forming a channel. We took our first steps tentatively. The structure held beneath us. After a few minutes, we spotted the first gap—a hole about thirty centimeters wide that penetrated all the way through, exposing the distant ground below. We gave it a wide berth.

I leaned against the southern wall and peered down. "This is amazing. To think that humans built this . . . and now most of us wouldn't even understand how it works."

"Remember why," Halli said. "Those people couldn't craft the elements like the alloys can today. Instead of learning to live in the hospitable zones, they chose to build things like this."

"It looks like this duct crosses the ocean," Somya commented. "I wonder how far it goes?"

"According to the plaque, they cover a lot of NorthAm," I said.

"Do you think we could ride our bikes on these," Somya asked, "instead of waiting to take a boat to Tequestan? It wouldn't violate the terms of the AC since the aqueducts are from the Human Era."

"You won't have a map without network access," Halli said.

Somya smiled. "That's okay. We know how to navigate by the sun and stars now, and we can follow landmarks. As long as we head west and north, we should get to the NorthAm mainland."

"It would save us some time," I said, thinking as I spoke. "We could cover the same daily distance on the bikes—maybe more since the ducts are level, and they're wide enough to camp on."

Somya met my gaze and raised their brows. I couldn't help a little thrill of excitement. As much as I loved being on the ocean, I didn't relish the idea of sitting around waiting for a boat. I much preferred to take our journey into our own hands.

The sun sank behind us as we made our way down to our bikes. When we reached the ground, we stood in awkward silence.

"I guess this is goodbye," Somya said. They embraced Halli briefly and stepped back.

It was my turn. Halli wrapped their sturdy arms around me and said softly, "I'll miss you."

"Same," I said.

We held each other for a few extra beats. As they turned to walk away, I asked them to wait. I rummaged in my sack and pulled out my wrinkled sketchbook.

"Here, something to remember me by," I said.

"But where will you draw?"

I flashed a smile at Somya. "I have another book that's only partially filled. I can use that one."

Halli held the notebook to their chest and bowed. "I'm honored." They gave us a nod and walked away toward the city.

Somya's hand landed lightly on my shoulder. "You like them." It wasn't really a question.

"I do."

"As more than a friend?"

"I don't know." I sighed. "It doesn't matter now. Come on. We should get moving. We don't have a lot of light left to get to the top and set up camp for the night."

I swung my leg over my bike and started up the ramp. I didn't look back.

# DAY 73

We spent the next four days riding, and we didn't see a single person the entire time. By our estimate, there was a descending ramp every hundred kilometers, most allowing access via a human-size valve in one of the sidewalls. Unlike the causeway at the start, these wrapped in a spiral around one of the support pieces. The ones along the ocean crossings ended in the water and weren't worth the effort, as we discovered after making the trek once. Luckily the islands in the area were all within a day's ride, so we could restock our food as necessary. Fresh water was tougher, but we discovered puddles large enough to fill our sacks, probably left over from the hurricane that had hit Oloubera.

Camping posed little trouble, except for the wind. We learned to pitch our tent against whichever sidewall provided more shelter. It rained on us once, for an hour or so during the day. The roots turned slippery, but the spongy base grabbed our tires harder and compensated. We covered ground as fast as we had in Asia, riding for about eight hours each day. The first day was the worst in terms of sore bottoms and muscles. Rune had insisted that I take a breather with me, and I used it whenever we had access to enough water. My pain level had pretty much gone to zero by then, but with the sudden exertion, I didn't want to take any chances.

On the morning of New Year's Eve, we rode across a fairly large island. Going by our map book, we guessed that it was Cubao, which meant we had a little over one hundred kilometers to the mainland.

"Less than half a day's ride," I said to Somya as we finished lunch.

To our east, clouds gathered on the horizon, and judging by the wind, they would eventually catch up to us.

"Maybe we can find shelter from the rain before it gets here," I said.

Somya nodded, their gaze fixed on the aqueduct behind us. They raised a hand to shade their eyes. "Do you see something moving back there?"

I peered in the same direction. "No, but your eyesight's always been better than mine. Maybe it's an animal?"

Somya laughed. "You'd like that, wouldn't you? Why would an animal come up here?"

"It could be lost."

I tried to recall what kind of fauna lived in this part of Earth.

"Whatever it is, I think it's heading toward us," Somya said. After a minute, they added, "It does look like it's walking on four legs."

"Hah! See, some poor creature wandered up a ramp, maybe in search of food, and we'll have to help it get back down." I grabbed their arm. "Som, maybe it's a horse! I remember reading that NorthAm has wild horses."

Somya packed up the last of our lunch items and swung a leg over their bike. "We may never know."

I started pedaling with reluctance. "Let's ride slowly. Maybe it will catch up."

"Aks—"

"We have plenty of daylight to reach Tequestan."

"Fine."

I looked backward every few minutes to check if the figure had gotten closer. It grew larger every time, and it definitely had four long legs. After a while, I could resolve enough detail to see that it wasn't a horse, much to my disappointment, and also that a human rode on its back. Perhaps a construct or alloy taking someone for a joyride? The aqueduct seemed like an unlikely destination for such a thing, but I didn't know enough about Earth to judge.

Eventually, the two of them were close enough that it felt rude to keep pedaling. We stopped to drink water and waited for them to catch up. The rider had medium-brown skin and dark eyes, with dark curly hair in a close crop. The four-legged creature was nonliving so I guessed it was a construct. To my surprise, no identifying information about either of them came up in my visual.

"Hello," Somya said with a smile.

The stranger came to a halt and gracefully swung to the ground. She introduced herself as Toypurina, and we responded with our names.

"It's an unusual but pleasant surprise to see others up here," she said. "What brings you this way?"

"And your companion is?" I asked, as delicately as I could in the face of her rudeness.

"Oh, this?" she said. Her round face broke into a smile. "Not a companion. A walker—a type of machine." She placed a hand on its back, which came up to her shoulder. "It's something of an heirloom, but it gets me around."

On closer inspection, I noticed that the legs had a similar construction to Lumo's walker-wagon. Perhaps the two devices came from the same era. The shape of the body resembled that of a horse, but in place of the head, it had a riser with a crossbar attached, kind of like the handlebars on our bikes.

"We're making our way to the mainland," I said, answering her question without giving away any real information. "What about you?"

"I'm returning from an annual pilgrimage. I come to Cubao every year to honor one of my ancestors and spend time with distant relatives."

"Do you live in Tequestan?" Somya asked.

Toypurina laughed. "Oh no. I have a long way to get home. I live on the west coast of NorthAm."

"We're headed that way, too," Somya said.

I tried to keep my exasperation from showing. We didn't know yet how much we could trust this person. At least she hadn't recognized us from the show.

"How far can your walker go?" Somya continued. "Perhaps we could travel together."

I groaned inwardly. I knew Somya's *this-person-is-attractive* face all too well.

"I can cover about four hundred kilometers per day at this time of year," Toypurina said. "Less when it's cloudy. What about yours?"

"We aim for about three hundred," I said. "We'd hold you back."

"I don't mind," she said. "I never have company on these journeys. It would be an interesting change to travel with someone."

She straddled her walker and waited for us to get on the bikes. The duct was wide enough for the three of us to ride side by side, but we ended up staggered after avoiding some soft spots. Somya and I had learned that the ground yielded more near a hole. Toypurina had clearly figured it out as well.

"So why are you up here?" she asked after a while. "I'm from an independent principality, and my family likes to minimize their involvement with modern ways. We use mounts except for emergencies."

This time, Somya glanced at me for approval before answering. I shrugged. I had no idea what we could offer that would seem plausible, but given Toypurina's attitude, perhaps we could trust her with the truth.

"Have you heard of the Anthro Challenge?" Somya asked.

"No."

After our explanation, Toypurina's demeanor didn't change. If anything, she seemed excited and impressed by what we were trying to do.

We spent the rest of the ride answering her questions about the places we'd seen and the troubles we'd faced along the way.

"I was here for the big storm," she said. "It wasn't so bad by the time it reached Cubao, but we still got plenty of wind and rain. Makes for nice travel conditions up here, though. When the lattice goes dry for a long period, the surface deteriorates in more places."

"The lattice?" Somya said.

"That's what we call the waterways. From orbit, they look like a giant lattice, and they go everywhere. I stay on them for most of my journey."

"All the way to the west coast?" I asked.

"Yes. You can reach many parts of NorthAm via the lattice. During the catastrophic years, people needed to move water around a lot, and then later, when the rivers were being rehabilitated, the lattices were the best way to distribute rainfall."

Riding on the elevated ducts had made our lives much easier, too. We didn't have to worry about unfriendly humans or hiding our gear at night, and with Toypurina at our side, we wouldn't get lost. The only downside was the climb down and back up when we had to resupply.

"We're trying to get to Tongvana so we can find another sailboat and continue across the Pacific," I said. "Do you know the way there?"

She laughed. "Yes, that's where I live. I'm happy to guide you."

Somya's face lit like it had when I said that Freni could go farther with us. I hoped that this time, things would end on a better note for my heartsib.

# DAY 80

Over the next week, we made good progress. Toypurina knew exactly where to go, which was a big help because the lattice followed topographic contours rather than a grid, making navigation a challenge. Toypurina—or Toya, as she preferred once we got to know each other—had made the journey enough times to know the way. She had marked some of the junction points with cloth during her first attempt, and the faded strips still hung in place.

When we arrived above Kado, we were about a third of the way to the west coast. We took turns with the supply runs, leaving one person with the bulk of our gear while the other two descended. At Kado, Somya stayed behind. As Toya and I rode down the spiral ramp, I got a better look at our surroundings. The land stretched out in every direction, flat as a geometric plane. From our position, all I could see were the tops of trees. They swayed in a rising breeze as clouds gathered in the sky above us. We'd experienced two rains already, both fairly heavy but also brief. The first time, I'd worried that the duct would fill up and we would have to stop riding until the weather cleared. Instead, most of the water had fallen through the spongy surface, leaving our ride wet but doable. Toya explained that the root structures solidified below us, forming a sort of pipe to carry the water. Every hole allowed that water to escape, though, so the aqueducts didn't function as well as they once had.

Using my bike and her mount, we descended quickly. We left our rides at the base of the ramp and headed into Kado on foot. The buildings in town looked so much like Vaksana that it reminded me of my parents. Chedi should have passed by Earth several days earlier, which meant that my maker and mother would have briefly reunited. I wondered what they thought of our adventures, and part of me wished I could spend a day with them.

I missed Halli's company more. Somya had worked their charms on Toya—no surprise—and the two of them had grown close. She had a more even temperament than Freni. During the day, she made a point to include me in conversations. Toya had a wide-ranging knowledge of the people and places we passed, but she didn't share the love for fauna that Halli and I had.

We approached a community garden after dark and didn't see any people around.

"Do you want to get the produce or the dried goods?" Toya asked.

I chose the latter. A modest storehouse squatted near the vegetable beds. In addition to picking up millet, cornmeal, and dried beans, I riffled through the selection of clothing. We were gradually accumulating items to replace what we'd lost to the hurricane. I found a hip-length shirt woven with bright geometric patterns that fit me, so I added it to my sack. A beautiful matching skirt tempted me, but it would have been impractical for riding, so I left it and grabbed a pair of simple brown leggings instead.

I emerged from the storehouse and scanned the area for Toya. A flash of light caught the corner of my eye. The clouds were soaked in deep purple and limned by the golds and pinks of sunset. A streak of lightning traced its way from one mass to another. I hurried over to Toya.

"Almost done?" I asked her. "We should try to get back before it starts to rain. That must be why no one's here."

"Yes. I was going to pick some custard apples, but we don't really need them."

We kept a brisk pace back to the lattice. Lightning illuminated the sky above us every few seconds, and thunder rumbled menacingly, but no rain fell. The wind blew cool and moist at our backs. As we neared the lattice, I noticed a strange gray cloud that stretched vertically between the lattice and the sky. It twisted and writhed like a living being.

I grabbed Toya's arm and pointed at it. "Is that a tornado?"

Her expression filled my stomach with ice. "No, it's smoke. We'd better hurry."

I had seen small fires on Chedi, but the scale of this one defied my imagination. I didn't know what it signified. Going by Toya's reaction, it was nothing good. We ran the rest of the way and rode our mounts as fast as we could up the ramp. The smell reached me first. It tickled my nostrils with its familiarity. After a few minutes, my throat grew dry and irritated, and as we approached the top, my eyes began to water.

Toya held out a hand and forced us to a stop.

"We need something to cover our noses and mouths. Maybe we can rip off the bottoms of our leggings."

I pulled out the new pants from my sack. "How about this?"

The fabric didn't tear easily, but with our combined strength, we split it in two, doused the pieces in water, and wrapped our faces. The makeshift mask didn't help my eyes, but the intense acridity eased from my breath.

At the top, smoke and heat buffeted us. To our right, flames licked at the dry walls of the duct, while clouds of gray and white billowed from the floor. In the other direction, the air was clear. There was no sign of Somya that way, but our campsite lay in the direction of the fire. We rode toward it, yelling out Somya's name. There was no response. We did our best to stay toward the center of the lattice and away from the flames. I coughed and blinked ash from my eyes. Our tent loomed, a triangular shadow, gray upon gray. Toya reached it first. She lifted the flap and ducked inside. I dropped my bike and followed her. Coughs racked both our chests.

Through the haze, I spotted Toya crouching next to Somya's supine figure.

"Help me carry them to my mount," she shouted over the crackle of flames.

I nodded and grabbed Somya's legs. Toya took their shoulders. We managed to drape them over the front of the mount. I held them in place while Toya clambered up. She rode back toward the ramp, against the wind. I grabbed my bike, then hesitated as I spotted the breather. Somya had placed it next to my bedroll, where they always left it ready for me. I stuffed it into my sack and rode after Toya.

Their silhouette faded until I burst out of the smoke. Lightning flashed and threw the scene into unflinching clarity: Somya on the ground, still unconscious; Toya nearby, wiping the soot from my heart-sib's face with the damp pant leg. I flung my bike to the ground and yanked the breather from my sack. With trembling hands, I hooked the hose up to my water bladder, turned it on, and placed the mask over Somya's mouth and nose. Only then did I notice Toya's fingers pressed to Somya's wrist. I met her gaze. I couldn't ask the question out loud.

She nodded at me. "Their pulse is weak, but it's there."

With a shaky breath, I sat back. Time froze as the first drops fell from the sky. *Wake up, Som! You have to wake up!* I stared into the turbulent sky. No indriyas—not surprising considering the weather. Calling for help meant going back to Kado. How long could a person safely be unconscious from smoke? I would violate the challenge if I connected to the network to look up medical information. I thought we had learned all of the essentials, but we'd never considered fire or smoke exposure. Toya still had her hand wrapped around Somya's wrist.

*What should I do?*

I closed my eyes. The Anthro Challenge wasn't worth my best friend's life. I formed the thought-command to activate my public network access. A cough interrupted me. My eyes snapped open. Somya had rolled onto their side. Their eyes were open, and their arms propped up their torso as spasms shook them. They yanked off the mask and retched. When they finished, Toya held her water bladder up to Somya's lips. They sipped, spit, and broke into another coughing fit. After catching their breath, they pulled the mask back on. I burst into tears.

Somya pulled me into a hug. "I'm all right," they rasped. "It's all right."

I wept into their shoulder for a minute before calming myself. Somya smiled wanly as I pulled back. They turned and embraced Toya as well.

"Thank you," they murmured.

The rain increased in intensity. Our clothes quickly became soaked. The flames died out soon after, but the smoke lingered like a stubborn, unwanted guest.

"We need to get somewhere dry," I said, shivering in the cool night air.

Somya tugged on Toya's sleeve. "Your tent—still in your pack."

She nodded. "I'm glad, but it would be better to get you away from the lattice. If the wind shifts, it could blow smoke this way."

"We could head to the bottom of the ramp," I suggested. "Some of the ground below will be protected from the rain."

Toya nodded. "Good idea. Let's you and me go back and get your bedrolls and cooking gear."

"I can help," Somya said, starting to rise.

Toya pushed them firmly back down. "You need to give your lungs time to clear out all that smoke before you exert yourself. Akshaya and I can handle it."

We left Somya with an *I-don't-like-this* expression on their face. The wind picked up and blew raindrops into my eyes. Wispy gray smoke swirled like fog around us. At the campsite, we didn't bother loading up the makeshift trailer, instead shoving the essentials into the storage bags on the flanks of Toya's mount. We returned for Somya—they rode atop the walker with Toya—and made our way carefully down the wet, slick surface of the ramp.

By the time we had a pot of millet and beans cooking, my stomach rumbled like the last of the thunder. I had crushed many of the fruits and vegetables in my earlier rush to stow the breather, and the combined flavors made for a strange but not terrible stew. The warmth of it soothed my raw throat.

"Ahh, that natural smoked flavor," Somya commented with a grin.

Toya and I laughed. My heart lightened to see Somya's good mood. The fire had been a close call, but if they could crack jokes, they would be fine. We had less than ten days until we reached Tongvana. I closed my eyes and sent a silent prayer to anything in the universe that was listening: *No more surprises, please.* Reaching the west coast was only the first milestone. Once there, we would have to find a boat and a captain who was willing to take us not only across the Pacific but across the equator via the Out of Bounds. *One problem at a time,* I reminded myself as we crammed three bodies into Toya's single-person tent.

# DAY 84

"This is one sight you cannot miss," Toya insisted. "It's worth a few extra hours, especially since today is Akshaya's birthday."

We arrived at Jadnut-Udebiga four days after the fire. Other than a nagging cough and more sleep than usual, Somya seemed fine. On the first day, Toya and I had forced Somya to ride on her walker while I towed their bike. Under the extra weight, the trailer didn't hold together as well as the fabricated one, and I had to stop periodically to tighten the fastenings.

"I'm returning the favor," I'd said, thinking back to our journey from Laietan to Nuberia.

We'd had to abandon the tent. In spite of the overnight rain and wind, it reeked of smoke, and none of us could imagine sleeping in it again. After that first night, I decided to let Somya share Toya's tent without me. My decision had the double benefit of giving everyone a little more room and allowing the two of them some privacy. Fortunately, the storm was brief, and we'd had clear skies since then, so bedding down in the open wasn't too uncomfortable. The nights were chilly, but they never got too cold, not like the temperatures we'd experienced in the OOB portions of Europe.

Jadnut-Udebiga lay in the middle of a long, dry stretch of land. The lattices had delivered water to these parts of NorthAm once upon a time, transforming an area that had been a desert into a more subtropical zone. Low-growing shrubs dotted the landscape, and convoluted rivers meandered through folds in the earth. We'd gained altitude, but the real mountains lay ahead of us, to our west, their peaks gleaming with snow.

Toya led us to the entrance of the famous caverns. She held Somya's hand as we walked down a zigzag ramp. A cabinet at the bottom contained gloves and shoe covers. Oils, dirt, and bacteria could affect the growth of the cave's formations, and a printed sign instructed us to stay on the walking path and avoid touching anything.

For the first few minutes, we had the whole place to ourselves. I felt like I'd entered another world. Crystalline stalactites descended from the ceilings while conical stalagmites rose from the ground. Here and there, massive columns—bigger than I could wrap my arms around—had formed where the two had fused. Tubes of bioluminescence in pinks, greens, and blues lit the formations in gentle hues that complemented their natural grays, whites, and browns.

We walked into a second chamber, where a couple of midsize alloys with elongated faces and webbed feet stood well away from the path. They turned to look at us.

<Do you know who they are?> one flashed to the other in phoric.

<None of them has their network active,> the other replied. <I don't think they're here for research.>

<Why else would they come?>

<Why do you care? They're just humans. By the way, I'm not finding any sign of algae in this region, but there's quite a bit of HFA precipitate. Can you scan for microbial activity, especially those that oxidize iron and arsenic?>

The first one turned back to the surface in front of them. Their conversation shifted to their work and a bunch of scientific terms that I didn't recognize. I was tempted to flash a retort to them, something to the effect of humans having more right to these caverns than a couple of alloys, but I resisted the urge. I had done enough harm with my accidental reveal at the hot springs. Unlike the bounders, two fully networked alloys could spread the news of my chromatophores to everyone in the CDS at the speed of light. I didn't want to imagine what would happen after that.

Somya, Toya, and I continued on, winding our way past calcite formations that ranged from needle sharp to pillowy round. Some locations had small plaques with whimsical names like "Hall of the White Giant" and "Chocolate High." If we'd had our public network access enabled, we might have found tags with all kinds of additional information. I mentally added Jadnut-Udebiga to my list of places to revisit.

We stopped at the lowest point—Lake of the Clouds—and listened to the slow chime of water drops echoing around us. I walked a little ahead of the other two, and when I turned back, Somya and Toya were wrapped in a kiss. Their relationship had a gentleness compared to the one Somya and Freni had shared, one that I didn't mind so much, though it did sometimes make me feel lonely. Toya didn't act threatened by my close friendship with Somya, and she seemed to like me as well, but I couldn't help missing Halli in that moment. I'd liked them best of all our traveling companions, and I regretted that I would never see them again. Did that mean something more than friendship? I still had no answer for Somya's question.

I left my friends to their romantic moment and strolled along the textured pathway. Like everything around me, the surface under my feet was either damp or wet. Moisture infused every breath. I shivered as I ascended a narrow staircase. Toya had insisted that we wear some extra layers and hats. I was grateful for that. I hadn't realized how cold a cave system could get. It reminded me of the ice shield in Chedi's outer hull, and I felt a sudden longing to be back there again, sitting on a walkway with Huy and Cariana with nothing to do but pass the time.

I shook myself free of nostalgia and focused on my surroundings. Earth had such wonders. Would Meru have anything like this? Even if it did, Meru didn't have enough population for someone to make such a cavern easily traversable for humans. Why would my mother want humankind to inhabit a planet so devoid of beauty and wonder? But as I came back in sight of my friends, it occurred to me that few people on Earth cared to see these marvels. The cave should have been filled with visitors. Instead, it sat empty and largely neglected.

Did my mother really think Meru could harbor a society that made room for human curiosity without the associated damage? And if not, then what did that say about someone like me? Was I a danger to Earth? The Anthro Challenge had imperiled several lives, including mine, but we hadn't caused much harm to the planet. Why couldn't we build a more tolerant human society on our home planet? The OOBers, including people like Halli, already lived without much alloy assistance or interference. Lumo and the other bounders traveled without trashing the places they went. Humans had changed a lot since the Alloy Era began. Couldn't we change a little more, recover some of our ambition without rolling our natures all the way back to our destructive origins?

"What do you think of it?" Toya asked as she reached my side.

"Amazing," I said. "I wish more people could experience it."

Somya squeezed past me, took three steps, and slipped. Their arms windmilled for a moment, then they fell backward into the lake and disappeared under its surface.

"Somya!" I cried out at the same time as Toya.

She acted faster, wading into the water as I stood and stared. Somya's head popped up a moment later, then their torso. Toya took them by the hand and hauled their dripping body out.

Somya lay on the slippery path and coughed. "I'm fine."

Toya and I frowned at them.

"Really, I'm okay. A bruised ego at worst, and plenty of shame to go with it."

"Be more careful," I scolded. I didn't know what else to say.

Toya heaved Somya to their feet. Somya winced. Their hand gripped Toya's arm as they grimaced, tried to put weight on their left leg, and hissed with obvious pain.

"I don't think I can walk," Somya admitted. "Sorry."

Toya frowned. "Akshaya, help me support them."

We each looped an arm under Somya's shoulders. Using us as supports, they took a few tentative steps, putting almost no weight on the bad leg.

We made our way out of the cavern with excruciating slowness. The alloys had disappeared by the time we reached the second to last chamber. I was grateful for that. If they had noticed Somya's injured state, they probably would have tried to help us. We returned our gloves and shoe covers and emerged under a sky blazing with deep-pink streaks from the setting sun.

"Aside from Somya's leg, that was a perfect outing," I said.

"Don't worry, I'll be fine," my heartsib said. "Happy birthday, Aks."

The tension in their back muscles told me something different.

"Happy birthday," Toya added.

"Thank you both."

On Chedi, our village would have hosted a small celebration, and my parents might have given me some small items, like hand-picked fruit or a new set of clothes. Somya would have come up with some fun new challenge for us. I hadn't wanted to call attention to the date because I feared that Toya would find it awkward, and it wasn't like we could do much to celebrate, but the caverns had exceeded any birthday I could think of.

"Let me take a look at your leg," Toya said.

Somya sat on the ground while she gently probed their foot, ankle, lower leg, and knee.

"I can't tell if you've broken anything, but it seems possible," she said. "Just in case, we should make a splint for it."

"A what?" the two of us said in unison.

"It's a way to immobilize a broken bone. We'll need some fairly straight pieces of wood and some strips of cloth."

We continued back to our campsite. As we walked, we scanned the ground for sticks that met with Toya's approval and gathered them in our packs. By the time we got Somya up to the top of the lattice, night had fallen, and Toya had to work by the dim glow of a lantern. We sacrificed a shirt for the splint. Toya tied the wood into four bundles, and with my help, used the remaining cloth to secure them around Somya's leg.

"When we get to Tongvana," she said, "my relative who is a doctor can take a better look, but until then, no more walking or pedaling. If it is broken, you could make it worse."

Somya shot me a mortified look. "I'm sorry, Aks."

"It was an accident," I said. "Nothing to apologize for."

I tried to keep my tone light and pushed away the questions that had risen in my mind. Would Somya be able to ride the walker? Would I have to tow them on the trailer with their bike? Could I handle that, and if so, how much would it slow us down? Could the trailer handle the weight? Even if it worked well enough on the lattice, we'd be back on the ground for the final stretch to Tongvana. Would it hold together over bumpy terrain? *That's a problem for another day,* I told myself. Before that, we had to cover another thousand kilometers.

# JAYANTHI (DAY 87)

Jayanthi wished she could hold Akshaya on her birthday and tell her child how much she loved her. She reviewed the most recent footage from Nara one more time. After the fire, Somya seemed to recover quickly, but they had injured their leg during the visit to the caverns with their unknown companion. Reshyan's aerial recordings showed Somya with their leg in some kind of binding, while Akshaya gamely pulled the trailer. Worry creased Akshaya's expression like folds in the land.

Jayanthi quelled her concerns and recorded a message for Vaha. Chedi had passed Earth thirteen days earlier and was now only two hours away at light speed, so they could communicate a lot more often, but it was too long for real-time exchanges.

"Remember the fire from a week ago?" she said after some initial pleasantries. "We saw that Somya inhaled quite a bit of smoke. It looked like they had recovered, but now they've done something to their leg. Akshaya is pulling the trailer with the extra weight of Somya's bike. I'm not sure where they are headed, but I'm guessing it's somewhere along the west coast of NorthAm. At their current pace, they should arrive in the next few days. I discussed the situation with a medical constructed mind, and they recommend that Somya get their leg examined." Jayanthi chose her next words carefully. "If they've broken a bone, it will heal badly without treatment. We can't know that unless they get a scan, but I doubt they'll do so while they're in Loka. Vaha, you need to discuss this with Gamo and Zohel. It's their call whether to stop Somya from continuing on the challenge. This isn't a life-threatening emergency, but it could have long-term consequences for Somya, including extensive medical therapy later on. I've included some relevant snippets of the recordings, with Nara's permission. Let me know what Gamo and Zohel want to do."

Four hours later, Jayanthi received a reply. Her visual display showed Vaha and Somya's parents sitting in the second story of the grahin. Zohel's lips were compressed to the point that the color barely showed.

Gamo leaned forward, resting their elbows on their bent knees. "I'm conflicted. If we intervene prematurely, we'll void all the progress they've made."

"So what?" Zohel demanded. "They've risked too much already—the river, then the fire, and now a possible broken bone. Are we supposed to wait until they're at death's door? What if they're somewhere in the middle of the Pacific Ocean by then?"

Jayanthi sympathized. Somya's health ought to take priority, but the children had survived everything the Earth had thrown at them. She wouldn't be surprised if they came through their latest difficulty as well. Akshaya would never forgive her if she called off the challenge without sufficient cause. Jayanthi wished her child could understand why Meru mattered so much. She also suspected that forcing the issue, especially via alloy interference, would sabotage any chance of opening Akshaya's mind.

"I don't think we should intervene," Vaha said, as if predicting Jayanthi's thoughts. Zir phores glowed with concern. "I don't know if you've seen it, but many people—alloys especially—have started to follow the journey. A good subset of them are talking about the need for exile reform, and several have already proposed amendments to current policy."

"What does that have to do with making sure our children are safe?" Zohel snapped.

Vaha's phores flashed white.

"I'm sorry," Zohel said. "I know you mean well, but I don't see what a legal or political movement has to do with the current situation."

"I should have made myself more clear," Vaha said gently. "People have pledged to vote in favor of abolishing the practice of exile if Akshaya and Somya succeed in the Anthro Challenge." Zie held up a hand as Zohel started to speak. "That's not our responsibility, of course, but I thought it might be an added incentive to avoid interfering with the AC until we're certain that it's necessary."

Jayanthi knew exactly where Vaha's mind must have gone—to zir friend Kaliyu, convicted of intentionally dropping a contaminant on Meru's surface and trapped in exile for three times the duration of Vaha's. Jayanthi herself had prevented any lasting harm from the contaminant, and Kaliyu had later helped her and Vaha reunite from across the galaxy. Kaliyu's sentence had devastated both of them. If Vaha could free zir friend, zie would do it.

"Did you sign the pledge?" Gamo asked.

"I did," Vaha replied.

Gamo put an arm around Zohel. "Let's trust the children to contact us before the situation gets dire. They've managed a lot of setbacks already. Somya is strong and smart. We can see that they're resting and doing their best to take care of themself."

"I don't like it," Zohel said.

"I know," Gamo said. They drew Zohel in closer. "But we should take it day by day. Jaya, please reply as soon as you have any new information. We'll be on Earth in a week."

The recording ended shortly after. It irritated Jayanthi that Vaha hadn't discussed the pledge with her before signing it, though it didn't surprise her. She'd been so focused on watching the children's journey that she hadn't spent any time looking at people's reactions to the show.

She hoped that Akshaya and Somya didn't know about the pledge. They didn't need additional pressure to finish their ridiculous quest. Jayanthi thought about sending Vaha a message to express her feelings on the matter but decided to look into it first.

Someone had nicknamed it the SomAx Pledge, and the label had stuck. Alloys had connected the dots between the title of Nara's show and the detrimental effects of exile on Jayanthi's family. Fans had dug up other instances of alloys whose loved ones had suffered during their absence from society, and Jayanthi could see momentum building for legal reform. Some proxy voters with a large number of constituents had signed the pledge, and the number of people following *In Exile* had grown along with the reform movement.

Now that Vaha had signed the pledge, she wondered if zie expected her to do the same. On the one hand, she hoped that Akshaya would somehow fail the Anthro Challenge naturally and come quietly to Meru. On the other, she would be glad to see Kaliyu freed. Some other alloys—like Pushkara—not so much, but Kaliyu had redeemed zirself when zie confessed zir crimes in order to convict Pushkara. The pledge's success depended on Akshaya and Somya completing the Anthro Challenge. If Jayanthi signed it, would that make her a hypocrite?

She stood, stretched, and stepped outside for some fresh air. Her old walking route beckoned, and she followed its call to the top of the hill behind her parents' house. The more she'd watched of Nara's recordings, the more she understood her child's fascination with Earth. Seeing the world through Akshaya's travels had revealed treasures that Jayanthi had only read about, if she'd known of them at all. In her own youth, all her thoughts had bent toward space and living like an alloy. She'd ignored the wonders, both natural and human built, that had lain within her reach. Jayanthi could feel her resolve wavering. She'd held on to her dream of Meru for nearly two decades. Was she being unfair in forcing Akshaya to share it?

# DAY 89

Tongvana was the largest city I had seen on Earth. It took us an entire day to ride from the outskirts to the coastal hills where Toya's family lived. Clusters of buildings formed small villages that made up the larger whole, which Toya described as a subsovereign region within Loka. The people of Tongvana could set their own local laws as long as they didn't negatively impact the surrounding ecology. They had chosen not to accept alloy assistance in their daily lives, including their housing, which didn't resemble the structures we'd seen elsewhere. Their homes had strong lines and mud-brick walls, more like Human Era construction, but they favored tapered pyramidal shapes rather than blocky rectangles. Colorful woven tapestries hung from the windows and doorways. Thin tendrils of smoke rose from the larger buildings—the cookhouses, according to Toya—which were shared by multiple families.

"My people lived on this land long ago," Toya said as we rode through a grove of coconut palms. "We were decimated during the European colonization of NorthAm, but enough of us survived to reclaim it after the compact. About two hundred years ago, we submitted a proposal to allow us to resume some of our original ways of life, and it passed. My ancestors knew how to live in balance with the Earth. It took some work to figure out how to do that again, but for the most part, we've succeeded."

We crested a low hill and pulled to a stop. Ahead of us, a wide expanse of sliver-blue spread to the horizon under a wintery sunset. High clouds glowed with hints of pink and gold.

"The Pacific Ocean," Toya announced.

"At last," Somya said. "Now all we need to do is find a boat."

"I think I'll be doing all the finding," I said.

Somya's leg still couldn't bear their weight, and their ankle bulged as if a plum had grown under the skin. Toya's splint hadn't done much in the five days since the accident at the cavern. She had tried to adjust it to wrap around Somya's foot like a boot. When Somya removed their shoe, they couldn't bear the pain of putting it back on. Chedi had always used modern methods for injuries, and her injected microconstructs made repairs within a week or two. I had no idea how long Somya's healing would take with human-era techniques.

We needed to find someone with a sailboat who could carry us across to Australia and Asia, either from Tongvana's harbor or at Cueva, in CentralAm, where the Pacific flowed into the Atlantic. The latter meant an overland journey along the west coast of NorthAm. If I had to tow Somya and our gear and do all the work at camp, we would not make it that far. The alternative was almost unthinkable—to leave Somya behind and continue on my own to Cueva. The likelihood of finding passage from there was higher than in Tongvana. Would the pledge hold if Somya quit the AC? Would the deal with my parents?

*One problem at a time,* I reminded myself.

Toya's family house had several conical rooms connected by sinuous, arched passageways, all made of the same brown clay that lay in the soil around us. She led me to a separate, smaller building and pulled aside a tapestry that hung across a double-wide doorway. The air inside smelled of dried sage, which hung from wood beams that crossed the ceiling.

"You can store the bikes and trailer in here," Toya said.

She parked the walker in an empty space and indicated another gap that would hold our gear. Somya stood awkwardly near the entrance, balancing against the outer wall.

"I'll sort through our things and bring in what we need," I said.

Toya nodded. "I'll help Somya inside."

Somya kept one arm around Toya's shoulders and supported themself with a sturdy stick with the other. As I repacked our clothes and toiletries into our daypacks, a blanket of weariness settled across my shoulders. We were a little more than halfway through our journey. Our days had alternated between interminable tedium and extreme stress. So much had happened that I could barely remember the person I'd been at the start. The urgency of avoiding life on Meru had faded. I was so tired, I wanted to curl up in a ball and never move again.

Instead, I forced myself to my feet, pulled the packs over my shoulder, and walked back toward Toya's home. The first stars sprinkled the deep-blue twilight above. An orange glow marked the line where the ocean met the sky. I inhaled the scent of the sea with a long, deep breath, held it, and let it out. I pulled aside the privacy curtain and stepped into the dim glow of bioluminescence. Mouthwatering aromas of onions, herbs, and other foods I couldn't identify made my stomach gurgle in anticipation.

I followed the sound of voices through one of the curving, arched hallways and into a room. The chamber held two single-width beds and a couple of sling chairs made of some light-colored wood that I didn't recognize. Somya rested upon one of the beds. Toya stood near a window and argued with someone named Pensa. They spoke to each other in a language I didn't know, and Toya's tone was raised in anger, which I hadn't heard before. When they noticed me, both of their expressions cleared.

Toya gave me a tight smile and said in Terran, "Akshaya, please meet my mother. She and I were just discussing the best way to care for Somya."

Pensa walked toward me and held out her hands, palms upward. She was plump with graying black hair and a round face. I placed my hands in hers.

"Welcome to our home," she said. "My life mate has almost finished cooking dinner. Please, join us. Toya will bring food back here for your friend so they can rest." She kept hold of one of my hands and led me through another door.

Toya followed us out into an open courtyard. We crossed it and entered a room with a round dining table surrounded by eight chairs. Two children—I guessed their ages around seven and ten—bustled in and out of the room with their hands full of dishes. I would have preferred a bath before eating, but I didn't want to make everyone wait on me, so I took the chair that Pensa offered. The two little ones were Toya's younger siblings. Another sib who looked close to my age joined us at the table, their gaze distant and focused on their visual. Toya's parents sat down, and Toya reappeared and took the chair beside me.

After some words of gratitude to the land and water, everyone reached out and grabbed a dish to serve themselves. The younger siblings began to argue in loud voices, and the teenager started a conversation with their father. The family seemed unfazed by my presence. No one mentioned the show or the pledge, much to my relief. They asked me a few questions in Terran, but mostly they talked among themselves in their own language. It reminded me of communal dinners in Chedi, and after a while, I relaxed and soaked in the easygoing atmosphere.

Toya leaned close and explained what the dishes were. Two contained fish—something the Tongva people traditionally ate and had special permission to do. I had drunk bhojya that contained nutrients derived from animal products, but I'd never eaten the real thing. Alloys had figured out ways to produce the necessary ingredients for their bhojya without having to hunt and kill. Out of curiosity, I tasted both dishes. The texture of the fish didn't exactly resemble anything I'd had before. A cross between certain mushrooms and chewy breads was the best comparison I could come up with.

The meal ended with more commotion. I tried to help clean up, but Pensa instructed Toya to get me a bath and set me up for bed. Toya led me to an outdoor shower with two private stalls. Somya had washed with a basin in the room so that they didn't have to remove the splint. Toya and I each occupied a stall. Rivulets of brown water ran into the drain at my feet. I rubbed a sweet-smelling liquid into my hair to get the last of the smoke out and scrubbed at the caked dirt under my nails.

As we dried off, Toya said, "I'm sorry about earlier. My mother thinks Somya will need more help than Elogio—our local doctor—can provide. People here expect outsiders to get help from the alloys. Somya won't be under our care for life, and outsiders are . . . there's not an exact word for it in Terran, but it's like a disruption, a thing that throws life out of balance. My mother thinks we shouldn't risk creating more problems."

I put on clean basics—a yellow tunic with brown leggings—and stepped out of the nook. Toya emerged dressed in a white calf-length gown with bright-blue embroidery along the neck and hem. She wrapped her long hair in her towel. My own wet curls had grown a couple of inches and grazed my shoulders.

"Are you saying we'll have to violate the Anthro Challenge to get Somya treated?"

Toya made an apologetic face. "I hope not. I'll talk to Elogio tomorrow and let him know why you need his help. He's a good person. Maybe he can do something for Somya and also ease my mother's concerns." She made a *sorry-about-this* face.

We parted ways, and I returned to my room.

"You smell so clean," Somya said. The grin on their face faded as they caught my expression. "What's wrong?"

With no time to prepare an answer, I relayed what I'd heard from Toya.

"I'm sorry, Aks. If I hadn't gotten careless in the caverns—"

"Stop," I interrupted. "The fire wasn't your fault, and neither was the slip. Rune had to deal with injuries, too. It could have happened anywhere. I caused more problems by getting sick."

"Debatable," they said.

I lay back on the bed and sighed. "I never thought a mattress could feel so soft. Let's wait and see what the doctor says. Maybe we'll get lucky, and he'll pronounce your leg almost better."

"It doesn't matter, anyway. I can sit on a deck with one functional leg. I'm sure I'll be fine by the time we reach Asia and have to bike again."

That assumed we would find a ship. I didn't share my heartsib's optimism, but I had nothing else to hold on to. Outside the window, the stars shone bright enough that I felt I could reach out and touch them. *A disruption.* That's what humans had once been to the entire planet. Too many of us had behaved like Somya and me—driven by ambition and a sense of purpose, needing to make our mark. If we stayed on Earth, if we encouraged a new society to grow in the OOB rather than on Meru, would we repeat the mistakes of the past? Was there a way for people like us to maintain balance, or had our ancestors been right that we had to change our nature?

I thought of my mother, finding her way across the galaxy all alone, a far more dangerous journey than the AC. Space didn't suffer humankind gladly. She had sacrificed—no, she had *deferred* her ambition to give humans like me a place where we could start anew, a place without the burdens of historical injustice. *But also without the legacy of achievement.* That legacy had given birth to the alloys and taken people to the stars. I wanted the Anthro Challenge to mark the beginning of a life of accomplishment on Earth, but I couldn't do that in good conscience, not if my ambitions kept leading to pain and suffering. Neither could I quit, not with the potential reform of exile riding on our success. Would bringing about legal change be enough of an achievement for my lifetime? The changes my mother had wrought in her twenties hadn't satiated her ambition. We shared much of our DNA, so I suspected that I already knew the answer.

# DAY 90

Elogio had the same dark hair, eyes, and complexion as Toya's family. Toya had already explained to him why we couldn't go to the local alloys for help, so he arrived with a handheld scanner and other equipment that I didn't recognize. He unwrapped the splint and probed Somya's leg and feet with his hands. My heartsib winced and went pale. The doctor nodded to himself and scanned the injured area with his device. He held it up and showed us an image.

"Your fibula is broken here, near the ankle, and there is soft-tissue damage as well," he said to Somya. "As a doctor, I can't ethically refuse to help a patient, but I'm also responsible for the people in my community, and we have limited resources. The best I can offer is to lend you a supportive boot and some crutches. You need to keep your weight off the foot for another three to four weeks and spend plenty of time with your leg and foot elevated. Judge your progress by your pain level. You can use a cold pack to help with the swelling and pain." Elogio turned to Toya. "If you would take them to the alloys for modern treatment, they could have Somya's ankle fully healed in five days. Do you really want to put your friend through several weeks of pain?"

"She does," Somya said firmly. "We are not giving up on the Anthro Challenge, not yet."

"Very well. Toya, come with me to the supply building. I'll give you the items that Somya needs."

Elogio beckoned Toya. They left the room, but the earthen hallway wall carried their voices back to us.

"I'm sorry," Somya said.

"Stop apologizing!" I arranged my pillow under Somya's leg. "After Toya comes back, I'm going to ask her where the nearest harbor is."

"What am I supposed to do all day?"

"Rest, like the doctor said."

"Boring," Somya grumbled. "I can't use the network. There's no one to talk to."

I fished out Rune's book. "Here, you can read this again."

Somya shot me a disgusted look as they took it.

"I'll go make us some lunch."

---

A couple of rolling hills sat between Toya's family home and the ocean. We sweated our way along a dirt road, and the midday sun glared from above.

I dabbed at my forehead. "How was it so cool in the morning and now this?"

Toya laughed. "That's winter weather for Tongvana. The air here doesn't hold a lot of humidity, in spite of the marine fog that often rolls in, so the temperature fluctuates a lot each day. Back in the Human Era, the land turned to desert a couple hundred kilometers to the east."

"We haven't passed through any deserts so far," I said. "Northern Europe was really cold and snowy, and everywhere else, we've been in Loka."

"You still are. Don't worry, the alloys make sure it doesn't get much warmer than this. The afternoon breeze will pick up soon and start cooling us off."

She handed me a water sack. I swallowed several mouthfuls before giving it back. We threaded our way between shrubs that grew to shoulder height. Atop the first rise, I paused to catch my breath and was delighted as a family of quail ran in front of me. Sparrows chittered from all sides, and a hawk circled far above. A brown lizard the length of my palm did push-ups on a flat stone. Metallic insect constructs glittered here and there, reminding me that nonliving creatures inhabited this world, too. I wished I had brought the field guide, but not enough to go back and get it. My leg muscles had a pleasant burn going. My body had held up reasonably well, considering the extra weight I'd towed, probably because I'd used the breather whenever possible, but I didn't want to push my limits.

We topped the second hill, and my heart soared at the view. The Pacific Ocean stretched to the horizon, deep aquamarine near the coast and brilliant sapphire in the distance. Tiny white-capped waves swept across the expanse. A large harbor with multiple docks nestled in a sheltered bay. A gloriously double-masted boat floated in one of the slips, and some smaller craft were moored nearby. They looked like toys from our elevated vantage point. Tongvana's harbor could have held a hundred ships. We made our way down to a road and through a small village that abutted the harbor.

"Do you have regattas here?" I asked.

"What's a regatta?"

"A large group of boats that sails together, sometimes as a race," I explained.

Toya shrugged. "I haven't heard of one. I pay my respects to the sea near home, but I don't get up this way very often, so it's possible that I wouldn't know."

"Why else would the alloys maintain such a large harbor?"

"They consider the breakwater and the lighthouse to be historic structures." She pointed at a round white tower that sat upon the end of a long, narrow stretch of rocks that extended from the land in a straight line before bending left via an equally unnatural right angle. "This was once the Port of Los Angeles, one of the largest in NorthAm during the Human Era."

"Do you mind if I talk to someone on the big boat?" I asked.

"Of course not. I'll wait here."

Toya planted herself on a flat-topped stone wall. Gentle waves lapped at its base. I continued until I reached the dock that led to the ship.

From the base of the gangway, I called out, "Hello? Is anyone aboard?"

After half a minute, someone emerged from the cabin, leaned over the railing, and squinted at me. According to the information that appeared in my visual, his name was Kaimi. He was the biggest person I had ever seen, and his deep brown skin gleamed with sweat and oil.

"Hello," I said with an uncertain wave. "My friend and I are looking for passage to Australia and Asia. We're experienced sailors. Any chance you're heading that way and could take us on as crew?"

"I thought you looked familiar," he said. "You're that kid from the show, *In Exile*."

I nodded and hoped that the recognition would work in our favor. "So you know what we're trying to do and why. Will you help us cross the Pacific?"

He waved his arms in a warding gesture. "Sorry. I'm not getting involved in anything illegal."

I tried to think of what he could mean and failed. "We're not doing anything that breaks the law."

"Not yet." He gave me a *you-know-what-I-mean* look. "There's a new law being proposed. It would ban journeys like your Anthro Challenge. A lot of humans in Loka are making noise about it, and I need the goodwill of the people I meet in port. Quite a few of them don't like what you're doing." He shrugged. "Nothing personal. You seem all right, but taking you aboard puts me at too much risk."

I recalled Ebra and her family's reaction to hearing about our journey. It made a kind of inevitable sense that others had found it objectionable after seeing the show. How did their numbers compare to those who had signed the pledge for exile reform?

"Do you know if there are any other boats in the area, or heading this way?" I asked.

"Not without checking the network. Wouldn't that violate your rules?"

"It would," I admitted.

"Plenty of craft pass through here. I'm sure you'll see more in a day or two. Might get luckier with the next one."

I nodded, though my heart sank. "Thanks."

We had seventy-five days to get home and catch Chedi's final shuttle from Earth. Two and a half months to sail across the Pacific Ocean and then make our way back to Vaksana. Based on the estimates we had made with Rune, we couldn't afford to lose another day, but without a boat, we had no way forward.

# DAY 100

For ten days, I'd gone to the harbor every afternoon. Somya would accompany me until their arms got tired from the crutches, and Toya would come along when she didn't have work to do. Most days, I found only small boats, except for another large one that showed up, but its captain gave me the same story as the previous one. People—both alloy and human—had serious objections to the challenge. They didn't like that our wheeled bikes and trailer caused erosion damage. They thought that we used resources in unpredictable ways and endangered lives. Ebra and her family had helped start the protest movement, Toya learned. Unlike the pledge to reform exile, the petition to outlaw the AC wasn't contingent on us finishing it. Alloys took their time to make new laws, often spending decades before enacting change, but there were provisions for emergency measures. How badly did people want to prevent me and Somya from going on, and how many of them felt that way? I wished I could look up the answers.

Somya and I sat in the courtyard and discussed our options. We shared a wide stone bench covered in cushions. Sunshine warmed us intermittently as heavy broken clouds sped by overhead. A cool wind gusted through our sheltered space, but I didn't sense rain in its passing. I marveled at the fact that I had the confidence to predict the weather. Our time on the *Svapna* must have sensitized me to changes in pressure and humidity—another skill I would lose if I had to leave Earth, which appeared increasingly likely.

"You have to leave me here," Somya said. "I'm sure people will honor the pledge if you finish the challenge on your own."

"I looked at the maps this morning," I said. "From here to Cueva is roughly sixty-three hundred kilometers. If I keep a really good pace, I can make it in eighteen days, but more realistically it will take closer to twenty-five. I'll have to do all the work—making and striking camp, cooking, cleaning, towing the trailer on my own. We have only two months. Even if I found a boat to take me across from Cueva, I wouldn't make it home in time."

Somya's expression turned stubborn. "Then we wait here, and you keep checking the harbor every day until it's absolutely too late."

"The more time that passes, the more captains who learn about the anti-AC law and the lower our chances of finding a ride." I shook my head and looked my heartsib in the eyes. "Som, at some point we have to accept that we've failed. I want to finish the challenge, I want to see the pledge go through, but I don't see a reasonable way forward at this point."

"How much longer can we wait here for a boat?"

"Four days."

"Then we don't give up yet." Somya crossed their arms and shot me a *you-can't-change-my-mind* look.

I shrugged. "Okay. I enjoy the walk to the harbor. I'll humor you for a few more days, but nothing will change."

"See you in a few hours."

Somya headed back inside. Toya and her teenage sister were foraging, so I headed out alone. I tried to take solace in the rolling hills and the glorious views of the Pacific. The sea had moods that changed often, sometimes by the hour. The patchy clouds and brisk onshore wind lent the ocean a temperamental air. Waves tossed around white tips, and the water had a deep-silver-gray color that reminded me of oxidized jewelry. I would have to leave all of it behind.

I slowed my steps when I reached the village road. Fisherfolk carried baskets with their catches and walked in the opposite direction. I stopped at a window where the resident handed out tea and coffee to passersby. I requested my usual, a hot spiced coffee. A few houses farther, people queued up for hot fried fish.

A few minutes later, I was holding a cup that warmed my chilled fingers. The aroma of cinnamon, rosemary, a hint of cacao, and steamed milk eased the sting of daily failure. As I swallowed my first sip, I spotted a tall person with a blond braid in the fish-fry line. For a moment, I thought I was dreaming.

"Halli?" I cried. "Is that you?"

They turned toward me, and their startled expression was replaced by a smile like a sunbeam piercing a cloud. Halli closed the distance between us with a few rapid steps and wrapped me in their arms. A bit of coffee spilled on my hand. I laughed in surprise and delight at the unusual display of affection.

"I'm so glad to see you," they said as they pulled back. "We didn't know if you and Somya would be here, and Tongvana is so large. I had no idea where to start looking."

"We? Rune is here, too?"

Halli nodded. "We fixed up the *Svapna* faster than we expected, so we sailed through the strait at Cueva and up the coast. We've searched for you at every port we put into along the way."

"I am so happy to see you," I said. "We've been stuck here for over a week, and the boat captains refuse to give us passage because of a new proposal to outlaw the Anthro Challenge."

Halli nodded. "We've been desperate to find you. Rune and I caught up on the show and all the surrounding activity. I added my name to the SomAx pledge. That's what people are calling it now. I remembered what you told me about growing up in exile, and I figured you'd approve of abolishing the practice."

Tears prickled the back of my eyes. I blinked a few times before choking out a soft word of thanks.

We stepped back into the fish-fry line. People glanced at us with curious expressions. If they recognized me or Halli from the show, they didn't say anything. I lowered my voice and told Halli about Somya's broken leg.

Halli received their paper-wrapped food and turned to me. "Let's go see Rune. He'll be relieved to know that we've found you."

We moved at a brisk pace. I was shivering in the full force of the sea breeze off the exposed harbor when I spotted the *Svapna*, tall and regal in her dock, the only sailboat in sight. I would have known its contours anywhere.

We found Rune belowdecks with Paasha, who greeted me by rubbing against my leg. The old sailor grinned and pulled me into a fierce hug.

"Where is Somya?" he asked.

I repeated the abbreviated story I'd shared with Halli and promised both of them all the details once we set sail. I paused. "That is, if you'll have us aboard."

Rune cocked an eyebrow. "Why else would we have come all this way? We should get going as soon as possible."

"Thank you," I said, overwhelmed by emotion. "I'll head back to Toya's house and tell everyone the good news."

"I'll come and help you," Halli said.

Was there more than kindness to Halli's offer? I put the thought aside. Plenty of time to sort out my feelings while we crossed an ocean.

---

There were no tears when Somya and I said our goodbyes to Toya and her family. The younger children took their leave and returned to their studies. The older sib didn't seem overly bothered, as was their personality. Toya's parents had kind smiles and some small gifts of food and artwork for us. Toya gave Somya a ride on her walker as Halli and I followed on foot with the bikes. I thought of Somya's pain when leaving Freni. Toya and Somya hadn't grown as close, in part because of Somya's limited mobility, but also because Toya had a very different personality. She was more reserved, and she'd kept her distance by staying busy helping her family.

By the time we arrived at the harbor, the sun had dropped behind a mass of clouds on the horizon. Rune heard us on the dock and helped get our gear loaded and secured. The *Svapna*'s hull looked as if the storm hadn't touched it, the new sections of woven wood seamlessly integrated with the old.

Toya hugged me goodbye. Somya handed her the crutches and their boot, along with many promises to sit still after getting settled on the deck. Toya kissed them gently on the lips. I turned away and busied myself with preparing for our departure.

"Safe travels to you all," Toya said as she stepped back onto the dock.

A seagull cried out and landed atop the main mast like a proud mascot. Toya waited until we unmoored and started to motor away. I waved to her one last time and shifted my attention to the journey ahead. We had no margin left for error or natural disaster, but we had the *Svapna* and Rune and Halli. As long as the wind and sea cooperated, we could reach the Hawai'ian islands in ten days. After that, we would turn southwest toward Falealupo and then onward to Vanuatu and Ganjdija. I hoped the Pacific wouldn't live up to its name too much, that we wouldn't get becalmed like the sailboats of old. The *Svapna* had a solar-powered motor, but its top speed was only half of what she could do with a healthy wind in her sails.

I sat beside Somya and put an arm around their waist.

"Feels good to be out on the water again," they said.

I matched their grin. The wind tugged at our hair and carried the scent of kelp and fish and brine. We cleared the breakwater, and the boat began to roll with the waves.

"Guess you won't be needing your sea legs for a while," I said.

Somya grimaced. "It's not my legs I'm worried about."

I laughed. "I'm sure the fish have missed seeing your face over the rails."

They peered down. "Is that right?"

I leaned my head against their shoulder. "We have to finish this, Som. Between the pledge and now this counterproposal, we might never get another chance."

"We will. Don't worry. We've jumped across every hurdle this planet has placed in our way so far, and we'll get over the rest."

I stared out over the endless expanse of the sea. The horizon rose and fell and beckoned us with promises. I intended to make sure it kept every one.

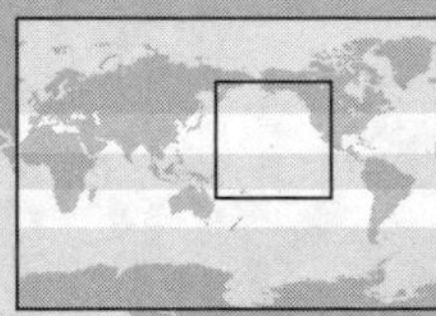

OUT OF BOUNDS
Jadnut-
Udebiga
Tongvana
LOKA
Hilo
Tabakea
OUT OF BOUNDS
Falealupo
Nabouwalu
LOKA

# DAY 111

We came upon the lava flows of Mauna Loa a little before sunset. Glowing blobs of orange oozed from the crusty land and dripped into the sea, creating plumes of white steam where the two met. Halli and I were on shift. Rune was below making dinner, but he popped out after we dropped anchor to take in the view before returning to meal preparations.

Our journey west had taken one day longer than we'd hoped—not bad considering that calm waters had sometimes stranded boats for a week or more. We'd sailed through a couple of minor squalls without incident. The weather had kept the breezes strong and the ocean relatively calm. I hoped it was an omen of good fortune for the rest of our journey.

The route from Tongvana to Hawai'i had kept us within the borders of Loka, and we witnessed alloys in the sea and air, along with native Earth life. I spotted quite a few mola, a flat, elongated fish almost as large as some whales. We'd seen plenty of the latter as well—grays, humpbacks, and a lone blue that stretched almost twice the length of the *Svapna*. Massive pods of bottlenose dolphins would accompany us for up to an hour at a time, their dark black eyes staring with curiosity and intelligence into mine. Stingrays spread their wings and glided through the water like two-dimensional birds. I couldn't wait to get underwater for a closer look.

We decided to anchor offshore for the night and go for an evening dive. Rune thought that I should stay on the boat in case people in Loka recognized me. The released episodes of *In Exile* hadn't caught up to our trek across NorthAm, so even if people identified Rune or Halli, they wouldn't obstruct them the way they might with me or Somya. My heartsib wasn't quite ready to walk off the boat anyway. They had spent the journey on deck because they couldn't descend the stairs into the cabin. The sunshade provided basic protection from the rain, and the cushioned benches at the stern made for a decent bed. Somya's foot had mended quite a bit, though, and they had started walking on it for short amounts of time.

That evening, we dined with the most unique view in the world.

"We're witnessing creation," Rune said. "The union of fire and water produces land and also feeds life. Without magma, the earth would have barren rock."

"That's part of what makes Meru special, too," Halli said. "The level of geothermal activity creates conditions similar to ours."

"And if we leave it alone, one day it might develop complex life," I said.

People had discovered cyanobacteria in Meru's oceans, enough to oxidize the planet's atmosphere to twice the level of Earth's. Moisture, heat, and single-celled organisms formed the basis of evolution, so why would Meru's fate be any different from Earth's? I could understand why so many alloys had voted against allowing people—including humans—to inhabit the planet's surface.

"You could have both," Halli countered. "Evolution on Meru won't stop because of our presence, unless we actively force it to. What if humans could safeguard the life there, nurture it, and watch it grow into greater complexity, like we do here? We could form an entirely new kind of society."

"Like the people of Tongvana," Somya said, "and their philosophy of coexistence rather than maintenance. Instead of seeing ourselves as caretakers, we should act like the integral parts of the environment that we are. Our presence in a place makes us inseparable from it, so rather than isolating and preserving Meru's existing life, we accept that we'll affect it and that it'll also change us."

Halli looked at me. "That's already true of the humans who live there, right?"

I nodded. Why was everyone else more excited by the prospect of living on Meru than I was? *Because for them, it's not an option, much less a destiny forced upon them.*

"So where are we going to dive?" I said, deliberately changing the subject.

"About half an hour away, around the west side," Rune said. He stood and started to gather up the empty dishes. "We should get underway now that the sun has set."

We had two breathers, and Rune felt a little tired, so Halli had offered to take me. Rune promised that the world beneath the surface held at least as much beauty in the dark as it did in daylight. The journey to the dive site took as long as predicted, and we dropped anchor a few kilometers off the coast near an underwater atoll. Halli stripped down to their underwear and pulled on their dive vest. They activated a switch, and the outlines of their garment lit with golden bioluminescence. They pulled the second vest out of the storage bin and handed it to me.

I held it uncertainly, remembering what happened with the bounders when I removed my clothing. Nobody who had watched *In Exile* had mentioned anything about my chromatophores, so I guessed that Nara had edited those parts out. I was afraid to face the same animosity from Halli and Rune that I had from Lumo and the others, though my instinct told me that I could trust them with my secret, and my instincts had always been right in Chedi.

"You can dive in those clothes if you're shy," Rune said.

I locked eyes with Somya and saw my doubts reflected in their gaze. They gave me the faintest of shrugs. *Do what you want,* their gesture said to me.

"I'm not shy." I took a deep breath and pulled up my sleeve. "I have some DNA that isn't human." I repeated the words in phoric. The light from my skin glowed in the evening with unmistakable bioluminescence, and the brilliant chartreuse hue betrayed my concern.

Rune's bushy eyebrows rose. "Chromatophores? I've only seen those on alloy skin."

"I'm not an alloy, I promise."

He nodded. "I believe you. Is this another gift from your mother, or is it an unexpected mutation?"

"My mother."

I worked up the courage to look at Halli. Their expression held wonder and a hint of delight.

"I guess you won't need these," Halli said and gestured at the lights on their vest. The corners of their eyes crinkled with amusement.

Somya laughed, Rune grinned, and the moment of tension dissipated. I sighed with relief and began to undress. My phores glowed purple with happiness. I didn't try to suppress them.

Halli dropped off the side of the boat first. I stared into the inky water for a minute, took a deep breath, and stepped away from the deck. The ocean surrounded me like a lukewarm bath. I gave Halli the hand sign that I was okay. With a tap of the wrist unit, the vest adjusted my weight until I sank slowly beneath the bobbing surface. I adjusted my ear pressure as we dropped, using the method Rune had taught me on the boat. Halli's illuminated torso guided me toward the shadowy form of the atoll. Oval forms flashed by, some in muted colors, most silvery. Halli made the sign to go neutral, and I adjusted my buoyancy again.

We hung in the water, suspended. In addition to the breathers and dive vests, we carried small lanterns with internal mirrors to illuminate anything that seemed interesting. Halli trained theirs toward the atoll. I spotted the long face of an eel before it pulled back into its cave. A large round shadow swam above me, and one oblong flipper passed through the beam of my light. *A sea turtle!*

Startled, I reached out and grabbed Halli's shoulder. They turned, waved at the turtle, and took me by the hand. As our bare skin met, I felt a spark of happiness. I held tight as we swam forward into the dark waters, away from the eyes of the world, and trusted Halli to guide me. The world of the surface disappeared from my thoughts, along with all concerns for the future.

# DAY 118

We passed the boundary of Loka on the third day out of Hawai'i, and four days later, we crossed the equator for the first time. Rune made us lemonade to celebrate, and we raised our glasses for a double toast over dinner. Not only had we checked off an important requirement for the Anthro Challenge, but Somya could walk without pain. They had climbed down into the cabin earlier that day.

The wind picked up after our meal, and Halli supervised while I let the *Svapna* heel to a forty-five-degree angle for the last hour of their shift. Rune had gone to bed a little while earlier, but he gave us his blessing, saying that he would use a hammock so that the conditions didn't bother his sleep. After a couple of hours, Halli went off duty and Somya took a shift for the first time on the Pacific.

"I've got my sea legs back," Somya crowed.

I laughed and eased up on the sails. The two of us lacked the skill and experience of Halli and Rune, so I let the boat resume a more upright stance. The wind had grown relentless, gusting to thirty knots, and clouds began to stream across the stars.

I watched the barometer drop and warned Somya. "I think we're heading into a storm. We need to change course."

We reefed both sails and tried to get ahead of the low-pressure system, like we had on the way to Nitaynoa. After half an hour of bearing away, we failed to find calmer conditions. In the moonless night, we could only see as far as the circle illuminated by our bow light. Walls of gleaming onyx loomed over us as we crested wave after wave. The boat rose and fell with sharp lurches. I guessed that the swells had risen to at least four meters, maybe five. The wind battered the sails, which were already down to a third of their full height.

Somya yelled something that I could barely hear over the noise. I assumed they were telling me that we should take the sails down fully. I agreed and grabbed a harness from its storage bin. I slipped it on, clipped myself to the deck rails, and took the jib down. Somya did their best to steer into the barely visible waves, but the deck pitched and rolled under my feet. Before dealing with the main, I staggered back to the bin and pulled out a second harness.

"Put this on," I shouted and thrust it at Somya.

The wheel was an angry creature that fought their grasp. I left them to battle it and took down the main sail.

I returned to their side and yelled into their ear, "I'll go get Halli."

Somya nodded. At least it wasn't raining. Without the sails, the ocean would take us where it willed. I unclipped my harness and pushed my way through the cabin door, holding on to the ladder rails with a death grip. The door swung into my shoulder with a crack. I winced and latched it closed. Halli and Rune stood over a table looking at a print map that showed our recent positions and headings. The sea roared as loudly below as it had above. I lurched over to them.

"We took down the sails," I said. "Can't see a thing out there. What should we do?"

"We'll have to ride out the storm," Rune said. "Drop the sea anchor."

"I'm not sure how—"

"I'll do it," Halli said.

I followed Halli up the ladder because I wanted to learn. The gale tore at me as soon as I stepped through the cabin door. I grabbed my harness line and clipped on. Through squinted eyes, I watched Halli flip two switches. Under my feet, a motor rumbled to life, winching the anchor down, I presumed.

Rune braced against the cabin doorway and peered up. The clouds had thickened. Stars shone through a countable number of gaps. The *Svapna* tipped from side to side like a child's toy. Halli kept a white-knuckled grip on the wheel. Somya dropped to their knees on a port-side bench and threw up over the railing. A whooshing noise came from the same direction, and the rest of us turned toward it.

A wall of glossy black rushed at the side of the boat.

"Som!" I cried in warning.

The rogue wave crashed into the *Svapna* and sent it careening to one side. I fell backward. My tailbone hit the deck with a sharp crack. A body slammed into mine. Instinctively, I wrapped my arms around it, and we slid until the clip line yanked me to a stop. My arms strained around the bony frame—*Somya.*

The water receded, and the boat returned to a more vertical position. *That was a knockdown,* whispered a voice in my head—a term we'd learned from Isin back on the *Zephyros* that meant a sail or mast had touched the water. We hadn't practiced dealing with one because Isin thought we'd never need to. I pushed dripping hair from my eyes and looked around. The cabin door flapped. The steering wheel spun freely. Rune and Halli were nowhere in sight.

Somya crawled out of my arms. A hole gaped in their harness where the clip line had torn free.

"Don't!" I yelled. I grabbed at their arm and pointed at their torso. "You're not attached to the boat anymore."

They turned. Their eyes gleamed white and round. I had never seen such terror on Somya's expression, not even at the Euphrates.

"Go below!" I pointed at the door.

Somya nodded. We lurched upright, leaning upon each other for balance, and I helped guide them to the doorway.

"Rune? Halli?" I called down as Somya climbed down. "Are you all right?"

"Here," a voice answered—*Rune*. "Bumped my head, but I feel okay. Watch your step when you come down. It's a mess."

Water reflected the dim glow of the bioluminescent lighting in the cabin. Somya staggered as they stepped off the ladder and splashed onto their knees. Paasha warbled in distress from the bed at the bow.

"We'll have to pump this place out," Rune said. He peered up at me as he helped Somya up. "Where's Halli?"

"I thought they were down here," I said.

Rune's expression told me everything I needed to know. With a set jaw, he climbed toward me.

"Get me a harness," Rune said, one hand clutching the doorframe.

I moved cautiously to the storage bin, making sure my clip stayed secure, though after seeing Somya's harness, I knew I couldn't count on it to save me if we were knocked down again. Rune waited at the top of the stairs until I handed him the gear. I moved to the starboard side and worked my way along the railing, searching the water. A voice in my head said it was impossible. *Look at those waves. You'll never find Halli in that.* I ignored it and headed toward the bow. From the corner of my eye, I saw Rune do the same from the other side.

The *Svapna* heaved under our feet. We had given up on trying to steer. Perhaps the rogue wave had damaged the rudder. We wouldn't know until we'd passed through the storm. Rune's hand fell on my shoulder. He turned me to face him and shook his head. He gestured to go back to the cabin.

I repeated the painstaking walk aft. I couldn't take my eyes off the sea. *Just in case.* My stomach hardened to stone. Rune stood at the stern with a lamp held aloft like a prayer.

Could we get the alloys to help us? Nothing mattered more at that moment—not the Anthro Challenge, not exile reform, not Meru—nothing except rescuing Halli.

I put my mouth close to Rune's ear. "Can we get network access? Call for help?"

And then I remembered that we were in the Out of Bounds. Even if we could find a connection in this storm, would they come?

Rune turned toward the cabin door without a reply. Next to the door, the round life buoy hung like an empty promise. I flung it out behind the boat in an act of desperation and hope. Rune nodded and motioned me down the ladder. He followed and latched the door behind him.

Two grim expressions bore into me in the dim glow. Seawater lapped at my ankles. In the background, the bilge pump wheezed, and the *Svapna* kept up a steady chorus of creaks, groans, and judders.

Rune took my hands in his. The warmth of his fingers contrasted with my chilled ones.

"We could probably get network access," Rune said, "but even a watercrafter would struggle to swim in these conditions. By the time they got here . . ."

He didn't finish the sentence. He didn't have to. Somya let out a choked sound of denial. I freed myself from Rune's gentle grasp and sat on a bunk. I should have felt a tempest inside me, with ten times the rage of the one outside, but all sensation had fled.

Rune looked as if he were going to be sick. He had an arm around Somya, whose shoulders shook with quiet sobs. Something nudged at my foot. I looked down and saw the green sketchbook. It had flipped open to a water-logged drawing of a pelican. I picked it up, closed it, and held it against my stomach.

Halli couldn't have disappeared. Not really. They would step through the cabin door at any moment with a mild expression and chide us for our distress. Or maybe they had grabbed a breather before being washed overboard. They could ride out the storm underwater. Maybe they were swimming beneath the *Svapna* at that very moment. It would explain why we saw no sign of them. They would come aboard in the morning, when the sun shone and the Pacific lived up to its name once more.

*The breathers are inside a latched storage bin,* said a traitorous voice in my head. *Even if Halli had thought to grab one, the wave passed in seconds. They could've knocked their head on a railing as they went over. An unconscious person can't swim.* I told the voice to shut up. I wouldn't give up on Halli. I couldn't.

# DAY 119

The rain ended overnight, and dawn brought low clouds and a steady breeze. The voracious waves of the previous night subsided and left behind a messy gray churn with excellent visibility. Beams of sunlight broke through the overcast sky like spotlights. I wanted one of them to reveal a small figure clinging to the life buoy, but no miracles occurred. Halli did not appear. Instead, an isolated mass of white clouds rose on the horizon—a sign of land.

The rudder had taken damage, along with the boom and the freshwater filter. Somya and I helped Rune with makeshift repairs, enough that we could steer our way to shore. We worked in grim, monochromatic silence. Halli's loss had leached all color and muted all sound, and yet somehow, impossibly, we had to live. My mind insisted on seeing them everywhere on deck, a ghost more solid than reality. A thousand whys and what-ifs overflowed my thoughts, and I kept telling myself to focus on the task at hand. Sometimes it worked, but more often I would realize after a few minutes that I'd frozen while holding a tool, lost in a black hole of thoughts. I'd catch Somya and Rune in similar positions of stillness.

We eventually figured out that the storm had thrown us off course only slightly, putting us less than half a day behind schedule. We arrived at Arariki, a small island in the middle of the Pacific. The lone human outpost had a tiny pier with a cluster of homes that barely constituted a village. Rune went ashore first, and nobody mentioned anything about the show or the pledge or the protest, so Somya and I followed to help him. We stocked up with some jugs of fresh water, fruit, and coconuts. In exchange, we left a few items of clothing that we didn't need. Rune insisted that Somya and I eat. I forced myself to chew and swallow, but I tasted none of it. After a while, I noticed that Rune didn't touch any of the food himself.

I overheard him telling a few of the residents about Halli and how to reach Rune or Halli's family if they came across anything. The listeners' faces wrinkled with sympathy, but they offered no words of assurance. The storm had flooded the island and brought damage with its winds. They didn't say it out loud, but it was clear they didn't think anyone could have survived it.

I didn't see a single alloy anywhere, not even in the ocean. Would they have come to help if we had called them the night before? Life in the OOB was risky. Everyone knew that. Unlike exile in space, where other alloys would take care of you, on Earth, you had no guarantees outside the boundaries of Loka. Maybe they wouldn't have endangered themselves to save a lone human washed away during a voluntary activity.

We gathered natural materials that would help repair the *Svapna*, even if it meant cutting down trees. We had arrived at a place so remote that the people relied on skills and ways of life from the Human Era. Residents had more leeway to use the land as they wanted. Rune seemed familiar with the lack of constraints, but he moved as if he felt the weight of his years in every motion. He gave instructions to me and Somya, and we did as he asked. We worked until nearly sunset.

"Enough," Rune finally said.

He carried a basket of flowers and led us to the far side of the breakwater. Waves lapped at the stones as gently as Paasha's tongue. You would never know that a ferocious storm had blown through less than a day earlier.

"It's time we acknowledge Halli's death," Rune said.

"No," I whispered. The sea breeze snatched the word away.

Rune's lined face sagged further. "I'm sorry. I had hoped"—his voice broke—"I hoped that Halli would take the helm of the *Svapna* in the coming years. They were one of the kindest and cleverest sailors I have had the privilege of knowing, and their absence leaves a void in my heart." He flung a handful of flowers into the sea.

"They were my friend," Somya said. Tears trickled from their eyes. "They taught me to sail and dive, and they cooked excellent fish."

Somya gave their offering to the water and passed me the basket. I didn't want it, but I took it anyway. I didn't know what to say. I couldn't cry. I felt numb and blank and empty. Somya's arm wrapped around my shoulder. Their gaze, like Rune's, was not on me but fixed to the horizon.

I opened my mouth. "It's all my fault. If I hadn't done the Anthro Challenge, if I hadn't wanted to avoid Meru so badly, none of this would've happened. Halli would still be alive."

"I agreed to the challenge, too," Somya said.

"And Halli was my responsibility," Rune added. "I should've come up on deck with them. I thought I'd taught them well enough, but the fact that they didn't use a harness—I failed." After a few seconds of silence, he sighed. "Accidents happen, even in Loka, but especially here in the OOB. It's part of life. We can spend our days in regret and what-ifs, blaming ourselves for everything we could have done differently, but that won't bring Halli back to us." He cupped my chin and gently turned my head to face him. "They would not want you to spend your time on self-reproach. The best way to honor Halli's memory is to get back on the sea, to keep sailing, and to finish the challenge."

I heard Rune's words, but I couldn't *feel* them. I grasped the remaining flowers in the basket, cast them into the waves, and watched them disappear.

---

That night, Somya and I shared the double-wide bed in the bow. Rune took a hammock. I awoke from a deep sleep with my heart pounding. I sat upright and peered around, but I saw nothing. After a few seconds of stillness, I heard a low moan. Somya slumbered quietly beside me, so I knew it must have come from Rune. I considered whether to go to him. He'd known Halli a lot longer than I had. What comfort could I give?

I heard the telltale creak of wood followed by the click of the cabin door. I scooted out of the bed and stuck my head into the darkness of the cabin. Rune had left. Had he heard me? Maybe he was avoiding us, trying to look strong so we wouldn't worry.

"Aks?" Somya said softly from behind me. "Everything okay?"

"Nothing's okay."

"Yeah." After a minute, Somya spoke again. "Was there—did you and Halli—I mean, were you more than friends?"

I let my phores do the talking in the dark. <We never said so to each other,> I flashed, <but after the night dive, I felt like maybe we had the start of something. All I know is that right now, my heart hurts.> The edges of my phores glowed with deep yellow.

"I'm sorry," Somya whispered.

And somehow that was enough. The tears began as a trickle and grew to a flood. Somya wrapped their arms around me as I shook with sobs so violent, I thought I might vomit.

I had never experienced true grief before then. My mother had. Her best friend, Sunanda, had died when I was eight years old. I hadn't known what to do with my mother's anguish, but I could recall the first three or four days after the funeral—her frequent crying, the long hours in bed, my maker sitting by her side and holding her hand, the pain crisis that followed a couple of weeks later.

<I'm glad you're here,> I flashed. I didn't have the breath for speech.

"Me too," Somya said.

We sat that way until fatigue overwhelmed the waves of emotion. My breathing slowed. We lay back down in wordless agreement, and Somya draped their arm over me as they had during our sleepovers in Chedi. Somehow, I would have to get up in the morning and keep moving forward, even though I wanted the world to stop. When I closed my eyes, I saw that moment—Halli fighting the steering wheel, the rogue wave crashing over us. My body shuddered. Somya hugged me closer. The images played over and over in my head while sleep receded into the horizon. I wondered if I would ever sleep again.

# DAY 124

We pushed on from Arariki the day after we finished our repairs. We headed south toward Vanua Levu, the first major island back inside the bounds of Loka. The *Svapna* held together. We hadn't mended the boat so much as cobbled together solutions to keep it going. I felt the same way—on the brink of falling apart and yet moving forward. The smaller OOB Pacific islands used old methods of shipbuilding. They didn't have replacement parts for the *Svapna*, nor could they produce them. Rune thought the odds of finding what we needed on Vanua Levu were slim, but it was the most populated island in the area and a destination for people sailing from Australia, so we had a better chance there than anywhere else.

We hopped through smaller atolls and villages along the way. At each stop, we begged for fresh water, our greatest need. The filter had completely quit. We emptied every wide-mouth container on the boat and set them on deck to catch rainwater, but the precipitation was minimal. No storms, and only the briefest of tropical showers. After a couple of stops, I forgot to worry about the anti-AC petition. No one this far out cared about us or what we did.

I stopped using the breather. I could only think of Halli and our night dive when I looked at one. To place it over my face took a strength of will that I didn't have. Somya and I took separate shifts, and Rune split his sleep time so that he could help us, though the weather made his supervision unnecessary. Our smiles had no real joy behind them, only kindness or sympathy. Somya and I spent a lot of time sitting shoulder to shoulder in the cockpit. I saw reminders of Halli everywhere. At one point, I considered jumping into the ocean to escape it all, but that also made me think of them.

My body started to ache somewhere around Falealupo. The pain came on so gradually that at first I assumed I was working my muscles too hard, but as it increased, I started to suspect that my sickle-cell disorder was flaring up again. I should've used the breather. I should have asked for more drinking water. I shouldn't have ignored the alerts from my bodym. Instead, I welcomed the pain.

Despite Rune's words at Arariki, I couldn't help blaming myself for Halli's loss. We were caught unprepared in that terrible storm because of the Anthro Challenge rules. If we had used the public network, Rune would have known to avoid the bad weather. Worse yet, Somya and I steered the boat right into the mess. I deserved to suffer.

That's why I didn't tell Somya or Rune about my building symptoms—the trickles of lightning that shot through my limbs, the stabbing pains deep in my muscles. Exhaustion built day by day. Busy with our own tasks, none of us did much talking, so hiding my problems wasn't hard.

We dropped anchor in the bay at Falealupo on the western tip of Savai'i after a very long day at sea. Coming off a sleep shift, I should have had plenty of energy, but when I stepped out of the dinghy onto shore, I couldn't hold myself straight.

"Land legs," I mumbled when Somya steadied me.

By the time we returned from the village with supplies, Somya and Rune could tell that something was wrong.

"Sit down," Rune said. He pointed at the sand.

I gently set down my sack of fruit and lowered myself onto the sunbaked softness of the beach. Somya and Rune sat, forming a triangle with me.

"What's the matter, Akshaya?" Rune asked. "You are clearly unwell."

Somya's eyes narrowed. "You haven't been using the breather. Are you having pain?"

I opened my mouth, but the excuses stuck in my throat. What could I say in my defense? The truth was that I had stopped caring—about myself, about the AC, about the pledge. Nothing mattered in the face of Halli's death. I had watched my friend get washed away, and I hadn't been able to stop it. They were gone. The pain from my bad blood helped distract me from the greater agony of loss. I would continue to welcome it.

Rune placed a hand on my knee. "You're still alive," he said, as if reading my mind. "You have to take care of yourself." He sighed. "I'm sorry. I've been lost in my own grief, but that's no excuse. As the adult, I should've paid more attention, and I will, to both of you." He extended his arms and pulled us both in. "You two are my spiritual children, like Halli was. I loved them dearly, and I miss them terribly, but this is not my first encounter with grief. It will get easier, I promise. You'll never stop missing them, and it will never stop hurting to think of them, but your hearts will heal."

I had cried so much in the previous days that I thought I'd spent all my tears. I was wrong. We sat there for a while, Somya and I holding on to Rune as if we had been thrown overboard and he was our life preserver.

"I don't want to do this anymore," I whispered.

"You don't have to," Rune said.

Somya pulled back. "Yes, you do." Their words had a harsh note that I'd never heard before. "What Rune said before was right. Halli would want you to keep going. People throughout the world are counting on us to see this through. We have a chance to make a difference. It would be selfish to give up."

"*Selfish?* Do you think I want to end up on Meru?" I glared at Somya through my tears. "Halli's dead because of the Anthro Challenge. You broke your leg. I'm sick again. We abandoned Freni on the bank of a river. We offended the bounders who helped us, and we've damaged Rune's boat twice. Quitting would be the least selfish thing we could do!"

Somya's face went pale. "If we quit," they said through tight lips, "and you go to Meru, I'll be all alone. Don't leave me, Aks, not after everything that's happened."

Their words struck me like a gust of wind. I had already lost one friend. I didn't want to abandon another, especially my heartsib, and I didn't want to fight them, but I was so very tired of pushing forward.

"If I could make a suggestion," Rune said, gentle as moonlight. "Let's go as far as Vanua Levu. It's only a few days away, and it'll put us back in Loka. I can get some fluids for Akshaya there. We can make sure your leg has healed, Somya. Once you both feel better, you can decide what to do, okay?"

I looked into Somya's eyes. We didn't need words to know what the other was thinking, and I saw agreement in their gaze. We turned to Rune and nodded.

"If you decide to continue the challenge," he said, "I can look for one or two more people to join our crew. We might find someone in the borderlands who enjoys adventure and supports what you're doing. In the meantime, Akshaya, please use the breather as much as possible. I can make an electrolyte solution for the medical sleeve to help with hydration. Everything is harder when you're exhausted and sick."

I forced myself to pick up my sack and follow him and Somya to the dinghy. The sun had disappeared behind a bank of gray clouds. Tendrils of fog blew past us, toward the island, as we made our way back to the *Svapna*. The rise and fall of the deck beneath my feet felt like home and, at the same time, like someone had wrapped a fist around my heart.

# RESHYAN (DAY 127)

Atolls dotted the ocean below Reshyan. The atmosphere was clear, with minimal turbulence, and flying was a joy, especially since zie was working alone. Zie towed a sensor net in a three-dimensional grid pattern. It sampled air composition and flow as it moved. Another half an hour and the measurements would be complete.

Somewhere below, the indriyas zie had deployed at the start of the day were capturing close-up footage of the *Svapna*. The two documentary subjects had sailed on in spite of their distress. Reshyan couldn't imagine the internal conflict of trying to concentrate on work while mourning a death. No healthy alloy would do such a thing. If only the humans could have adjusted their bodies' hormones, like an alloy, they could have mitigated the severity of their grief. Human ambition was a strange phenomenon. Reshyan could understand why it needed external regulation.

The boat had crossed back into the border of Loka, which made it easier for Reshyan to keep it in sight. Zie had incorporated the flights into zir research again, rather than taking personal time to patrol the Out of Bounds. With one final zigzag pattern, zie finished the sensor sweep of the area. Zie hovered while the net spooled back into the rectangular storage device at zir waist. With that done, Reshyan folded zir wings and dove down. Gleeful violet glowed from zir phores. Fortunately, no one was there to witness it. Zie extended zir wings and leveled off, maintaining an altitude where zie would appear as no more than a speck to a human on the surface. From there, zie recalled Nara's indriyas.

As the devices flew back toward Reshyan, zie received an incoming call request. Zie slow-blinked and issued a thought-command to accept it. The face of zir project manager, Chalin, appeared superimposed in zir visual. She wore an elaborate headdress that resembled braids of human hair, a fashion among the residents of the Primary Nivid. Reshyan's hands twitched with an urge to tie the strands into a neat bundle.

They exchanged a few tedious pleasantries, which Chalin seemed to find necessary.

<The real reason for my call,> Chalin flashed at last, <is that Olanma informed me of your assistance with the recordings for *In Exile*.>

Reshyan's body flooded with stress hormones. Zie fought to suppress the reaction, sending thought-commands to mitigate the effects on zir physiology. Was zie about to lose zir research position? Olanma had been right about zir contract. Reshyan needed approval before taking on additional work as a service alloy, but Nara's project didn't fall under that category. Technically, Reshyan had done nothing wrong. Zie accessed zir extended memory for the verbiage that zie had prepared in case Olanma questioned zir again.

<The work I'm doing with Nara,> Reshyan flashed, <has no impact on planetary conditions or the lives of any humans. It's not under the purview of the Ground-Based Service Committee. I'm not using any of our project resources for it, either. Nara has provided all of the equipment, and my flights are either part of my research work or done on my own time. None of it conflicts with my contract.>

Chalin's phores flickered with mild amusement. <Don't panic. I'm not here to ask you to stop. In fact, I'm rather curious about Somya and Akshaya. Are they doing well?>

Reshyan failed to keep the mint-green skepticism from zir phores. <Why do you want to know?>

<To be honest, I'm a fan of the show,> Chalin flashed. <I was hoping to get a preview of what's coming. In the last episode, the two of them were about to head south from Tongvana over land, but your flight paths for the last three weeks have taken you over the Pacific Ocean, far from the coast.>

<My contract with Nara prohibits me from sharing the raw footage with anyone except Akshaya and Somya's makers.>

<I don't need to see what's happening. Just give me a quick summary of their status. In exchange, I'll overlook any . . . irregularities in your performance on our project. For example, if you might have adjusted atmospheric parameters to favor their journey.>

Was Chalin trying to blackmail zir? Did she plan to do something unethical with the information, or to tempt Reshyan into manipulating the humans' fate? Akshaya's health had worsened again, and the boat had lost a crew member during a storm in the Out of Bounds. The humans tried to gather rainwater, but East Asia needed more precipitation, and the moisture had been redirected there. Little had fallen over the boat's route, and none would come for quite a while, not until the rice paddies in Loka had sufficient hydration. Regardless, Reshyan hadn't compromised zir morals or the Anthro Challenge, and zie wasn't about to start.

<I'm sorry,> Reshyan flashed, <but unless you can show me an agreement with Nara, I can't reveal anything to you. You're welcome to use the public observation equipment like everyone else to deduce what you can.>

Chalin's phores flickered again, though their edges glowed apricot. Reshyan could understand her frustration but not the amusement.

<I had to try,> she flashed. <I'll be keeping a closer eye on your flights and data collection to ensure that you're not abusing your research position. You understand, right?>

<You won't find anything.>

<Of course not. I look forward to your next status report.>

Chalin ended the call with cordial words. Reshyan gathered the indriyas, which hovered nearby, and stowed them in the pouch at zir waist. Zie had been tempted to precipitate some rain for the *Svapna*, but that would have meant a violation of the Anthro Challenge rules, and if anyone discovered it, the SomAx pledge would fail. Exile reform depended on the two humans' success, and they had demonstrated remarkable resilience, so Reshyan forced zirself to trust that they would continue to do so.

When zie reached zir berth, zie grabbed a tube, sipped at some bhojya, and called up the flight plans from the recent weeks, as well as zir upcoming routes. A quick scan showed nothing untoward. To make certain of it, Reshyan submitted the records for review by the Ground-Based Services Committee.

Chalin's implied threat left a bitter hue in zir mind, and it built the more zie thought about it. Without mutual trust and respect with zir coworkers, atmospheric research would not hold the same joy. Reshyan had experienced a similar loss of satisfaction during the latter portion of zir extra-solar travels. Circumstances had pointed to a coming end to zir work then, too. Perhaps it was time to consider what zie wanted for the next chapter in zir life.

# DAY 129

We docked at a small, very old pier in the town of Nabouwalu on the island of Vanua Levu. I didn't take in many of the details because in the four days it had taken us to sail there from Falealupo, my sickle-cell disorder had flared worse than an unstable binary system. In spite of Rune and Somya sacrificing their water, in spite of round-the-clock breather usage and liters of electrolyte solution, my body decided to quit functioning. By the time we arrived, I could barely stand, much less work the boat or take in the sights.

I was curled in a ball of misery when Somya came to get me.

They put a hand on my arm. "The borderlands have something in common—hospitals. There's one in town here, and they have hydration equipment."

"The protest," I grunted in response.

"We're close enough to the border that they're on our side. Rune checked. It's all right."

Somya put their arm under my shoulders and hauled me to a sitting position. It took all my willpower not to cry out in pain. I kept it to a whimper, and involuntary tears pooled in my eyes.

"I'm sorry," Somya said. "You have to do this."

I nodded and did my best to move myself. Getting up the ladder was the worst part. I didn't notice the swaying of the gangway or the bobbing of the floating pier. Rune held me on one side and Somya on the other. I hobbled between my two friends as best as I could. It took us ten times as long as a healthy pace would have, but eventually we reached the entrance to a squat elongated building with coral-pink doors.

A human nurse attended to me. He took all three of us to a small room with a window overlooking the beach. It had a simple cot and two chairs. He left the breather over my face and hooked me up to a passive device that pumped me full of clear fluids. I let my eyelids fall.

"What she really needs is a blood exchange," Somya said. They went on to explain what they understood about my sickle-cell disease. "Do you have one of those machines?"

"Not here," the nurse replied. "There's a much better facility at Ganjdija, about three thousand kilometers to the west."

"In Australia," Rune added.

"I can give you the name of the place," the nurse offered. "In the meantime, I'll do some research during my break and see if there's anything we have here that could help."

"Thank you," Somya said.

I heard someone leave, presumably the nurse.

"I'm heading back to the boat, but Somya will stay here with you," Rune said. "We'll take turns at your side."

I wanted to say that they didn't need to watch over me like a child, but the mere thought of arguing made me tired, so I kept quiet and nodded.

The room went silent after that. Sleep came in fits and starts, usually interrupted by the fire in my body whenever I moved. I had no idea what Somya was doing to occupy their time. I drifted in and out of awareness, unsure of whether minutes or hours passed. At some point, I noticed that my pain level had dropped. The fluids must have included some kind of analgesic. The relief brought with it a deeper sleep, though still in nap-size bites, and a general sense of detachment from reality.

The light clatter of dishes and utensils brought me out of a dream about swimming through space in a bubble of seawater . . . with Halli by my side. Reality and remembrance landed on me like a lead cape. I wished I could reenter the dream, but the images in my mind fled.

"You should eat something," the nurse said.

I cracked my eyes open. Outside the window, night had dropped a curtain over the world. Bioluminescence traced the walls and ceiling inside the room with a warm yellow glow. A rolling tray table made of regen walnut held two bowls of chunky stew, some bread rolls, and a mug of clear liquid.

The nurse helped me sit up and slid the table across my lap. I inhaled steam from the bowl, and to my surprise, my mouth watered. I clutched the spoon and took a tentative bite of the stew. It tasted like home, rich with the aroma of cumin, turmeric, and ginger. I held the second bowl out to Somya, who took it and sat on the edge of my cot.

"I was able to find some information on sickle-cell disease in the Nivid," the nurse began. "Hydration, pain mitigation, and oxygen—all of which we're doing—will help, but you were right. An in-kind blood exchange provides the best therapy. I'm sorry we don't have access to that here. I could ask an alloy to fly a machine in from orbit—"

"No," Somya and I said together.

"We're doing something called the Anthro Challenge," Somya explained. "The rules don't allow any kind of assistance from alloys or technology developed after the end of the Human Era."

"Of course, I forgot about that." The nurse smacked his forehead lightly. "The one other treatment I came across is gene therapy." He looked at me. "Would you be interested in that?"

"She's not old enough," Somya said before I could answer.

"At that hospital in Ganjdija, there's a doctor who will do it for anyone . . . including people who are underage."

"The alloys don't object?" I asked.

"They don't interfere at that facility because so many OOBers come across the border for help. So far, everyone who goes there has kept the secret. If you're interested, I can give you her name and contact information. The only requirement is that you're in good health before you start the therapy."

"Thank you," I said. "I'll think about it."

As soon as the nurse left the room, Somya turned to me. A rare frown creased their brow.

"Aks, there's nothing to think about. Not only would you be breaking the law, a change to your DNA is permanent. You're not an alloy."

I swallowed and said quietly, "I know."

"You'd never be able to live on Meru."

"Less than a week ago, you begged me not to go."

An expression of *pain-sadness-regret* spread across Somya's face. "I've been thinking about that," they said. "It was selfish. You're my heartsib, and I'll always want you by my side, but Meru is your birthright. Even if you spend the next ten years here on Earth, you should go there one day. If you get rid of your sickle-cell DNA, you'll never have that chance, and if you get caught taking illegal gene therapy, the CDS might force you back to Chedi or send you to the Out of Bounds."

"I'll take Chedi over spending the rest of my life on a planet I have no interest in. As for the OOB, that would mean we get to forge ahead with the destiny you want, right?"

Somya ignored my question. "Halli liked the idea of you going to Meru."

How had Somya known that? Had the two of them talked about me? In what context? I stared into my nearly empty bowl of stew and tightened my fingers around the rim.

"Don't use Halli's memory against me," I said through taut lips.

"They were my friend, too."

I lifted my gaze to Somya's. I could only see them in profile, but their pain was clear. I had gotten so lost in my illness and grief that

I had neglected their feelings. Shame rose like acid in my throat. It mixed with anger to create a caustic brew, and I couldn't bring myself to apologize. After all, I was the one having a crisis. I was the one who had finally made a connection with someone on Earth. Didn't I deserve more sympathy than Somya?

"Finishing the Anthro Challenge matters more than where I end up living," I said. "A lot more, because of the potential for exile reform. If we fail, there's a good chance we'll never get to try again. All the people who signed the pledge are counting on us. We owe it to them—and Halli—to see this through, and that's what I'm going to do. If gene therapy means I stop getting sick like this, then it's worth the risk."

"Fine," Somya said.

It clearly wasn't fine, but right after they said it, the nurse poked his head into the room. "All done with dinner?"

I nodded. Somya moved back to a chair and picked up a book. The nurse collected the tray and dishes. I lay down with my face to the wall and closed my eyes. The argument had worn me out. I didn't want Somya to be upset, but at the same time, I didn't want them or anyone else telling me how to live my life. I had always planned to get the gene therapy once I reached adulthood and left Meru. If someone could give it to me sooner and in the process get me everything else I wanted—finishing the challenge, improving my health, and ensuring me a long life on Earth—then it made perfect sense to take it.

---

Later that night, I woke up feeling somewhat more myself. The fire in my muscles had reduced from an inferno to a moderate blaze. I sat up slowly, exhaling as my joints protested, and proceeded to stretch. *Definitely less pain than yesterday.*

Rune dozed on the other side of the room, his feet propped up on the second chair, his head lolling on a pillow against the wall. True to his word, he and Somya had taken shifts, never leaving me alone. Somya and I hadn't spoken again about our argument, but when I discussed the gene therapy with Rune, his reservations had to do with my parents and their feelings. I knew they wouldn't be happy with me, but all I could think about was finishing the Anthro Challenge. Success would make the pain of Halli's loss easier to bear.

Through the window, a moonless night filled half my view and cast starlight over the inky ocean. A stretch of sand and shrub created a shadowed barrier between me and the water, and a lone palm tree stood like a guardian silhouetted against the glittering sky.

Rune snorted and shifted. His eyes opened a little and then, upon seeing me, opened fully. "You're awake." He yawned.

"I am, sorry."

"It's all right. I'm used to odd sleep hours, and I'm happy to see you more upright. How do you feel?"

"Better," I said with a small smile. "Not back to full health, but not as bad as when we arrived."

He raised his bushy gray brows.

I nodded. "Well enough to move on in a day or two, I think, if I don't have to take full shifts on the *Svapna*."

"I'm sure we can manage that. Somya's an experienced hand now, and as long as we don't hit any trouble, we should reach Australia in about a week. I haven't had any luck with recruitment here, but I'll try again at Ganjdija. It's a good-size city for the borderlands of Australia."

I had spoken with the nurse after Rune took over for Somya. I was too much of a coward to tell Somya of my decision, and I had asked Rune to keep it to himself until I told my heartsib. I hated the barrier it created between me and them, but I didn't know what else to do. The nurse had given us a name and directions to the hospital where I could get gene therapy. He also promised us a sufficient supply of hydration and pain packets to last us the week's journey there. He emphasized that I needed to rest and avoid any other illness if I wanted to be ready for the treatment on arrival at Ganjdija. We didn't know the weather forecast, so the only potential complication would come from overly calm or stormy seas. Given how quickly I had recovered from my previous pain crisis, I expected to feel well by the time we reached Australia.

"I'm sorry I can't help you get ready for the journey ahead," I said to Rune.

"That's why you have me and Somya."

"And I should probably stay on the boat during any resupply stops so I don't catch anything."

"Akshaya," Rune said.

I looked at him.

"One day at a time, remember?"

I smiled. Between his own experience and our time together, Rune could practically read my mind.

He stood and patted my leg. "I don't think you need us here round the clock anymore. Am I right?"

I nodded.

"Good. Then I'll head back to the *Svapna*. Somya and I will start stocking up in the morning. If you're still feeling well in two days, we'll sail on to Australia."

"My numbers already look better than they were back at Nuberia. I'm sure I'll be fine." I didn't add that I had no choice.

After Rune left, I did a rough calculation. A week to reach Ganjdija, maybe a few days there to start the gene therapy, then another three weeks to reach home and catch the last shuttle to Chedi. All I needed was to get my sickle-cell disease corrected. After that, nothing would stop me from finishing the Anthro Challenge and spending the rest of my life on Earth.

# VAHA (DAY 133)

Vaha floated in Chedi's zero-gravity viewing bubble. It bulged out of the megaconstruct's central axis like a clear drop of condensation and gave Vaha a perfect view. At their current distance, Earth was just another dot in the backdrop of stars. The final shuttle run would depart from Chedi the next day. Jayanthi would be ready to ride it back, but what about Akshaya?

Nara had been sending daily footage to Jayanthi and Vaha, and what Vaha had observed on the *Svapna* had sent zir incarn's heart toward its stomach. Unlike the previous sailing journeys, Akshaya had hardly been on deck since the storm. What few shifts she pulled were much shorter than before, and when they stopped for supplies, she never left the boat. Close-up views of her face revealed shadows under her eyes and hollows in her cheeks.

Vaha played the latest message from Earth.

"She's having a flare-up," Jayanthi said with no doubt in her voice. "And she looks worse than last time." Worry lined zir life mate's face.

Vaha wished zie could reach out and hold her—hold Akshaya, too. Growing up in space, zie would never have imagined that zie would one day have a human family, but Jayanthi and Akshaya had occupied zir heart. Vaha couldn't imagine life without them.

Zie agreed with Jayanthi's assessment. They had expected Akshaya to recover after her stay at the hospital, as had happened in Europe, but it seemed like she was getting worse.

"I have an idea." The grimness on Jayanthi's face made Vaha's heart race. "Maybe we need to give up on Meru."

Vaha's phores flashed in surprise, though no one was around to witness them.

"I've been thinking about it," Jayanthi continued. "Akshaya is doing this because she wants to remain on Earth. If she destroys her body for the Anthro Challenge, she's not going to have much of a life anywhere. I think we should let her out of the deal we made. Tell her she can stay here as long as she wants. That way she can quit the challenge, we can get her to orbit, and the alloys there can give her the treatment she needs." Jayanthi looked away from the camera. "I'm afraid I've done to her what your maker did to you."

Vaha understood what she was getting at. Zir maker had designed Vaha to be a multimodal pilot, and Vaha had struggled for years to fulfill that destiny. In the end, zie had let it go in order to find true happiness. Jayanthi was nothing like Veera, who had abandoned Vaha when zie proved a disappointment to Veera's hopes. Vaha couldn't imagine zir life mate treating Akshaya that way, and Jayanthi's proposal proved it. She would sacrifice her dreams of Meru to give Akshaya the best life that she could.

The recorded message continued. "I've managed on Earth and Chedi for my entire life. Akshaya should have that option. What right do we have to ask her to go to Meru? It's our dream, yours and mine. Not hers. I made her the way an alloy makes a child, giving her the genes I wanted her to have. She's seventeen. By alloy standards, she'd be on her own and able to remake herself if she wanted to. Maybe it's time we let her decide what to do."

*And what does that imply about you and me?*

Jayanthi had anticipated the question. "It leaves us with a decision. You know the choices as well as I do. It breaks my heart in every way, but I don't know how else we can help her."

If they stayed on Earth, Vaha wouldn't get to spend much time with zir child. Zie could apply to create a different incarn who could serve on the planet's surface, but that wouldn't let zir live among humans. Meru was the only place outside of Chedi where the three of them could be together as a family.

"She can stay with my parents," Jayanthi said. "You and I could still go to Meru. With time in a womb to heal your tail, you could fly in microgravity again. You'd be strong enough to bring us back and forth to visit."

All kinds of sensations washed over Vaha's incarn. Vaha wished zie could regulate zir human body the way zie could with zir true body. It was so hard to think straight when zir physiological systems went into overdrive. Zie had made peace with zir broken tail before Akshaya was born. Did zie want to revive those long-dormant skills?

The months Vaha and Jayanthi once spent on Meru had turned into a hazy fiction, the way human—and all organic—memories did. At the time, Vaha had briefly conquered all four modes of flight, just as zir maker had intended. When it later became clear that zie would have to go into exile, none of zir piloting abilities—or lack thereof—mattered. All zie wanted then was to stay with Jayanthi and watch their child grow, and they were all Vaha still cared about. Zie needed zir family. To allow Akshaya to live on Earth meant splitting them up, and every cell in zir incarn body rebelled against the thought.

"I know you'll want some time to think it over," Jayanthi said, gazing into the camera. Her demeanor exuded regret and sadness as clearly as if she had chromatophores. "Reply as soon as you can."

They would need to speak to Somya's parents and tell them about Jayanthi's suggestion. If they allowed Akshaya to quit the challenge, Somya would also face a choice—to give up with her or to go on alone.

The round-trip message delay to Earth was now seventeen hours. Vaha could imagine Jayanthi's impatience. If she could sacrifice everything she'd spent two decades waiting for, then zie could consider going back to a womb and learning how to pilot again. No matter what decision they arrived at, one thing was clear: zie had to go to Earth. Akshaya needed time—they all did—and the pressure of traveling together on Chedi created a deadline that served none of them.

Jayanthi hadn't mentioned the SomAx pledge at all. Had she signed it? Vaha hadn't asked, and she hadn't volunteered. Zie didn't want to pressure her, and they always had more immediate concerns, which made it easy to avoid the topic. Kaliyu's continuing exile pained Vaha, and zie wanted to see the practice reformed or ended. Zie felt even greater heartbreak at the thought of living without Akshaya in zir daily life, but their child's health had to take priority over all other considerations. On that, zie agreed completely with Jayanthi.

Vaha recorded a brief message to Jayanthi. "I love you and Akshaya, not Meru, not the pledge. I'll figure out a way to ride with tomorrow's shuttle and come to Earth. Whatever you and she decide to do, I trust you both to make the right choice. See you in a month."

By the time Jayanthi received the message, Vaha would have departed from the megaconstruct. Zie hoped that she trusted zir to choose well, too. Once underway, zie would be too preoccupied for communication, especially with the added complexity of using the shuttle as an assistive device for microgravity flight, but it didn't matter. Vaha didn't need messages to know what zie would find upon arrival at Earth—zir family, the most important thing in zir life.

# NARA (DAY 135)

Excitement filled Nara with an energy that he channeled into his mindspace, doing lazy circles over the trees of his office. Reshyan watched with bemused irritation seeping from zir phores.

<I'll need you to deploy an array of indriya recorders,> Nara flashed, <including a couple with tracers to follow Jayanthi in case she's indoors when it happens. We have to capture the moment when Akshaya sees her mother in Ganjdija from every angle. I have Jayanthi's permission to record in full immersive mode, so don't worry about invasion of privacy.>

<And what is so important about this meeting,> Reshyan asked, <that you want me to take two days away from my research for it?>

Nara's phores shone with a mixture of smug satisfaction and glee. <Jayanthi and Vaha have decided to release Akshaya from their original bargain in exchange for getting her the medical treatment that she needs.>

When Jayanthi had told Nara what she planned to do, his mind went into overdrive. The audience for *In Exile* had built with every episode, and it had grown exponentially along with the number of petitioners for exile reform. Billions had signed the so-called SomAx Pledge. How would they react to Akshaya's parents undermining the effort? Nara could only imagine the sense of outrage warring with the empathy built by the show.

Meanwhile, millions of humans clamored to outlaw the Anthro Challenge. This could be Akshaya's one and only chance to complete her circuit of Earth. Nara intended to emphasize Akshaya's illness and suffering to tug on the audience's heartstrings, and he had already decided to accelerate the story so that the next episode ended with Akshaya facing the biggest decision of her life. The previous episode would climax with Halli's disappearance. The events in between, including Akshaya's hospital stay, involved minimal drama, so zie could easily condense that and focus on Jayanthi's reunion with her child.

<They're going to allow her to remain on Earth?> Reshyan flashed. <What about her health?>

<What do you mean?>

<She keeps getting sick. It's obvious even to me, and I don't know anything about human physiology. The child belongs on Meru, according to her genetic design.>

Nara shrugged. <Why should that affect anything that we do? It's a matter between Akshaya and her makers, not our concern.>

<Have you ever thought that this whole endeavor is wrong? That we shouldn't turn a human child's life into entertainment?>

Mint-hued astonishment saturated Nara's phores. What had gotten into his stoic cameraperson? <It's a bit late for second thoughts,> Nara flashed. <Besides, I have the full consent of her makers. We're not exploiting a minor.>

Colors played across Reshyan's phores, too fast for Nara to process the jumble of feelings running through the pilot.

<If Akshaya accepts Jayanthi's offer,> Reshyan flashed at last, <she won't finish the Anthro Challenge.> Zir phores saturated with crimson and mint green.

<That's what makes it such a good development,> Nara enthused. For a moment, he was puzzled why the pilot would be so incredulous and angry, and then he remembered. Reshyan had more invested

in Akshaya's journey than a contract for labor. <Did you sign the pledge?>

Reshyan gave Nara a single, curt nod.

<At least you'll find out Akshaya's response sooner than the rest of the world.> Nara's phores flickered with amusement.

<You shouldn't allow Jayanthi to interfere like this.>

<Whyever not? It's too delicious for me to dissuade her. She, Vaha, and Somya's makers have already received many messages from fans of the show, offering support for their children. Imagine how much more they'll get after people find out about this! And who knows, perhaps exile reform will take on a life of its own, regardless of what Akshaya and Somya decide to do.>

<If the reform movement fails or if they quit, I'll hold you to our original agreement. You'll owe me a series devoted to the subject.>

Nara held up his hands in placation. <Of course. I may do that as a follow-up to this anyway. It would be interesting to document the politics and votes as they happen, and it would make for a good historical record.>

Reshyan's phores still rioted with negative emotions. Nara shrugged mentally. There was only so much he could do to convince Reshyan to see the narrative the way he did. A weathercrafter couldn't really understand the nature of directing a show.

<I've already ordered the indoor recorders,> Nara flashed. <They'll arrive at your station tomorrow. They're not large, so you should be able to carry them easily and deploy them when you need to.>

<Very well,> Reshyan said.

The pilot's drab figure disappeared from the mindspace. Nara turned his attention back to the latest episode, which needed finishing touches. The musical score and color saturation for Halli's loss didn't evoke enough heartbreak, never mind the shock value. Alloys didn't get to see much about human existence outside of Loka. Nara filed away an idea for a future series as a title coalesced in his mind: *Life on the Edge*, all about the dangers to humanity in the Out of Bounds. He already had a perfect cameraperson in Reshyan, and with the undisputed success of *In Exile*, Nara would never have to worry about finding an audience again.

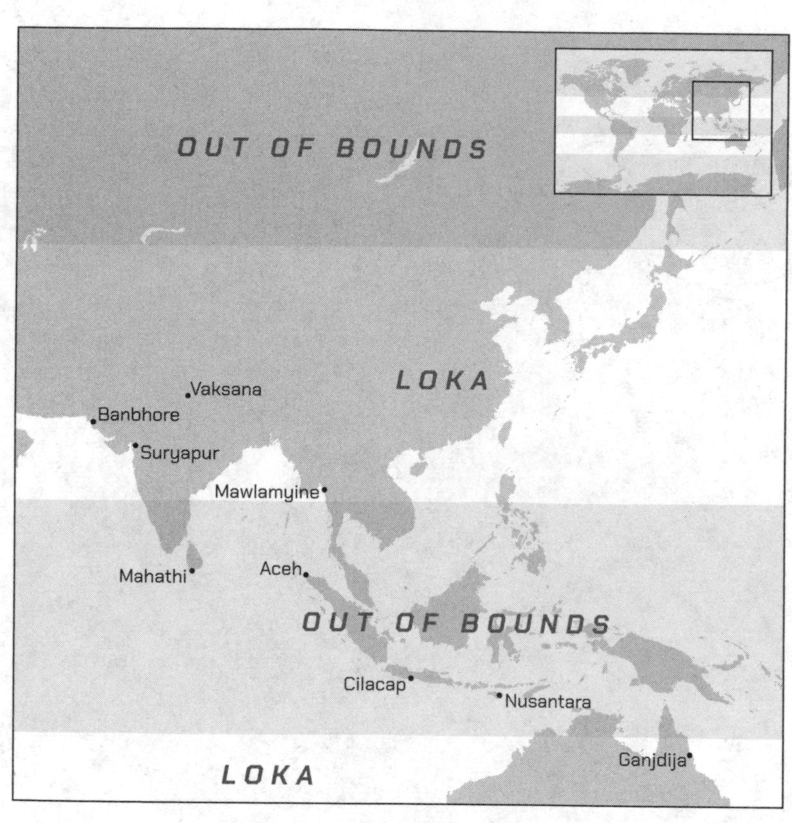
OUT OF BOUNDS
LOKA
Vaksana
Banbhore
Suryapur
Mawlamyine
Mahathi
Aceh
OUT OF BOUNDS
Cilacap
Nusantara
Ganjdija
LOKA

# DAY 140

The worst part of our journey to Australia wasn't my deteriorating health. It was the growing distance between me and Somya. We spoke to each other on the way, but only the minimum necessary to take care of the boat. More than once, I considered trying to talk to them, but then I would imagine our conversation. Would they expect me to back off from taking the gene therapy? I felt no need to apologize, except for my heartsib's anger. I had to do what was right for my life. According to my bodym, I had pushed myself past the limits of what hydration and oxygen could repair, and since I didn't have access to blood exchanges, the only way to finish the Anthro Challenge was to modify my DNA. I couldn't understand why Somya didn't see that.

One night, about eight hundred kilometers from Australia, Rune was up top and Somya below. I had gone to bed but couldn't sleep. The unsaid words between us weighed on me like a too-hot blanket, so I got up and made my way to the galley, where Somya was cleaning up from dinner.

"Why are you so opposed to it?" I said without preamble. "You should be happy that I can get rid of my sickle-cell disease. It means I can stay on Earth without any health problems."

Somya's shoulders tensed. They placed the metal pot back in the sink. "You have never understood how special you are. How lucky! You were born for a reason, Aks. There are humans of all kinds on Earth, but not one of them could go to Meru and start a new kind of society. I used to think that we could do that in the Out of Bounds—"

"Used to?"

"There's no way to make it happen." Somya rotated to face me. "You saw how people behave there. They're scavengers. They have no real ambition or drive to make the world a better place."

"Maybe they're too busy trying to stay alive."

"That's not the point," Somya said. "My old idea—my sense of purpose—it's not realistic. The OOBers would reject us, same as everyone else."

"So . . . what? Because you're afraid to try and fail, I should give up on my dreams?"

The words hit hard. I knew they would, and I regretted them as soon as I saw the pain on Somya's face.

"I think you should keep your options open, that's all." Somya resumed washing a dirty pan. "Not risk gene therapy using Human Era technology from some borderlands doctor."

"Doesn't the pledge matter to you?"

Somya set the clean pan in its storage cabinet, shut the door, and slammed the latch into place. "It's not our pledge, okay? The Anthro Challenge was supposed to be something we did for us, not for a bunch of politics about exile."

"Politics that matter a lot to my maker," I snapped. "And to me. Exile ruined my life, or did you forget that?"

"Sure it did. You go on believing that if you want to."

Somya left me and went above deck before I could respond. I hurled myself back into the V-shaped berth at the bow. What had they meant with that parting shot? It was easy for them to criticize me. They had spent more than half their life on Earth. They'd gotten to visit their family when Chedi passed through the Solar System. They'd tromped through jungles and swum with fish and caught raindrops on their tongue. I'd had none of those experiences until the past few months. Why did I have to give that up for some strangers on a planet two hundred light-years away? If we finished the Anthro Challenge, we could make sure no one else—neither human nor alloy—would have to suffer the consequences of exile again. Surely that was worth risking my health, which was terrible anyway. How much worse could I get?

It took me a long time to get to sleep that night, and the next one, too. I could hardly meet Somya's gaze in the following days. Rune watched our strained interaction with sad eyes, but he left us to make peace on our own. We weren't children, after all. But as we approached the harbor at Ganjdija, peace seemed as far away as home.

Australia marked the fourth continent on our journey. It didn't look all that different. The buildings that clustered around the bay had raised foundations and walls of woven wood, much like the hull of the *Svapna*, but they were painted with brightly colored patterns. The air felt warm and humid, as it had since we'd entered the equatorial OOB, and a light sea breeze dried the sweat on my brow. I watched Rune and Somya bring us into a dock. I couldn't do more than sit and breathe while the mask over my face softened the edges of reality.

That's why, when I set foot on land with Rune and Somya supporting me on either side, it took me a moment to recognize the person who stood in front of me. An array of spherical devices floated around her head like a silver aura.

"Akshaya." My mother held out her arms.

My brain tried to align her presence with my expectations, and after a few seconds of utter confusion, it succeeded.

I pulled off the breather. "Ma?"

Until her arms surrounded me, I hadn't realized how much I had missed my mother. My eyes stung as I relaxed into her grasp. The pain of her embrace made me wince, but she didn't let go, and I didn't pull away.

"It's all right," she murmured. "You're going to be fine."

"Hospital," I said, my mind still whirling. "Dr. Kirra. I have to see her. I'll explain there."

She frowned and looked as if she wanted to say something, but then decided against it. My mother took my right shoulder while Rune took the left. I glanced back at Somya, who trailed behind us. Our gazes locked for a second, and I saw my confusion mirrored in their face. What was my mother doing in Ganjdija?

---

Dr. Kirra looked about the same age as my mother, but she had darker brown skin and gray-green eyes. Her black hair was cropped close around her head, giving her face a hardness that softened when she smiled.

"So, the famous SomAx duo have decided to grace my hospital," Dr. Kirra said as she stood in our room. An intricate wheeled construct, about the same height as the doctor, waited beside her.

Daylight dappled the stone floor through small round skylights. Unlike most of the other buildings in Ganjdija, the hospital featured Human Era architecture, which surprised me, considering that we were inside the border of Loka. I would've expected the alloys to have demolished and digested the place long ago, but they had a minimal presence in the area, perhaps due to the remote location. Other parts of the city had relics of the past, too.

A nurse had brought the four of us—my mother, Somya, Rune, and myself—to one of the many rooms in the hospital. Only a quarter of them had occupants, so I had my own private room with a comfortable bed, two sling chairs, and a desk. The special indriyas that Nara had sent with my mother accompanied us inside. They arranged themselves near the ceiling to capture every part of the room. My mother and Rune had taken the chairs, and Somya perched on the desk.

The doctor glanced around and fixed her gaze on my mother. "You're Jayanthi, right?"

My mother inclined her head in assent.

Dr. Kirra's brows rose. "I wasn't expecting to see you here." She turned toward me. "I've been following your show, *In Exile*. I take it you're here because of an illness. Is it your sickle-cell disease again?"

I nodded. How could I explain the full situation in front of my mother? The weight of her expectations combined with Somya's disapproval and trapped the words inside me.

"I need treatment," I said.

The doctor's expression said *slightly-curious-and-concerned*. "Perhaps we should start by examining you. If you could lie back on the bed, please." She motioned with her hands, and the machine rolled over to us.

"No constructs," Somya and I said simultaneously.

"Don't worry, this device is based on old technology," the doctor said. "It lacks sufficient complexity to be considered a being. We have to be self-sufficient this far from the populated areas of Asia and Australia."

I tracked the machine's movements with my eyes. Five of its eight articulated arms moved over my body, grasping gently at my arms and legs, touching various spots on my torso and head. Its behavior resembled a construct's enough to make me uncomfortable. It was hard to imagine that humans had once relied on such devices for all kinds of tasks with no regard for their well-being. Everything in the universe had some consciousness, but my ancestors only recognized it in the most complex life on Earth. The device examined me with silent efficiency. Everyone waited until it rolled away from the bed and stood beside the doctor.

Dr. Kirra's gaze went distant, accessing her visual. I tried not to fidget. I accidentally locked eyes with Somya, and the corner of their mouth twitched upward. *It's too quiet,* they mouthed at me. I matched their tiny smile. Part of me relaxed. If Somya could make a joke, then our friendship wasn't entirely lost. Maybe they had come around to seeing my point of view. Maybe they approved of my decision to take the gene therapy.

That thought gave me the courage to speak up. Before I could lose my nerve, or the doctor could say something to change my mind, I blurted, "We would like to invite you to dinner."

Dr. Kirra's focus snapped back to me. "I see." She blinked a couple of times. "I'm free tonight, and I would be glad to accept."

Behind her, my mother's face took on a puzzled frown.

"In the meantime, then, let me provide you with pain medication. I'd like to add nutrients to the hydration sleeve that you're wearing, and I suggest that you continue to use the breather at high oxygen."

She left the room to get the supplies.

"Dinner?" my mother said.

Somya, Rune, and I exchanged glances, which only drove my mother's brows higher.

"I'll explain on the boat," I said. "We don't want to talk about it here."

I examined the indriyas above us. Would they follow my mother everywhere? I didn't want to endanger Dr. Kirra by revealing her secret work to the world, but how else could I tell my mother the truth?

After the doctor returned and loaded up the sleeve with what I needed, she lent us a wheelchair. My mother insisted on pushing it, and as we walked, I asked her if she could turn off the recording devices.

She couldn't.

"But you can ask Nara to remove certain parts for my safety, right?" I asked.

"Yes."

That meant I could ask for the conversation about Dr. Kirra's gene therapy to stay private. It wouldn't make what I had to say any easier, though. I wanted to permanently change the DNA that made my mother and me unique—the genes that she had chosen to give me. I knew it would feel like a rejection to her, but I had to make her understand that I wanted this for myself, that it had nothing to do with her or her dreams and everything to do with my own.

---

I rested for a few hours, unable to string two sentences together as pain spiraled through my body and sucked away my energy. By the time relief kicked in, the sun was setting and Dr. Kirra had arrived at the boat for dinner.

The five of us arranged ourselves around the stern of the boat. My mother was to my left on the starboard bench. Dr. Kirra and Somya sat across from us, and Rune took the cockpit chair. The indriya recorders settled on the masts or floated above my mother's head. I wondered if our alloy minder flew somewhere above us, too. *Thank the stars this isn't going out live!*

I took a deep breath, focused on Dr. Kirra's seafoam-colored eyes, and got right to the point. "I heard that you give gene therapy using Human Era technology. I want to get rid of my sickle-cell disease."

Dr. Kirra tilted her head. "I do sometimes offer that service to OOBers who have no other option, including their children, but you don't fit that profile."

The nurse in Nabouwalu hadn't mentioned those constraints.

"But you can do the procedure?" I pressed.

"There's a difference between *can* and *will.* Your medical scan shows a severe amount of sickling in your blood. Before we can consider something as traumatic as gene therapy, we'll have to improve your baseline health. At the very least, you need a blood exchange."

"Akshaya," my mother said in a remarkably even tone, "what do you think you're doing?"

I forced myself to face her. Disbelief inscribed every muscle in her body.

"It's the best way to finish the Anthro Challenge, Ma. Every time I get sick, we fall further behind. I owe it to Halli, to Som—"

"Don't drag me into this," my friend interrupted, their expression bland. "I didn't agree with your decision."

"—and to everyone who's signed the pledge," I continued. "We have less than thirty days before Chedi's last shuttle leaves from Earth. Gene therapy will give me the best chance of getting home in time to catch it and fulfill my bargain with you."

"You can only take this therapy once," my mother said. "You're not an alloy. You can't change your mind later and restore your original DNA."

"I know. The entire way here from Nabouwalu, that's almost all I've thought about." I thought my mother would react with anger. Instead, I saw tears in her eyes. "There's no other way. I have to do this."

She took my hands in hers. "You're wrong—there is another option. Your maker and I talked it over and"—she took a deep breath—"we're willing to let you stay on Earth for as long as you want. You don't have to finish the Anthro Challenge. You *definitely* don't need to risk gene therapy with Human Era technology. All we want is for you to come home and get healthy again. Nothing matters to us more than that."

My world shrank to my mother's gaze, locked unflinchingly on mine. I could see worry in the lines of her face, the sacrifice she was ready to make for me. All the words I'd prepared, the arguments to persuade her—all of them fled my mind. My parents were ready to let me live my dream. All I had to do was let go of the Anthro Challenge, the struggle that had consumed me for nearly half a year, the journey that had caused so much pain.

"Well, that makes it all easier," Somya said. Their voice had a lightness to it that I hadn't heard since Halli's death. "Come on, Aks, it's not even a choice at this point. We've done most of what we set out to do—we've sailed across two oceans, survived a hurricane, visited the Out of Bounds, climbed mountains, crossed rivers, and now you can stay on

Earth. We can do the whole thing again and do it right. You wouldn't have to push your body past its limits. We could climb everything that can be climbed. Just say yes!"

"Not if the counterprotest succeeds in outlawing the AC," I pointed out. "The Committee for Intercontinental Travel might never approve of this kind of journey again. And if we don't complete the challenge, the people who signed the pledge won't support exile reform."

"You're seventeen years old," my mother said. "You don't need to take responsibility for that. People will understand that you had to prioritize your health. Let Nara and the proxies figure out how to put the right spin on it."

"And remember what I said," Rune added. "Things like this can take on a life of their own. If people are truly moved to change the system, they won't need you to destroy your health over it."

Part of me wanted to accept, to allow my mother to take charge, as she always had, and to put aside the burden of such a big decision. But as I tried to imagine quitting the Anthro Challenge, I thought about what my future would look like on Earth. I wouldn't have accomplished anything that Somya and I had dreamed about in Chedi. Replicating Rune's journey. Finding an OOB location to recreate the megaconstruct lifestyle. Understanding what it meant to live like a human being.

I recalled Halli's words. How I loved to explore, and how I failed to see Meru as the pinnacle of that. Could I make the life that I wanted there, rather than in the Out of Bounds? Would a society that allowed all kinds of people—humans, alloys, constructs—accept my hybrid nature? At a fundamental level, humankind had turned me away, just as they had turned against their own former nature, in order to save themselves. I had begun the Anthro Challenge expecting that I would prove my fitness for Earth, but I'd done the opposite. If I quit the AC with no hope of doing it again, what purpose would remain for me on Earth?

Dr. Kirra broke the silence. "I can see that you need some time to discuss this further."

She stood and my mother rose.

"Before you go, Doctor," my mother said, "you mentioned the need for a blood exchange. I brought an emergency supply that we've been culturing, just in case. Could you provide the machine?"

"Of course," Dr. Kirra said. "I'll stop by the hospital and have it delivered here."

"Thank you," my mother said.

Rune walked Dr. Kirra off the *Svapna*. Above us, stars glittered like diamond dust across a clear night sky. Somya leaned over and tapped the switch on the cockpit to turn on the deck lights. Bioluminescence glowed in primary colors from the masts and the railing.

My mother sat down and turned to me. "This journey has changed you." She smiled wistfully. "You don't need me to tell you what's right anymore. That's your decision, and I trust you to make it for yourself, but it's a big one. Maybe you should sleep on it?"

"I want to talk it over with Som first," I replied. "Alone, please."

Without a word, my heartsib walked to the cabin door and held it open. My mother gave me a gentle squeeze and let go.

Somya's face remained impassive in the dim lighting belowdecks. The silence between us made my heart ache. I had never fought with them before, not like that, and I simultaneously wanted to shake sense into them and beg their forgiveness.

"You already know how I feel about the gene therapy," Somya said quietly. "What is there to talk about?"

"I have another idea," I said.

"I'm listening."

"The blood exchange will make me feel a lot better. I'll do the exchange, skip the gene therapy for now, and then we finish the AC."

Somya's expression relaxed into thoughtfulness. "Do you think it'll be enough for you to continue?"

"We're only a month away from home. I bet I can make it back before I get worse again."

"It's definitely a better idea than risking gene therapy here."

"There's only one problem. I'll need time to recover after the procedure, at least a week. That means—"

"We'd miss the shuttle back to Chedi."

I nodded.

"But it doesn't matter now. Your mother said you can stay here."

"What about you and your parents?"

Somya made an *oh-right-that* face. "I don't know what they'd do. They might keep going on their own. I have family here, adults who can look after me. It wouldn't be any different than you living with your grandparents. It might even work to our advantage. We could visit each other as often as alloy transport allows, or live together and take turns at our family homes."

"That would be amazing," I said. "Som, I've hated the way we've been since . . . since the rogue wave." I couldn't say *Halli died* out loud. "I don't know if staying on Earth is right for me anymore. All our dreams about starting a new kind of society in the Out of Bounds—none of that seems possible, not with my health and the way the OOBers treat me. What if nobody on Earth wants me because of what I am?"

Somya placed their hands on my shoulders. "I'll want you, and I'll be here with you. Rune will, too. You know that."

They enfolded me in a very tight hug. I blinked away the tears that prickled behind my eyes and pulled back.

"Maybe I shouldn't stay," I said. "Maybe I should go where I truly belong."

"Where you belong . . . do you mean Meru?"

"Yes," I whispered. "I don't know anymore. When we started all this, I was so sure about everything, so sure that the Anthro Challenge would give me the life that I wanted. Now, I have no idea what's right—for me, for you, for the planet, for all the humans who don't fit."

Somya took a deep breath, blew it out, and then laughed. "Okay, that is all too much to carry on your scrawny little shoulders right now. One day at a time. One problem at a time, right? You don't have to figure everything out right now. First, get better. Then we finish the challenge. Then you can worry about whether or not to stay."

I exhaled and nodded. "You're right."

"Of course I am."

"And my shoulders aren't scrawny."

"Yes, they are."

I swatted at Somya's head, and they dodged it easily.

"Now go lie down and get some rest."

They were right about that, too. The conversation had used up the last of my strength. I crawled into the bed at the bow and closed my eyes. The next thing I knew, my mother's hand was on my shoulder, waking me. The blood machine had arrived, and she'd brought it to me, along with the breather. I sat and pulled up my sleeve.

As my mother attached the equipment to my arm, I said, "I've decided not to take the gene therapy." Her hands stilled for a second. "But I am going to finish the Anthro Challenge," I added before she could interrupt. "This treatment will help, and it should get me the rest of the way home. You know how I feel about exile. I can't let the chance to reform it slip away, and I know it'll mean a lot to Maker."

"I signed the SomAx pledge, too," my mother said.

My phores lit with surprise.

She traced one of the glowing spots on my arm. "The world will see these soon. Nara has footage from when you revealed your chromatophores. I told him he can use it in the show. He said he's waiting for the right moment, and I don't know when that will be, but you don't have to worry about hiding yourself anymore."

I leaned against her shoulder. "Thank you, Ma."

She kissed the top of my head. "I'm sorry I put so much on you. Given what happened between your grandmaker and your maker, I should have known better than to burden you with expectations. Life is a gift, and you are free to decide what you want to do with yours. I'll support whatever you choose."

For the second time that night, I repressed the urge to cry. I didn't tell her about my conversation with Somya. The Anthro Challenge had shown me exactly the opposite of what I'd hoped for at the start. I couldn't have adventures on Earth without damaging my health. At the same time, there was so much more of the planet that I wanted to explore, so much about humanity that I hoped to understand. If I went to Meru, I had no idea how long it would be until I could return, nor how long I could stay on Earth when I did.

I lay down in the bed and pulled the breather on. "Will you remind me about Meru and the project? I've forgotten a lot of the details."

After a moment of surprise, she said, "Of course. But first, let me tell you about the time I taught your maker how to skip stones on a lake. You'll understand why when I'm done." She gave my hand a gentle squeeze. "It was before I knew that I was pregnant with you. Your maker hadn't spent time on a planet before Meru, so for fun I taught zir how to skip stones. Naturally zie was terrible at it." She smiled. "Afterward, we talked about a dream that one day we would live together there and raise a family. I could *see* it, Akshaya. Our child—you—in the open air of the planet, climbing rocks and trees. Me and your maker walking behind you, hand in hand. That dream took root over time.

"There's nowhere else in the universe where humans, alloys, and hybrids"—she shot me an *I-said-that-on-purpose* look—"can share a planet on equal terms. We have a chance to do it right this time, to avoid the mistakes of our past." She stroked my hair, and her voice grew softer. "You are a direct result of that dream. I had assumed that you would share that vision with us. I never meant for it to become an obligation, and I should have considered that you'd be your own person. Until you become a parent, you won't understand how difficult it is to let your child grow up." She settled herself beside me and kissed my head. "The project parameters don't necessarily apply to our family. People are curious whether your body will behave differently than those of the womb-born children on Meru. It's likely that you have congenital factors that they don't. Even if you go there years from now, you can contribute useful information. There's no rush. And if you decide to change yourself to suit the Earth, your maker and I will be sad, but we will support you as much as we can from afar. Take as much time as you need to understand the path you want to walk, because that, more than any destination, will define you."

# DAY 150

We spent two days in Ganjdija's harbor while a machine removed and replaced my sickled blood. While there, I told Dr. Kirra that I wouldn't be needing her "other" services, after all, and she looked pleased at my decision. It took another three days before I felt comfortable without a steady stream of pain medication, and two days after that before we were ready to depart. To my surprise, my mother decided to sail with us. We had to go north around Australia and then west, through the Arafor and Timor Seas, into the Indian Ocean, then north again for nearly two weeks before we would reenter Loka. Between our schedule and potential hostility from Loka's residents, we decided to skip the overland portion that would take us near Somya's family. We would put into port as close to Vaksana as we could.

"We'll be spending most of our time in the Out of Bounds," I pointed out to my mother. "And you'll have to follow all the rules of the AC."

"I can handle it," she said. "I've been through worse."

"That was a literal lifetime ago by my measure."

She grinned with a gleam in her eye that I had never seen. "That's exactly why I want to come along. Besides, I've never had the opportunity to sail before. I'm not about to pass it up."

Her sickle-cell condition had always been more sensitive than mine, so she couldn't do as much physical work as I could, but she was a quick study. Quicker than I expected, if I was honest. Initially, Rune and Somya split the shifts, with my mother and me acting as seconds. On the third day, as we passed the island of Moa, I felt well enough to take command with my mother backing me up. It felt good to sit in the cockpit again, listening to the snap of fabric, the clanking of fasteners, the rush of waves—holding the wheel lightly under my hands as I gazed up at the telltale ribbons blowing steady and true. At the start of our journey, I would never have thought a boat could feel so much like home.

The ache of Halli's absence had eased enough that I could look around, see their ghost, and not tumble into instant despair. Sailing onward felt like fulfilling a promise. I hadn't made up my mind about what to do after the challenge, but with every passing kilometer, I found it easier to think of places beyond Earth. If we built a sailboat on another planet and learned its waters, wouldn't that be the ultimate way to honor Halli's restless feet? If they'd lived, would they have spoken against the renegade gene therapy, like Somya? Would they have invited me to stay with them on Earth's oceans?

My mother's hand on my shoulder interrupted my ruminations.

"Can I have a turn at the wheel?" she asked.

I stood and invited her to take my seat. "Want to learn some maneuvers?"

She arched her eyebrows. "I'd love to."

I spent the next hour teaching her how to turn, how to keep the wind in the sails, and how to work the controls. Her mistakes made me realize how much I'd learned since the day I set foot on Isin's *Zephyros*. I found it hard to believe that only four months had passed since then. After we got the boat back on course, we took a break to nibble on green grapes and pale-yellow cheese.

"I can see why you're enamored with this lifestyle," my mother said. She sighed. "I've missed you. It's been hard the last few months, not having you or your maker with me." She stroked my head. "I don't know how I'll manage only seeing you every year or two."

"You did the same thing to your parents," I pointed out.

"That's true. I didn't feel so wistful then, and I imagine you don't now." She smiled. "You could stay on the *Svapna*, you know, if Rune would have you. He seems to enjoy your company. You might not get another chance at the Anthro Challenge, but sailing would give you a way to keep seeing the world, and I'm sure Rune could use some young hands."

After a moment, I said, "I wish you could've met Halli."

"Me too."

"They loved the sea." I could understand why Halli's loss would spur people to make journeys like ours illegal. And yet, Halli had loved the adventure. They had grown up in the Out of Bounds, with its inherent risks, and had chosen their lifestyle. "If the CDS outlaws the Anthro Challenge, they should also stop letting people live in the OOB," I said. "It's inconsistent to allow one but not the other."

"Inconsistency is the hallmark of biological beings," my mother said with a wry smile. "Our actions are often at odds with our best interests. It's part of what makes us human . . . or alloy or hybrid."

"Why did you decide to stop hiding my chromatophores?"

"Because my original idea—to wait until we were settled on Meru—might never happen, and after everything you've gone through on this journey, you're practically an adult."

"You started treating me like one after I turned fifteen."

"In some ways, yes, because of your maker's mindset. Alloy habits die hard." She said it with a fond smile. "But now I think you've earned it as a human being, too. You shouldn't have to hide your true self anymore. Nara said that he's saving it for the right episode, whatever that means. I'm sure we'll know as soon as it goes public. I only hope that the laws against double jeopardy will protect me."

"What do you mean, *protect you*?"

"The gene modifications I gave you go against tarawan standards."

I shrugged. "Isn't my very existence illegal?"

"Not your existence, but definitely your conception, and also your DNA."

"Besides, you're not a tarawan, so why should their rules apply?"

My mother had once dreamed of being a genetic designer, the first human allowed to practice in that field, and she had made me illegally while on Meru. The law eventually changed to allow human tarawans, but by then, my mother had gone into exile as punishment for bringing me into the world. She would never get a license to practice, or so she'd always told me.

"Genetic engineering rules exist for historical reasons," my mother said. She tucked a loose curl of windblown hair behind her ear. "They apply to everyone, regardless of professional status. Much like with Meru and space travel, I think enough time has passed that some of those reasons no longer hold true. Just because we couldn't safely create hybrids centuries ago doesn't mean we still can't. You're evidence of that."

"Do you think," I said, choosing my words with care, "that they'll allow others like me—other hybrids—to be made on Meru?"

She took a minute to think it over. "People might have an easier time accepting the risks if they're away from Earth. Many see Homesite, the human village, as an experiment already."

What if I could live with others who had chromatophores or similar genetic changes? People whose bodies didn't incorporate the extra chromosomes of an alloy but who weren't entirely human, either. My uniqueness hadn't bothered me in Chedi because everyone there treated me like one of them, but the humans on Earth had found me unsettling.

I wanted a home where I could do more than exist. I wanted to integrate seamlessly with every form of consciousness in my surroundings, as Toya's people did, and to thrive in ways that inspired others rather than worried them. I wasn't going to find that in Loka or the Out of Bounds or even in Chedi.

And yet . . . and yet . . . I wasn't quite ready to make the decision. When I tried to form the words, I couldn't speak them, even though I knew they would make my mother happy. The thought of starting all over on Meru with no friends depressed me. The few humans at Homesite were either my parents' age or several years younger than me. I thought about Halli, about that first hint of feelings that went beyond friendship. On Meru, I'd have no one to pour my heart out to. I didn't fit on Earth. I had no purpose in Chedi. Meru would benefit my health and allow me to live adventurously, but what was the point if I had to do it alone?

# DAY 160

For the next week and a half, we sailed without any major problems. Our route traced the western arc of the Sunda islands in Southeast Asia, and we had plenty of sheltered coves to anchor in during rough weather. We encountered strong winds, but no storms bad enough to damage the boat. My mother got her sea legs and became a competent sailor, though she didn't love it the way Somya and I did. Rune seemed to appreciate her company, perhaps more than ours, and they spent a lot of time talking. Rune especially enjoyed hearing about her stays at the Primary Nivid, the only permanent structure in all of CDS space, and the one place off Earth that he wanted to visit. I'd never had a strong urge to go, but after watching Rune's face light up as he listened to my mother's stories, I felt a small pang of regret at not seeing it.

As we neared the island of Nias, we crossed the equator again. All we had left to meet the requirements of the Anthro Challenge was to get home. I almost didn't want to celebrate the milestone, given that the previous crossing occurred on the same day as Halli's death, but we put into port at Nias with clear skies, and Rune wouldn't allow me to indulge my superstition. After dinner, we toasted to the memory of our friend and our arrival in the northern hemisphere.

The next day, we turned westward toward Mahathi. Somya and I were on the night shift when we noticed a fog bank like a puffy wall across the horizon. At first, I thought it might indicate the presence of an island, but there was nothing on the map for a hundred kilometers in any direction. We confirmed our location as best as we could, then locked the steering wheel and hoped that the wind wouldn't shift as we headed into the mist.

The vapor around us glowed a pale bluish white. At first I attributed the light to the moon, but the waxing crescent didn't seem bright enough, and the luminance grew stronger as we sailed. Suddenly the water ahead of us shone with a matching color. I had a sense of vertigo as the ocean and sky merged into a solid mass of pale blue. Were we sailing or flying?

"What is this?" Somya breathed from the railing.

I joined them and gazed outward, trying to recall whether Rune had mentioned anything like this in his book. A different reference surfaced in my mind.

"I think this is the milky ocean," I said, keeping my voice soft. I felt like my speaking would disturb the illusion. "I read about this somewhere in the *Field Guide to Earth Flora and Fauna*. It's a kind of bioluminescence that can stretch over huge spans of the water's surface. The fog makes it a lot more strange."

I rolled up my sleeves and tried to get my phores to match the glow around us. Somya laughed at my efforts, which had far too much violet, but eventually I calmed down enough to get it right.

"I'm impressed," they said. "You look like you have ghostly arms."

<If I could practice more, I'd be better at this,> I flashed. Then, aloud: "My mother gave Nara permission to reveal my hybrid nature. He hasn't done it yet, but she's sure it'll happen before the end of the series."

I explained her reasoning to Somya, who nodded in approval.

"What will you do once everyone knows?"

"I'm scared," I admitted. "After the way Lumo and the other bounders reacted, and what happened with Ebra and the protest, I'm not sure whether I'll be allowed to bare my arms or have to keep them hidden. I don't want other humans to look at me as if I'm not one of them."

"Is it really so bad if you're not?"

I replied using my chromatophores. <I wish I felt more welcome here.> I didn't know how to say *Earth* in phoric, which seemed ironically appropriate. I gathered up the shreds of my courage and flashed, <There's only one place I can be myself.>

A light came back into Somya's eyes. "Are you considering going to Meru?"

I nodded.

Somya smiled.

"Would that make you happy?" I asked aloud, my phores edged with orange. "Didn't you beg me not to leave you? Which, by the way, is not something I'm excited to do."

"You're not the only one who gets brilliant ideas." They grabbed me by the shoulder and turned me to face them. With a dramatic flourish of their arms, Somya said, "What if I came with you to Meru? Think about it! There won't be a law against the Anthro Challenge there. We could be the first to circumnavigate it!"

I pointed out the obvious. "You can't thrive there. You'd get sicker than I do here."

"Unless . . ." Their smile widened into a grin.

"Unless what?"

"Unless *I'm* the one who gets gene therapy."

Understanding slowly dawned. Adults who relocated to Meru had their DNA altered to introduce sickle cell and other changes that would help them stay healthy in the high-oxygen atmosphere. Somya could sign up to do the same.

"You could never undo it," I said. I couldn't keep the dismay from my voice or my chromatophores.

"Worth it."

"And you'd have to wait until you're twenty-one."

"We already know that isn't true." They held up a hand as I started to protest. "If Dr. Kirra can successfully give gene therapy to humans under twenty-one, then so can Chedi, and Chedi sets her own rules. She returns to the Solar System every two years, so we'll have to wait that long, but that's better than five years."

Everything Somya said was true. Chedi might choose to ask Somya's parents for approval, but strictly speaking, the sovereign megaconstruct wasn't bound by the laws of the CDS within herself. She could treat Somya, and when they were ready, send them off to Meru. We could live there. Adventure there. Fulfill our dream to start a new kind of society there.

My heart felt five times too large for my chest. The world around us reflected my joy in its gentle radiance. I flung my arms around Somya and said, in a choked voice, "Together or not at all."

"Together," they said and held me tight.

# NARA (DAY 167)

Nara gathered the show's entire staff in mindspace. They floated in what he liked to call the assembly room, which had walls of deeply oiled rosewood arranged in a spacious cube with pale-pink veins that illuminated the group. Most of the crew had dressed for the occasion in elaborate tunics worked with embroidered designs. Metalwork snaked up their arms. Gems studded their throats and tails. Headwear followed the latest trends—long, floaty, and full bodied.

Reshyan stuck out both literally and figuratively. The pilot floated just far enough from the others to make it clear that zie didn't consider zirself one of them. No clothes. No decorations. No headwear.

The inconsistency pained Nara. He did his best to put aside his irritation. If *In Exile* concluded with Akshaya and Somya completing the Anthro Challenge, Nara wouldn't have to work with Reshyan much longer. The SomAx pledge gathered momentum like a black hole passing through a nebula. It was possible that the practice of exile would be outlawed entirely instead of reformed, at which point, Nara would have discharged his obligation to Reshyan. He still considered the political movement good material for a documentary, but he'd much rather create it for pleasure than from contractual obligation.

Nara pulled his thoughts back to the moment. The experienced staff—the ones who'd worked with him before—knew to expect a pep talk before the final episode, but even they had no idea what Nara was about to propose. They suspected something, though, given that more than half the group were newcomers. As the popularity of the project had grown, numerous people had reached out to Nara asking if they could work with him. He'd contracted with his favorites as the penultimate episode approached. He would need them.

<This is it, people,> he flashed, his words glowing with urgency. <In about seven days Earth time—that's six kaals for us—the crew of the *Svapna* should arrive at the port in Suryapur. The second to last episode will go out the day before they reach land. After that,> he paused dramatically, <we go live.> Phores around the room lit with surprise. <Yes, live, for the remainder of the show. We'll have multiple indriya feeds to choose from, and I will be working every hour that our subjects are awake to decide what footage to use. The assistant directors will make the final edits on their nighttime activities, which should be minimal.>

The live broadcast would have less than one hundred seconds of delay. It would need music and lighting effects and a hundred other little touches, and the crew would have to make quick decisions with little opportunity for oversight. A constructed mind would translate human speech to phoric and manage the technical side of broadcasting the feed from Earth to the rest of the Solar System.

<What this means for all of you,> Nara continued, <is round-the-clock shifts for three to four kaals, which is how long we estimate the overland journey will take. I've tried to distribute the more experienced people across each team, but every one of you is here because I trust that you have the skills and dedication to pull this off.> Nara rotated to face his most essential collaborator. <Reshyan, what did your project manager say? Do you have permission to take a week to devote to this?>

<No,> the pilot flashed. <She denied my request. I decided to resign from that project in favor of this one.>

Nara didn't try to hide his surprise. He hadn't expected that much dedication, but he had no time to question it.

<Happy to hear that you can devote your full attention to this,> he flashed. <Obviously you can sleep when Akshaya and Somya sleep.>

<Yes.>

Nara turned back to the group. <With Reshyan's help, we'll deploy and recall indriyas in real time. Few people have dared to release a continuous live documentary of humans from Earth. This is our chance to join their ranks. I'm sure you won't disappoint me. Any questions?>

The newest producer flashed, <What do we show when they're asleep? Nobody's going to want to immerse themselves in that.>

<Good question,> Nara replied. <I'd like to compile snippets from previous episodes, as well as fan reactions in the form of interviews, especially from people who are in-body.>

It was easy to get the attention of alloys who lived in stasis. Much harder to chase down those who were flying around the system or, worse, inhabiting an incarn on the Earth's surface.

<What about humans?> someone flashed.

<Especially the antichallengers,> someone else flashed.

Conversations lit up all around the room, too fast for Nara to keep up, but he let the discussion go for a bit. Part of the reason for bringing everyone together was to exchange ideas. After a suitable amount of time, he brightened the lights until they washed out people's phores. Once he had their attention, he dimmed the room back to a comfortable level.

<Lots of good ideas,> Nara flashed. <For the overnight teams, you'll have more leeway in putting together interesting content. I suggest you get a head start now. For everyone else, please find your shift assignments in your calendars, along with those of your crew members. I've scheduled a follow-up meeting for one kaal from today. That should give everyone enough time to get their bearings and come back with a coherent set of concerns and suggestions.>

Nara waited to see whether anyone had strenuous objections. No one did. The excitement in the room was clearly visible. Nara issued a thought-command to disband the group, and they vanished from his view. He switched to his usual office environment, called up the bubbles for the upcoming episode, and sent a note to his first assistant director. One of the overnight streams would contain a flashback to Akshaya's accidental reveal of her chromatophores. At some point before she reached Vaksana, the world would see the full extent of her genetic modifications. All that remained was for Nara to choose the right moment.

# DAY 174

Two weeks after experiencing the milky ocean, we arrived at the harbor in Suryapur. The Out of Bounds weather had continued to treat us well, to the point that I confronted my mother about it. She denied knowing of any alloy interference, though that didn't put my suspicions completely to rest. A weathercrafter who was against the pledge could sabotage the Anthro Challenge by interfering with the atmosphere or the ocean, but why would anyone modify conditions in our favor? Would it count as a violation of the AC if we hadn't requested or known about it?

When Somya and I had first dreamed of doing the challenge, the rules had seemed so straightforward. My weeks on Earth had shown me how wrong we'd been. Unlike life inside a megaconstruct, life on a planet was complex and chaotic. Alloys and humans didn't exist in separate bubbles. They were linked as closely as the sheets and sails on a boat. Even in the Out of Bounds, humans couldn't escape the effects of alloy actions, and vice versa. Everything was connected—from the rope under my hands to the wood of the hull, to the saltwater that carried us, to the ocean floor and the magma beneath, and somewhere along the way, to Halli's body—just as the Principles of Conscious Beings indicated. In turn, our actions affected the sail and the wind and the clouds, and beyond, to space, to my maker's true body, and to Chedi, zooming through the system. My breath. Somya's. My mother's hip nudging mine. Rune's laughter in my ears. Sunlight warming my skin. All of it linked in the inextricable dance of the universe.

As the first light of dawn touched the top of the main mast, we secured the *Svapna* to a floating dock in Suryapur's harbor. Rune, Somya, and I unloaded our things. My mother's health had noticeably declined. I could tell from the way she held her body and the shallowness of her breaths. She insisted on continuing with us, and for the first time, I understood why my recklessness had caused her so much concern. Her health problems had always scared me when I was little, and I found myself feeling protective of her. It was a strange and unsettling position that reversed our usual dynamic.

When everything was ready, Rune turned and pulled me and Somya into a group hug. "I will miss you both very much. You are the wind in my sails and the water 'neath my hull. Anytime you want another day on the sea, just ask."

"Thank you," Somya said.

"I'll miss you, too," I said simultaneously.

With a smile and a wave, Rune turned and headed back to the *Svapna*. I watched until his teal hair disappeared into the cabin. He was my last connection to Halli, and part of me didn't want to walk away from that. I tried my best to fix the scene in my mind—the placid blue water, the great masts reaching for the sky, the intricate texture of the woven-wood hull, the memory of Halli standing on the deck with the wind in their hair.

"Ready?" my mother asked, touching my shoulder.

Somya strode to their bike. I helped my mother get settled on the trailer before taking my position. We pushed off and pedaled around the outskirts of Suryapur, heading north and east toward Vaksana.

My mother had tempered her reaction when I told her about my decision to go to Meru after all. I could see a million what-why-how questions in the crinkle of her eyes and the quirk of her brow, but all she said was, "If you're sure, then I'm glad." She had embraced me, and

I squeezed her extra tight in thanks for not pushing me to explain it all. I would tell her at some point, preferably after sorting out Somya's fate. Maybe after they joined me on Meru.

With each passing kilometer, an invisible rope tugged at my heart, urging me back toward the coast, toward the *Svapna* and the lingering ghost of Halli's presence. I forced myself to focus on Somya's back. My heartsib had offered a great sacrifice to be with me on Meru, and I couldn't throw that away to ease the ache in my chest. We would have to find a way to memorialize Halli once we got there. In the meantime, the best way I could honor them was to finish the Anthro Challenge.

---

The strangers showed up when we stopped for lunch. Two humans walked down the trail from the direction we were headed and stood a few meters away. My mother waved at them, but they didn't react.

"Curious," she said.

One of the indriyas moved to hover above them.

"Is Nara doing something that we don't know about?" I asked in a low voice.

"Not that I'm aware of," she replied, equally quiet.

"I bet they're saying something on the public network," Somya said.

Before my mother or I could respond, Somya walked over and cheerfully explained who we were and that we would be on our way after lunch. The two humans said nothing. They stared straight ahead with the distant gazes of people focused on their visual displays.

Somya turned back toward us with a baffled shrug.

We did our best to eat our meal and clean up as their silent gazes prickled our necks. They did nothing to interfere, though, and they made no move to stop us as we pedaled away.

High wispy white clouds filtered the spring sunshine. Wildflowers dotted the plains and surrounded us with their heady aroma. My mood lifted as we got farther from the strange couple. We saw alloys along the way, but they ignored us and focused on their work—tending to plant life, breaking down rubble from old structures, taking samples of land and water.

As we skirted the only good-size city on our route, we spotted more human bystanders. Once again, they did little except silently watch us go by. A few shook their heads at us. More showed up as the day went on, and by the time we neared our planned stopping point, all three of us felt unsettled.

"Maybe we should find a spot farther from the trail," my mother suggested in a low voice. "Somewhere more private."

I pointed up at the indriyas. "They'll be able to find us wherever we go, thanks to Nara."

"Those are recording devices," my mother said. "Only Nara and Reshyan have access to them."

"Somehow they've anticipated our route," I said.

"I wish they would tell us what they want," Somya grumbled.

"I think we should push on," I said. "We should be able to cover another hundred and fifty kilometers today, which will put us halfway to Vaksana. That's four more hours. If we do another thirteen-hour stretch tomorrow, we can reach home."

"Can you handle that much?" Somya asked.

I shrugged. "It's only two days, and once we reach my grandparents' house, I'll have access to my mother's blood-exchange machine. It won't matter if I arrive exhausted."

My mother nodded in agreement. "I don't know what these people intend, and the sooner we can find out, the better."

"Maybe they're supporters of the pledge," Somya theorized, "and they're not communicating because they don't want to break the rules?"

"They could safely cheer us on," I said. "If they're anti-AC petitioners, that would explain the lack of enthusiasm, but why bother to stand along our route?"

We set aside our speculations and continued onward, riding north and east as the sun dropped behind us. Shortly after it set, we arrived on the outskirts of the small town of Chithor and set up camp near the banks of the Berach River. Somya pitched the tent while I assembled the stove and started on our dinner. By the time we finished our meal, fourteen silent visitors had gathered nearby. I counted them as I rinsed our dishes clean. Would they stay overnight? They had nothing to sleep on, so I guessed they must have come from the nearby town.

"Good thing we don't have to restock," I said as I lay down to sleep. I pulled the breather mask over my face. My mother insisted that I use it since I'd been active all day.

"I don't like this," she said from beside me. Her hip pressed against mine. "Maybe I should separate from you so I can find out what's going on."

"And then what?" I asked. "You can't tell us without breaking the challenge rules, and we'd have to leave you behind."

My mother made a frustrated noise.

"One more day," Somya said with their usual cheer. "So what if we have a silent audience for the final stretch? Maybe they're going to throw us a big party at the end."

I snorted. My mother sighed. We all adjusted ourselves, getting arms and legs into the most comfortable positions we could with three people and the breather. We'd picked up a new tent at Ganjdija, but the best one we could find on short notice was intended for two. I didn't mind the cramped quarters too much. With my mother's back against mine and my arm across Somya's torso, I felt the first semblance of peace in a long time.

# DAY 175

Our answers came at dawn, in the form of an alloy who approached me as soon as I emerged from our tent. I woke up first, and I had slept in the middle, so crawling out was easy. Getting past the deerlike figure that sat in my way was less so. At first, I thought it strange that a wild animal would stay so close to human smells. Then I noticed the thicker, shorter neck, and the flattened shape of the face. Identification popped up in my visual. She was an alloy named Kamma.

The spots on her neck lit up. <Greetings. I am a friend,> she flashed in slow, clear phoric, as if to a child.

In my barely awake and slightly shocked state, I didn't know how to respond. I acknowledged her words with a small bow and left to answer the call of nature. When I returned, I found a human sitting beside the alloy. His name was Dhira, and he explained that he had come to support us.

"How come you're talking to us but those other humans won't?" I asked. Hastily, I added, "Don't answer that if it violates the Anthro Challenge rules."

Dhira grinned through his dark beard, the bottom of which grazed his chest. "I wouldn't dare after you've come so far. Those people think you have serious behavioral problems and should be genetically treated or else expelled from Loka. Their presence is a demonstration of their feelings. They don't have much love for your mother or your friend

Somya, either, but you represent the worst because, well, you aren't entirely human." He said the last part apologetically, as if he didn't want to admit that it was true.

So Nara had finally revealed my chromatophores. Making the Anthro Challenge illegal was no longer enough for my detractors. They wanted me gone—exiled in Earth's way, by sending me to the Out of Bounds or permanently changing my behavior. The situation shouldn't have taken me by surprise. Would it satisfy the residents of Loka to see me leave for Meru? I wondered what the residents of Chedi thought about my hybrid genes. Would they also reject me?

"This part of your journey is going out live," Dhira added, "and viewers can tell that you're worried about the human protesters. Some of us support what you're doing. We came to encourage you to keep going."

"Thank you," I said. I rolled up my sleeves and flashed my gratitude to Kamma. <I appreciate you being here.>

The alloy expressed surprise at my fluency and flashed, <As someone who signed the SomAx Pledge, I am grateful that your journey has sparked so much discussion about exile. I wish you a successful finale.>

I excused myself back to the tent. Both Somya and my mother were still sound asleep, so I shook them awake. I relayed what I'd learned from Dhira and Kamma, to their relief, and then made breakfast while they struck camp. We had to get an early start in order to reach Vaksana before nightfall. I no longer doubted that we would finish. Silent demonstrations of disapproval might sway less determined humans—which included many of them, from what I'd observed—but it wouldn't stop the three of us. Still, it was nice to know that we had people on our side. Six months earlier, it would've pained me to get more support from alloys than from humankind. On Meru, I would get to live side by side with all kinds of people, and none of them—I hoped—would see me as someone who didn't belong.

---

All day long, we gathered people like iron shavings to a magnet. The silent protesters outnumbered our supporters by five to one, but nearly fifty of our new friends ran beside us, the alloys carrying the few humans in their midst. The closer we got to Vaksana, the larger the numbers, and we had to slow our pace to allow our new friends to keep up. I was glad for their presence as the density of soundless bystanders grew. I couldn't decide if it was better or worse that I didn't know what messages played across the public network. Would the negativity turn people away from the SomAx Pledge? Would all our sacrifices to finish the Anthro Challenge end up meaning nothing?

As we ate lunch, my mother reminded me that the answers to my questions would not come quickly. "Alloys have the luxury of time, especially when it comes to changing law and policy. Pledge or no, it could take years before exile reform gets enacted, especially at the scope that people like your maker hope for." She smiled at my growl of frustration. "It's hard to be patient, especially when you're young and eager. Just remember that you've already accomplished a lot."

Somya elbowed me in the side. "Aren't you glad now that we agreed to Nara recording our journey?"

"Yes, fine, you were right," I said in a mock grumble.

Dhira, who was eating with us, laughed and said, "I, for one, am very happy that Somya talked you into doing the show. Nara is an amazing director, and he's really outdone himself."

One of the indriyas above us whizzed around in a circle and bobbed up and down, as if to thank us. I'd grown so used to the passivity of the immersive recorders that I kept forgetting they were broadcasting live.

I looked around at the clusters of people who sat nearby. It was strange to think that in a few more hours, our journey would be over. I would leave Earth and head to Meru for a different set of stars and skies. I couldn't begin to imagine what my life would be like, but I knew that

I had to go. As Halli had seen long before I had, it would have been a betrayal of myself not to.

On Meru, we wouldn't be able to disregard the laws of the CDS, but we would have an opportunity to avoid repeating the past. Living beings would always follow the axioms, but unlike our ancestors, we could adapt ourselves, and we could strive to do better. We would make mistakes, of course. That was inevitable. But if humans and hybrids, alloys and constructs, rocks and water and plants, could coexist for long enough, then perhaps one day our boundaries would blur, and all of us could see the true nature of the universe.

By the time we rode into Vaksana, twilight had draped the sky. Our supporters walked alongside, shielding us from the silent masses that lined the streets. The chromatophores on the alloys shone with violet hues of cheer. The humans waved light sticks that glowed with a rainbow of bioluminescence—reds, blues, greens, and yellows. They helped lift my spirits and keep me from focusing too much on the protestors. Our detractors lined the roadways from the edge of the city all the way until the final hundred meters to my grandparents' house. They stood silently, but many of them held up signs with lettering in glowing paint: **You Have AAD** and **You Are Dangerous** and **Ban the Anthro Challenge** and **Hybrids Are Not Humans**. The isolation of Meru looked better and better. Not only would I be healthier there, but I could escape the scrutiny of so many strangers. With two hundred light-years between Meru and Earth, news and information arrived only sporadically by courier. I could ignore the rest of the CDS if I wanted to.

As we turned onto the road that led home, Somya called out, "Race you back!" They took off.

I cursed and pedaled as fast as I could. We left everyone behind. For a few minutes, it was just us and our bikes and my mother bouncing on the trailer.

Four human figures waited for us in front of the house. Somya and I rode most of the way toward them before we recognized them in the dimness of twilight. When Somya saw their parents, they leapt off their bike and ran to close the distance. I abandoned my bike as well. My mother stood and walked the last few meters beside me.

Gamo and Zohel pulled Somya into a hug. My grandparents embraced me and my mother. Cheers sounded from up the road. When I turned, I saw the phores on the alloys flashing with congratulatory messages. I matched their deep-purple joy with my own. Somya grabbed my hand, raised it above our heads, and pulled me down into a bow. We waved at the indriyas and the crowd. I flashed a greeting to my maker and told zir that I loved zir. I assumed zie would see my words via the live feed.

My mother held aside the privacy curtain and motioned for me and Somya to enter first. All was quiet and cool inside.

I turned to face my heartsib. "We did it. We finished."

Somya blew out a long, incredulous breath and laughed. "What now?"

Nowhere to go. No campsite to set up or food to prepare. We had completed a feat that few humans had ever done, before the Alloy Era or since. Whatever happened with exile or the legality of the Anthro Challenge, no one could take away our sense of accomplishment. I could step into the next phase of my life knowing that I had survived everything the Earth had thrown my way, that I had seen more of the planet than most of its residents, and that I could shape my destiny however I chose.

# YEAR 2

I shaded my eyes and peered into the cloudless violet sky of Meru. The speck that was my maker grew until I could see zir blue-black body and golden wings. In the year since I had arrived with my parents, my maker had practiced atmospheric flight until zie had grown adept at it once more. Zie carried precious cargo within zir body: my heartsib.

I hadn't seen Somya since I left Earth. They and their parents had waited there for Chedi's return. The megaconstruct made an earlier-than-usual turn around to pick them up from the Solar System, and with the blessing of Gamo and Zohel, Chedi had provided gene therapy so that Somya could live and thrive on Meru. It took two or three months to send messages between star systems, and I'd spent a year in a painfully slow exchange with my friend. Once Chedi entered the Pamir System, where Meru was located, our communications got faster, but the final month until Somya's arrival passed impossibly slowly.

I felt a hand on my shoulder. I glanced back and saw my mother, a wide grin on her face. She closed the gap between us and put an arm around my waist.

My maker's immense true body glided toward an empty stretch of ground. Zie landed about once a month, and I hadn't lost any awe or delight in watching zir do it. Zir golden wings gleamed in Pamir's light. Two air bladders on either side of my maker's torso bulged as zie used them to control zir airspeed. Zie slowed to a hover, blowing dust across

Meru's rocky brown surface, and used zir arms to settle zirself gently on the ground. One enormous amethyst-colored eye winked at me. I waved in response and approached zir face with my mother at my side.

A minute later, my maker opened zir mouth. A small human figure emerged. I quickened my pace and left my mother behind. Somya looked exactly the same except that their braid hung lower down their back. They pulled me into a tight hug and lifted me off the ground.

"Welcome to Meru," I said when my feet touched land again.

"Thank you," Somya said. They squinted and pointed at the brilliantly purple sky. "The immersives don't do it justice."

"I know."

"Welcome to your new home, Somya," my mother said.

She embraced them briefly and then gave me a hug before walking into my maker's mouth. Zie would take her to orbit for a week, something zie did on every other visit. I would usually join my mother, but with Somya's arrival, I had more important things to do.

The two of us headed toward the small human-scale settlement with the unimaginative name of Homesite. It was built around the same spot where my parents had stayed during their first visit. Twenty-seven adults and five children, plus myself, lived in the village. Rounded stone buildings sat around a dome-shaped greenhouse, their shapes blending into the red-and-brown boulders that dotted the area. To the north, a larger structure acted like our grahin, a gathering place for social activities, and next to that was a medical facility that included a womb.

"You picked a good day to arrive," I said. "The newest addition will be born later today."

Somya's brows rose. "Do we get to watch?"

"Yes, but only because my mother is heading up to orbit. She's allowing me to stand in her place as tarawan. Usually it's just her and the parent who receive the baby. Shun—he's the parent—said he didn't mind if you wanted to come. He arrived from Earth about three months ago, so he's glad to have another new person around."

I stopped in front of a house with a rust-colored privacy curtain. A sign above the door read, **The Hybrid Family.**

"This is home," I said.

A sense of uncertainty weighed on me as we entered. Somya and I had practically lived together in Chedi, but they hadn't officially been part of the family, and people in Chedi didn't use enclosed houses. Would Somya be happy on Meru? Would they like the simple living conditions?

Somya gazed around the front room. The sling-chair frames, like all of our rigid structures, were made of lightweight resin that used the silicates and minerals found on the planet. The fabric was woven from plant fibers, the same material that went into our clothing. All manufacturing happened in orbit, as it did around Earth, to preserve the planet from any toxic by-products, and everything had a similar palette of reds and browns.

"We're still working on growing plants for dyes," I said apologetically. "That's why everything's so plain."

"It's great," Somya said with sincerity. "Where's our room?"

The houses had similar layouts, with a front room and a single bathroom flanked by two bedrooms. The kitchen and food were in the communal building. We peeked into my parents' room. My maker's incarn lay on the bed in a state of suspended consciousness. Zie would wake at some point after zir true body reached a secure berth in orbit.

I led Somya into our shared room, which had two single cots, one against each wall, as well as a window, a skylight, and two wardrobes for our personal items. Somya had sent over the design they wanted ahead of time, along with the items to stock it. They placed their small bag of personal things on their bed.

"What next?" Somya asked.

"How about a hot meal? It's nearly lunchtime."

"Yes, I'm ravenous."

---

At lunch, Somya met the other residents, including Shun. He didn't eat much and blamed his lack of appetite on nervousness. The three of us headed to the womb soon after the meal. I didn't have to do anything unless Shun asked, but his jitters infected me anyway. I'd gone inside the womb only once before. As with the first time, it took my eyes a minute to adjust from the brilliant light outside to the gentle glow of bioluminescence inside.

I let Shun turn the handle and open the door to the inner chamber. The room was large enough to receive a newborn alloy up to a meter long. The actual gestation happened inside an equally large space on the other side of a smooth partition broken only by an orifice. The walls around us held an assortment of equipment, some of which I'd seen my mother use for her genetics work.

"Greetings, Shun, Akshaya, and Somya," said the womb's constructed mind through speakers embedded in the walls. "Shun, please disinfect your hands in the sink and then bring the receiving tray to the delivery orifice."

He did as the CM directed. As a backup, I stood next to him with my arms ready to catch the tray. The orifice dilated to roughly ten centimeters. A small head covered in dark hair and bodily fluids emerged, followed by a tiny male body.

Shun's face broke into a smile. "Welcome to the world, Mikoto," he said.

"Akshaya," the CM said, "if you would please hold the tray so that Shun can cut and tie the umbilical cord."

I did as directed.

"Amazing," Somya breathed from beside me.

The infant let out a reedy, staccato cry, and spots on his arms and neck glowed in a riot of colors. Somya looked at me and raised their brows.

"My mother's design," I confirmed. "The second hybrid to live on Meru."

I had known what to expect, but I hadn't anticipated the immediate sense of kinship I felt with this tiny person. I had wished that my mother would have another child, a true sibling, but after seeing Mikoto, I knew that I could love him as a sib. Homesite had become my extended family, and in terms of DNA, Mikoto had as much in common with me as the other humans. I allowed my own phores to glow a steady violet and hoped that the newborn's eyes would see the color and respond in some instinctive way.

The CM talked us through cleaning and bundling the infant. The womb had an ambulatory construct that could have done all this for us, but my mother had already told me that it would act only in case of emergency. Shun allowed me and Somya to hold baby Mikoto for a minute. I couldn't believe how tiny he was.

We accompanied Shun back to his house, which he shared with two other adults, and got Mikoto settled into a cradle. After we left, Somya put an arm around my shoulders and squeezed.

"That was really incredible," Somya said. "Thank you."

I shook my head. "You got lucky with your timing. I had nothing to do with it."

I led Somya around the greenhouse and back toward our home. From there, I grabbed the sack that I had packed earlier with food and water, as well as the bag that held a surprise for Somya. We had already planned to head to the boat in the afternoon. Witnessing the birth was a nice diversion, but it had taken only an hour, and we had plenty of daylight to go for a short sail.

Somya reached for the sack, and I pulled it away.

"You don't need to do things like that for me here," I said.

"Right. That's a habit I'll have to break."

We kept a brisk pace as we headed south from the village toward the coast.

"How can you tell where you're going?" Somya remarked. "Even with the route overlay in my visual, everything looks the same."

"It's like navigating by dead reckoning. I've memorized the rock shapes, I know the bigger landmarks, and I have a good idea of how fast I walk. You'll get used to it after a while."

Meru had no plant or animal life outside of Homesite. Cyanobacteria populated the ocean, and constructs had found other single-celled organisms in some of the larger freshwater lakes, but nothing more complex existed, other than what we'd brought. The laws had changed between my mother's first visit and the establishment of the village. They allowed us to mingle freely with the local biota, and more recently, they had allowed my mother to practice as a tarawan and make more hybrids like me. The birth rate had strict limits, but the population would grow over time, and if Somya and I had our way, at some point more alloy incarns like my maker would live on the surface alongside the humans, hybrids, and constructs.

The Anthro Challenge and my time on Earth had made it clear that historical customs would not only slow down the pace of change but make those changes less acceptable to society. It was hard to embrace new ways of living when the old ones were front and center in your daily experience. On Meru, we could truly make a fresh start. The challenge was to do it in a way that avoided the mistakes of our ancestors, both past and present.

We arrived at a stretch of beach covered in small round pebbles. The land curved inward from our right to form a natural harbor, with a pier that I'd modeled after the ones we'd seen in Loka. Two boats bobbed in the water—a small dinghy that I used to teach others to sail, and a single-masted sloop. Somya had helped me with the designs. We'd made the sloop fifteen meters in length, with two sails and a cabin that could sleep four—large enough to cross Meru's oceans. Since I couldn't use fallen tree limbs for the construction, I had asked for fabricated resin that mimicked the woven texture of the wood. With some calcium carbonate mixed in, the hulls had a light-honey color. It complemented the furled sails, which had the same rust tone as our privacy curtain at home.

Somya stepped onto the floating pier and nearly lost their balance. "Need to get my sea legs back."

I sauntered over to the gangway and leapt onto the deck with exaggerated nonchalance.

"Show-off," Somya called out.

I laughed and held out a hand as they made a *disgusted-with-myself* face.

"I asked Chedi to reduce my motion sickness with my gene therapy," Somya explained. "Figured I might as well, though she insisted on doing some ear surgery as part of the process."

"Good thinking."

I set the sack on a bench and extracted some fruit and a water pouch. We sat and crunched on apples in silence for a minute.

"So it's just you and me," Somya said. "No couriers or electronics between us. What do you really think of life here?"

"It's strange," I said slowly. "This planet is so vast, and there are hardly any people here, but they make me feel like I belong in a way that I never did in Chedi or on Earth. Throughout the Anthro Challenge, I thought if we could find the right place, somewhere free of alloys, we could build a perfect society, but that never happened. Meru is far from perfect. No plants. No animals. Nothing to add to my notebook except landscapes that—as you noticed—are largely the same. As for alloys, there are more of them on the surface than humans. The constructs outnumber us, too. Maybe because they got here first, or maybe because it's a different relationship than the one they have with Earth, but when I do interact with them, they're friendly. Did I tell you that Reshyan's here?"

"No. When did that happen?"

"About six months ago. Zie made an incarn who could live underwater, and zie's working with an ocean-research project. Zie told me that zie had left Earth soon after I did and spent some time at the Primary Nivid visiting zir maker, but zie kept getting requests for interviews to the point that they became a nuisance. That's when zie decided to apply for a position here because, and I quote, 'two hundred light-years and a very small population means no one will bother me.'"

Somya laughed. "Sounds like you and Reshyan would get along."

"We *are* getting along. Zie is mapping ocean currents and sending me the data for a future circumnavigation."

"It's good to see you happy, Aks. Maybe it's less about the perfect location and more about finding people who can accept you for who you really are."

I nodded. "We're gathering and birthing more people like that every year. Coming here was the right choice. Now, it's time for your surprise. I decided to wait until you got here to put the name on the boat, assuming it meets with your approval."

From inside a storage bin, I pulled a makeshift scaffold and hung it from the railing on the stern, the traditional location for a boat's name. I took the bag with the letters from my sack and laid them out on a bench.

"What do you think?" I asked.

"It's perfect," Somya said softly.

I grabbed a tube of fixative and clambered over the railing onto the scaffold. Somya handed me one letter at a time. After I attached the final character, I leaned back and examined the results. In contrast with the pale-honey-colored hull, the dark metal letters spelled out a single word: **Halli**.

Our old idea of creating a freer society on Earth had been naive. We had dreamed of a place where people didn't have to limit themselves to the behaviors defined as acceptable in Loka. What we hadn't realized was that no such place could exist. We could go as far from Loka as we wanted . . . all the way to Meru or beyond, but we wouldn't find it, because fundamentally, no one is alone in the universe. Every action creates a cascade of reactions, and every decision ripples outward with a multitude of consequences. The only existence is coexistence.

My maker had once tried to describe what a reality transit felt like in zir mind. Zie said that entering the state of shashtam made it clear that physical boundaries were an illusion. I was beginning to understand what zie meant. Our bodies didn't have a true end. Subatomic particles bounced between skin and air continually. So what did that make me, or any person? If I coexisted with everything and everyone, then part of me was also part of them, and vice versa. To some people, I would never be human enough. To others, I would always be too human. In the end, I had no choice but to be myself.

# ACKNOWLEDGMENTS

This was the most difficult book I have ever written, not because of the story, but because it's the first long-form work of fiction I wrote under the constraints of Long COVID–induced ME/CFS. I've always been a slow, deliberate writer, so a very limited ability to write each day made me feel like a tortoise crawling through mud. I have the utmost gratitude to my editor, Adrienne Procaccini, for her patience and understanding, and to my agent, Cameron McClure, for her sound advice as I navigated my way through these new waters.

When I embarked on this novel, I was inspired by my experiences as a parent, as a disabled person, and most especially, by my child. Adolescence is a time of change, of chrysalis, and self-actualization, and it's an amazing privilege to witness it firsthand. I tried to bring some of those observations along with my own memories to Akshaya's journey, both metaphorical and literal. I also channeled my love for travel and adventure, taking the opportunity to vicariously experience parts of the world that are difficult or impossible for me to visit right now.

A massive thanks to my structural editor, Jason Kirk, for helping ensure that the visions in my head made it to the page and that I told the story as well as I could. Thank you also to Hannah Buehler, Kellie Osborne, and Jill Schoenhaut for double-checking the many fine details of the book; to Mike Heath, who somehow read my mind for the cover design and paired it beautifully with *Meru*; and to the entire team at 47North for helping deliver this book to the world.

To Eric McClure and Darusha Wehm for sharing their love and knowledge of sailing with me: thank you, and I hope I did justice to your experiences! Any technical errors are entirely my responsibility. I would also like to thank Kathryn Eberle, Jennifer Purrenhage, Anusha Srinivasan, and Shaker Srinivasan for their beta reads and feedback. Last but never least, thank you as always to my family for supporting me in my writing endeavors.

# ABOUT THE AUTHOR

*Photo © 2022 David Perry Photography*

S.B. Divya is the Hugo- and Nebula-nominated author of *Meru* in the Alloy Era series, *Machinehood*, *Runtime*, and the short-story collection *Contingency Plans for the Apocalypse and Other Possible Situations*. Her stories have been published in various magazines, such as *Analog* and *Uncanny*; on Tor.com; and in several anthologies, including *Seasons Between Us* and *Rebuilding Tomorrow*. She holds degrees in computational neuroscience and signal processing, and she worked for twenty years as an electrical engineer before becoming an author. A lover of science, math, fiction, and the Oxford comma, she enjoys subverting expectations and breaking stereotypes whenever she can. For more information, visit www.sbdivya.com.